"STEADY, LADS ... STEADY."

Favian saw the men of the number two carronade stiffen and knew they were staring right into an eighteen-pound muzzle—and eternity.

He saw Hibbert suddenly start moving, jerkily, as he felt the twitter of a musket ball near his ear.

Any second now. The number two carronade was drawing even with *Teaser*'s mainmast.

"Wait for the next sea to pass under us," Hibbert said. "Wait, wait. . . ."

The surge lifted *Experiment*, the brig rolling, wind whistling through the rigging.

"First section, ready . . . FIRE!"

THE RAIDER

Jon Williams

A DELL BOOK

Published by
Dell Publishing Co., Inc.
1 Dag Hammarskjold Plaza
New York, New York 10017

Dell ® TM 681510, Dell Publishing Co., Inc.

ISBN: 0-440-17357-4

Printed in the United States of America

First printing—September 1981

PART ONE:
United States

1.

Lieutenant Favian Markham, of Portsmouth, New Hampshire, was not yet quite asleep when he heard the knock on his cabin door. He had spent the morning watch, from four until eight, as officer of the deck; he'd sleepily eaten breakfast in the wardroom while trying to write a letter to Miss Emma Greenhow back in Portsmouth, had grown too sleepy to see his own handwriting, and then had retired to his cabin, with the intention of sleeping through at least the next watch, and if possible, the entire Sabbath. But now a summons had come. Resignedly he rolled over and acknowledged the knock.

"Captain wants you on deck, sir. Ship in sight on the weather beam."

"Thank you, Mr.—ah—Zantzinger," Favian said, peering uncertainly through the slats of the wooden screen that served as his cabin door. "Tell the captain I shall be at his service momentarily."

He heard the midshipman's footsteps on the companion as he swung his long legs out of the cramped berth, and felt a warning stab of pain from his touchy stomach as he groped uncertainly for his shoes. A ship, he thought. He brushed his dark hair forward. Too much to hope she was an enemy warship; but it would not be unreasonable to trust she was a fat Indiaman crammed with specie, like the one John Rodgers had captured a few months before.

Favian reached into his locker for his neckcloth and cravat, then decided against wearing them in the tropical heat and brought out his undress coat instead. He let his collar float loose, like Lord Byron. Taking his undress round hat from its peg, he held it in the crook of his arm and stepped

from the cabin, ducking his six feet four inches to avoid
ramming the deckhead beams with his forehead, looking,
he knew, the very picture of an ill-tempered executive officer—dyspeptic, approaching thirty, no longer hopeful of
promotion, and awakened in the midst of a profoundly
needed nap.

Scratching his long side-whiskers, he went up the companion. The berth deck was deserted, the gun deck above
almost barren of humanity. The word of the sighting had
passed swiftly among the crew, and except for a few shellbacks peering out the gun ports that had been opened for
ventilation, all were on the open spar deck above, adding
their weight to the weather rail and probably saving the
ship a few inches of leeway as they stared out at the
weather horizon. Favian buttoned his coat and donned his
hat as he came up onto the quarterdeck, feeling the warm
Atlantic sun on his shoulders.

Favian blinked in the strong tropical sunlight. Captain
Stephen Decatur stood on the little roundhouse aft, peering
to windward with his long glass, Midshipman Zantzinger
standing by, holding the captain's straw hat. Decatur wore a
black homespun coat, for he affected a carelessness of dress
as well a genial attitude with the crew, just as Favian, to complement it, insisted on formality. It was a kind of working
relationship that suited the two men well, and just as well
suited the ship.

Favian went up the roundhouse ladder and saluted his
captain with bared head. "You sent for me, sir?"

Decatur took his eye from the glass and looked up at his
tall, gangling first lieutenant with an easy, familiar smile.
"Sorry to get you up. Rub the sleep from your eyes and
take a look at this singular apparition."

"Aye aye, sir." Singular apparition indeed, Favian
thought. Favian put his hat back on his head, tipped it
back, took the long glass from Decatur, and peered through
the tube.

United States was on the edge of the Sargasso Sea, and
the water was a sour yellow. The wind was fresh and warm
from the south-southeast and blew into Favian's face as he
adjusted the glass to the movement of the rolling frigate.

Standing out on the bilious yellow horizon and into the blue, cloud-scudded sky were the three masts of a ship, traveling swiftly and easily under topsails and topgallants, sails that were etched against the blue sky in gently curved, classic lines, well cut and trimmed to perfection. Beneath the masts, barely visible above the wave tops, rode the black hull of a ship.

Favian lowered the telescope and faced his captain. Decatur's black eyes were calmly leveled at his, expectant. This was one of the little dramas at which Decatur excelled, Favian thought: that of the captain receiving dramatic news from his first officer—news that, Favian had no doubt, Decatur knew full well already. Favian had no intention of playing his own part badly. He knew that his words might go down in history, to be read by generations of boys who would promptly go out and make the same kind of mistake Favian had made at that age, and Favian had no intention of letting it be said that Decatur's hand-picked first officer was not equal to the occasion.

"A warship, Captain. She's got a new suit of white sails aloft, so she's probably just been overhauled and has a clean bottom." Before his words could be buzzed among the hands, he added, "May I recommend sending the men to quarters, sir?"

Decatur received the words with practiced self-assurance. "Not yet, Mr. Markham, if you please. Let's haul our wind and go for a closer look."

"Aye aye, Captain." Nothing like keeping an audience in suspense, Favian thought.

"Hands to the braces!" he called. "Smartly, now! Mr. Sloat, starboard your helm!"

United States turned into the wind with her accustomed sluggishness, Favian seeing the sails trimmed and the yards properly fanned. The motion of the ship changed abruptly, and Favian felt his breakfast tumble in his stomach, tasting for a second rice pudding unpleasantly mixed with bile. He fought the sensation and it swiftly passed.

Decatur was using the long glass, so Favian picked another from the rack and peered at the mysterious ship. She, too, had altered course, studding sails blossoming from her fore-topmast and top-gallant yards as she bore down in chase. She'd seen *United States*, and wanted a closer look—confirmation, as if any was needed, that the mystery vessel was a warship and looking for trouble.

"Mr. Stansbury, make our number." Decatur was speaking to the signal midshipman, who bustled to the flag locker and then to the halyards. The sliver of black that was the hull of the other warship rose slowly above the yellow horizon, and as Favian peered intently through the long glass he caught a glimpse, between tossing waves, of a yellow stripe on the black hull, broken by black gunports.

"She doesn't answer the private signal, sir," Stansbury reported.

"She's British, Captain," Favian said, returning the long glass to its rack. "She's painted in the Nelson checker. We don't have any ships with yellow stripes."

"I think you're right, Mr. Markham," Decatur said. As he lowered his glass, his lips twitched in a languorous, satisfied smile. "Clear the ship for action, if you please, Mr. Markham."

Even as Favian bawled the order, hearing the American trumpeter blow the call to action and the thunder of five hundred sets of feet respond, he appreciated the value of the moment as patriotic tableau: the calm, heroic Decatur, standing motionless on the little roundhouse in full view of everyone on deck, smiling and self-confident as the ship burst into frenzied activity around him. If they'd had a flag up over the quarterdeck to form a backdrop for the captain, the scene would have been perfect.

Favian fought a burst of impatience at these necessary preliminaries and wondered if Decatur, behind his casual, assured mask, felt the same. The whole of the naval officer's life was geared to those brief moments when he might be in combat; both Decatur and Favian had spent seven years of peacetime duty, of paperwork and drill, beef and rice on Sundays followed by pork and peas on Mondays— all aimed simply at those rare and fleeting moments when an American ship might lie yardarm-to-yardarm with an enemy ship, amidst the smoke and flame of guns, and the officers would at last discover whether all those years of drill had been in vain. Favian felt irritable and headstrong as he paced along the spar deck supervising the work of the crew, wishing he could fling himself against the enemy then and there, and somehow requite himself for those years of drill, bad food, scant pay, and no promotion.

But if time and tide wait for no man, Favian thought, neither do they speed. The wind would bring the ships together in due course. It was a pity, for fame's and promotion's sake, that Hull in *Constitution* had already beaten Dacres in *Guerrière*; for Favian's future's sake, it would have been best if *Unites States* had been the first American ship to meet and defeat an enemy. Charles Morris, Hull's first officer, had been jumped two grades of rank to captain. Would the Navy Department hand out another such plum in so short a time? But he was anticipating. The battle was yet to commence, and its outcome was by no means sure.

"Watch it there, Cassin!" Favian snapped out at a helpless midshipman. "I'll not have your section's lashings cast off in such a lubberly manner, strewn about the deck! Stow 'em away properly!"

His tension somewhat relieved by his little outburst of anger, Favian ducked down the companion to the gun deck, stooping beneath the deck-head beams, watching the gun crews at the business of making their guns ready to fire, casting the lashings off the long black twenty-four-pound guns, clearing away the side tackles, preventer tackles, and breechings, the gun captains heading up from the gunner's storeroom with their cartouche boxes, their priming irons stuck in their belts, while the ship's boys scattered sand on the deck to prevent seamen's feet from slipping on the blood that might soon anoint the planking. It was the familiar bustle, enacted at least once each day on the well-drilled frigate. But this time the air seemed taut, as with an electric charge; the glances of the hands were feverish, their speech terse.

"What d'ye think, Markham?" asked John Funck, the fifth lieutenant. He commanded the larboard twenty-four-pounders—the guns that would soon, if the other warship proved hostile, greet the enemy with a deadly hail of roundshot.

"It's a warship, and it's not one of ours," Favian said.

"She could be French, but a Frenchman would probably have run. There's a small chance she might be Portuguese in these waters."

Funck nodded. He was twenty-two, six years younger than Favian, too young to have fought off Tripoli. He seemed calm as he faced the prospect of his first action, but there was a muscle jumping in his cheek, and Favian knew how well looks could deceive. He remembered his own barely controlled terror as he faced his first man in a duel, at the age of seventeen, in that quiet orchard in Spain, and how afterward his friends had, to his immense surprise, praised him for his courage; he remembered also the strange, sudden paralysis of his arm on the morning before he stepped with Decatur into the ketch *Intrepid* to sail into Tripoli harbor to burn the *Philadelphia*. He flexed the fingers of his right hand at the memory.

It would be easier for Funck. A frigate action was less personal than a duel or a cutting-out party. He'd never see an enemy until it was over. A good first battle.

"She's British, all right," he concluded. "She's got to be. I'll be down when the time comes to open fire."

"Aye." Funck nodded tersely, and Favian passed by him, stepping carefully over the twenty-four-pounders' training tackles, which stretched back from the gun carriages almost to the deck's center line. The gun deck was as it should be, the screens between the captain's great cabin broken down to reveal the long black guns that shared Decatur's living space—the reminder, amid the captain's comparative luxury, of the single, deadly purpose of the ship's existence.

Favian heard cheering above; probably flags were being raised. He ducked down to the berth deck to take his sword from his locker, then carefully took from his chest the two balanced dueling pistols, a gift from his father, and loaded them. They were exquisite, with hexagonal barrels, so that he could take hurried aim along the top of the barrel if there was no time to aim properly. He stuffed the pistols into his waistband and strapped on his sword—this was another gift, from the town of Portsmouth, following the adventure in Tripoli harbor. Favian left his cabin and made his way to the spar deck, his head turning to windward involuntarily as he gained the deck, seeking the strange sails coming ever closer on the yellow horizon. They were larger, fore studding sails set, edging down the wind, the hull risen clearly from the waves.

"Mr. Markham, come look at this. It will amuse you." Decatur's voice floated over the spar deck. Favian, holding his scabbard carefully so as not to foul himself on the crowded, busy deck, joined his captain on the roundhouse and uncovered in salute.

"Ship cleared for action, Captain."

"Very well. I'll tour the decks presently. Take the glass and see if you recognize that ship."

Favian handed his hat to Zantzinger, took the long glass, and put it to his eye. The other ship leaped into focus: the sleek lines, the well-tended rigging, the yellow stripe down its side. "A little large for a Britisher, sir," Favian reported. "She's—good God! It's *Macedonian*!"

Decatur grinned delightedly from beneath his straw hat. "It is indeed," he said. "Captain John Carden, unless they've given her a new man."

Favian suppressed a grimace. Just a few months before the declaration of war *Macedonian* had visited Norfolk, and the officers of *United States* had played host to their British counterparts. Favian had not been impressed.

"Carden's a brave man, by all accounts," he said. It would not do to defame a fellow officer in front of the hands, even if the man was an enemy. "But you know him better than I. I spent my time with Lieutenant Hope, whose talk was all of flogging."

"D'you doubt we'll beat 'em now, Markham?" Decatur asked.

"Never did, sir." Another little dialogue for the benefit of Clio, the Muse of history. Favian might find himself quoted in some musty text as an example of the "spirit of the early Navy."

"Carden told me that a twenty-four-pounder was too large a gun for a frigate—that his eighteens could be worked faster and more accurately in a fight," Decatur said. "Besides, he said we had no practice in war."

Favian lowered the glass and looked down the length of the spar deck, seeing the men standing ready at the rows of deadly forty-two-pound carronades. "They've had all the practice they need to handle the likes of Carden, sir," he said. As you well know, he might have added. Decatur's habit of speaking for the history books could grow irritating. *United States* was a bigger ship, constructed more stoutly, and with an armament that could overmatch *Macedonian* both at short ranges and long bowls. *Constitution*'s victory over *Guerrière* had removed from American hearts any lingering doubts about whether an American forty-four could beat a British thirty-eight in a fair fight. As far as Favian was concerned, the question was not whether the American frigate could beat the British, but by how much. And, though he didn't quite admit it to himself, there was another question, of interest to at least one member of the crew: whether Favian Markham would survive the victory.

"I'll take my tour of the ship now, Mr. Markham," Decatur said. "I'd be obliged if you'd accompany."

"Of course, sir." The tour of the decks was as much a part of the ritual of battle as the raising of the flags, and it was the sort of thing at which Decatur excelled: going down amid his men, the sailors and marines, clapping backs, making jokes, giving little homilies and speeches, exuding self-confidence, bringing the ship's company to the proper pitch of battle. There would be nothing out of place, Favian knew, nothing Decatur would have to reprimand the crew about, or awkwardly choose to ignore, for Favian had made his own tour of the ship to prevent just such an occurrence. He considered smoothing his captain's path to be part of his job: Decatur, who so obviously felt the breath of history on his neck, had quite enough to think about as it was. Favian had known his captain for years, from Decatur's days as a reckless, headstrong midshipman to his more sober, stalwart days of 1812; and Favian knew that somewhere in this more solid version of Decatur the reckless youth was waiting to blaze out. Favian prudently considered that he wanted his captain to keep his head, and so he gave Decatur no reason for upset.

The tour went well. Decatur could hardly avoid the realization that while he was liked and respected by his officers, he was loved by the people. Dressed in his homespun coat and straw hat, he looked as much a foredeck hand as any of them, and he mixed well, while Favian, uniformed, with his presentation sword, pistols stuffed into his waistband, and collar open in the fashion set by Lord Byron, followed him over the deck, smiled obediently at his jokes, and glared with eagle eye to make absolutely certain the captain was not disturbed by the sight of gear not properly stowed or lashed down, rust spots not scoured out of cannonballs, or side tackles not overhauled and clear for running.

Toward the end of his procession Decatur was approached by one of the ship's boys, Jack Creamer, asking to be placed on the ship's rolls. He was only ten years of age, and the legal limit was twelve; young Creamer, the orphaned son of a dead crewman, had been put aboard unofficially after artfully pleading his way on board.

"Why d'you want to be on the muster roll, my lad?" Decatur asked.

"So I can draw my share of the prize money when we take the enemy, sir."

Cheeky little banker, Favian thought; but Creamer's reasoning provoked a laugh, and any laugh in the tense moments before battle was a good sign, so Decatur airily acceded to the request. Favian, as he made a mental note to record the boy's age as twelve on the muster roll, knew full well that it would not be Decatur who would have to answer the inevitable inquiry from the Secretary of the Navy as to why and how a small boy had suddenly appeared aboard the *United States*, in mid-Atlantic, in the moments before a battle. Such correspondence was entrusted to the executive officer as a matter of course. Favian, anticipating the volumes of paperwork this little patriotic tableau would generate, ground his teeth and tried not to think of how much his life would be simplified if, in the ensuing action, little Creamer's head were knocked off by a cannonball.

Decatur went up the companion to the spar deck, joked with the marines, the trimmers, and the crews of the spar deck carronades, and then returned to the roundhouse, peering at the *Macedonian* through his glass. The British frigate was still about three miles off, edging down slowly; she had raised three battle flags—spots of color against the white sails, the blue sky—visible to Favian without the use of a telescope.

"I don't like her having the weather gage," Decatur said, his eye fixed to the long glass. "I'd like to try our rates of speed."

"We could go about and try to take the weather position, sir," Favian offered.

"Ye-es," Decatur said slowly. "Wear ship. We'll see if Carden wants to keep the weather gage."

"Aye aye, sir. Mr. Sloat, stand by to wear ship!"

Sloat, the sailing master, nodded and sent the trimmers running to the sheets, tacks, and braces. "Manned and ready, sir," he reported.

"Rise tacks and sheets." As Favian gave the order, he could see Decatur out of the corner of his eye, standing with the long glass tucked under one arm, staring pensively at the enemy ship, paying no attention to the efficient work of the sail trimmers as they clewed the big mainsail up to the yard. Favian wondered if Decatur was remembering the discussions in *Constitution*'s wardroom, years ago, off Tripoli, where Favian, the young Decatur, Favian's friend William Burrows, Thomas MacDonough, and others of the youthful junior officers later known as "Preble's boys" would hold forth endlessly about naval tactics and the best methods of matching ship against ship. Burrows, perhaps the best technical seaman among them, had always held that it was foolish to engage a single enemy without a trial of sailing first, in which an acute officer could discover his enemy's strengths and weaknesses. Perhaps Decatur was remembering Burrows now, that awkward, eccentric, misanthropic young man from South Carolina, Favian's only real friend in the service—perhaps Decatur was remembering Burrows's advice as he commanded the sluggish *United States* against a weaker, but swifter and more maneuverable, enemy. It might become important to know just how much swifter, and how much more maneuverable.

"Wear-oh!" Favian shouted.

"Port yer helm!" Sloat roared. "Brace the yards square to the wind!"

United States rocked uncertainly as her bow fell from

the wind, spray curling up over her stem. From a position with the wind coming over her larboard side, *United States* would swing through an arc of perhaps two hundred twenty degrees to come up close-hauled on the starboard tack, with the wind coming forward of the starboard beam. *United States* and *Macedonian* would then be heading in nearly opposite directions, and unless *Macedonian* wore as well, she would let the American frigate get upwind of her and take the weather gage, seizing the initiative for the upcoming battle.

"Shift the heads'l sheets! Set the spanker!"

The big American ship lumbered through her turn, the yards being progressively braced around as the wind shifted. "Careful there! You on the t'gallant braces!" Favian called, and Sloat barked out a reprimand. Because of the difference in the purchase of the braces, the topgallants tended to get a little ahead of the rest.

"Set the mains'l!" *United States* was on her new tack, plunging into the waves, the brisk, warm Atlantic wind blowing into Favian's face as he cast his eyes over the braces, the buntlines and clewlines, making certain all was coiled down properly.

"D'you have your watch, Markham?" Decatur asked, his eye once again glued to the long glass.

"Aye, sir."

"Let's see how long it takes Carden to respond to our maneuver."

Favian glanced at his watch, then followed carefully with his eyes the black sliver of British oak being driven along under its cloud of canvas; the black sliver seemed to hesitate, then swept slowly around in its turn until it looked like a mirror image of itself a few minutes before, edging down on the wind with studding sails set, yet still anxious to keep the weather gage.

"Twelve minutes, sir."

Decatur's smile affected laziness, but Favian saw triumph in his black eyes.

"Very well," Decatur murmured, for once more to himself than to any hypothetical audience. "Very well, in truth."

Favian saw a fore royal blossom on the enemy yards as the British frigate, eager to regain lost ground, added to her spread of canvas. She was still two miles off. Favian calculated relative positions, speeds, angles, and with a sudden shock realized why Decatur was so pleased.

"We'll wear again presently," Decatur said, his eyes bright with calculation. "Not yet. I'll give the word."

"Aye aye, sir. Mr. Sloat, keep the trimmers at their stations."

Favian repeated his mental calculations, his mind filled with angles, surfaces, wind strengths. By God, he'd been right: *United States*'s maneuver had caught Carden by surprise, and it had taken him a long time to decide upon an adequate response. In another fifteen minutes or so, unless *Macedonian* changed her angle of approach, Decatur could wear again, and *Macedonian* would again be forced to follow suit, but this time the British frigate would put herself in an awkward position. Any attack made on Decatur would come slowly, allowing *United States*'s lower battery of twenty-four-pounders to hammer at the British frigate at long range before *Macedonian*'s eighteen-pounders could be expected to enter the fight successfully. Favian smiled. Burrows, discoursing long ago in *Constitution*'s wardroom, had been right. The trial of sail preceding the combat would be critical, unless Carden saw his danger; and when Favian had met Carden and his officers a few months before in Norfolk, none of them had struck him as an acute man.

The minutes crept by. *Macedonian* sailed her way into the trap, none the wiser.

"Wear her again, Mr. Markham," Decatur said, his eyes glowing.

"Aye aye, Captain. Mr. Sloat, stand by to wear ship!"

"Manned and ready, sir."

"Rise tacks and sheets."

"What wouldn't our fathers give to be here, eh?" Decatur asked, and then his eyes saddened. "And poor James, of course."

"Aye, sir," Favian said. "It's what they'd all fought for."

His words were diplomatic, but Favian knew his own father too well ever to think that old Jehu Markham would wish to stand here by his son. Both Jehu and Decatur's father, Stephen the elder, had been privateers in the Revolution; Jehu, with his brothers, Josiah and the legendary Malachi, had made himself a tidy fortune in property and prize money with their squadron of privateers, and even now Favian's cousin Gideon Markham, Josiah's son, was continuing the family tradition, commanding a New Hampshire privateer schooner against the British. Favian had been the first to break the tradition of a nautical but independent family and join the young Navy, the first naval man in the family since Tom Markham had deserted from a Royal Navy man-of-war in Boston generations ago; Favian's had been an uninformed choice made at the patriotic, impressionable age of sixteen, and since regretted at leisure.

But no, Jehu would not want to be here. He had turned his back on the sea, retired from his shipping interests about the same time young Favian had entered the service, and now lived the life of a squire some miles from his old home at Portsmouth. He had never shown signs of regretting his choice.

But from what Favian had heard of Stephen Decatur the elder, he was certain the old captain of the *Fair American* and the *Royal Louis* would wish to be here with his son. And of course Favian had known the James whom Decatur had mentioned: James Decatur, the brother who had been treacherously killed at Tripoli, and whose life had been so bloodily avenged by his infuriated brother, by a maddened Favian, and by a host of ragged, wounded, but enraged American tars. It had been one of those rare moments, Favian remembered, when he had actually seemed transported, losing all consciousness save that of fury; he had become a living embodiment of vengeance, storming aboard the Tripolitan gunboat at the head of a party already weary with wounds and fighting, to hack with a cutlass at its perfidious commander and drive its crew howling into the sea. Decatur had gone mad as well, Favian remembered, but he'd gone after the wrong boat in the milling confusion of battle, and had a wrestling match with a formidable Tripolitan captain before managing to draw a pistol and shoot the Moor through the heart. That inci-

dent—the lucky shot while he was sprawled on the deck
with a maddened enemy pinning him to the planking in an
effort to cut his throat with a curved knife—showed the
reckless, youthful, and charmed Decatur as well as any.
And it showed something characteristic of his admirers as
well: In the same fight a seaman, Daniel Frazier, with
both arms wounded and hanging helpless, had interposed
his head between an enemy scimitar and the grappling Decatur, saving Decatur's life at the cost of a vicious, and
potentially fatal, wound. A man who inspired that kind of
devotion was a man worth watching, many had concluded,
but then, Decatur had been so marked from the start—
unlike Favian Markham, and so many others.

"Set the mains'l!"

Sloat's final command shook Favian from his memories,
and he forced himself to recall the fact that the enemies he
now faced were far more dangerous than the Tripolitans
had ever proved to be, and that the kind of fighting madness that had fallen over him off the coast of North Africa
would never work successfully here, not in the careful, pre-
cise maneuverings of a frigate action. Favian turned his
eyes to the enemy, then took out his watch and made note
of the time in case Decatur wanted it.

Macedonian was not slow this time, evidence that she
had expected *United States* to wear again, but even so she
was late. Her approach would be long, and all of it in the
deadly arc of the American frigate's twenty-four-pound
guns.

"Very good, Mr. Markham." Decatur returned his glass
to the rack; he had learned all he needed to know. "We'll
shorten down to fighting sail and wait for them. Mr. Sloat,
steer her rap-full."

"Aye aye, sir."

That would lay the mizzen topsail aback, slowing the
ship but increasing its stability as a gun platform.

"Captain," Favian said, "unless you need me here, I'd
like your permission to go below to the gun deck and supervise the firing."

Decatur looked upon Favian with an indulgent eye.
"Aye, go down. I'll probably join you presently. Fire on my
signal."

"Aye aye, sir." He bared his head in salute and made his way to the gun deck.

The guns had been given affectionate nicknames by their crews, and Favian had allowed them to paint the names on the port sills above the guns: Glory, Lion, Brother Jonathan, Jumping Billy, Nelson, Happy Jack, Long Nose Nancy . . . the guns Favian had drilled for two years, day in and day out, until he knew each as well as—better, really, than—he knew his own hand. One of his chief jobs as first lieutenant was to supervise gun drill, and Favian had always made gunnery the subject of regular study; Decatur, finding their ideas in general agreement, had let Favian have almost a free hand in training the crews, and had supported him in his long-running skirmishes with the Navy Department, who could never understand how so much powder and shot could be expended in peacetime. The guns were tested, the men trained to be able to load and fire in their sleep, and Favian was immodest enough to know that he had done superbly.

"All right, lads!" he bawled as soon as he'd made his way down the companion. "Larboard battery, out tampions, load, and run out! Round shot—the smoothest and roundest iron you can find!" There was a cheer of satisfaction and anticipated triumph as the gun crews bent to their work. The choice of shot had to be made with care, since not only did uncertain casting methods result in irregularities in the spherical shot, threatening to produce errant flight at long ranges, but American shot in particular tended to be short weight. Favian had discovered, and immediately had consigned to the hold as ballast, so-called twenty-four-pound shot that weighed less than eighteen pounds. As the battle would open at long range, it was especially critical that the best shot be used first.

The gun deck filled with a menacing rumble as the men leaned on the side tackles, the long black iron guns thrusting themselves from the ports and into the bright sun. United States's corkscrew motion through the water altered slightly as the forty-two tons of broadside guns were hauled by main strength out the gun ports. Favian parked his round hat on a cutlass rack forward of the captain's pantry and walked along the row of guns, stooping to avoid the deckhead beams, peering through the ports at the British frigate coming down the wind toward them. *Macedonian* had shortened to "fighting sail," topsails, jib, and spanker, and Favian grinned: Even now Carden hadn't realized the trap into which Decatur's maneuvers had lured him.

The clatter of feet on the companionway announced the appearance of a midshipman. It was Archibald Hamilton, the young son of Paul Hamilton, current Secretary of the Navy; Hamilton came forward, hopping over the training tackles, and doffed his hat in salute.

"Captain Decatur will wear two points in a few minutes," Hamilton reported. "His compliments, and he hopes you are ready to open fire."

"Tell Captain Decatur it's too blasted early!" Favian almost roared, knowing the broadside was going to be wasted, but he bit his uncourteous reply back and simply nodded. The reckless Decatur had triumphed momentarily over the cunning; perhaps it was best that there be a whiff or two of powder to take the edge off Decatur's eagerness, even if the carefully chosen shot in the larboard guns were lost.

"Very well. Tell the captain that the range is only a little less than a mile, but we're ready to try it if he wishes."

"Aye aye, sir." Hamilton uncovered again, his fair hair, bleached almost white in the Atlantic sun, gleaming briefly in the dark confines of the gun deck; then he put his hat back on and turned to return the way he had come.

The *United States* began to alter her motion even before Hamilton's foot had touched the companionway. Favian frowned at Decatur's impetuosity and called Hamilton back. "Take careful aim now, boys!" he told the gunners. He stationed himself behind the first gun in the third section, the one known as Nelson because its crew was composed of the crew of the famous admiral's boat, all born Americans pressed into British service, and all deserted en masse sometime after Trafalgar to join the young American Navy. They were men who had served England unwillingly, but who still revered their former admiral and had named their gun after him.

"The range is a bit long, Mr. Markham," said the captain of the gun, Nelson's former coxswain.

"The captain wishes us to shoot, Timberlake," Favian said simply, and the man nodded: What Decatur asked of his crew, they would try their best to perform.

"Sir? You wanted me?" Hamilton, head bared in salute, had returned at Favian's call.

"In a moment," Favian said impatiently. The frigate's movement had settled to an easy roll as the waves came broadside; the gun captains knocked the quoins from their pieces to elevate them, trained them with the side tackles and handspikes, then each in turn raised a fist into the air to indicate he was ready.

"Ready now, lads, on my signal," Favian shouted. "On the uproll, lads! Wait for the roll. . . . Larboard battery, fire!"

The gun deck filled with smoke and flame and the roaring of giant beasts; there was a general impression of an iron stampede as the lunging guns recoiled to the limits of their tackles. The smoke poured back in the ports, carried by the wind, obscuring the results of the guns' handiwork: the disadvantage of the leeward position.

"Now, Hamilton," Favian said to the midshipman, his ears ringing, and trying not to cough in the lung-scorching smoke, "tell the captain, with my compliments, that as that broadside missed, I respectfully suggest we wait before firing another."

"Aye aye, sir," Hamilton said. He hesitated a moment. "How d'you know it missed, sir?" he asked finally, coughing. "We can't see a thing."

"If it didn't miss I'm a Turk," Favian said. "Get along with your message now!" He turned to the gun crews. "Choose your shot carefully, boys! I'll not ask you to waste them again!"

Hamilton made his way over the training tackles to the companionway. The thick smoke gradually cleared as it poured from the lee ports, revealing the British frigate sailing as before, apparently unharmed, her flags like bright dabs of paint against her matchless white sails. *United State*'s gun deck filled with growling as the guns began to run out, darkening the white square of each gun port.

Hamilton was back. "We're going close-hauled again,"

he said. "The captain wishes you to delay the next broad-side."

Favian bit back a scathing reply, and instead merely nodded. Hamilton returned to the deck above.

United States lumbered nearer the wind, resuming her former course. Favian paced along the gun deck, feeling impatience mount, easing his own nervousness with motion. The sound of the guns had set the blood roaring in his ears; and even though he knew it would be premature, he almost longed for the command to commence the action again. Though he realized that this impatience was the same reckless eagerness he had just deplored in Decatur, it fretted him all the same, and he was relieved when the closing of the range offered him the opportunity to vent his mounting eagerness with the roaring of guns. He called for Carr, one of the junior midshipmen.

"Cut along to Captain Decatur, give him my compliments, and tell him that if he will fall two points from the wind we will oblige him by chancing a broadside," he said. The midshipman, his eyes gleaming with the same impatience Favian felt within his own heart, uncovered in salute, turned, and almost ran for the companionway.

Favian stationed himself by Sally Mathews, the aftermost gun on the larboard broadside, and peered out of the port. "Aim low, boys!" he roared. "Aim for the yellow stripe!" The motion of the ship began to change as the helm was put up, the enemy frigate—handsome, larger now, and an unmistakable target on the yellowish sea— swinging into the view of the men crouched behind the guns.

Now we'll show Carden who has practice in war, Favian thought savagely, surprising himself with his own vehemence. "Ready, first division!" he called out. *"Fire!"* The roar of the guns was like a score of thunders in the low, confined deck. "A little low!" Favian called, seeing the shot sparkle on the waves twenty yards before the British frigate. "Second division, ready! Fire!" Flames lapped from *United States*'s gun ports, the bellowing guns leaping back to the limits of their tackles. "On target!" Favian roared delightedly. "Third division, ready! Fire! Fourth division . . ."

Again and again the five divisions, each of three guns, spat out their twenty-four-pound shot, then leaped back into the confined deck like enraged iron beasts. Gunsmoke poured in the windward ports and shrouded the deck in midnight blackness. Favian, Fifth Lieutenant Funck, and a pair of midshipmen walked along the line of thundering guns, keeping the men steady, reminding the gun captains to keep their pieces pointed low into the enemy hull, straining their vision peering through murky gun ports to catch a glimpse of the yellow Nelson hullstripe that served as the aiming point. In the darkness Favian caught brief glimpses of the men he commanded, illuminated by gun flashes, instants frozen in time, unforgettable: a muscled pair of arms holding a handspike; a jagged profile of a seaman, his head wrapped in a handkerchief to lessen his chances of being deafened by the echoing guns; the skeletal grin of some old shellback, once pressed into the British navy and flogged within an inch of his life, baring his teeth at the enemy he had escaped.

A hand clapped down on Favian's shoulder, and he jumped, knocking his head against a beam in his surprise; he saw through dazzled, smoke-blinkered eyes that the hand belonged to Decatur, come to inject the gunners with his brand of infectious optimism. Favian raised his hand to take off his hat in salute, then realized that he'd left his hat parked forward of the captain's pantry; he continued the gesture self-consciously, raised his hand to his forehead, and dropped it.

Decatur had come at a particularly bad moment, with torrents of smoke from the guns reducing visibility to a few feet. Gun captains were firing almost blind, or at glimpses of the enemy when the cloud parted at a wind's eddy, or firing at phantom frigates in the smoke, by mere guesswork.

"I believe we should cease our fire till we see the enemy, sir!" Favian howled into Decatur's ear. "Firing blind'll get us nowhere!"

He couldn't hear Decatur's words, but he understood the nod. "Avast firing!" Favian shouted. "Pass the word! All guns, 'vast firing!"

The weary gunners gratefully ceased their labors, leaning on their rammers and cartridge ladles. Favian felt his ears ringing in the silence, and then over the ringing heard gunshots, randomly spaced percussions. The enemy must have been firing for some time, but Favian hadn't noticed: None of the British shot had as yet struck *United States*'s gun deck.

"I'm proud of you, boys!" Decatur called out. "We're cutting 'em to ribbons. A little breathing space, and a little wait for the smoke to clear, and then we'll go at 'em again."

Probably only Decatur could have raised a cheer with that speech, but raise a cheer he did. His progress across the deck was like that of a monarch amid his devoted subjects; the powder-streaked gunners reached out to touch his hand, strained their ringing ears to catch his words, worship plain in their eyes. Favian had long ago ceased to feel any jealousy of his captain's success with his men; Decatur was clearly above most of the laws applying to officer and sailor, and Favian accepted the hands' worship of Decatur as some sort of inexplicable natural phenomenon, like snow in July.

There was a rending crash above, signifying an enemy shot striking home on the spar deck. Through the clearing smoke Favian saw the sails of the enemy frigate and, below them, the black hull, obscured by *Macedonian*'s own gunsmoke. He saw occasional flashes that signified the British guns roaring their answer to the American challenge. He watched carefully as the smoke dissipated, as Decatur made his royal progress through the deck; he counted the enemy flashes, pleased that the British were firing their smaller, lighter guns much more slowly than *United States*'s crew were firing their heavier, more awkward weapons. Part of that was superior American equipment: The United States Navy had recently begun issuing sheet-lead powder cartridges, more efficient than the old flannel ones. A gun firing the old flannel cartridges would have to be wormed and sponged after each shot, to remove flaming fragments of flannel that might prematurely ignite the next cartridge; with the sheet-lead cartridges that danger did not exist, so the guns had to be wormed not at all, and sponged

only every half-dozen shots or so, quickening the firing
process by the elimination of two tedious steps. Yet the
swiftness of *United States*'s gunnery was not entirely superior technology: Favian had drilled these men for two
years, every day, and the drill showed in their smoothness,
the ease with which they repeated their movements, and
the quickness with which they fired by divisions—Favian's
particular innovation. *United States*'s guns were also
sighted, and British guns usually were not: another advantage.

As Favian peered out the port, he saw also that winking
flashes of gunfire were issuing most often from the second
and third gun ports on *Macedonian*'s side, and he heard
after one such flash a rending above that meant a shot
striking home.

"With your permission, I'd like to open fire, sir," Favian
called out. Decatur waved his assent. Favian turned to the
crew.

"I want you to aim at the second and third ports on the
enemy side," he called. "You can see 'em plainly against
the yellow stripe. Don't raise your fists until you're ready."
He gave them a professional, invigorating smile. "There
isn't another crew in the world who can fire so fast they
blind themselves with their own smoke on such a brisk
day!" he said, and heard them cheer in answer.

He knew as well that there was probably no other ship
on earth whose gun crews could find it possible to obey an
order such as the one he'd just given. The battle had not
been won on this day alone, but on every day throughout
the preceding two years, every day that he'd drilled his
men at firing by divisions and firing live guns at a mark—
the tedious and daily exercises that had sharpened his
crews to the point where they could spot a cask bobbing in
a high sea at five hundred yards, and in ten shots be certain to smash it to splintered fragments.

"First section, ready!" he called, seeing the gun captains
blow on their slow matches, the burning ends glowing
cherry red. "Fire! Second section, ready! Fire! Third section, ready . . ."

Favian gave *Macedonian*'s second and third gun ports

three rounds from each of his guns, until American accuracy was spoiled again by American smoke. And then the roaring guns were directed at random into the enemy hull, until a wind-torn gap in the smoke showed that the enemy mizzen topmast had been shot away near the caps; the mast had pitched forward into the enemy's main rigging, and lay like a drunken sailor in a tangle of canvas, cordage, and torn battle flags. Favian led the men in a cheer at the sight and, standing behind the gun called Nelson, heard Timberlake, Nelson's captain, turn to Torment's captain just aft of him, his mouth set in a leering grin. "Bill, we've made a brig of her!" he laughed.

Favian turned to walk forward and saw Decatur standing there, and knew from his grin that he'd heard Timberlake's comment. "Take good aim, my lads, and she'll be a sloop," Decatur shouted, loud enough for history to hear, and the gun deck rocked with laughter.

"She needs a little more hulling," Favian corrected after his chief had passed, hoping Decatur's joke hadn't been taken as an authorization to fire high at enemy masts. The guns roared out, Nelson and Torment and Long Nose Nancy, aimed at the yellow stripe with which the enemy had so conveniently decorated their planking.

United States suddenly lurched to starboard, the gun deck echoing to a long, splintering crash from the spar deck above. Through the haze filling the deck Favian caught a glimpse of Decatur running hotfoot for the companion, hopping oddly over each training tackle. Favian glanced hastily about and saw Funck, the fifth lieutenant, directing the guns of his battery, all coolness now, as calm as if it were a Sunday service instead of a Sunday battle.

"Carry on, Mr. Funck!" Favian shouted. "I'm going topside for a spell. Keep hulling 'em!"

Funck nodded, and Favian ran for the companion. The air on the open spar deck, filled though it was with gunsmoke, seemed clear in comparison to the atmosphere a deck below. The mizzen topgallant had gone, lying across the starboard rail, rolling and pitching with each toss of the waves, the jagged stump thrusting like a shivered spear across the deck. Axemen were working to cut the mast free and get it overboard. Favian glanced up at the mizzen top and found himself staring into the awed eyes of the marines who had been in the top when the mast had been chewed away over their heads and crashed over without doing them harm.

Decatur was directing the axemen, the damage was minor, and the situation obviously well in hand; so Favian climbed the larboard horse block, shaded his brow with his hand, and studied the enemy. Without having to peer through a small gunport and strain his eyes through a deck filled with smoke, Favian could see the *Macedonian* clearly, and he just as clearly saw a ship in trouble: the dangling mizzen topmast was gone, probably fallen and thrown overboard, and the stump of the mizzen as well, probably shot through below decks. The rest of the rigging seemed in good condition, but the hull had clearly been badly battered. Even without a glass Favian could see that the second and third gun ports had been pounded into one.

Flame flickered along the enemy side, and Favian held his breath: There was a crash below, and a shriek above as a pair of shot streaked over the deck. A severed buntline coiled down onto the planking. Favian felt a smile of grim triumph spreading over his features. The British gunnery was slow, slower than it had been, and their aiming simply poor. Favian must have made of their decks a charnel house.

As he watched, the enemy forecourse blossomed whitely and filled with the brisk Atlantic breeze. *Macedonian*'s course altered slightly, her silhouette narrowing as she bore up. She was coming straight down toward *United States*, placing herself in a position where the American guns could pound her during her long approach without a hope of a British gun being able to bear in answer.

"Captain!" Favian called, jumping down from the horse block. "She's bore up, and coming down on us!"

Decatur turned from his axemen, absorbed the information, then called the sailing master. "Mr. Sloat, lay the main tops'l aback. We'll wait for Captain Carden, if he's that anxious to bring us to close quarters."

"I'll go below for the present, sir, if I may," Favian said. "Until we can use the carronades."

"Aye, Mr. Markham," Decatur said abstractly. The last shrouds parted and the mizzen topgallant slid overboard with a final wooden shriek, bobbing astern. "Do your duty."

Favian ran for the companion. Putting the main topsail aback would drop *United States*'s speed to zero, making her a perfect aiming platform, while *Macedonian* was making of herself the perfect target: almost bows-on, unable to fire a gun in reply, and raked by Favian's twenty-four-pounders from stem to stern.

The gun deck was brown with smoke and echoed with the roaring guns. The guns were so hot they leaped three feet or more into the air with each shot, dropping like juggernauts to the deck with tormented, plank-buckling crashes. The guns, to Favian's surprise, were firing at will, as fast as they could be loaded and run out, rather than by section. "Avast firing! 'Vast firing till I give the order," Favian shouted, in his fury kicking an intruding water bucket, spilling it across the deck, angrily looking for Funck to give an explanation.

"Funck, where the hell are you?" he demanded. "Blast you, anyway!"

In the sudden silence of the gun deck he found his answer, as litter bearers loomed through the smoke, carefully negotiating their way across the row of training tackles, carrying a white-faced casualty: It was Funck, the fifth lieutenant, splattered with his own blood. Lying on the litter was the oozing form of his left leg, separated at mid-thigh by a roundshot. His eyes were closed, and a midshipman held each of his hands.

Favian felt his blazing anger turn to shock as Funck was carried by, knowing the young officer had little chance of survival: The odds were badly against surviving any kind of traumatic amputation, but even the best surgeons hesitated to perform an amputation above the knee, knowing it meant almost certain death. And it was Funck who had been commanding the gun deck while Favian had run up to help deal with the fallen topgallant mast; if the mast had not fallen, Favian might have been standing where Funck had been standing, encouraging the men at the guns, when a British roundshot widened the number four gun port and

passed through the deck. For the first time Favian felt a
claw of fear touching his nerves.

"Funck's been wounded, sir." It was Nicholson, the
fourth lieutenant, the man who commanded the starboard
broadside that had not yet been fired during the course of
the battle. "Shall I take command here, sir?"

Fear is a luxury, Favian told himself. It can be dis-
pensed with. The odds were against Funck's being hurt,
against anyone's being hurt. Silly to be afraid now, with the
enemy beaten.

"The deck is yours, Mr. Nicholson. I'll help you,"
Favian said, hoping his face had not inadvertently betrayed
his hesitation. He clasped his hands behind him and spoke
quickly, turning to the task at hand, hoping simple me-
chanics would occupy his suddenly timorous mind.

"Is the third section ready? At the hull now . . . fire!"

Again the guns roared in their sections; again the decks
filled with smoke and angry, leaping artillery. Favian,
walking along the gun deck, felt the fear ebb, the moment
of apprehension replaced by a moment of disengagement.
He felt strangely detached, analytical; carefully he prodded
his own consciousness, trying to discover the source of that
unlikely, inconvenient trepidation. It seemed to have vanished; its source seemed undiscoverable. In the meantime
he continued to function as an officer; he spoke encourag-
ingly to the hands, pointed out targets, reminded the gun
captains to allow for windage and relative motion. The reflexes of the serving officer had been built up for years,
and had taken over now; he spoke the right words, made
the right decisions, stood with the proper impassivity as
Macedonian yawed to fire a broadside and enemy shot
crashed into the American frigate's timbers. The rest of
Favian seemed quite detached, uninvolved, watching the
mannequin of an officer do its job. Favian searched the pit
of his soul for his own thoughts, his own reactions, triumph
or vindication or pride in his work—even an outburst of
temper or another hint of fear. But there was nothing: The
mannequin was empty, filled with a soulless wind, as if his
effort to suppress his fear had resulted in the suppression
of all else, everything that was his own. The face of the
proper officer, the talented subordinate, had eroded en-

tirely whatever it was that lay within, and Favian felt a
detached sorrow that there were no longer any real choices
in his life, that his course had been charted at sixteen,
when he'd made the mistake of joining the Navy and ad-
hering to the granite, unforgiving code of the serving officer, and discovered within himself the ability to counterfeit
so well the face of a member of the American elite.

Macedonian yawed every so often to deliver a broadside,
showing that she had only about half her guns remaining in
the fight. From the occasional motion of his own ship, recorded so well by that automaton which the outer Favian
had become, he knew that Decatur had been alternately
backing and filling the main topsail, sliding away from the
British frigate. Both the British yawing and the American
easing off prolonged *Macedonian*'s approach, keeping her
in ideal pounding distance of the gun deck twenty-four-
pounders, but eventually the range narrowed, and Favian
left Nicholson in charge of the gun deck and came up the
companion to supervise the spar deck carronades.

These short, light guns threw a forty-two-pound shot,
perhaps the largest weight of shot ever fired from a frigate;
but they threw it only over a short distance, and thus far
had not been fired. Favian, walking up the companion and
blinking in the strong sunlight, saw the men and their officers standing by the short, squat carronades, waiting impatiently for their orders. Decatur, imperturbable and confident, stood on the roundhouse, watching with anticipation
the British frigate descending on them.

"With your permission, Captain, I'd like to fire the
smashers," Favian called. Without waiting for Decatur's assent, Favian turned to the forty-two-pounders' crews.
"We've swept their foredeck clean," he said, "so we don't
need to pay any more attention to their fo'c'sle. It's amidships I want you to aim, and at the mainmast." The mannequin, the officer's mask, had made these observations
below and was now translating them into action. He felt as
detached as if he were watching another man play himself
at chess.

"First   section . . . fire!   Second   section . . . fire!
Third section . . . fire!"

The carronades spoke, flinging their awesome projectiles at the enemy. The number five carronade, amidships, flung itself muzzle up as it recoiled on its slide, a constant problem with these short guns whose trunnions were lower than the guns' center of gravity. With a seemingly cheerful, professionally feigned grin, Favian flung himself at the carronade to bring the barrel low again. Another two shots from each carronade section and the British frigate's main topmast was shot away at the caps and came down in an avalanche of splintering spars and torn new canvas. The enemy topsail swathed the British gun ports, preventing them from firing their guns without certain danger of setting themselves ablaze. While they coped with this difficulty, Favian shifted his fire forward and brought the foretopmast down as well. *Macedonian* was a helpless ruin, virtually a hulk; her main yard was in its slings and unusable, her foresail so riddled as to be almost useless. Decatur filled the main and mizzen topsails and *United States* surged ahead.

"Shall we rake her, sir?" Favian asked, knowing it was perfectly possible for them to station themselves off *Macedonian*'s bows and tear her to bits without a hope of receiving a shot in return.

"No—cease your firing, Mr. Markham," Decatur said with a slow smile. "We'll put our ship in order and give them time to *think*."

"Aye aye, sir. 'Vast firing, there! 'Vast firing, all! . . . Mr. Stansbury," Favian said, calling to a midshipman. "Pass the word below to cease firing."

"Give them time to think," Decatur had said. Favian himself would have seized the advantage of the *Macedonian*'s dismasting and raked her mercilessly, but he saw at once how Decatur's astonishing grasp of human nature had produced a plan that would work much better. Raking *Macedonian* might have produced a hopeless defiance in her officers, but Decatur would let them have time to realize, without the distraction of guns and screams and crashing masts, that they had lost. They were rolling their gun ports under with every wave. The wounded would be in agony from the motion. There was no hope of resistance—not with only one torn sail. They were probably taking on water as well, rolling all the shot holes under. No hope, he thought. She'll sink like the *Guerrière*.

United States forged ahead and hove-to three cables from her enemy. The hands were called up to knot and splice the rigging, replacing the torn mizzen topsail with fresh canvas, setting another jib in the place of one weakened by shot holes. Then the American frigate tacked, showing herself fully capable of maneuvering and renewing the fight, and ranged up under *Macedonian*'s lee; and, without a word being spoken, the British battle flag raised on the stump of *Macedonian*'s mainmast was lowered in surrender.

"Mr. Markham!" Decatur called from the roundhouse. "You may congratulate yourself and your gunners on a job spectacularly done! Find a boat that can swim and go take possession. Take Mr. Nicholson with you."

"Aye aye, sir." Favian turned to the crew. "Three cheers, lads, for Captain Decatur!" he bawled, waving his arms like an orchestra conductor; and the men cheered their hearts out for their captain, while Decatur stood in his homespun black coat on the roundhouse, waving his straw hat in acknowledgment of their applause. The inner Favian watched his professional self lead the cheers, a little awed by the hands' devotion. *Devotion*: It was a sentiment he did not understand; yet he knew that some of the men were devoted to him with almost the same fervor they felt for Decatur, and as a professional officer he knew how to use that devotion to contribute to the well-being of the ship—and, if necessary, to his own less scrupulous ends.

As the hands cheered, Favian became aware of a sickening ache in the pit of his stomach, an ache that swelled even as he stood on the deck and waved his arms. *Dyspepsia*. It had come, and it would stay, a reminder of his own imperfection, for days. By this time he knew it well. The profession of sailor ideally demanded a stomach of iron, and in this piece of necessary equipment Favian was sadly lacking.

Favian made arrangements for one of the whaleboats to be lowered and manned, then ducked below decks to arrange his appearance. "Mr. Nicholson," he called. "Get yourself below and into a clean coat and hat. We're going to take possession." Nicholson looked up at Favian with eyes reddened by smoke, and perhaps by sorrow.

"Funck's dead," he said. "Funck and five others. Six wounded. I just heard the butcher's bill."

"He was a good man," Favian said. He wondered how often he had confronted the death of a brother officer with the same stiff resolve he knew he was displaying now; he knew so well how to handle himself, how to approach the grief of others. He touched Nicholson's shoulder. "At least he died in victory. His guns did well. The British dead will have no such consolation." He could see Nicholson's young face slowly absorbing the words. "Now we're going aboard the enemy frigate," Favian said. "I want you with your good coat and hat, your face cleaned of gunpowder, your dress sword and white gloves. I don't want them to guess about Funck. I don't want them to know they even made us *sweat*."

Nicholson looked at Favian in slow surprise, and then nodded. Unite and present an imperturbable front—that was the way of the service. Never let the enemy see grief, joy, anger. Be dispassionate at all times, even in killing. Favian intended to step aboard the beaten ship impeccably dressed, unruffled, superior, establishing his ascendancy over the beaten enemy, letting them know that there was no possibility of resistance, and that there had never been any other possible outcome.

Favian's cabin on the berth deck, below the water line, had not been disturbed when the ship cleared for action. Favian stepped through the door, threw his powder-streaked uniform onto the bed along with his trousers and shirt. He washed his face thoroughly in a fire bucket and was careful to take off the least traces of dirt and sweat. His long side-whiskers were brushed, the elegant little spit curls on temple and cheek, demanded by current fashion, were moistened and combed into place. Over a clean shirt went his neckcloth and cravat, then the heavy full-dress coat with its bullion epaulet on the left shoulder. He strapped his sword into place over the coat, dropped his pistols into the pockets, then put his good cocked hat into the crook of his arm and stepped from the cabin, dressed as if he were sitting for a portrait. It was not for nothing he was the son of Jehu Markham, one of New England's most prominent men of fashion, and one of the most imperturbable. He knew he looked good in full dress, the blue coat and gold epaulet that accentuated his slim figure and showed his broad shoulders to advantage. He started up the companion, then turned to go back for a pair of kid gloves.

Nicholson waited on the spar deck, less well accoutred, but still looking as if he were outfitted for a dinner at the home of one of the Navy's commodores. Favian stepped up onto the spar deck, nodded at Nicholson and the boarding party that stood ready, and stepped up onto the roundhouse. Decatur was still there, seeing to the splicing of cordage, the fishing of wounded spars. "Don't take Carden's sword, Mr. Markham," he said. "I'll be along presently to do it myself."

"Aye aye, sir." Favian took an American ensign from the flag locker, uncovered to Decatur and the flag over the quarterdeck, and stepped to the entry port. His stomach ached with every step. The whaleboat was having difficulty in the high seas, trying to keep near the frigate's side without smashing itself against the bilge. Favian timed his leap carefully, holding his scabbard in his hand so that it wouldn't flail about and injure the boat's crew, and jumped down to join Nicholson in the whaleboat's stern sheets.

The whaleboat shipped a lot of water as it rowed, heavily laden, over the steep seas. *Macedonian* was a handsome ship even in defeat, even with her gun ports rocking under and bloody salt water sluicing from the scuppers. The whaleboat passed under the figurehead of Alexander the Great, then made its way to the entry port. Favian could hear a weird chorus, screams and moans and crashes, snatches of laughter and song. So this is what a beaten ship is like, he thought. I have never been on a beaten ship. It sounds as if half the crew are deranged. He donned his kid gloves. As the whaleboat slid to the entry port, Favian recognized one of the men in cocked hats who stood by the port to help him in.

"Hello, Hope," he greeted.

"Hullo, Markham."

Favian timed his leap and jumped for the entry port,

soaking himself to the knee as *Macedonian* rolled water aboard. David Hope, the beaten frigate's first officer, saluted hand to hat. One of his uniform sleeves was missing, the exposed arm red-stained and bandaged; there was another bandage beneath his hat, and blood on his collar. Favian doffed his hat in the American salute. The well deck was slippery with blood and spume, corpses and parts of corpses rolling from one bulwark to the other as the ship rocked, flesh tossed in a little lake of red. Favian put his hat back on.

Hope cleared his throat loudly. Favian looked down and saw that Hope was offering his sword in surrender, the sword of one first officer given in defeat to his victorious opposite. *Macedonian* shipped another sea, and the corpses rolled. Nicholson jumped aboard and stared in shock at the horrid scene as the red slowly climbed his white dress trousers.

Favian reached out a glove to the British sword, and took it.

Triumph, and vindication.

2.

In his ill-spent year at Harvard, when Favian was fourteen, he had read a translation one of the professors was making of an Icelandic saga. It had afterwards struck him, when he had been in the Navy for some years, that the berserkers about whom he had read in the saga were a kind of primitive version of the naval officer. The lives of both revolved around those few hours in which they were actually in combat; and the rest of existence, in contrast to those whirlwind, bloody moments, was tinged slightly with the unreal. The Norse berserkers lived only for battle; in combat they would often foam at the mouth, throw off their armor, and charge like mad animals, like bears or ravening wolves, straight for the terrified enemy. In times of peace they were out of place, drank heavily, were morose, quarrelsome, sullen, and most dangerous.

The naval officer was a more cultivated form of the same animal, Favian thought, but the resemblance was more than casual. Naval officers were as high-strung as the thoroughbred racers Jehu Markham raised on his land in New Hampshire, and as nervous. For seven years Stephen Decatur and Favian Markham had worked toward the ends accomplished in ninety minutes of battle with the *Macedonian*—the vindication not simply of their tactics and their place in the service, but of their very existence. For seven years they had endured the tedium of peacetime service, the humiliation of serving in useless, unseaworthy gunboats while fine American frigates were neglected; they had survived the purges of officers, where some of the best had been sacked to serve the Republicans' political ends, or simply because the Navy was to be reduced and there were too many. The overall monotony of service had been broken by quarrels, by duels, and by the massive rupture over the court martial of James Barron for the peacetime capture of his *Chesapeake* by the British *Leopard*—for months the Navy had been divided into two camps, as ready to battle one another, like a collection of drunken Norse, as to avenge their humiliation by the British. Like tempered steel, they were in need of constant honing to keep them sharp. The constant battles for precedence, for advancement, the duels with one another or with officers from other navies, other nations, kept them on their toes, and served to remind them of the deadly purpose of their existence. It weeded out the dull or the cowardly or the simply unlucky, and kept the rest on the razor's edge of danger, where a misstep could plunge them into peril or death.

Favian remembered well the infamous suggestion, after a duel had narrowly been averted between the twenty-year-old Midshipman Decatur and Richard Somers, that Somers was "too fond of the lee side of the mizzenmast," whereupon Somers had no choice but to call out every other midshipman in the ship, with the chivalrous Decatur acting as his second. There were six opponents altogether, and Somers proposed to fight them all in one afternoon: The first wounded his right arm, the next his thigh; he fought the third sitting down, Decatur holding up his wounded arm so that he could fire his pistol. The other midshipmen apologized, and afterwards no one questioned Somers's courage. But Favian wondered if that accusation had been in Somers's mind later, on that dark night in Tripoli harbor, on a hopeless, foolish mission to demolish the harbor with a boat crammed with gunpowder, when Somers, refusing to surrender, had put a light to the powder train, blowing up himself and his crew and his enemies in one glorious, fiery spectacle, illuminating the pages with which Clio would inscribe the record of his once blotted, oft vindicated courage. It had been a Viking funeral worthy of the greatest berserker.

Favian knew that Decatur still carried part of a ring that Somers had broken into thirds on his departure: a third for Decatur, a third for Charles Stewart, a third for himself. Two thirds of the ring were still in the service: a piece of

Somers's carried by Decatur on the *United States,* another
piece with Stewart in Washington, or wherever that talented, brilliant man was now. The other third had blown
up gloriously, lighting the way by example. *This rather
than disgrace,* Somers's action had clearly stated; and the
service was filled with men who would endorse the action,
particularly after James Barron had been forced to surrender *Chesapeake* to *Leopard* in peacetime and had undergone such degradation since. No one knew where Barron
was now; some said Europe. It didn't matter. As far as
anyone in the service was concerned—with the exception
of what remained of the Barron-Elliott clique—he might as
well have died aboard the *Chesapeake.*

The officers of the young Navy—mostly young, battle
tested, high-strung, fiercely competitive—constituted,
Favian knew, an elite, although they were an elite drawn
from the egalitarian ranks of a republican society. They
lived in monklike isolation behind their wooden walls, conducting their lives by a code that few outside their brother-
hood could ever hope to understand. None in the civilian
world—not even any in the Army—had ever submitted
themselves to the testing undergone by the young naval
men. The presence of the naval elite was looked upon with
unease and distrust by the American republic; Jefferson
and his Democratic-Republicans had won office partly on
a platform of restricting naval expansion, if not eradicating
the junior service altogether. Jefferson, exponent of equality, hating any elite that wasn't Virginian, had purged the
Navy's ranks, and Favian himself had almost been flung
from the service on account of his civilian brothers' uncompromising federalism; but somehow he had been allowed to
remain, and he suspected that this was because of the inter-
vention of Decatur and old Commodore Preble.

Favian hated the Navy. It was not the elitism he detested, for he was an elitist himself, and politically a Federalist, though not so fanatic a one as Alexander Hamilton,
and not so public a one as the officers who had had the
misfortune to be cashiered because their opinions differed
from those of Thomas Jefferson. He hated the Navy for
what it had done to him. He had joined, at the age of six-

teen, because he was without a profession, and by the age of seventeen or so, young Americans were supposed to have settled into the avocation that they were to practice for the rest of their lives. He had tried a year at Harvard, and found the education there redundant after the brilliant tuition he'd had under his father and mother, and his studies had suffered because he'd had it all before. He'd tried reading law and found it dull; he'd entered the family business and found it worse. His parents had sought through consultation to discover the answer. The ministry? Jehu and his wife were freethinkers, close to atheists. The sea? It was the old family profession, before the Markhams had become more concerned with investing the old money than making the new. Favian's cousin Gideon was already serving as an officer on one of the family flotilla.

But Favian had also been brought up within his family's martial tradition. Jehu had been a Revolutionary privateer, as had his brothers, Josiah and Malachi, and their example had infected Favian with a youthful fantasy of himself on the quarterdeck of a man-of-war, a sword in his hands, and pistols stuffed into his belt. Malachi in particular provided an inspirational example—the hellion brother, mercurial and passionate, who had cut for himself a brilliant career amid the smoke and flame of battle. He was one of the few privateersmen to defeat Royal Navy ships, placing his name alongside the immortals, Joshua Barney and Silas Talbot; he had wrecked the enemy frigate *Melampe*; taken home the crack Indiaman *Royal George*, with her holds choked with spices, porcelain, and silver; and then, in command of *Royal George*, captured *Bristol*, a fifty-gun British man-of-war—a battleship with two tiers of menacing heavy guns, and larger than any ship the United States had yet built for her Navy. The vast memory of the *Bristol*, the new American flag floating over her shot-scarred decks, had inspired the young Favian to ask his father to send him to sea, not in a Markham ship, but as a midshipman in the new Navy.

His father had approved. Jehu Markham had been educated at two schools, Oxford and the sea. He had married the Honorable Anne Fairbank, daughter of a baronet, and possessed certain traditional ideas concerning the employment of younger sons. The Navy had just embarked on the war with Tripoli, and promotion might come fast for the bold and the talented. Jehu had always been just a bit defensive about family history. He had transformed Tom Markham, the able seaman who had jumped ship in Boston to found the New England branch of the family, into "a naval gent in the Dutch Wars." And privateering, in which the Markhams had made most of their fortune, was a profession tainted with self-interest. Privateers were often accused (with considerable justification) of piracy, and they were accused also—and this was far worse from Jehu's point of view—of not being gentlemen. Pay in the new Navy could only be described as miserly: A captain in the American service earned only twelve hundred dollars per annum, less than one fourth that of his Royal Navy counterpart, and he also took a far smaller share of the prize money. Favian's decision to volunteer was clearly made without pecuniary consideration and could be taken as the act of a person devoid of self-interest and high in patriotism; annexed to his name, the initials USN could scarcely refrain from reflecting honor upon the rest of the family. And the Navy was a genteel service as well; Truxtun and Preble both insisted on raising mannerly officers as well as fighters, in direct contrast to the rough-and-ready tradition handed down by the old Continental Navy.

And so Favian was sent to the war with Tripoli, on the corvette *Boston* under Captain Daniel McNeil. A year later, under another captain, he still had not seen Tripoli, but he had stood amid a fragrant orchard in Spain, a pistol in his hand, ready at the drop of a handkerchief to kill a Spanish midshipman as terrified as he was. The world of the naval officer had made him its own.

And for this he hated the Navy. For if the service encouraged some traits, it denied others. If it encouraged bravery, it denied the reality of fear. If it admitted war, it refused anger. If it upheld an ideal, it also refused to admit the existence of anything contrary to that ideal. Favian had believed in the myth, once—until those seven years of peace had given him a dose of another sort of reality. He could not believe in it again; but if he hid from others his moments of doubt, his secret self-loathing, perhaps he could become one of the gods of the new cult, one of the Prebles, Decaturs, Somerses, or Stewarts.

But now Favian was confronted by the British version of the serving officer, which had at first been imitated, then surpassed, by the American variety. The British had been beaten, and were plainly mortified; the stunned white faces of the officers looked out at him with the eyes of poleaxed oxen.

After Favian brought his prize crew aboard, he'd been conducted to the quarterdeck to meet Captain John Surnam Carden. Carden looked thoroughly defeated, shrunken in his powder- and blood-streaked coat, the antithesis of the confident, proud, somewhat boastful man he'd met only months ago. Like the other officers, he wore a stunned look on his countenance; unlike them, he showed resentment and anger as well.

Favian saluted. "I think we should get a new foresail up, Captain Carden, don't you think?" he asked. "If you will send an officer to conduct my men to the sail locker, we can get it set up and relieve this rocking."

"Do as you like!" Carden snapped, and turned away. Favian waited stiffly for an apology, then saw it was not coming.

"Mr. Hope," he said. "If you'll conduct us?"

The way to the sail locker passed through scenes of unimaginable horror. Dead men lay strewn along the path, rolling in their own gore and in the salt water that cascaded down the hatches; the survivors seemed demented, some lying weeping on the decks, others dancing hornpipes in perverse celebration of their own survival, their every footprint reddening the planks. At one point a group of tars armed with capstan bars tried to block their path, intent on exacting retribution for their dead comrades, but Hope burst into anger, shouting as furiously as if he, too, had gone mad. His roaring was difficult to understand—these British officers seemed to have developed some new, affected way of talking, as if there were a grapeshot in their mouths, and Favian supposed it was imitative of the prince regent, in the same way that the previous generation of officers, with all their hemming and hawing, had imitated

George III. But Favian caught the words ". . . flogging
. . . lash . . . grating . . . backbone . . " and so supposed that Hope was threatening them with his favorite
punishment. The British shellbacks, defiant, tried to answer back; but Hope left them no breathing space, and
eventually they retreated. The old forecourse was roused on
deck, and the American prize crew sent aloft to knot and
splice the damaged foremast rigging and then get the sail
aloft and spread.

The British seamen stood about and watched, impassive
or hostile. Crews of another nation, more used to defeat,
would perhaps have better accepted their downfall, but the
British crew simply felt cheated out of a triumph that
rightfully belonged to them. The officers seemed scarcely
better; Carden was uncivil, and Hope's cooperativeness
barely concealed a rage that had already exploded once,
and that took fire again when Favian sent the fifteen-
striped American flag up the repaired foremast halyards.

"It's British deserters that won you this triumph, I'll
warrant," Hope said bitterly. "Traitors who will turn on
their own kind."

"There is not an Englishman aboard our ship," Favian
replied coldly, deliberately putting an edge to his voice, reminding Hope of where he was and with whom he was
speaking—the man to whom he had surrendered his sword.
"And if there are," Favian continued, "it shows only that
Englishmen under American officers fight better than they
do under their own."

Hope glared at him, then abruptly turned and walked
away, as Carden had done. Favian realized that he'd spoken too harshly, and that Hope's turning away had been
self-control asserting itself. If Hope hadn't done so, he
might have struck Favian, and then there would have been
no choice but pistols somewhere, in some dawn, and a blot
on the whole business. He'd have to be more careful.

The foresail was bent and caught the wind and was
trimmed as it turned the beaten frigate's stern to the waves;
the hellish roll turned to an easier pitch, and *Macedonian*'s
well deck ceased to ship water. Now the well could be
sounded and the pumps manned. With Yankee backs bend-

ing to work the pump handles, and seawater gushing from the pumps, Favian, Nicholson, and a party of their men began a tour of the ship, descending into the bloody chaos of the lower decks. The surgeon's cockpit had entirely overflowed with wounded, and they were stacked up in rows on the berth deck, men rudely bandaged and awaiting treatment mixed with those who would now require no attention at all. Favian descended into the cockpit, seeing the surgeon, naked except for his bloody leather apron, working feverishly by candlelight. "We've got sail aloft, so it should be easier for you, sir," Favian said, trying to picture how much worse this scene had been with the ship rolling uncontrolled at every wave.

The surgeon looked up, his face baleful in the light of the candles. "You fellows have made wretched work with us, Mr. Markham," he said, evidently recognizing him from his earlier stay in Norfolk.

"Shall I try to send for our surgeon, sir?" Favian asked.

"I should think he'd have enough work, Mr. Markham. You there, bring the light closer, so I can stitch this artery."

"Not at all, sir," Favian said. "We had only six men wounded, and I'm sure they've been cared for long since."

There was silence in the cockpit as the surgeon, his mates, and the many conscious wounded absorbed the shocking news. The only British consolation for their defeat had probably been the thought that the American frigate, too, had been badly punished. But only six men wounded? The scope of the victory was stunning.

"We've another table for your surgeon, if you will send him, sir," the surgeon said.

"Yes, sir," Favian said. "Mr. Nicholson, go on deck and try to hail *United States* to bring Mr. Trevitt aboard. Or use a signal hoist if you can remember the number. The rest of you, follow me."

They walked along the orlop, examining the damage at the ship's waterline. *Macedonian*'s carpenter had made a good job of plugging most of the holes, at least to the point where their leaking was under control; and now that the rest of the shot holes were no longer shipping water steadily, he and some of his mates, aided by Favian and his men, patched up those remaining. When Favian returned to the deck, he was informed that the pumps had begun to make headway against the water in the hold.

United States's big thirty-six-foot pinnace was crawling over the water toward them, and Favian, recognizing Decatur's straw hat, met his captain at the entry port. Decatur, incredibly, was still dressed as he had been during the battle, still in his black homespun coat and blue trousers; he would step aboard the beaten frigate looking as much a farmer as a successful captain. Favian smiled at the irony. He had tried his best, white gloves and all, to show himself the proper officer, treating the occasion and himself with all the dignity he could muster. Decatur, in black homespun, would be undercutting Favian's dignity; but more importantly, he would be showing himself, by contrast, as unique. It was a clever piece of psychology, demonstrating himself not only as rudely dressed in plain republican clothes, but in stark contrast to his officers; he would be showing himself off the more, adding another piece to his legend. Favian almost laughed. It was too perfect.

Decatur came up the entry port, followed by Archibald Hamilton. Favian saluted with bared head. "Captain Carden is on the quarterdeck, sir."

Decatur's black eyes gleamed with eagerness. "Aye, I'll meet with him presently," he said, virtually brushing the idea of Carden aside. "What of the *ship*? Will she swim, Mr. Markham?"

"She'll swim as long as we care to keep her afloat," Favian said. "The pumps are undamaged, and gaining. We won't have to evacuate her in a hurry, like *Guerrière*."

"Will she swim as far as Rhode Island, d'you think?" Decatur asked.

Favian was stunned. Take the prize home? Across the Atlantic, in October, with the mizzen shot away below decks and the fore and main topmasts gone? He had assumed they would empty *Macedonian* of her crew and useful supplies, then burn her, as Hull had burned *Guerrière*.

"Th-the hull's sound, sir," he said, stammering with surprise. "I don't think there's enough in the way of spars."

"Survey the spare spars. We have spares in the *United*

States, in any case," Decatur said. He looked over the decks, and for the first time absorbed their horror, the dead lying in pools of water, the living wandering aimlessly over the planks, or weeping over their fallen comrades. Decatur sobered instantly, his eyes reflecting the misery of the men on *Macedonian*'s decks.

"I've brought enough men with me to start cleaning this up, at any rate," he said quietly. "You've done a good job, Mr. Markham, with what you had. I've brought the surgeon with me. Now where's Captain Carden?"

Carden was still on his quarterdeck, clearly still stewing in his own hellish misery. Still, recognizing Decatur, he endeavored to do his duty; visibly steeling himself, he unclipped his sword from his belt and walked to Decatur to surrender it.

"Sir, I cannot receive the sword of a man who has so bravely defended his ship," Decatur said, to Favian's utter surprise. "But I will receive your hand."

Such high style coming from a man in a homespun coat! In Favian's professional judgment, Carden deserved to lose the sword if ever a captain did; his tactics had been abominable and his manners worse. Favian felt the weight of David Hope's sword clipped to his own belt, and grimaced. There was no way to get out of this situation with credit. If he returned the sword, he would look foolish; if he kept it, he would seem churlish. But Hope seemed to have disappeared, allowing him to postpone his decision.

"My God," Carden was saying. "I'm the first British naval officer ever to strike his flag to an American. What will they do to me?"

Knight you, probably. Favian thought. That's what they did to Pearson when he struck to John Paul Jones. The ranks of the service would close over one of their own; Carden would be court-martialed, but extenuating circumstances would be found, and he would be complimented for his bravery, and probably given another ship to lose. So much the better for us, Favian thought.

"You aren't the first, sir," Decatur was saying. "Dacres surrendered *Guerrière* to the *Constitution* in August. You hadn't heard, sir?"

Carden scarcely seemed to credit the news, chilly comfort though it was. "No," he said. "I had not."

But Decatur had already turned to Favian. "I'll take the ship's officers off," he said. "Have Nicholson survey the spars lashed down on the well deck. You can make some effort to clean up here, and perhaps get a maincourse up."

"Aye aye, sir."

"Pass the word for the British officers to gather their belongings and assemble at the entry port in five minutes."

"Aye aye, sir." Favian uncovered to Decatur and Carden and went down to the waist, where he set the men Decatur had brought to securing and fishing the mainmast, and sent messengers to find *Macedonian*'s scattered officers. Hope returned in a few minutes, red faced, as he argued with the messenger Favian had sent after him.

"Admit it, man!" Hope almost shouted. "It's no secret, not once you open your mouth."

"I was born in Harrisburg," the man replied. "How many times do I have to say it?"

"Blast it, man, you're lying!" Hope replied.

"What's the difficulty, Mr. Hope?" Favian asked, conscious of the two swords rattling at his waist; he'd have to make his decision soon. "What's Ewald here supposed to be lying about?"

"I've never heard a clearer Northumberland accent in my life!" Hope said. "But this man won't admit he's a traitor."

"I've never been a traitor to nothing in my life!" Ewald roared. "I was born in Harrisburg! That's in Pennsylvania, you blasted lunatic!"

"I know that dialect—" Hope began.

"Heinz Ewald an Englishman?" Favian asked, amazed beyond all measure that any British officer could mistake the Pennsylvania Dutch ship's corporal for any man of his own island.

"Proof, Markham," Hope said triumphantly. "I knew there were Britons behind those guns."

"I ain't never even seen England!" Ewald said. "Let alone North Bumberton, or wherever it is you say I come from."

"He comes from Pennsylvania, Mr. Hope," Favian said. "He's been on board for at least two years."

"Five!" Ewald snapped.

"And he's clearly speaking with a Dutch accent. His parents were immigrants, and Harrisburg is an area with many Dutch and Germans."

"Protect him if you like, Markham, but it is futile," Hope said placidly. "I know what I know."

"Fuck what you know," said Ewald.

"Ewald, that is enough," Favian interposed. "Mr. Hope is a British officer, and he may believe what he pleases." Even if it is contrary to fact, he thought, but did not say it.

British officers, many with their gear, were bundled together in the battered waist of the frigate, looking like schoolboys on a holiday who had somehow involved themselves in combat.

"My dunnage is being used as an operating table by your Mr. Trevitt," Hope said. "I hope you will not send me away without my baggage."

"I hope you don't take us for pirates," Favian said. Hope would get his blasted chest back later.

"I am sure," Hope said, his anger breaking out at last, "that I don't know by whom I have been taken."

You've just lost your damned sword, my boy, Favian thought with savage satisfaction, and he felt a roar bursting from his throat. "Into the boat with you, Hope!" he shouted. "There are no conditions to your surrender, and if I want your *balls* I'll have 'em!" There was a shocked silence at this enormous breach of courtesy. Then Hope and his fellow officers, without regard for precedence, were bundled into the boat; Decatur followed, with an apologetic, yet secretly amused, smile; and the pinnace returned to *United States*, leaving *Macedonian* to Decatur's fuming first officer.

Later, hours later, Favian became grateful for the chilled feeling of detachment that had come over him during the battle and had continued, despite his single outburst, throughout the night; he was thankful for the reflexes of the trained officer, which seemed to function automatically, in the place of his own percipient mind. He set Decatur's men to assembling corpses, laying them out on the

deck preparatory to burial at sea, the men trying to find
the bits of arm or leg or gut that belonged to each body.
Most of those who had died in the fight had been flung
overboard so as not to hamper the working of the ship, but
nearly all of them had been killed by roundshot, which
meant mutilation, and pieces of them inhabited the deck,
along with the bodies of other men who had died since the
fighting ended. Favian recruited some of the Macedonians
to sew up each body in sailcloth, with a roundshot at its
feet, preparing them for burial. The Americans were set to
work securing the mainmast rigging, and then the mainyard, which had been shot away in its slings. After the
yard was secured and fished, a new mainsail was got aloft,
and the running rigging rewove. A piece of twelve-inch cable was run from the bowsprit to the foretop, and a staysail
run up. Macedonian could now sail downwind, albeit
slowly, and maneuver if it had to, though within a narrow
range of limits.

And then it was discovered that the Macedonians had
broken into the spirit locker and become reeling drunk,
both on rum and on the eight hundred dollars' worth of
Madeira that had been brought aboard just a few days before. Favian was forced to lead a party of men below,
armed with belaying pins to brain a few of the more bellig-
erent Britons, and secure the locker, under the guard of
two teetotaling Yankees—preparatory to heaving overboard, the next day, every bit of spirit that could be found,
in case the thought of those waiting casks tempt not only
the vanquished, but their conquerors.

In the meantime the Macedonian's surgeon, aided by Dr.
Trevitt of the United States, continued to operate on the
lines of wounded filling the cockpit. Their drunken comrades danced above the wounded, singing old melodies,
conspiring to get the injured drunk as well. Their caco-
phony—old songs mixed with the shrieking, moaning
wounded—and the babbling of those driven mad by defeat
or horror, continued through the next morning, when
Favian, stomach burning with dyspepsia, trying and failing
to snatch a few hours' rest in Carden's shattered cabin, finally gave it up and returned to the deck. Drawing on his

gloves, he found them stiff with dried blood—when had that happened?—and threw them into the sea.

The morning also brought a cessation of the anarchy aboard the *Macedonian*: The crewmen, weary with wounds or debauch, had fallen asleep in the ship's corners, few managing to make it to their hammocks. Nicholson brought the results of his survey on the state of the spare spars, which had been stowed, as was the custom, on the well deck: Almost all smashed, Nicholson reported.

"Why does the captain need a report on the spare spars?" Nicholson asked, bemused. "Does he want to make sure we all get our proper share of whatever Congress gives us in lieu of prize money?"

"Captain Decatur intends to rerig *Macedonian* and take her home," Favian said. "We're going to run the British blockade to New England."

Nicholson's eyes widened. "Good lord," he said.

"Aye, it's almost beyond belief. But I think it can be done. We're going to make a bark out of her."

Favian had been considering the matter since Decatur had first made his intentions known the day before, and had lain awake, with the howls of the wounded in his ears, calculating stresses and purchases, running through his mind the inventory of *United States*'s own spare spars. Getting topmasts up and down was not an unusual procedure in itself; but doing so on a totally dismasted ship—with the chain plates, the pin rails and fife rails smashed by roundshot, as well as the bumpkins and chesstrees and other fixtures to which the standing and running rigging, which supported the masts, were fixed—and doing so without the aid of a well-equipped dockyard—was, to say the least, uncommon. Favian, who considered himself a scientific sailor, who operated a vessel through the power of reason and not with what seemed to be the mystical, instinctive approach of the old shellback, felt that the job could be done, if the weather stayed mild.

"We can do it," Favian said, allowing his face to assume an expression of manly confidence.

"I'm certain we can, sir," Nicholson answered; there was a certain abstract withdrawal in his eyes, and Favian knew that he, too, was totaling *United States*'s inventory of spare spars and masts.

"Mr. Nicholson, I've discovered something that may be of interest," Favian said, turning to a small locker set abaft the barricade, the rail between the quarterdeck and well deck. "A mechanical log, Nicholson," he said, opening the locker and removing a case covered in fine leather and brass. "Have you seen one before?" He opened the case to reveal a long, arrow-headed machine of gleaming brass and copper, and heard Nicholson's gasp of appreciation.

"'Massey's Recording Log, A.D. 1810,'" Nicholson breathed, reading the label.

"We should search the master's cabin and the wardroom to see if instructions for its use can be discovered," Favian said. "Its principles are clear enough, but I'm not certain how the dials are supposed to be read."

The *United States*'s logs were the traditional sort, of wood, trailed astern at the end of a knotted line. One operator would invert a sandglass, usually of twenty-eight seconds, while the other would count off the number of knots as the log line ran off its spool, stopping when the sand ran out of the glass; a routine calculation would result in the speed of the ship, in "knots," through the water. Massey's Recording Log was obviously designed to simply record the speed at which it was trailed astern, dispensing with the calculations needed by the traditional logs. There was a wedge-shaped head equipped with three dials protected by a sliding cover; behind the head, attached by a half-inch brass wire, was a projectile-shaped length of copper, with three fan blades made of brass, clearly designed to be turned by the water as the machine passed through its element. As the rotating part spun, it would turn the brass wire connecting it to the head of the machine, which would in turn record the number of revolutions and translate the information into knots per hour. Favian found himself enchanted by the beauty and usefulness of the thing; it was the sort of invention he had long maintained would be standard equipment in any rational, more scientific American Navy—it was a pity the British had invented it first. But Massey's Recording Log had been made a lawful

prize, and Favian had a suspicion that this particular recording log was going to have a long life aboard the *United
States*—after, of course, Favian had studied it thoroughly,
and made it the subject of a monograph addressed to the
Secretary of the Navy, expressing its usefulness and perhaps
recommending improvements.

Favian, standing on the quarterdeck explaining the log's
usefulness to Nicholson, heard a burst of French from the
deck below, and saw a group of men carrying instruments,
drums and fifes and trumpets, appear on the well deck.
"What in blazes is that?" he asked, amazed.

"Oh. I forgot to tell you, sir," Nicholson said. "It's the
French band. Carden captured them from a Frenchie some
time back and wouldn't let them go. He let them hide in
the cable tier during the fight. He let the Frenchmen hide
below," he said, indignant, "but he made the Americans in
his crew fight us. Three were killed."

"D'you have the names of the survivors? We can invite
them to replace our casualties."

"I have their names, aye, sir. But what I forgot to tell
you was that the band wishes to play us a concert."

"Now?"

"Aye, sir. To celebrate their freedom."

"Send them to the *United States*. We don't have time for
concerts here."

But the Frenchmen had already struck up the "Marseil-
laise," and Favian had no choice but to respect the anthem
of a co-belligerent, or whatever France was: France and
the United States were fighting the same England, but
were not allied; Madison was being careful not to involve
his country in wars against France's other European adver-
saries, Spain, Portugal, and Russia, with whom the United
States had no quarrel. But American privateers sheltered
in French ports, and the Revolutionary anthem deserved
respect on that count at least; Favian doffed his hat and
called his crewmen to attention. The French anthem was
followed by a brave, if unpracticed, rendition of "Yankee
Doodle." The American prize crew seemed stunned by the
sight of the French band rendering patriotic songs on the
scarred, bloodstained deck; those few British crewmen pres-

ent scowled, no doubt feeling another betrayal—if *Macedonian* had been the victor, the same eight-piece band would be playing "Heart of Oak" and "Britons, Strike Home."

As "Yankee Doodle" wound to a well-deserved halt, Favian quickly interrupted before another tune was begun and thanked the musicians in French for their playing, asking them to hold themselves ready to be sent aboard *United States* to play for its brave and victorious captain, Stephen Decatur; he then told them to dismiss. There was a great deal of work to be done, and although music might have made it go faster, or at any rate more pleasantly, there was so much to do that there was no place for the band to stand in peace and play.

For instance, the *Macedonian* had to be very thoroughly cleaned, from the orlop upward; the action of the tropical sun on the bloody decks, the bits of flesh and bone still scattered about from the action, would soon have the frigate smelling like a charnel house, and there would be risk of contagion. The channel pumps were manned and the decks rinsed with seawater. Swabs and holystones were brought out, and the decks cleaned, then scoured thoroughly with vinegar and gunpowder.

Then the *Macedonian*'s guns were properly secured. A number had been shot from their tackles during the fight, but had been tripped up by their British crews to lie on their sides, preventing them rolling about the ship with each wave like mad, brazen bulls, perhaps rolling into the main hatch and crashing through the ship's bottom. New tackles were rove, and the guns carefully righted and lashed into place. Favian tried to shift as many as he could to larboard, to keep the damaged bilges as far out of the water as possible, for the next item on the agenda of repairs was to replug, more permanently, the shot holes that had been temporarily plugged the day before.

The business of the shot holes took two days, with one crew working from inside the battered ship, another hanging down *Macedonian*'s tumblehome in rope chairs, and yet others working the pumps in shifts. In the end *Macedonian* still leaked, but in a normal sea a half hour's pumping out of every twelve sufficed to keep the bilges reasonably dry.

The task Favian dreaded came next. *Macedonian* still lacked a mizzenmast, and had no spar remaining long enough to serve as one. Masts were usually lowered into ships by a sheer hulk, a mastless ship with a crane that was warped alongside, able to drop a mast into a ship gingerly and without trouble. Favian would have to do without one, and he would also have to improvise a mizzenmast out of a spar originally designed for other work. For this Favian had himself rowed to *United States* to consult with Decatur, while Nicholson supervised further repairs. It would be some days yet before any masts could be put in; until Favian could be certain that the chain plates and other fixtures supporting the masts, and without which a mast would rock out at the first wave, were thoroughly surveyed and repaired, he did not intend to add so much as a royal mast to what *Macedonian* currently carried.

"It won't be an easy job," Favian reported to Decatur, "but we can do it. We'll bark-rig her and take her to Rhode Island for the antiwar Federalists to gawk at!"

Decatur's black eyes twinkled merrily. "Imagine what those who claimed the Navy could never hope for victory against the British will say when a genuine Royal Navy thirty-eight comes sailing to New England! Now which of our spare spars will you need?"

Favian explained his needs while Decatur made notes, then concluded.

Decatur smiled. "Thank you, by the by, for the band. They provided a luncheon concert today for the hands and for our guests, although I suspect the medley of patriotic tunes was not to the liking of Captain Carden and company. That band is surprisingly good. I'm tempted to keep 'em aboard, like Carden, when we reach port."

"I'm glad you enjoy them, sir," Favian said smoothly. "I'm certain they would look impressive leading a victory parade in New York."

"Aye, they would," Decatur said, absorbing an idea that, though it had not occurred to him first, clearly pleased him greatly.

"And how are our guests overcoming the boredom of the passage, sir?" Favian asked.

"Ah, they wander over the ship, making notes which it

pleases them to hide," Decatur said offhandedly. "Lieutenant Hope has claimed to have recognized sixty British subjects aboard, either from listening to their speech or some such reason, or because they serve the guns we named Nelson and Victory. He turned white when he heard Nelson's crew were deserters, and refused to believe they were born Americans; he talked of flogging and hanging till nightfall."

"He claimed Heinz Ewald was British," Favian said. "You should have seen the Dutchman glare!"

"We should probably encourage the British in their illusions," Decatur said. "It will prevent them from discovering the true cause of our victory." His amused eyes turned serious. "I mean to see you promoted for this, Favian," he said quietly. "I won't rest until you have your command. You've deserved it, these last seven years, and I won't forget your loyalty."

"Thank you, sir," Favian said. "It has been a distinct privilege to serve under you."

And strangely, Favian found that it was true. Though he saw through much of the Navy, he had still spent every year, since his sixteenth birthday, in the uniform; he had helped to make, and certainly lived by, its growing body of tradition and myth, and he was not entirely immune to it. He felt a clear, unalloyed pride at being the hand-picked subordinate to the most famous hero of the Navy, knowing it was perhaps the most singular honor that could have been bestowed on an officer of his rank. And as he felt Decatur's level gaze and heard his words, spoken not for the benefit of Clio but as simple truth, he felt the same kind of boyish, glowing achievement he'd felt when the crew of the *Constitution* had run aloft to cheer them when the *Intrepid*, Decatur at the helm, had returned from Tripoli harbor.

It was the same way he'd felt when old Preble fed him one of his rare compliments, light-headed, a tad wobbly. Strange, the return of this puppy conceit. He doffed his headgear.

"Sir, I think I should return to *Macedonian* to supervise the repairs."

"Very well. You seem to be holding your hand over your stomach. Is it the old problem again?"

"Aye, sir."

"Have you spoken to Mr. Trevitt?"

"No, sir."

"Do so. We can't afford to have you ill."

Stephen Decatur watched his subordinate make his way out of the cabin, then turned to the stern windows, seeing *Macedonian* pitching on the sea, battered, scarred, the American gridiron flag flying bravely from its stump of a foremast. Favian Markham's plan would put sail on her, topsails and topgallants, royals even, a regular pyramid of sail to drive her across the Atlantic and to New England, where she'd be taken into the United States Navy to fight against her builders. Perhaps one day Favian would command her in battle with the British, once Favian achieved command rank.

Decatur had always found Favian correct to a fault: punctual, reliable, a scientific sailor, gifted, a good conversationalist at dinner, and a learned one. In action he had never seen Favian hesitate; it was as if Lieutenant Markham had plotted every move several turns in advance. Perhaps his mind was too facile, too intelligent; perhaps, with Favian's ability to so clearly see all sides of an issue, he would have made a better judge than he made a naval officer. Or possibly Favian found that judicious pose convenient; perhaps he so glibly adopted the attitudes expected of him as a way of maintaining his own inner reserve, keeping his own self separate.

Decatur knew human nature well; he knew it instinctively, as some men knew the sea or the tangled affairs of politics, and he knew that Favian, for a long time now, had been keeping a part of himself back. There was nothing, of course, that Decatur could be expected to do about it; as long as whatever face Favian chose to present the world was competent and did its job, Decatur knew it would not be proper to intervene. Everyone, and perhaps most of all the men aboard a crowded man-of-war, needed a little piece of privacy apart from everyone else: a private journal, a secret treasure trove, filled with trinkets and souve-

nirs, bits of scrimshaw, a musical instrument into the playing of which the individual could withdraw. . . .

But Decatur had seen Favian's look before, and it had
usually been on people who had given up the Navy, thrown
it up to become something else. Favian had stayed with the
Navy, though, even in those frustrating gunboat years,
when his reserve had grown, and when any day Decatur
had expected him to fling down his resignation. Perhaps
one day the resignation would come, but until then Decatur
would compliment him, and work for his promotion, knowing he was giving his first officer only what the man deserved. Favian's talents were undeniable. How he would
handle a command of his own was anyone's guess—there
were other ways of leading men than Decatur's, and Decatur knew it—but Decatur knew that Favian had the technical skill, and the experience, to make for a promising commander. In any navy not so continually purged, from
within and without, and in a service that hadn't had to
tread so carefully in Washington, Favian would long since
have been given a command, even if it was only a paper
promotion to lieutenant commandant and the command of
a schooner. But the Federalist connection had worked
against him, and even after the thaw in political and naval
policy that had come with Madison's presidency, Decatur
had been unable to secure Favian a promotion. But now,
with *Macedonian*'s capture, Lieutenant Favian Markham
could no longer be overlooked. And Decatur had a plan,
one simmering in his political brain, to make that notice
stick.

Still, it would be interesting to discover what kind of a
commander Favian would make. Would he create another
persona for himself, Decatur wondered, an artificial captain into which, like hand into glove, he inserted himself?
Or would something of the real Favian Markham, whatever it was, come forth at last? It will be interesting to
watch, Decatur thought.

Favian's launch bobbed on the sea, curving toward *Macedonian*'s battered bulk. The sun gleamed from Favian's
single epaulet. Decatur sighed. He was having the British
officers to tea in his cabin that afternoon, and he was already tired of them. It would be captured tea, of course.

3.

"I wish I was a cabin boy aboard a man-o'-war.
Sam's gone away, aboard a man-o'-war.
Pretty work, brave boys, pretty work, I say.
Sam's gone away, aboard a man-o'-war."

The chantyman's baritone boomed over *Macedonian's*
deck, the men at the capstan singing along on the chorus.
Favian's strange engine rose over the pitching quarterdeck,
lines dangling from its peak.

"I wish I was a purser aboard a man-o'-war.
Sam's gone away, aboard a man-o'-war.
Pretty work, brave boys, pretty work, I say.
Sam's gone away, aboard a man-o'-war."

Favian had improvised sheers out of a pair of *United
States's* spare topmasts: Sixty-four feet long and lashed together near the masthead, they formed a triangle with their
heels spread apart as far as the width of the poop would
allow, and secured by temporary shorings and tail tackles
leading fore and aft. With the heels planted on the deck,
the triangle, which had been lying on the taffrail, jutting
out over the stern, was being lifted by the power of men at
the capstan until it lay directly over the hole where the new
mizzenmast was to be placed. The head of the sheers rose
slowly to the strains of the chanty, revealing the complicated lashing and the series of blocks and lines necessary
for the work: a fourfold block to raise the mast; a girt-line
block at the end of one of the masts, to hoist a man in case
of an emergency; four guys, two leading forward, two aft,

to support the sheers once raised, and to make slight adjustments to their position. It had taken two days to prepare *Macedonian* to receive its new mizzen, and another day to transfer the spare spars from *United States* to the captured frigate. Favian, his flesh pale and ill through his sun-brown tan, stood on the quarterdeck, giving fretful, nervous instruction to the men at the guys as the jury sheers rose.

> "I wish I was an officer aboard a man-o'-war.
> *Sam's gone away, aboard a man-o'-war!*
> Pretty work, brave boys, pretty work, I say.
> *Sam's gone away, aboard a man-o'-war!*"

That chantyman had chosen an unaccountably tedious melody, to be sure. The paired topmasts lurched skyward, helped on occasion by the surge of the sea beneath *Macedonian*'s counter. From above, Favian thought, the quarterdeck would look like a mass of gaping, upturned faces, as everyone watched the engine rise.

" 'Vast heaving, there!" Favian barked, and the chanty cut off in mid-chorus. The sheers hung mute over the poop, the blocks swaying. Favian walked beneath them, peering upward. "Give the forrard guys a haul, there!" he said, perceiving a minute adjustment necessary, and the sheers edged forward. "Belay! Belay, all!"

That part done, anyway. The fall was unrove from the capstan, and the jury mizzen was tugged, cursed, and kicked into place; the lower purchase block was lashed on a little above the mizzen's center of gravity, to cant it upwards. Once again the hands marched to the chantyman's baritone, the capstan pawls clacking into place, and the jury mizzen rose from the deck, swaying dangerously with the scend of the sea.

The mizzen had started its existence as one of *United States*'s spare foreyards, eighty-two feet long; one end had been carved with the carpenter's adze to prepare it to fit the step below, bolted to the keelson; the other end had been given trestletrees, for the men to stand on while they fixed the rigging in place. The spar rose, clearly looking the improvised piece of furniture that it was, and for a moment Favian felt a lurch of doubt: This will never work. . . . But of course it will, he assured himself. A spasm of pain shot through his stomach, just below his breastbone, and he pressed his hand to it.

" 'Vast hauling! Tail on to the backrope! Haul away, smartly!" The head of the jury mast rose until the mast was nearly vertical. "Ease the purchase fall. Handsomely, lads!" Slowly the mast descended, sliding into place. The carpenter was sent below to help ease the mast's heel into its step. The heel of the mast was guided carefully through the four decks until howls from below stopped the entire procedure. It seemed the mast would not fit. His stomach rumbling like Vesuvius, Favian ordered the mast raised a foot while the carpenter did some hasty adze work; the mast was lowered again, and this time it fit snugly into place.

Cheering hands went aloft; the standing rigging was set up, and the rake of the mast adjusted. While Favian saw to the lowering of the jury sheers, he would leave Nicholson to rig the running rigging and the driver—it would be a loose-footed driver, because there was no spare boom, but it would at least allow *Macedonian*'s rig to be balanced, so that the frigate could do other than sail downwind. For the topmasts of which the jury sheers had been composed, Favian had other plans.

The hands were given their midday dinner and grog and then cheerfully went back to work. A new lower cap—the massive piece of wood that actually bound lower mast and topmast together—was swayed up the mainmast, its forward, round, leather-padded hole widened to accommodate *United States*'s bigger topmasts, its rear, square hole carefully checked to make certain it would fit over the top of the lower mast when the time came.

The masts of a warship were built in three sections: the lower mast, towering seventy or more feet above the deck on a *United States*–class frigate; the topmast, rising perhaps another sixty-five feet from the lower mast and supported by the trestletrees and the cap; and the topgallant mast, an equally long though lighter mast fixed atop the topmast. Each mast in turn was supported by an intricate network of stays and shrouds, which kept it from whipping right out of the ship at each wave, and supported the mast when sail was set aloft.

Getting up a new topmast meant, first, maneuvering its sixty-five-foot length to the right place on the deck. Hoisting it the length of the lower mast, pointing it so that it would rise through the lubber's hole on the maintop, then lashing it to the lower mast while the proper lines were rigged to get it up farther, and the cap was placed above it. Then the mast would have to be threaded like a sixty-five-foot, straight, solid piece of yarn through the padded leather hole on the cap, the needle's eye. Once it was threaded, it would be lifted almost its full length up the mast, where it would be fidded into place, and the shrouds and stays that normally kept it from rocking out would be rigged. And then the same procedure would have to be repeated for the fore-topmast.

Between the time it was hoisted into place and the time the first shrouds were rigged, there would be nothing whatever supporting the topmast should it decide to whip out of the ship. There would be no yards aloft, and certainly no sail, so wind pressure would be minimized; and the operation would be done in good weather, with a following sea, so that the mast shouldn't be tempted to roll out; but still, the thought of that sixty-five-foot piece of wood standing unsupported, atop a ship floating nearly dismasted on the open sea, gave Favian a pronounced ache somewhere near the back of his skull.

A deep breath. "Let's begin. Rig the hawser." A stout twelve-inch hawser was led forward from the capstan, up to a block on the head of the lower mast, then down, lashed along the length of the topmast so that it would keep the mast's head uppermost during its ascent, brought through the fid hole in the topmast's heel, brought up, and hitched around the head of the mast. Members of *United States*'s complement were assigned to the capstan, the maintop, and the deck. The work began.

"Sway away!" the chantyman's baritone rang over the ship, feet stamped, capstan pawls clattered. The hawser sprang taut; the topmast trembled, lurched, and began to rise. There was a faint cheer from the men on the deck. Scraping its heel across the planking, leaving a deep gouge that would require hours of holystoning to smooth, the top-mast lurched skyward. Favian's eyes narrowed as he looked into the bright sky.

> "I wish I was a bosun aboard a man-o'-war.
> *Sam's gone away, aboard a man-o'-war!*
> Pretty work, brave boys, pretty work, I say.
> *Sam's gone away, aboard a man-o'-war!*"

Good lord, that chanty was tedious. The men at the capstan trudged in their endless circle, and the topmast rose. His neck craning back, Favian saw the head of the mast approaching the maintop.

"'Vast hauling!" he snapped. The chanty died, and the tramping. "Bear the head into the hatchway." This was the easy part. The men in the top lashed lines to the head of the topmast and, timing their movements to the pitch of the ship, pointed the topmasts by main strength to the lubber's hole. "Sway away, handsomely." Capstan pawls clacked slowly, the mast inching upward, until a shout from aloft told Favian the job was done. "Avast! Lash the topmast to the lower mast. Timber hitches, lads." The lashings would support the weight of the topmast while the arrangement of the hawser was changed. "Fix the cap to the lower masthead."

The heavy cap was wrestled up and dropped over the mast's square head. Top mauls banged it into place, the hollow drumming echoing over the sea. Favian's stomach was surely afire. "Rerig the hawser." The hawser was cast off while the timber hitches supported the topmast's weight; the hawser was rerove from the capstan forward through a snatch block, up to the maintop, through a block hanging from the larboard underside of the cap, down again to a sheave at the very base of the topmast, up again to where it was lashed near the top of the mast to keep it head uppermost, up still to another block beneath the starboard underside of the cap, then down to the deck. It looked like a giant, slightly irregular rope letter, Favian thought—the letter M.

Favian looked at his watch: almost four o'clock. Time to feed the prisoners, then his own men. This job was going to be finished after dark. Astern he heard a squealing of sheaves; Nicholson was experimentally hauling aloft the new driver gaff. "Mind the vangs there," Nicholson was saying. "Very well. Belay."

"Mr. Nicholson—it's almost time for supper!" Favian called.

"Aye, sir. Shall we resume this after we eat?"

"Aye, may as well. Good work, all. You're dismissed until we feed the prisoners."

Favian went without supper: He had been fasting for two days, trying to starve his dyspepsia into submission, thus far without success. He had suspected the tactic would be futile, but it had worked once, some years ago. The only sure cure was the use of opiates, over a forty-eight-hour period, but the last thing Favian needed was to be lurching about the prize giving orders in an opium daze. Supper, feeding the Britons and then the prize crew, took two hours. Then Favian reassembled his gang in the fading light of the westering sun. The hardest part remained: threading the needle.

"Maintop detail aloft. Cast off the timber hitches. Man the capstan. Sway away! Handsomely, lads . . . handsomely!"

"I wish I was a captain aboard a man-o'-war. . . ." The chantyman sang out again, but at a reduced pace; the capstan pawls clicked over slowly. The sheave at the heel of the topmast uttered an attenuated squeal that made Favian shudder as if fingernails had been drawn over a blackboard. The topmast inched its way upward, the men at the top dragging, by main strength, its head through the leather-padded hole in the cap. Favian squinted upward against the bright sky. The blue he could see through the cap's hole seemed to be narrowing. Was it done? Yes—no blue at all now.

"She's threaded, sir!" a man at the maintop roared.

"Avast!" Favian shouted. " 'Vast hauling!" Glorious. Favian, exhaling profoundly, discovered that he'd been holding his breath.

"Very well," he said. "Cast off those lashings. And be careful casting off the lashing on that hawser—it's going to snap out straight, with the weight of the topmast on it, and I don't want anyone cut in half or flung from the ship."

"Aye aye, Mr. Markham. We'll be careful." A man lowered himself cautiously into the lubber's hole, one foot braced on a futtock shroud, and leaned toward the lashing. Favian felt a cramp beginning in his neck from the strain of looking skyward.

The lashing was cast off. The topmast dropped three feet, the hawser snapping straight with a bass *thrumm* that reverberated throughout the captured frigate, awesome in its power. Nothing was holding the mast upright but the fact of its being threaded through the cap.

"Masthead, there!" Favian called. "Is all well?"

The crewman rose through the lubber's hole to stand on the maintop. "Deck there—aye, sir, all's well."

"Sway away, then!" Favian shouted. "Cheerily, lads!"

The dreary chanty rose again, and massively the topmast began to slide skyward, its sheave shrieking, threatening to drown the voice of the chantyman. As it rose, its tip pitched slightly from wave motion, and Favian gnawed his nether lip: If the damn thing pitched out now . . .

It stood ninety feet above the deck, then a hundred, then a hundred ten. Favian massaged the aching muscles of his neck, blinking sweat from his eyes. He knew the British captives on *United States* would be watching, Carden and Hope and the rest, anticipating some Yankee clumsiness that would bring the whole jury rig down in ruins. The mast rose above the trestletrees.

"*Avast!*" The mast had been raised high enough. Its head whipped slightly in the breeze. The maintop hands wrestled with the heel of the mast, bringing it into place.

"Lower away!" The mast dropped a foot, then found its place. The hawser slacked. Top mauls echoed as they banged the fid into its place.

"We have a topmast, lads!" Favian roared, and the hands cheered. "Aloft with you, to rig the standing rigging!" Favian ran to the shrouds with the men, climbing the main shrouds slowly, a bit unpracticed, but steadily enough; he used the futtock shrouds, dangling inverted over the sea, disdaining the lubber's hole, and swung himself into the tops to be met with grins by the swifter and more proficient seamen.

Favian was either in the maintop or hanging from a shroud until two hours past midnight. The hands worked by the light of the stars, the moon, and a few inadequate lanterns, and in the end the main-topmast was secured, shrouds and backstays and topmast stays supporting its great length against the attack of the elements. Even after the work was done, and he was below in Carden's cabin, pressing his hand to the place below his breastbone where the pain had lived for days, Favian was unable to rest easily. The final piece of work was done at night, by tired men; perhaps he had allowed them to make a mistake. Were the larboard deadeyes turned too tight—or perhaps not tight enough? What if the new rigging went slack, as new rigging often did?

Favian was irritable the next day, snapping at the men, shouting at the chantyman when he commenced the same tedious song. The fore-topmast was got up in a similar fashion in the morning, and rigged in the afternoon. The next day, topsail yards and topgallant masts were swayed up, and more sail set; *Macedonian* began to speed through the waves, a growing bone in her teeth. Favian took the wheel to get the feel of her; she fought the helm, but eventually answered—in any case, she answered better than she had with only fore and main courses aloft. Favian sent up the fore-topgallant the next day and was delighted with the success of it; the main-topgallant followed. To set royals or not? Using *United States*'s big topmasts and spars, *Macedonian* was setting much more canvas than with her own, more modest original equipment, and the royals might put too much strain on her. Though the driver in him urged the experiment, Favian kept the royal yards down; he'd save them for an emergency.

The new rigging slackened, as Favian had expected; but it was noticed and the slack taken up. Nicholson and Archibald Hamilton kept tireless watch alongside Favian, going aloft to feel with their own hands the tension on the shrouds, keeping a sharp eye on the oversize spars and canvas. Some two weeks after *United States* captured *Macedonian*, and having lost some ten pounds from his normal weight, Favian finally allowed himself Dr. Trevitt's prescription, and stayed abed for a full twenty-four hours with his head and guts swimming. The pain in his stomach abated, and he returned to duty, dosing himself carefully. It would be weeks yet before *Macedonian* would see land.

The frigates' course took them with the trade winds on a long sweep through the tropics, outside the Bahamas and inside the Bermudas, careful to avoid both Hatteras and the squadrons of British warships blockading all the southern ports and Sandy Hook. *Macedonian* sailed well, despite a tendency, from the improvised sail rig, to gripe; she was a beautifully made ship, probably copied from some French original captured by the British. The weather was kind, even after the tender northeast trades gave way to the brisk winter westerlies, which sent the prize crew scurrying for the deadeyes to slacken the contracting rigging. Not a single sail was sighted.

A few minutes north of latitude 41 degrees north, calculated by dead reckoning in a dense fog with the aid of Massey's Recording Log, the leadsman brought up coarse sand at nineteen fathoms, then coarse gravel at eleven, and the two frigates hove to, knowing they were just south of Martha's Vineyard. The fog clearing, they weathered Gay Head, passed The Sow and Pigs, The Hen and Chickens, and sailed for Providence Sound. It was the sixth of December, 1812, and New England was about to go mad with joy.

4.

The *United States* entered Newport full dressed, flags flying from every stay and halyard, minute guns booming to call to the town's attention the fact of *Macedonian*, scarred, bark rigged, royals missing, sailing into harbor with the Stars and Stripes flying triumphantly over the White Ensign. Favian observed through his telescope that Decatur had not chosen this moment to wear homespun: The captain's cocked hat was decked with a cockade, and gold flashed from his buttons and bullion epaulets. The faint sound of band music floated above the steady booming of the minute guns as the French orchestra earned its grog. By the time the two frigates dropped anchor, all of Rhode Island seemed to be lining the shore, and every house seemed to be flying a flag.

That night there was a dizzying, improvised reception in the town hall, leading citizens vying with one another for the cherished place of honor next to Decatur, but Decatur insisted the place be given to Favian. "I want 'em to *know* you, Mr. Markham," he smiled. "Know you for a sailor, and for a New England man. And it may be handy for you to know *them*."

So, during the rounds of toasts, the speeches, music, and applause, Favian applied himself to cultivating the congressman he found at his elbow, a tobacco-chewing Federalist of the Peace faction, who, Favian knew, had (unlike most Federalists) consistently voted against naval appropriations and (hewing to the party line) also voted against any measure likely to antagonize Great Britain, and against the war itself. Favian found himself cynically amused at the man appearing at all, but supposed that the profession of politician required, first of all, the sacrifice of any sense of dignity; and his politically minded brothers and cousins had taught Favian the virtues of public exposure. So he supposed that by showing himself at a victory banquet the congressman was trying to show himself in a favorable light, associating himself with victory and courage, a hero by association.

Favian mentioned, offhandedly, his Federalist connections, the work his brother Lafayette and his cousins Obadiah and Jeremiah had done for the party in New Hampshire. The congressman's eyes gleamed at the mention of Lafayette Markham, and Favian, finding the gleam a little unpleasant, wondered why. Was the congressman, perhaps, an enemy of the family? Or was he simply grateful to be able to fit Favian into some political pigeonhole?

But there was little time to wonder about the congressman's thoughts and motivations; the banquet itself demanded attention. A certain amount of regard had to be given to the speeches, so that the correct replies could be framed. There were a lot of toasts, and even Favian, who was used to this kind of thing on shipboard, began to feel his head swimming. Newport was on the brink of relieved hysteria. New England had opposed the war, knowing it would be New England ships captured by the enemy, New England commerce wrecked, and New England that would, if all miscarried, be invaded through Canada. New Englanders knew that their chief hope of relief from these mischiefs—the Navy—had been gutted by the Jefferson administration, over all their objections. None of these facts led to sanguine expectations, and at first the worst had come to pass. Detroit had surrendered, along with an American army, through sheer cowardice on the part of its commander. Fort Dearborn had been taken, and every man of the garrison killed and scalped by Tecumseh's Indians. One American force was cut to ribbons on the Niagara while another American force stood by and watched, refusing to aid the comrades who were dying in plain sight.

And then a trickle of good news had begun to appear. *Constitution* had beaten and sunk the *Guerrière*, *Wasp* had captured the *Frolic*, although the United States sloop was taken itself by the British shortly thereafter. Now *United*

States had captured *Macedonian* and actually sailed her
into an American port, to be added to the American forces.
New England could actually look out its windows and *see*
victory swinging from its cable, to and fro with the tide,
the gridiron flag floating over the White Ensign in mute
proclamation of the triumph. Decatur's grasp of human nature had once again proven sound; he had known that a
captured British frigate the population could actually *see*
would be worth three enemy warships destroyed after capture—and of course it would be of value to the Navy after
it had been refitted and given an American crew.

It seemed as if all New England had crammed itself into
the banquet hall. There was an additional local reason for
the scope of the enthusiasm, it seemed: The two frigates
had appeared, by sheer chance, on the anniversary of Newport's capture by the British in 1776. The formal banquet
ended, and unrestrained celebration began. Favian found
himself thankful to be separated from the congressman, but
discovered to his dismay that he had been made prize to an
elderly merchantman with four marriageable daughters, all
of whom appeared properly awed by his professional accomplishments, and who seemed to require a gunshot-by-
gunshot description of his career from Tripoli to the present. Decatur at last rescued him from this reluctant
exercise of egotism, and took him briefly aside. "I'm going
to take *Macedonian* down the coast to New York," he said.
"The British will be reading of our appearance in New
England newspapers ere long, and I want to get the prize
out before they blockade us."

"Aye, sir." Favian pictured what a sensation *Macedonian*
would make, decked out and sailing past Hell Gate to the
great city.

"We'll stay here to put off the British crew and take on
supplies. Perhaps give her a proper mizzenmast."

"Aye, sir."

"I'm sending you and Hamilton ahead by pilot boat to
New York. You'll be leaving on the afternoon tide tomorrow. I'll need you to carry my official dispatches to Washington City, along with *Macedonian*'s flag."

"But the *Macedonian* . . . !"

"Nicholson can do it. In New York you'll see my prize agents, Wheeler and Tazewell, who will give you an advance for the trip."

Favian was too stunned to stammer out an assent. Going with dispatches from New York to Washington would mean riding overland over miserable December roads, and the importance of the dispatches would mean haste. The normal passage by sea would be in danger of interdiction by British ships, which were blockading most American ports from Sandy Hook south.

"I'm going to make 'em notice you, Favian," Decatur said. "Secretary Hamilton will wish to promote his son, and he won't be able to do it without promoting you as well."

"Th-thank you, sir," Favian said.

"When you reach New York, I want you to send back two damn good Hell Gate pilots. Tell them to meet us in New London. We'll be sailing there in a few days."

The celebration reeled on. The next day, Favian could remember the city of Newport running out of wine and offering less expensive substitutes; someone pressed a cup of pure undiluted whiskey into his hand, and afterward Favian could remember little, his memories like drops of foam thrown up by a ship's tossing stem, fine little jewels with nothing between them. There was the time Favian stepped outside for a breath of crisp winter air and discovered the congressman vomiting noisily in an alley. He remembered also receiving a note, delivered by a messenger who explained he was acting for a lady, whom he pointed out—her face was swathed in a veil, but her form was inviting, though a little buxom for current fashion. Favian read the note to discover it contained an offer of marriage.

While recovering from his surprise at this unexpected proposal, he found his elbow tugged by an old white-haired shellback, who, it turned out, had once been a crewman on the *Cossack* privateer under Favian's uncle Malachi; and Favian spent a fascinating half hour listening to the old man's fund of anecdotes—pity Favian could remember so few of them. But he recalled a firsthand account of the wreck of the British frigate *Melampe*, the capture of the *Royal George*, and an inexhaustible series of stories concerning Malachi's incredible seamanship: how he would navigate *Cossack* off an invisible lee shore by the seat of his pants, or would pick his landfall, after a two-thousand-mile journey outside of sight of land, within minutes. " 'Tis a pity, young man, that ye ain't a privateer yerself," the shellback had said. "That's *real* honor—and money, too. Not this button-polishin', monarchist naval service, as likely to get us into a war with all Europe just to secure themselves a few promotions."

It wasn't until Favian caught a glimpse of a veiled woman stalking angrily out of the hall that he'd remembered the note in his hand. I have been very rude, he'd thought with a drunken clarity.

It had not been until dawn that the officers of the *United States* stumbled back to their bunks. Again there was time for only a few hours' rest, for Decatur had arranged for Favian and Archibald Hamilton to be aboard the pilot schooner *Seaconnet*, under Captain Holland, at noon.

Favian was still slightly drunk as he approached the schooner in one of *United States*'s whaleboats, Nicholson and Hamilton accompanying him in the stern sheets; and Favian found himself lecturing Nicholson like an overpossessive parent on the need to take care of *Macedonian*'s masts and yards and to make sure that, at sea, the sails were reefed down at night in case of a sudden December gale appearing from the darkness, and on the need to take advantage of their stay in Newport, making certain of the repairs to the hull, some of which had worked loose on the long voyage. Conscious suddenly of his own absurdity, Favian abruptly broke off his lesson, wished Nicholson the best of luck and weather, and came aboard *Seaconnet* just as its crew was manning the windlass to heave her cable short.

Holland was a compact, muscular man in his mid-forties. His hair was tied in a short, slightly old-fashioned queue. Vigorous and knowledgeable, he was nevertheless very aware of having naval officers on board, and was determined that *Seaconnet* should prove as efficient a vessel as any in the Navy. The five days' journey to New York—which would have been shortened to a single night had not westerly December gales forced the schooner to run for New London and New Haven on separate occasions—gave him plenty of opportunity to demonstrate his abilities. Favian found the trip a blissfully peaceful vacation. Despite the bad weather and the irritatingly close confines of the pilot boat's accommodation, despite Holland's aggressive insistence on pointing out how well things were done aboard his vessel, Favian was delighted that he had nothing to do. For weeks he'd been worrying over *Macedonian* like a mother hen over her brood, almost frantic that the jury rig might not hold up, or that a British squadron would appear and render their work pointless, or that *Macedonian*'s original crew might rise and try to retake the ship. Now his only worries were those of a passenger: whether or not dinner could be cooked and served hot during a gale, or the remote possibility that *Seaconnet* might not be able to outrun a British cruiser—and Holland, justly proud of his swift clipper schooner, refused to admit that possibility at all—or that they might find themselves aground somewhere, or dismasted, blinded by the gales.

But Holland was a good man; he knew when to fight the sea and when to seek shelter; *Seaconnet* passed Hell Gate without incident, and Favian found himself again in the world of naval routine.

Commanding the New York Navy Yard was Isaac Chauncey, one of Preble's boys and a diehard New England man who had commanded the frigate *New York* off Tripoli and maneuvered *Constitution* during the bombardments, when Favian, the Decatur brothers, Somers, and the rest had been battling hand to hand with enemy gunboats.

"Favian Markham, by Jerusalem!" Chauncey exclaimed as Favian stepped into his office and uncovered in salute. "And young Hamilton! I thought ye were at sea! Come, sit by the fire; ye look soaked through, as if ye'd just stepped ashore—d'ye bring news from Captain Decatur?"

"We do, sir," Favian said. "It's good news. *United States* took the thirty-eight-gun frigate *Macedonian* in October, and brought her home to Newport. We're carrying the report to Washington City."

Chauncey's portly frame was almost dancing with excitement. "That's another blow for the flag, by thunder!" he barked out. "And perhaps soon there will be another— Bainbridge has taken *Constitution* out again, with the *Hornet*. Perhaps Old Ironsides will take another frigate."

"I pray she will," Favian said. "I pray we all may."

"Amen to that," Chauncey said. "Though my own chances are slim. I've just received word from Secretary Hamilton that I'm to ride to Sackett's Harbor—a sleigh ride it'll be, in this weather—to take command on the Great Lakes. No frigates there, I'm afraid."

"You may have to build some."

Isaac Chauncey's eyes gleamed. "I may at that, Mr. Markham. But what is it I can do for ye?"

"Commodore Decatur," Favian said, using the more prestigious, though entirely honorary, title, "hopes to be at New London with the prize in a week. Then he wants to take her to New York. His exact words were that he wants 'two damn good Hell Gate pilots' to meet him in New London."

Chauncey nodded. "I'll arrange for it."

Isaac Chauncey saying "I'll arrange for it" was the equivalent of most men swearing solemn oaths while standing atop a pyramid of bibles: Chauncey was universally conceded to be the Navy's most reliable figure. Favian thanked him, knowing the business was as good as concluded, and that Chauncey might well throw in a few extra pilots by way of being thorough.

"And we'll need horses for the ride to Washington," Favian added. "Can you arrange that, or shall I—?"

"When d'ye need 'em for?" Chauncey asked sharply.

"As soon as is practicable. Tomorrow morning we must pay a visit, on behalf of the commodore, to Wheeler and Tazewell."

"Prize money, eh?" Chauncey said. "That merchantman Captain Decatur sent in was brought before the prize court and returned to its owners. Sorry to tell ye."

Favian hadn't been surprised. Decatur had seized a Philadelphia-bound merchantman a few days before encountering the *Macedonian*, and on quite flimsy grounds made a prize of her.

"When I heard of it," Chauncey went on, "I thought to

myself, Aha, Decatur's so eager for action he'll be sending in fishing smacks next. Hope he finds himself a worthy frigate to sink. Never thought he'd actually bring it home. That's always been Captain Decatur's weakness—that eagerness."

"Yes, sir," Favian said tactfully, knowing Chauncey was substantially correct. Decatur had been itching for action and was willing to treat even a harmless merchantman as an enemy, at least until the real thing came along. Favian remembered that impetuous first broadside that had so completely missed: too eager. He had fought a cunning battle afterward, though, as if that one broadside had taken the edge off.

"Well, ye can't wait here till Christmas," Chauncey said. "I'll have horses here at the yard by noon tomorrow."

"Thank you, sir. I'm sure we're most grateful."

"And I'll speak to the mayor about the celebrations we'll arrange for *Macedonian*'s arrival," Chauncey went on, his mind briskly assembling the consequences of the victory. "We'll try to arrange for a parade, perhaps a theatrical performance. Illuminations, certainly; swords and medals for the officers—a pity I'll be at Sackett's Harbor by then. A great day for the Navy, Mr. Markham, when *Macedonian* was made prize. Mr. Hamilton, it will make your father's job a good deal easier."

"I hope it will, sir," Hamilton said respectfully. When confronted by the awesome majesty of a full captain, midshipmen like Hamilton were supposed to speak only when spoken to.

"And now, gentlemen, if ye've warmed yerselves sufficiently, I'll take the liberty of bringing ye home with me for supper. Let me send a message to Mrs. Chauncey."

Favian and Archibald Hamilton watched in comfortable amazement as the Navy's most conspicuous paragon of efficiency arranged the next twenty-four hours of their lives. Clerks were summoned to write orders that would send the pilots to New London, arrange for several horses to be waiting in the yard at noon the next day—Favian and Hamilton to have their choice—and a memorandum was sent to Mrs. Chauncey on the size of the supper party.

Chauncey maintained a superb cook in his household, as

his stout figure demonstrated, and he had a good cellar as well. His servants proved to be better drilled than many a ship's crew, virtually leaping back and forth from the kitchen, snatching empty plates from under surprised noses, refilling wine glasses without being bidden. Apparently Chauncey was as brisk about eating as he was about everything else.

The table talk was almost entirely service gossip—consisting chiefly, on Chauncey's part, of battles with stupid contractors, crooked suppliers, and ignorant subordinates. Chauncey was diplomatic enough to avoid mentioning any wrangles with Hamilton's father, the Secretary of the Navy. Archibald Hamilton, responding to Chauncey's questions, related the history of the fight with *Macedonian*, sparing no praise for Decatur or Favian. Respectfully, Favian kept out of the conversation altogether, except when he was asked a direct question; he appreciated Chauncey's interrogative skill in asking the junior member of the company about the action, receiving thereby the opinion least likely to be colored by loyalty or service prejudice.

But chiefly, throughout the meal, Favian wondered just what it was that Isaac Chauncey lacked. Perhaps if he hadn't spent the last seven years as Decatur's subordinate the question would never have arisen in his mind; he might not have been so thoroughly aware of some strange, half-spiritual difference between his plump host and the illustrious Decatur. Chauncey was, like Favian, a master of detail; he was sociable, friendly, and obviously intelligent. Unlike Chauncey, unlike anyone else Favian knew, Decatur possessed what the Greeks would have called charisma, the divine grace that made him a natural leader. Few commanders possessed such qualities as Decatur, but they were still good men. Yet, this obvious lack aside, there was still something missing in Chauncey.

Favian had never known Chauncey well, even when they served together off Tripoli, and their paths had not crossed since. Young Lieutenant Chauncey's coolness, his competence, in quenching a magazine fire that had panicked his captain, had raised him well above Favian's level before Favian had ever met him. When Favian was a midshipman, dreaming of glory in *Constitution*'s gun room, Isaac Chauncey already commanded the corvette *John Adams*, and later the frigate *New York*. It had been Favian who fought dirty melees from one gunboat to another, while Chauncey had taken over the sailing of the *Constitution* into the fight, with Commodore Preble directing its gunfire; Chauncey's job had been clean by comparison, and much tidier.

Perhaps Isaac Chauncey might have been helped by a slower advancement, and by being in those gunboats that had been forced to fight such a messy war. Perhaps it would have given him a certain steel that Favian suspected he lacked. Chauncey was intelligent, and knew his job well; there was certainly no reason to doubt his courage. But Favian suspected he wasn't a fighter. Criticizing Decatur for his eagerness, when most Navy men would have thought it admirable, was quite possibly the key here. Isaac Chauncey had not been through quite the same school as the rest.

Favian hoped the Navy Department hadn't been wrong in sending Chauncey to Sackett's Harbor, but he suspected they would have made a better choice in someone like Johnston Blakely, now wasting his talents in command of the *Enterprise* brig, or Thomas MacDonough, who, Favian had last heard, was rotting his time away commanding a gunboat flotilla in Maine.

It was not an easy job to which Chauncey had been assigned. His principal command was on Lake Ontario, where the United States had a single boat to oppose a formidable Canadian squadron. Chauncey's responsibilities would also extend to Lake Erie, where the British had another squadron, and the United States no vessels at all; the lack of American naval strength had already made its mark in the surrender of Detroit.

But it was hardly courteous for a guest, treated so royally, to have such doubts about his host, and Favian consciously suppressed his speculations. The conversation, continued over cigars and mulled wine in Chauncey's study, went on long into the night, and then Favian and Hamilton were shown to their rooms.

"A splendid fellow, this Captain Chauncey," Hamilton

laughed the next day, as he and Favian stood on the ferry
bringing them and their horses across the Hudson. Off beyond Sandy Hook, on this clear December day, they could
see the topsails of two patrolling British frigates, probably
the advance guard of Broke's squadron, reminders of the
royal might brought to Manhattan's front door.

"He's had food packed in our saddlebags, in case we
can't find decent meals at an inn," Hamilton went on.
"And a bottle of his best hock! That's a measure of how
long he's been on shore," he reflected. "To think that anyone living for months on hardtack and salt horse could
think inn food bad!"

"Aye," Favian agreed. "I hope his men on Lake Ontario
eat as well as we shall in the next few days." His eyes
slitted as he watched the British topsails. We've taken two
of them, he thought. Eight hundred to go.

Overland from New York to Washington would be at
least three hundred miles, all on horseback over the most
miserable roads in the United States. Most of the good
roads led into the interior, permitting immigration to the
West and bringing western goods to the port cities for ex-
port; north-south traffic was usually by sea, until Admiral
Warren's blockade closed off all the ports south of New
York. Favian was a good rider, but Hamilton, like most
sailors, was not. Allowing for bad weather, Favian calculated, they would be lucky if they did not spend the rest of
December on the road.

And so it almost proved. Hamilton, after a few days of
agony, became an accomplished horseman; but storms
brought them to a halt several times, and colic struck Hamilton's horse in New Jersey, and it had to spend a day resting. At Philadelphia—where Favian had spent the dreari-
est, most disillusioning years of his life commanding
Gunboat 182 on the Delaware—they stayed for one night
courtesy of the Navy Yard, exchanged their horses for
fresh mounts, and plodded onward through the December
mud. The stagecoaches promised service from Philadelphia
to Washington City in thirty-three hours, but in fact it took
four days; Christmas Eve and day were spent at a snow-
bound Maryland inn. Favian considered continuing the letter to Miss Emma Greenhow that had been interrupted by

Macedonian's appearance, but instead he spent the time polishing his monograph on Massey's Recording Log, and trying to stay out of the way of the two other travelers who had been crowded into a room already small for the two naval officers.

"No doubt the horses have better stabling," Hamilton commented, raising to his lips the jug of whiskey he had bought to sustain himself during his stay, and which was destined to be left empty in the room when they left. Hamilton's company proved to be Favian's only consolation on the journey; his irreverent stories of political figures, gathered no doubt from his father—the story of John Merry, His Britannic Majesty's minister to the United States, in full dress uniform, medals, ribbons, breeches, silk stockings, and buckled shoes, presenting his credentials to Thomas Jefferson, in an old brown coat and heelless slippers, was one of his favorites—provided some amusement, and fueled Favian's already considerable cynicism about the way the war was likely to be managed.

Hamilton was an able young officer, eager, intelligent, ambitious, and altogether typical; he seemed to show no resentment at being honed into the Navy's idea of a proper member of its elite. But then Favian had shown no resentment, either, at Hamilton's age; that had come only later, in Philadelphia, when Favian was obliged to practice the blockading skills he'd learned at Tripoli on ships of his own nation, enforcing the Embargo Acts by keeping United States vessels bottled up in their own ports, leaving seamen to starve and the merchants bankrupt; it was then that Favian began to grudge the mold into which he'd been cast, the honed, pristine edge of America's cutting blade.

Their horses stumbled into Washington three days after Christmas. They found rooms at Blodget's Hotel, a ruined edifice once boasting the only Ionic pilasters on the Potomac and now housing, among other things, the Post Office Department and the Patents Bureau. Part of it was still operated as a hotel, chiefly for peripatetic civil servants and hopeful office seekers, but the collection of inventions belonging to the Patents Bureau was slowly encroaching on the guest quarters.

Favian demanded a bath and got one, then carefully unpacked the dress uniform he'd carried with him, attached the epaulet to its left shoulder, combed his hair and side-whiskers, collected Hamilton, also in dress, and marched to the Navy Department, just west of the Executive Mansion—or the President's House, the White House, the Presidential Palace, or whatever else the pile was called.

"Mr. Hamilton is out, sir," said a withered clerk, as Favian stood in the foyer with mud dripping from his boots. "He is preparing for the Naval Ball tonight, where Captains Hull and Stewart will be honored. If you will leave a card, I shall give it to His Excellency on Monday."

"Isaac Hull? He's here?"

"Yes, sir," the clerk said, looking disapprovingly at Favian's footprints on the threadbare carpet of the foyer. "Now if you will just leave your card . . ."

"The Naval Ball—where is it?"

The clerk scowled at the ignorance of this young officer, who had probably come to beg for a job, but he loftily announced that the ball would be at the Navy Yard, and Favian fled the place before he was asked once more for his card.

The clerk's mention of the Naval Ball had set Favian's head spinning. President Madison would be there, of course, along with his fabled wife, Dolley; the foreign ministers would be there, the cream of Washington society, the secretaries of war and the navy, most of Congress. . . . Favian's head swam with names and titles. The guests of honor would be Captain Isaac Hull, late of the *Constitution*, victor over the *Guerrière*, and Charles Stewart, a man whom the professional side of Favian honored immensely. And of course the enormously influential Captain Thomas Tingey, superintendent of the Washington Navy Yard, would be present with his staff. Favian clapped Hamilton on the shoulder and brandished Decatur's report in his other hand. Hamilton looked surprised at Favian's sudden exuberance.

"So Stephen Decatur thinks he's the only one who can make a grand gesture, eh?" Favian laughed. "We're going to board the President and his lady tonight!"

Favian had not been apprenticed to a master of dramatics for nothing. No one in Washington knew of his muddy entrance, and word of *United States*'s victory had not yet penetrated by word of any blockade runner. The news, in the proper setting, could cause a sensation.

Favian suspected that Decatur would approve of his plan.

5.

"Blasted Washington," Archibald Hamilton muttered as he received the salute of the sentry at the gate of the Navy Yard. "Mud in winter, dust in summer. Dust and malaria." He grinned. "Be thankful you're here at the best time of year. You'll probably only get a flux."

"I'll bear it in mind," Favian said, urging his horse along the path, its hooves pulling from the mud with unpleasant sucking sounds. The Naval Ball demanded even more formality than had the visit to the Navy Department; instead of his blue trousers Favian was wearing white breeches and silk stockings, and he hoped he wouldn't enter the ballroom to discover his legs were splattered with mud from the three-mile ride from Blodget's Hotel.

"You've seen the public buildings—the President's House, the Capitol?" Hamilton said. "They look like mud huts in this weather. Particularly the Capitol, with that plain board gallery between the two wings. Washington's so unimpressive, the European powers scarcely keep as much as a single embassy here, just consular offices, and often as not they sell those duties to Americans. At least the French have their own minister here."

"I expect we'll change that, don't you think?" Favian said, riding to the door of the rambling building holding the ball. The faint sounds of the Marine Band came from inside. Favian dismounted into the muck, handed the horse to a black groom, and stepped up onto the sheltered porch. He examined the package containing *Macedonian*'s flag and Decatur's dispatch, which he'd kept from the wet under his cloak; he brushed sleet off his hat and cloak, and scraped the mud from his shoes. Hamilton followed suit, took off his hat, shook his fair hair. They stepped inside.

The Marine Band was playing a polka, and the foyer leapt to the tread of the dancers inside. Soft candlelight glowed through a wide interior door. Black men in livery took their cloaks, and Favian saw, in the candlelight, men and women dancing; many of the men wore blue coats and epaulets, both Army and Navy.

"Shall I take your sword, baas?" a majordomo asked, a stout, courteous black tugging at his own waistcoat.

"No, I'll keep it for the present. Has Captain Thomas Tingey arrived?"

"Oh, yes, baas. First of all."

"Will you give him this message?" Favian drew it from his cuff; neither the elegant cut of his swallowtail uniform coat nor the lines of his tight white breeches allowed for such things as exterior pockets.

Thomas Tingey was delayed until the end of the polka; apparently he'd been dancing. He was a New Jersey man who had been sacked in the Jefferson purges, but somehow had talked his way back to his former rank, and now, as head of the Washington Navy Yard, was the only non-seagoing captain in the Navy. He was a popular figure, loquacious, persuasive, honey-tongued. He had the ear of the politicians, was always ready to give advice, and convincing enough so that his advice was often taken. It was a pity, thought Favian, that Tingey's advice was so often bad.

"Favian Markham! Young Hamilton! Your parents are here, you know, Hamilton—have you seen 'em? They'll be delighted!" Tingey, large framed, jolly, held out a hand, and Favian clasped it. His voice was a remarkably melodious baritone; Favian remembered he had been famous for his parties, at which he'd sung duets with his late wife.

"Your note spoke of important news. Let's hear it."

"Captain Decatur has captured a British thirty-eight. It's probably in New York by now."

"By God, that's news! Hull is here—have y'told him?"

Favian, in a low voice, explained his plan. Hamilton listened with surprise, then admiration. At the end Tingey whistled appreciatively.

"By Jerusalem, that's an idea! Board the President and Dolley! We're going to enjoy reading tomorrow's newspapers, young man. Leave it all to me. Wait for a drumroll, then enter."

"Aye, sir," Favian said, then hesitated. "How will I know Mrs. Madison, sir? I've never met her."

Tingey laughed. "She's the one standing by the flags, young man! They set off her complexion so well. Y'can't miss her."

"Yes, sir."

The band was playing a reel, a statelier sort of dance which allowed the older members of the throng to recover their breath after the brisk polka. Favian waited impatiently, fidgeting while he unwrapped the package, and handed Decatur's report to Hamilton.

"Are you sure you'd prefer to carry the flag?" Hamilton asked insinuatingly. "I can do it, if you like."

"Seniority hath its privileges, Mr. Hamilton. You are to carry the dispatch."

Hamilton sighed. Favian fidgeted. What if he was confused, and picked the wrong lady? Madison he knew from engravings, but his famous wife had unaccountably been left out of the pictures. Perhaps the illustrators had given up hope of ever depicting her properly. The reel came to an end at last. The crowd gave scattered applause. Favian took a deep breath and hoped that when the time came he wouldn't stumble over a spittoon.

There was a single trumpet call, bringing the murmuring, applauding crowd to attention. A nice touch—the band leader must have improvised. A long drumroll began. Favian tugged at his uniform and advanced into the room.

It was lit by hundreds of candles, glowing gold on the faces of the guests. Hamilton's marching steps echoed behind him. Faces turned toward him in surprise, in anticipation, in merriment. In one corner were bearded faces, turbaned heads, and Turkish costumes, and Favian was puzzled until he remembered that a Tunisian envoy had recently taken up residence. Somewhere there was a shriek, and movement among the crowd to his left. Favian risked a glance, saw the familiar figure of the Secretary of the Navy supporting a limp bundle. It appeared that Hamilton's

mother had fainted at the sight of the son she had supposed
to be at sea.

British banners draped the walls, the ensigns of the corvette *Alert*, which had surrendered to the *Essex* after firing
a single musket shot *pour l'honneur du pavillon*, and the
great flag of the *Guerrière*. Beneath the flags, surrounded
by an invisible aura of power and respect—what in a mon-
archy would have been called presence—was a short, lean,
white-haired man in a plain black coat whom Favian recognized as James Madison, principal author of the Constitution and of an unpopular war, former Federalist turned
Democratic-Republican, President of the United States.
Beside him was a plump, lively-seeming woman, dressed
rather extravagantly in a pink, ermine-trimmed satin robe
with gold chains and clasps, topped by a white satin turban
with a jeweled crescent and ostrich plumes, who Favian
assumed was the famous Dolley Madison—she had *better*
be Dolley Madison, and not a dependent of the Tunisian
delegation, Favian thought, or his career was as good as
over. Her mouth was parted, her eyebrows raised in an
amused anticipation, wondering what little surprise had
been arranged by the Navy Department. Probably the Secretary of the Navy was wondering the same thing, if he
wasn't too distracted by his limp wife in his arms.

Favian cleared his throat as he approached, hoping his
voice would not crack. He swept *Macedonian*'s flag out
with a snap of his arm, the flag sailing out to its full twelve-
foot length, the riddled White Ensign billowing at the feet
of the President's lady. Dolley Madison stared at the flag
in dawning comprehension. Favian knelt.

"I beg the honor, madam, to lay at your feet the surrendered flag of the British frigate *Macedonian*, captured in
battle by Captain Decatur two months ago." Favian's voice
rang in the candle-lit stillness.

Sensation. Bedlam. Favian had intended Act Two to be
Archibald Hamilton's presentation of Decatur's official report to the President, but whatever Hamilton said was
drowned out by the pandemonium of men calling for three
cheers, wild applause, shrieks of enthusiasm, and the Marine Band's sudden fortissimo booming of the new anthem,
"Hail, Columbia." Dolley Madison said something unheard

in the sudden turmoil, but she was clearly asking Favian to rise, and he did so. She took the ensign from his numbed hands, and with a graceful gesture threw it over her own shoulders, draping herself in it.

The audience went mad. Favian, awed, realized with admiring surprise that he was in the presence of someone who knew at least as well as Decatur how to stir a crowd by a simple, eloquent gesture. She kissed Favian's cheek (to more cheers) and then the President, as thin as Favian but a good deal shorter, began to pump his hand. "Congratulations, young man. We'll speak later," the President almost shouted, and Favian nodded respectfully.

He glanced over the President's head and saw a milling, stampeding crowd; Dolley Madison parading with the ensign draping her shoulders, her ostrich plumes nodding; Archibald Hamilton engulfed in the arms of his mother, who had, it appeared, recovered thoroughly from her fainting fit. Secretary Paul Hamilton shouldered his way through the crowd, shook Favian's hand, and bent to shout into Madison's ear: "Never forget that it's to Captains Bainbridge and Stewart that we owe these victories!"

Damned if it was! Favian almost raged. It was Decatur's seamanship and my gunnery! But he bit it back, savage temper still filling him at the cheapening of his spectacle. What was the secretary driveling about? But then there were more handshakes and claps on the back as Favian was surrounded by a crowd of blue-coated naval officers.

"Congratulations, sir!" It was Isaac Hull, conqueror of the *Guerrière*, a plump man with a genial expression and one of the best technical sailors in the world, a man who had outrun a British squadron in a dead calm by towing *Constitution* with boats, then splicing together all the cordage in the ship to kedge her to safety. He'd returned to Boston to discover that his uncle, the man who had raised him, had surrendered Detroit to an army one third the size of his own—a disgrace Hull's battle with the *Guerrière* had done much to erase. Favian had also heard that Hull had split the seat of his tight trousers when he'd given the order to fire, and, looking at the cloth that was trying gamely to protect Hull's portly frame, he could well believe it.

"Thank you, sir," Favian said, still seething inwardly,

and was then engulfed by the arms of another officer and hugged until he gasped for breath—and until he found his brief flash of anger gone. Not even the discipline of the service had kept the Irish from Charles Stewart.

"It's a timely victory you've brought us, Favian!" the redheaded captain shouted. "I'll explain later."

"What's this about owing our victory to you and Bainbridge?" Favian demanded.

"Later, my son, later."

Dolley Madison returned from her procession and gave up *Macedonian*'s shot-torn ensign to the officers, who draped it from the wall between the flags of *Guerrière* and *Alert*. Favian and Archibald Hamilton were crowded into the place of honor next to Stewart and Hull, the President and his lady standing next to them. A procession of citizens, some of whom Favian recognized as congressmen, senators, Cabinet secretaries and their wives, judges of the Supreme Court, appeared to shake hands and offer congratulations. Thomas Tingey appeared with a girl he introduced as his fiancée; she was strikingly beautiful, and at least thirty years younger than her husband-to-be, and Favian revised upward his opinion of Tingey's reputed eloquence.

Between handshakes and salutes Favian heard from Stewart the meaning of Secretary Hamilton's strange remark. At the beginning of the war William Bainbridge—the competent, aggressive, but totally unlucky captain who had, through no real fault of his own, lost his first command to the French, and later the *Philadelphia* frigate to the Tripolitans—had been in Washington, haunting the doors of the Navy Department for a command; and Stewart, following a furlough of some years, during which he had been earning his bread as a merchant skipper, arrived on much the same errand. The news Paul Hamilton brought them was stunning: The Cabinet had decided to keep the entire Navy in harbor for the duration of the war, striking their yards to save cost of upkeep and using the big frigates as floating batteries. It was not thought possible for American ships to meet the British in open combat. Bainbridge and Stewart protested; Hamilton was convinced and went to the President; and Madison, after long wrangling, had overruled the skinflint Gallatin of the Treasury Department and the rest of the Cabinet, and sent the ships, among them Decatur's *United States*, in search of enemies to conquer. Isaac Hull, in the meantime, had simply ignored the order to stay in port, and on his own initiative, and at the peril of court-martial, commenced the voyage that had resulted in the capture of the *Guerrière*. Stewart and Bainbridge, since Hull's victory, had spoken before Congress, and had almost convinced the legislature to vote the money for four new ships of the line, seventy-fours, and six new *Constitution*-class frigates. The vote was expected any day.

Favian was stunned. It was the Navy every serving officer had been praying for for twenty years. "Well, sir, I thank you and Captain Bainbridge, wherever he may be, for your persuasiveness," Favian said.

"Bainbridge has already been thanked by the secretary," Hull said. "He's been given my old command, the *Constitution*. I had to leave her. My brother died, and I must settle his affairs."

And your uncle and stepfather is about to be court-martialed for treason, Favian thought, and that's reason enough to keep off a ship for the time being.

"I'm sorry to hear it, sir," he said.

"And they've given me *Constellation*," Stewart added. "She's here in Washington."

"A lucky ship, sir. Congratulations."

"We'll need all the luck we can find to get her past the British blockade. Captain Hull and I are staying at The Indian Queen. Come for a consultation tomorrow afternoon."

"I'll be happy to, sir."

The Naval Ball, its festivity increased to a near hysterical pitch by the news of the victory, careened onward into the early hours of the morning. The Madisons left at a respectable hour, as did Thomas Tingey, his bride-to-be, and his prospective in-laws. But for the most part the men present, especially the young officers, seemed inclined to toast the victory until they dropped from exhaustion; and the departure of the President and many of the older, more respectable citizens was not calculated to suppress their celebrations. The floor surrounding the many spittoons began to grow slimy from near misses; white and stainless collars and neckcloths began to collect sweat stains; waistcoats began to be streaked with tobacco. Favian, fixed like a mannequin in the place of honor, found his hand sore with congratulatory handclasps, and his voice tiring from responding to toasts and speeches. It was not until two in the morning, when the Navy Yard claimed to have run clean out of rum punch, and the Marine Band packed its instruments and made its way out, that the party began to disperse.

Hamilton had long since vanished in the company of his parents. Favian collected his hat and cloak, shook a few more parting hands, and called for his horse. Standing next to him on the veranda as he waited was a smiling, well-dressed man, who introduced himself as the owner of the most resplendent, most discreet, best-appointed, and most absurdly expensive brothel in the city, and who offered Favian, apparently from motivations of patriotism, the use of his establishment free of charge. Favian smiled—it was a weary, cynical, and knowing smile—and then he accepted.

6.

Favian's harlot was a long-legged free octoroon named Zenobia, whose infectious giggle, widely spaced, faintly Egyptian eyes, and smooth, delightfully cool skin—the color of coffee with milk—kept him entranced until dawn. She spoke with the lovely cadences of the West Indies and said she came from Nevis. There was a minor cut on one brown shin, presumably from bumping into a piece of furniture while making a nocturnal professional visit to a strange house. She was altogether as enchanting a young whore as he had ever found, in all his lifelong journey through the bordellos of the world.

"You're too skinny," Zenobia said, in a pause between carnal interludes. Her practiced fingers outlined the hollows between Favian's ribs. "My hipbones are going to give you bruises."

"I shan't mind," he said.

"I'll see if I can fatten you before you go."

Favian was vaguely surprised to discover that she was succeeding, rather sooner after their last encounter than he'd expected, in fattening at least a part of him. It was not long before her wandering fingertips discovered this as well, and with a cry of wonder and surprise she bent over the phenomenon, and began to nurture, with a series of playful experiments, its growing tumescence, after which Favian laughingly tumbled her onto her back and thoroughly, protractedly possessed her.

It was one of the many contradictions by which Favian lived that as one of the elite of a republic dedicated to the expansion of personal freedom, he, personally, experienced so little liberty. If there was, in his mind, a conscious intention to appear to the world nothing other than a conscientious, dutiful, professional officer, reflecting nothing but those ideals and enthusiams to which an officer might aspire, so there was also an equally conscious intention to seek out those blissful, well-deserved moments when the whole intractable burden might be let slide and he could relieve himself of propriety and consequence. Wrapped in Zenobia's brown limbs, he could forget, for the span of a few hours, all the tedium, frustration, and rigor of his profession.

"My God," Zenobia wondered some moments later. "What do they *do* to you in those boats?" Her fingers slid over his back, ran up to the gathering of muscles at his neck and shoulder, probed carefully. "I felt so much tension here when you came in. It's mostly gone now."

Favian wandered mentally over the last few months—the long voyage across the Atlantic, the battle, the struggle to get the prize home, his illness, the long, endless ride through the mud. What do they *do* to you? she'd asked. He laughed. There was no place to begin.

"It's a long story," he said.

"We have all night."

"It's a story longer than one night."

It was strange, this reversal of the usual question. He had learned, from whores encountered over the years, that the one question most asked by their customers was also the most obvious: How had they found themselves in such a profession? Favian had never asked it, for he had always known the answer. They had found themselves in brothels for the same reason Favian had found himself in the Navy, through a series of irrevocable mistakes. The details differed, from harlot to lieutenant, but the dismal outline was the same.

And now Zenobia was asking him for his history, instead of the other way around. He didn't mind; he felt talkative, enjoying his moments in bed with this long-legged, brown-eyed, agile woman, his hands wandering over the delightfully female form of her body, the compact, proud breasts, the chocolate nipples, the taut, admirably smooth curve of her belly. She had laughed, earlier, when he'd asked her simply to walk around the small room, and let him watch;

she hadn't realized that, locked away for months in close quarters with four hundred fifty other men, he might possibly forget what women looked like, how they walked—so refreshingly different from men—how they smelled, how they moved their arms, talked. Favian felt exhilarated, unfettered, the exhaustion of his long horseback journey melting away with his tension.

"You got a girl back home?" Zenobia asked.

"Yes."

"What's she like?"

Favian thought of Emma Greenhow, her slender form, pale blond hair, her long, aristocratic nose, green eyes, translucent pale skin.

"She's a little like you, I think," he said. Very little.

"You fuck her?"

Favian laughed at the unexpected question. "No," he said. "I most certainly do not."

"Why not?" Her limber hands massaged his nape, working at the tension remaining in the hard muscles. "It would do you good, here," she said, digging a thumb into his clavicle. He winced. "Do her good, too," she said.

"You haven't been to New Hampshire, I can tell," he said.

"No. Is that where you're from? You talk like you're English or something."

"I've been told that." The story of Jehu Markham's English education and his English wife was too lengthy, and too irrelevant, to go into, or how Favian had been carefully raised to keep his speech free from the New Hampshire dialect, which his parents considered graceless.

Her thumbs stabbed him again. "So why don't you fuck your girl?" she asked.

"Because New Hampshire girls do not—because that's not how things are done in New Hampshire society."

"Why is that?"

"I don't know. It's the way of things. The Lord did not consult me when he made New England."

"Are you going to marry this girl?"

"I think we have an understanding."

Zenobia began to giggle. "That'll be some wedding night, boy," she laughed. Favian felt a bubble of amusement rising in him, bursting from his throat. For some reason he began to cackle, trying breathlessly to speak through torrents of laughter.

"Are you—are you, madam," he whooped, "speaking with dis—disrespect of the venereal abilities of Miss Emma Greenhow, son of the Honorable Nicholas Greenhow, state assemblyman, of Spanish Farm, New Hampshire?"

She kicked her legs in midair, helpless with laughter. He buried his head between her neck and shoulder and kissed her, and her arms went around him. They panted breathlessly in one another's arms, and Favian found himself ridiculously at peace, all anger and resentment gone, evaporated in a burst of helpless laughter. Was peace for hire, he wondered, so easily purchased from a Washington bawd?

"I didn't understand the gentry on Nevis, either," she said. She raised a hand to scratch her knee, the sound of a leafy twig on paper. He rubbed his chin over her smooth shoulder. Emma Greenhow. He hadn't written her since before the battle. There just hadn't been time. Of course he couldn't expect her to understand that. There would have to be apologies. What do they *do* to you in those boats? She hadn't really wanted to hear his answer. And if she had heard it, she wouldn't have believed it. No one would.

In September 1801, Favian had made his second cruise to the Mediterranean, to join Commodore Dale's blockading squadron off Tripoli, in the new schooner *Vixen* of twelve guns, Captain John Smith. The blockade was not being carried out with any degree of thoroughness—this was before Preble had infected the young service with his uncompromising determination—and *Vixen*'s course took her on a sort of tour of the Spanish coast before joining Commodore Dale, showing the gridiron flag in every harbor. In Barcelona they moored near a big forty-gun xebec-frigate that acted as guardship, and when Captain Smith went ashore to present his credentials to the authorities, the xebec-frigate fired a broadside of eighteen-pound guns over his head and demanded that he come aboard. Smith ignored the command and rowed placidly to the shore to complete his errand, roundshot howling overhead; but the first lieutenant was incensed, and had a boat dropped into

the water for the purpose of seeing for himself whether
Spanish arrogance and contempt extended to lieutenants.

It was a Spanish challenge to the collective honor of *Vix-
en*'s crew and, by extension, to the American nation. The
Spaniards were trying to show that *Vixen* was composed of
cowards, gaining in honor at the expense of the Americans;
it was a rather typical Spanish trick, in fact, and the Americans supposed it had to do with the fact that the Spanish
had won precious little naval honor thus far in their battles
with the British. There was only one possible answer.
When another volley of shot splashed around the first lieutenant's boat, he rowed to the xebec-frigate and went
aboard, but only to denounce the officers of His Catholic
Majesty's navy as curs, cowards, and honorless rascals. He
denounced them, knowing all the time that he left them
little option.

No rum was drunk in *Vixen*'s gun room that night; no
one wanted unsteady hands or eyes in the morning. Captain Smith and his Spanish opposite had no official knowledge of the next step: better so. At dawn the next morning,
the first lieutenant, *Vixen*'s five midshipmen, and a surgeon's mate were rowed to shore and marched outside the
city walls to an orange grove, meeting the first lieutenant
of the Spanish frigate, five *guardiamarinas*, and a Spanish
surgeon. They all wore black collars and cravats, blue trousers, and black gloves so as not to show white and make
targets of themselves.

Vixen's lieutenant had carried a challenge from every
one of the schooner's officers to an equal number of Spaniards. The latter, outnumbering the United States officers,
had drawn lots for the honor.

Favian still remembered the scent of the orange grove,
the strange intensity of sound and color, the feel of the turf
beneath his feet. He had not been afraid, this seventeen-
year-old Favian, until after the moment when the seconds—the xebec-frigate's second officer and *Vixen*'s master—began pacing over the ground, running through the
checklist required by ritual: no unfirm ground, the rising
sun in no one's eyes, the pistols loaded carefully in front of
the seconds. Then the parties separated, stood in a huddled

circle around separate trees, and voided their bladders, to avoid medical complications in case anyone was hit in the abdomen. It was then, in that absurd situation—six young men standing about an orange tree and pissing onto the darkening bark—that the deadly purpose of it became clear to Favian, striking him cold like a handful of snow on his neck.

Twelve people were meeting in an open field, following an ancient ritual designed so that neither side should have an unfair advantage as they met for the express purpose of killing each other. *Fairness!* There were no tactics; there was no skill; there was no advantage given intelligence over stupidity. Nothing that Favian had learned in his career could help him. Two lines of men would fire at one another at the drop of a handkerchief, and it would be purely the gods of chance who would determine who was hit and who was not.

And when Favian found himself opposite his opponent, the outrageous unfairness of it all struck him. The *guardia-marina* was a tall, gawky creature in his mid-teens, with a nervous tremor in one pustuled cheek and at least the intelligence of a smart ox. Every midshipman's berth had a specimen: willing to learn but somehow unable, in whose mind the rudiments of navigation swam helplessly in a whirlpool of insensibility, whose arms and legs perpetually thrust hairy wrists or perpetually barked shins from outgrown uniforms—one of those incredible creatures with no necks who found buttoning their jackets a challenge and wounded themselves during sword drill.

And one of these incompetent gecks was standing fifteen paces from Favian, holding a pistol, commanded to kill at the drop of a handkerchief. Favian felt like throwing down the pistol and screaming in outrage. Why couldn't it have been swords? Favian would have carved his opponent like a side of mutton. *This lowbrow moron could kill him! Kill him by accident!* And dueling was supposed to be *fair*! That was the purpose of all the pacing, all the ritual, all the bickering about the position of the sun.

Anything that gave an ox an equal chance with a human being was not in the least fair, in Favian's fervently held, but unvoiced, opinion. But meanwhile he took his position and tried to assume the stance of the duelist: right side toward the enemy, to narrow the target, left arm dangling behind the body where it couldn't be hit, left leg shadowed by the right. The right arm was bent at a peculiarly uncomfortable angle, bent to shield the body from a shot, which brought the pistol almost to Favian's eye. His hand was shaking so wildly that he could barely distinguish the figure of his opponent over the dancing, unsighted barrel. His own breath rasped in his lungs. It was only through the most extreme effort that he could prevent his teeth from chattering. The scent of the orange grove threatened to smother him. Somewhere in the distance Spaniards were singing.

Why had he joined this absurd service? He was going to get killed in an orange grove without ever seeing the war he had come to fight. His first captain, Daniel McNeil, had been a lunatic. And now this. He had been misinformed by a cadre of official liars. He wanted to throw down his gun and make a protest. Eloquent phrases sprang to his mind. Let the captains fight their own duels!

"*Garde à vous!*" The Spanish second lieutenant was calling out the traditional commands in French, a neutral language. It was all worse than absurd. The sound of peasants singing was abruptly cut short, as if a band of orange pickers had suddenly seen a peculiar apparition in their orchard: men in neat, somber uniforms trying to murder one another.

Vixen's master had raised the handkerchief. Favian tried to line the neckless figure of his opponent over the barrel of his gun. The pistol was absurdly heavy; it seemed to require all of Favian's strength to keep it raised. What if it slipped from his sweaty palm at the last minute, and fell— would they have to go through the whole procedure again? Elbow cocked. Left arm out of the way. Stomach sucked in to narrow the profile. What had he forgotten?

The handkerchief dropped and the grove echoed to the sound of gunfire. Favian fired his pistol without conscious command, simply as a reflex of that white signal billowing in the light morning breeze. The recoil almost put out his eye. And then he stood there in the gunsmoke, his knees suddenly gone rubbery, blinking in astonishment. He caught a reflection of his own gaping wonderment in the face of his opponent. Both had missed. The air was full of smoke and screams. It seemed Favian had forgotten to breathe. He let the air out and almost fell, darkness swimming before his eyes. Perhaps his heart had forgotten to beat as well.

The Spanish lieutenant was down, and would take a long time dying, with a bullet in his belly. On Favian's immediate right, one of *Vixen*'s midshipmen had fallen with a ball in the leg and was screaming: a boy of Favian's age, who might as well have been Favian as far as chance and the orange grove were concerned. No one else seemed hurt. And suddenly Favian's *guardiamarina* sprawled on the grass. Perhaps he'd been hit after all, and it had taken his slow nerves a few seconds to realize it. But no. He rose, blushing scarlet, having simply tripped over his own elephantine feet.

Nothing was ever said about the matter aboard *Vixen* until many weeks later, but it was noticed that there was an increase in pistol practice among the midshipmen. The wounded boy, missing a limb, was sent home, his career over but his honor intact. None of them realized they had stepped over an invisible line, the first of many such lines over which they were to pass, the lines that separated the United States elite from the citizens they served. They had risked their lives for their country's honor; the first test had been met.

It was not until *Vixen*'s course carried them to the American squadron, and Favian saw for the first time the white walls of Tripoli and the brown, monotonous coast of Africa mottled with scrub and olive plantations, that one of Favian's fellow apprentice officers mentioned their fellow, the one whose leg had been forfeit to honor in the orange grove. "He never would have stood it here. Imagine! Screaming like a woman when he was hit!" And suddenly the midshipman was sprawling on the planks, Favian's fists having struck out, left-right-left-right, eye-nose-eye-chin, a combination Favian's father and boxing instructor had taught him years before, and Favian in his rage was shout-

ing, *"He stood the enemy's fire, damn you!"* There was
almost another duel, but a hastily convened court of honor,
headed by *Vixen's* lieutenant, had determined that each
should apologize to the other. Both apologies were given
and accepted gracefully. The boy whose eye Favian had
blacked lost his life a year later, trying to sail one of
Thomas Jefferson's leaky, unseaworthy gunboats across the
Atlantic to join the blockade of Tripoli, and so became one
of the honored dead, having passed the ultimate test, the
final proof honor and the Navy's mythos could demand. It
could have been any of them, just as the amputee invalid
sent home could have been any of them, just as the typhus
that carried off *Vixen's* lieutenant, later on that blockaded
shore, could have fallen on any of them. The line could be
crossed by any of them, at any time. It was a realization
that had served to temper them.

A few practical lessons had also been learned. When
Favian fought his next duel, with an American merchant
master who had smugly insulted the Navy within the hearing of Favian's epaulet, he made damned certain it was
with swords. He'd run the drunken bully through both
lungs and walked away without great regret, but that had
been just after his return from his third voyage to the Mediterranean, in the *Constitution* under Preble, when he'd had
his fill of hand-to-hand combat leaping aboard Tripolitan
gunboats in the face of waving scimitars—compared to that
one sodden merchant captain more or less hadn't seemed to
matter.

What do they *do* to you in those boats? Nothing much.
Nothing but point out a few sour realities that most people
rarely have to face, and force you to face those realities for
every minute of every day that you wear the uniform.
Those epaulets were heavier than they looked.

But there was nothing he could really say. Zenobia could
not be expected to understand. She could only sense his
need for relief, for the simplicities of bed and laughter and
musk, and these she was willing enough to provide. She
even provided breakfast, true to her promise to fatten him,
disappearing sometime after dawn and returning with a
tray that brimmed with eggs, toast, fried potatoes, butter
and marmalade, with coffee and a jug of beer to wash it

down—all the rich fare that kept the whores plump and happy and frisky.

She shared the meal with him, brushing crumbs energetically from the sheets. Her body was the color of rich honey in the dawn light, her belly creasing wondrously as she bent over the tray. She was an artist, this Zenobia; she had accepted Favian's jibboom with a knowing smile and a low chuckle, and had taken a seeming delight in arousing him repeatedly. "You're a nice change," she'd explained. "Most of the men who can afford this place are old." A creature of happy carnality, Zenobia, a princess of her profession. So much better than Favian's last harlot, that pink, plump, and somehow unsatisfactory Messalina for whom he had paid good silver dollars in Boston.

He finished his breakfast, and as Zenobia put the tray aside found that refreshment had awakened his desire. Zenobia's tongue tasted of butter and honey; he winced at the touch of her hipbones—he *would* have bruises there, by Neptune!—but that did not matter. He had time to be slow and tender. It was too early in the morning to be hasty.

Zenobia's fingers played running games on his spine, cupping his scapulae, caressing his nether cheeks. Blast it, there were still crumbs in the bed. His morning bristles made music against her neck. Prostitutes, by constant practice of their trade, have developed muscles that most women do not realize they possess. Favian was soon agonizingly aware that Zenobia had brought most of these into play, and that her satisfied, cooing moans, which he had been pleasantly listening to all night, had begun to develop an uncontrolled, slightly hysterical whine, the prelude to unfeigned bliss. Favian barely had time to enlarge his self-esteem—he was pleasuring her, by God! It's not in the contract, but it's nice when it happens—before the gallop began, a harrowing, mad steeplechase over hedge and gate and bouncy turf, rider and mount synchronized to each leap, each panting breath, swapping, somehow, their roles several times, rider becoming mount and back again, before the final spill at the final gate, horse and jockey, whose duties had by then become inutterably confused, tumbling headlong at the last obstacle, and into the shimmering, mirrorlike pool that reflected the final stretch, the green, the waiting steeple with its blank clock face.

They were both breathless and a bit crosseyed afterward; it took some time for things to come into focus. The bed was a wet chaos of sheets and sopping pillows speckled with crumbs. The sun seemed very high. Favian had to go, to get back into uniform and stagger weak-kneed to his meeting with Captains Hull and Stewart. He seemed very tender inside his tight breeches and wondered if he was going to walk splay-legged for days. He shrugged into his uniform coat. Zenobia smoothed the bedsheets and brushed crumbs from the downy backs of her arms.

"You've almost circumcised me, by God," Favian said, still breathless. She came into his embrace, her thorough-bred's breasts pressing against his double row of buttons. Her thumbs prodded his neck.

"All you did was put on the coat and already I can feel the tension here," she complained. "All my good work gone to waste."

"Never to waste." He kissed her. She swayed giddily, hanging from his neck.

"What's your real name, O Egyptian princess?" he asked.

"Sally Mathews, your honor," she said, and imitated a curtsey.

He grinned. "There's a gun on my ship with that name."

Her eyes rolled as she tried to think of a lewd pun having to do with naval artillery, but neither of their minds seemed to be working at proper capacity. Too early in the morning, perhaps.

He adjusted his neckcloth and strapped on his sword. Zenobia combed his hair with her fingers. Ouch!—he was very tender in his tight trousers. It was good that whores did not get excited with all their customers, otherwise you could tell their clients from their gait. Before he left, he asked her price, and calculated that if he watched his pennies he could afford another visit.

She rang the bell, to clear the corridors and stairs of any customers who did not wish to be seen by any other customers; he kissed her again and descended. There was something a bit sad about brothels in the morning, Favian reflected: sleepy-eyes whores, their hair piled carelessly, their powder flaking, wearing patched lingerie and showing too much thigh as they munched their breakfasts, while the air smelled of soap and steam as sheets were washed. . . . But this particular back stair was very discreet, opening into an anonymous alley, and Zenobia waved from her second-floor window. He went into the stable for his horse, discovered it was impossible to fit the saddle without agony, and so lengthened the stirrups and rode to Blodget's standing in them: bad form, but only sensible under the circumstances.

He had a few hours' rest at his hotel—one could not call it sleep—and then had the porter bring him hot water for washing. It was still unspeakably luxurious, hot water, after all those weeks of washing and shaving in seawater. He washed his face, neck, and hands, and, with one of his seven razors, each marked with a day of the week, scraped off his bristles. The sun was past its zenith. Time for his visit.

Favian preferred attending his bordellos incognito; wearing his uniform was a risk he rarely indulged. But last night had been special; there had been something to celebrate. In the Navy's midshipmen's berths, a fork was stuck in the table at four bells of the evening watch as a signal for the junior mids to clear out, so that the senior midshipmen and warrant officers could safely bring up the subject of depravity without fear of corrupting the innocent. Usually the juniors left under protest. Favian, during his spell as a junior, had never objected to his banishment, and was thought of as a prig. The real reason he had never minded was that he had precious little left to discover, having been well schooled in vice during his time at Harvard, when he had squandered his comfortable allowance at a plush brothel in Charlestown, beneath the shadow of Breed's Hill or Bunker Hill—with the rest of Massachusetts, he was confused as to which was which. When Favian had finally become a senior, he'd been disappointed in the fork talk: Even the senior warrant officers, grizzled men who had fought in the Revolution, seemed curiously vague about elementary female anatomy (about which Favian had taken pains to inform himself) and otherwise held some of the most surprising notions. Sailors seemed to be true innocents on certain matters.

Of how his fellow officers went about the business of correcting such errors, if they ever did, Favian was ignorant. He himself went about his venereal activities with perfect discretion. Dressed in a civilian coat, he would yawn to his fellows about being invited to some uninteresting dinner—"at the house of a Mr. Pillow—or was it Hillock? A merchant, I believe"—then take himself to the most elegant sporting club in the town, about which he had taken pains to inform himself by a few well-placed inquiries. He never visited the waterfront dives, or the bourgeois places where women tapped coins ostentatiously in the windows; they turned his lust tepid at once, with their bored, often shapeless, often undesirable women, with bruised thighs and mechanical smiles, who grew annoyed if one dawdled (time was money!), who yawned at awkward moments, who rarely bathed, and who always seemed to have leering pimps, eager to extort more coins, lurking about some corner.

Favian preferred the carpeted corridor, the bells that warned the discreet, the sanitary precautions that were maintained, the perfumed air and good cellar of the expensive stables, places that maintained pretty young women with straight teeth who at least knew enough to smile, and who were coached well enough to feign enthusiasm even if the hour was late and the customer's reflexes slowed by wine. . . . It was a difficult habit to maintain on his lieutenant's salary, but sometimes servicemen were given discounts, and in any case he had few other expensive hobbies. These places catered to gentlemen, of supposedly refined tastes and allegedly courtly manners, and it pricked Favian's vanity to consider himself among them; he had been raised genteelly, and though he could not afford to support himself in the mode of a gentleman, he was at least one by law. Officers in the services were gentlemen, if only by act of Congress, and they fought duels to prove it.

There was something sad, however, even about these well-appointed palaces, something a bit brutal about his relationships with these women, which Favian tried to assuage by gifts, by tipping as well as he could afford, and by adopting an aura of languid sophistication. But still there was a tang of melancholy revealed, like sad little lines around the women's eyes, in the light of dawn, and that lurked in the strained partings. Few encounters were as satisfactory as that with Zenobia. There was a residue of exploitation that Favian found he could not entirely get rid of—something nasty, like the taste of whale oil on his tongue.

But somehow it seemed more comfortable than the alternatives. Favian maintained proper relations with a number of respectable females of his own station, but he had never taken any of them to bed, even when a few of the less respectable ones, widows or wives or someone's petted daughter, had dropped some oversubtle hints over their sherbet. There was something Favian had never quite reconciled about how such affaires were supposed to work, about how to avoid complications: the missing monthly that would set everyone sweating, because a lieutenant could not support a bastard on his pay; the husband who could never quite be fitted into the picture; the rash and discharge that confirmed the fact that one was not alone in one's misery; the brothers or fathers who had gloves to crack across one's face, and bright new pistols that shot such uncomfortable lead. New England had not entirely gotten rid of the stocks, either. Positive examples were hard to come by, and negative ones hard to ignore, what with bawds being stuck in the pillory while strumpets cursed the merry crowd from their ducking stool. It was better to let these matters be taken care of quietly, in sanitary conditions, beneath colored lamp shades and accompanied by the sound of bells. So much less anxiety altogether.

It had been different, no doubt, in his father's day. Arranged marriages were more common, and the partners looked for love elsewhere. The Revolutionary generation seemed a bawdy lot by contemporary standards, the women freer than their daughters. Favian's uncle Malachi had merrily sowed bastards from one end of the watery globe to the other, and it was a family nightmare that these would show up in a body, white and mulatto and, for all anyone knew, half-Chinese, to claim their share of the patrimony. But, to the best of Favian's knowledge, that particular complication had not yet arisen.

And of course there was Miss Emma Greenhow. It was taken for granted that she and Favian would marry, as soon as Favian managed to acquire enough of a fortune to assuage her father's fiscal objections. Nothing formal had been arranged; no announcements had been made. But Favian and Emma had known each other for years; they had been raised in the same circles, and they understood one another well enough. It was a pity that Favian had been raised in genteel circumstances that his lieutenant's pay could never equal, but he could always hope for war and prize money, and in any case Favian's father, sooner or later, would leave him a stake of the family money. Miss Emma seemed content to wait and, in the meantime, had turned away a number of other suitors with better prospects than young Lieutenant Markham's.

Favian supposed that in the matter of Emma Greenhow he had little to complain about. There were no formal commitments, but then Favian was scarcely in a position to expect any. A man who might at any moment be thrown ashore on half-pay was in no position to enforce a demand that a woman pledge herself to him for life. Now that he could expect a few thousand in prize money—more than he'd ever made in his life, a fortune as far as his naval pay was concerned—perhaps he could begin moving in the direction of matrimony. The prize money could easily pay for a house and furnishings, and perhaps a small carriage. Outfitting a marriage was at least as complicated as outfitting a ship, even if the former contained only two people and the ship hundreds. Yet both wife and ship were necessary to the brand of success demanded by Favian's circles, and he had never been a man to swim against the tide. He would acquiesce to necessary destiny. As he had all along.

7.

Blodget's Hotel
Washington City
30 December 1812

Miss Emma Greenhow
Spanish Farm, New Hampshire

My dear Miss Greenhow:

I hope you will not be offended by my long silence. As you have no doubt heard, on the 25th of October we captured a fine British frigate after a short action. They fought bravely, but fortune and skill were with us, and we triumphed. The losses among our brave lads were mercifully light.

I was assigned the task of rerigging the enemy frigate and bringing her safely into a friendly port, which job accomplished I was sent posthaste to Washington to deliver dispatches. This afternoon I dined with the President and his Lady, who were both quite gracious, and solicited my opinion on naval matters. These they listened to, and I flatter myself that I may have contributed in some small measure to the enhancement of the naval Cause among the political denizens of this Capital. They are surprisingly informal at the Presidential Palace; any citizen may interrupt the President to shake his hand or offer advice, and quite often this impertinence is rewarded with dinner. Mrs. Madison is often obliged to play hostess to two score uninvited guests!

I beg you will forgive the lack of correspondence brought about by my activities. I know I have not had time to write a word, or draw a free breath, since the *Macedonian* was sighted. I hope to be able to take the honor of addressing you more correspondence in the future.

Since my arrival in this City, I have been much in the company of the Secretary of the Navy, Mr. Paul Hamilton, whose gallant son I had the honor of commanding in the battle, and with whom I journeyed to the City. Mr. Hamilton is a good-hearted fellow, and his behavior to me has been all kindness, but I think he is not a very well organized man, and the Navy suffers thereby; I also suspect his effectiveness is hampered by his deteriorating relationship with the Secretary of War, and possibly by his own habits of inebriety.

I have also spent time in the company of Captains Isaac Hull and Charles Stewart, whose compliments and benevolences I hope one day to deserve. It is entirely unfortunate that Captain Hull's victory over the *Guerrière* was so marred by the disgrace of his uncle at Detroit. He is much down in spirits, tho' I hope his forthcoming marriage—he was engaged just weeks ago in Philadelphia to Miss Ann Hart—will serve to brighten his life. I think that the war can but serve to brighten considerably the matrimonial prospects of Naval officers, probably at the expense of their Army colleagues!

As for Captain Stewart, he has been given command of the *Constellation*, a lucky old ship, and spends much time at the Navy Yard preparing her for sea. I have no doubt that you will hear more of Captain Stewart before this war ends.

I am myself assured of promotion, as it is the custom of the service to promote the first officers of successful captains, both as a compliment to the captain and to spread his success, as it were, upon the waters. The bill for my promotion is to be laid before Congress during the next term, and in the meantime I am given the acting rank of Master-Commandant. It is not the promotion to full Captain, such as the one they gave lucky Charles Morris, I had hoped for, but the lack of pay is probably attenuated by the chance of a command, which is more likely to come to a junior Master-Commandant than to a junior Captain. Even that likelihood, in all honesty, seems slim enough. Commanders have already been assigned to all the available ships, even the ones now building, but I shall continue loitering about the lobby of the Navy Department, and making a nuisance of myself, until Mr. Hamilton finds me a ship somewhere. Perhaps even now one of our cruisers is bringing a Prize into port, which it may be my honor to command.

I am sure you have been bored by this naval gossip. I would attempt to fertilize this missive with a compost of the latest anecdotes of Washington society, but the truth is that I have not been in this City long enough to absorb any, and I am already overdue for a reception at the Hamiltons'. I will write more thoroughly when the requirements of Duty are not so pressing. In the meantime I leave you with this titbit: the Turkish fashion seems once more in vogue, with Mrs. Madison affecting turbans, crescents, gold chains, and shawls. Please forgive the gap between this and my last letter, and commend me dutifully to your Father.

Your friend,
Favian Markham.

Favian blew carefully to dry the ink on the letter, reread it carefully, and hoped he had reached the bland, formal, essentially tepid standard considered suitable for an unmarried man addressing an unmarried woman not his sister. His difficulty of composition was complicated by his suspicion that Emma's letters were occasionally read, with paternal regard for the proprieties, by her father. The Honorable Nicholas Greenhow's manifestly clear intention had all along been to prevent any form of intimacy, even by post, until Lieutenant Markham had become rich, or until Emma's eye had been attracted by another, wealthier, prospect.

Favian, whose letter had not been cut short by a visit to the Hamiltons' but rather by a complete failure of suitable invention (as had all too clearly been demonstrated, he felt, by that absurd composting metaphor in the final paragraph), began to wonder, not for the first time, about the outrageous lack of reality demanded by this correspondence. It seemed as if any important message had to be diluted to the point of flat insipidity, if not eradicated altogether, before it was considered suitable to include in a letter to a woman with whom, damn it, he'd had a lifelong friendship and currently a certain unspoken understanding. The battle that Favian remembered—the roaring guns, gushing smoke, the thunder, cheers, and flames—was reduced to a nonrecognizable pap; the job of rerigging the prize had been edited to half a sentence; and as for the scenes of horror on board the *Macedonian*, they were best swept under the rug altogether.

The respectfully newsy part of the letter was intended to convey the following main points to Miss Greenhow and to Greenhow *père*: that Favian had achieved promotion; that he was moving now in high Washington circles, from which he might expect certain favors; and that, therefore, Lieutenant Markham was perhaps to be taken a bit more seriously in the department of matrimony. Favian thought that this ulterior object was perhaps too obvious in his observations regarding Isaac Hull's marriage, and how war was improving the prospects of the Navy, but he'd let it pass.

Favian had considered mentioning his prize money, and that perhaps it was time to buy a house in New Hampshire, but canceled the remark as being too obvious. State Assemblyman Nicholas Greenhow had not risen to his present position of respectability and influence by not being able to read between the lines of a communication: No doubt the thought of prize money would enter his mind without Favian's mentioning it. Greenhow had owned shares of privateers during the Revolution, including some of the Markham ships, and no doubt knew what a lieutenant's share of prize money was worth.

But hang it anyway! This business of writing to a father while ostensibly writing to the daughter, and of forcing oneself to carefully prune away any of the thorny branches of reality that might be considered unsuitable for a young lady of gentle upbringing, was unaccountably tedious.

At least Favian had been able to approach the truth in a letter he'd written to his father. "The scene on board the British ship was unimaginably horrible," he'd written, "and I now understand your reluctance to describe Bristol following Malachi's victory, where the slaughter had been as great. 104 of Macedonian's total complement of 301 were made casualty—over a third!—and over forty died. The battle was fought mostly at long bowls, and so the injuries were principally inflicted by round shot, which created horrible mutilations. Yet somehow I managed to work through these scenes of horror, and sometimes I wonder if I have not become a monster, able to inflict such destruction and then exist calmly for some weeks amid the results of my handiwork."

But that was to Jehu Markham, who had warred at sea in his time and could be expected to understand. Miss Emma Greenhow had never journeyed farther from Spanish Farm than Boston, and her acquaintance with death would have been made at staid Calvinist funerals, with corpses provided by heart failure or apoplexy, and not the work of roundshot or cutlass. There would be no point in disturbing the delicate unreality in which genteel women were expected to live. Favian suspected that if his world intruded upon hers, it would be his world, not hers, that would be banished from her thoughts.

There was a knock on his door, and he called for whoever it was to enter while he folded, sealed, and addressed the letter. Archibald Hamilton entered, with an invitation for a gathering at his parents' place, thus producing in fact what Favian had invented for the purposes of closing his letter. Favian accepted, donned his undress uniform and blue trousers, and, after posting his letters at the Post Office Department, which shared the hotel, followed Hamilton to the waiting carriage.

The pleasant supper with the Hamiltons did not prevent Favian from walking to the Navy Department the next day to pay his respects to the secretary and to remind him officially, by his presence in the office, that the new master commandant had no appointment. Favian, as he entered the Navy Department's foyer, and scraped mud from his boots with a contrivance bolted to the floor for the purpose, had no expectation of seeing anyone other than Hamilton, some clerks, and perhaps Archibald Hamilton pressed into temporary duty to relieve the pressure of the usual backwater of paperwork threatening to inundate the department. It was therefore with considerable surprise that Favian saw an old service friend—perhaps his only service friend—waiting in the lobby, his feet stretched out and ankles crossed.

Lieutenant William Burrows was dressed, as usual, in ordinary clothes—it had always been difficult to get him into uniform, and when he was not in civilian clothes, he was as often as not wearing the tarred hat, embroidered jacket, and ragged trousers of a common seaman—and he supported the *National Intelligencer* on his knee. A dour clerk, who was replacing Charles Goldsborough, the head clerk famous for his hospitality to sailors, while the latter was on holiday, glared at them both over the rims of his spectacles.

Burrows looked up from his paper. "Hullo, Markham," he growled. It was plain from his attitude that he seemed to consider Favian's entrance a resented intrusion. "I've been reading about you. I suppose you think you've made a great splash in the world."

"What water barrel did they drag you from?" Favian retaliated. "And how did they persuade you to dress like a human being?"

"This?" Burrows plucked at his jacket. " 'Twas placed topside in my dunnage. Don't know who put it there."

Burrows went back to his paper as Favian reported to the clerk, who sent his card in to Hamilton. Favian turned, walked across the lobby again in silence, and sat in the chair next to Burrows. Burrows folded his paper elaborately, then stuffed it into his coat.

"I suppose I shall have to thank you for my exchange," Burrows said. "I have spent the last few months as a guest of the Royal Navy."

"Indeed?" Favian said, his tone implying that the fact was of little concern.

"They captured our boat on its return from the Indies. Washington had the effrontery to declare war on them and not tell us. A scandal. Shall bring the matter up in Congress."

The clerk glared over the rims of his spectacles, then busied himself once more with his papers.

"I've been paroled," Burrows said. "There are so many British officers in our hands, and so few of us in theirs, that I shall be officially exchanged very soon. Probably with one of the *Macedonian*'s crew. So I thank—" His discourse was interrupted by a mammoth yawn. "—thank you for it."

"I suppose, sir, that you are welcome."

The clerk suddenly stood, snatched up a bundle of papers and his pen, and quit the room, leaving a splattered trail of ink behind him. Burrows raised an eyebrow. The clerk was apparently unwilling to abide the obscure and probably (in his mind) impertinent dialogue. It was clerks, not naval officers, who were supposed to speak in secret languages unknown to others; naval gentlemen were supposed to be silent, speak when spoken to, keep to their quarterdecks as much as possible, and exhibit proper deference when begging for an assignment.

"The fellow seems upset," Burrows remarked. "Can it be one of us, I wonder?"

"You might try bathing one day, and see if he acts any differently."

Favian, from the corner of his eye, caught a glimmer of amusement in Burrows's eye; and suddenly he was laughing helplessly, mirth roaring up from him without conscious volition, while Burrows looked at him with an absolutely immobile face that was at once vaguely curious, vaguely disapproving, and yet somehow strangely comical.

"I wonder, sir, that you do not see a doctor," said Burrows. "May I recommend a Dr. Keith, who, if memory serves, was once great help to my aunt—that would be Aunt Dotty—who suffered, like you, from fits."

Favian recovered his breath and then was assaulted violently by a bout of hiccoughs.

"Aunt Dotty, if memory does not fail me, was later done in by a Mr. Hound from Timmonsville, a drummer I believe, who we later discovered to be the Florence County Hatchet Fiend. It was a great shock. I fear Dr. Keith's prescription may not serve, sir. You appear to be in need of something stronger. Permit me to thump you on the back."

Burrows's thumps almost knocked Favian to the floor, but they served both to eradicate his hiccoughs and to awaken his wit.

"I am sorry about your Aunt Dotty, sir," he said. "Tell me: Do many in your family exhibit symptoms of—ah—lunacy—hmmm?"

Favian's ten-year friendship with Burrows had been handicapped, as far as Favian was concerned, by Burrows's ability to send Favian into unpredictable fits of laughter, while Favian had never been able to elicit as much as an involuntary smile from Burrows. Perhaps the reason for this was that Burrows's style was Favian's own carried to an exaggerated degree. Favian was known for being correct, aloof, scrupulously polite, technically accomplished, an ironist at home in most situations simply because of the measured distance with which he observed them. Burrows was all these things, but more so, and carried to such an exaggerated degree that he seemed almost a parody, not only of himself but of Favian. Where Favian was reserved, Burrows was completely misanthropic; where Favian made the technical details of his profession a specialty, Burrows made them an obsession; where Favian secretly distrusted the code by which he lived, and had never given himself entirely to the Navy, Burrows made no secret of his dislike for the officer's role, and his love for the fo'c'sle over the quarterdeck. In sartorial matters they differed: Favian dressed well, whether in uniform or not; but Burrows, even when he could be persuaded to don his uniform, looked like a scarecrow insufficiently stuffed with straw, his bony wrists winking from his cuffs, and locks of hair resembling dark wood shavings straggling from beneath his hat. Even when dressed as a common sailor, he looked unkempt alongside other sailors, few of whom had never been known as men of fashion.

Lieutenant William Burrows was Favian's only service friend; they had struck up an unlikely fellowship as midshipmen aboard the *Constitution* at Tripoli and cemented it under gunfire. He knew Burrows as an aloof, blunt, morose eccentric, and a man obsessed. Burrows, Favian suspected, hated the Navy as much as Favian did, but he was also obsessed by it; to Burrows, the Navy was like a demanding mistress whom he could not live without, even if she made him unhappy. Burrows's advancement, like Favian's, had been held up for political reasons: His father, the first commandant of the Marine Corps, had quarreled with Jefferson's secretary of the navy, Robert Smith. Convinced he would never be promoted by the service to which he had dedicated his life, Burrows had resolved to break with his obsession; he had taken a long furlough and voyaged to Canton as a merchant skipper. War had broken out while he was absent, and the first he knew of it was when the *Thomas Penrose* was brought under British guns.

And now, paroled—on his honor not to fight the British—and awaiting exchange, he waited in the secretary's office, apparently ready to resume his long, frustrating affair with the Navy. Favian was delighted to see him, but also concerned for his friend: Would Burrows find his requests for assignment again denied, and again wear a path in the floor of the Navy Department as he was shuffled, like a sheet of paper, from office to office, until he once again left in disgust, hoping to regain his self-respect in some other capacity?

"He'll see you both now." The clerk had returned, and spoke in tones that implied that he could not understand why Paul Hamilton did not have them ejected from the premises by the local constabulary.

Favian brushed a streak of mud from his trousers and walked with Burrows to Hamilton's office.

Hamilton rose affably from his chair, shook their hands, bade them sit. "I have some fine North Carolina whiskey, gentlemen," Hamilton beamed. "I hope you will take a glass."

"It's a little early for me, thank you, sir," Favian said. It was a few minutes after nine in the morning, and gaging from Hamilton's breath, the North Carolina whiskey jug had already suffered a loss of some of its contents.

"Not for me, sir," Burrows said, blunt as usual. The Secretary cheerfully poured a glass for himself and offered his guests a seat.

"Mr. Burrows, I am happy to meet you again," he said. "I have been reviewing your record."

Burrows's answer was an uncivil grunt; he was not a vocal man among those he did not know well. Hamilton peered at him oddly and then continued.

"Mr. Markham, I have a certain amount of good news for you, although it is tempered by qualifications. In short, I have a command for you, but it is a command which you may wish to decline."

Favian felt his blood race—purely an instinct, he knew, driven into him by years of hearing the special, awed way young officers inflected the words "a command," as if it were the equivalent of the Holy Grail (which, for officers at least, it probably was). But Favian hooded his excitement and answered cautiously.

"In what way, sir?"

"It's the old *Experiment* schooner, Mr. Markham," Hamilton said. "She's been converted to a brig and given new guns. She's been laid up for some years, but is being recommissioned and should be in the water in a month's time. It's normally a lieutenant's command, you know. You may feel it is beneath your station. I would not blame you if you were to decline."

Almost palpable sensations flickered through Favian's mind. *Experiment* was not a good command. He should have had a sloop of war, or at least one of the larger eighteen-gun brig sloops. But assignments to these had already been made; he would have to wait for someone to die or fall ill or resign, or for Congress to vote money for new boats; it would mean waiting on shore for years. In the *Experiment* he'd at least have a chance for prize money, perhaps even for glory. Then again, the fast twelve-gun schooners, now converted to brigs, were said to have lost many of their excellent sailing qualities, and the chances for their capture were high. The *Nautilus* and the *Vixen*, both in the *Experiment*'s class, had been lost to the enemy so far, both overhauled by greatly superior enemy forces and compelled to surrender.

Yet it was—it was a command! The hushed, awed, respectful tone with which the phrase was uttered by junior officers had been given years in which to impregnate him with its wishful meaning. He was not immune, despite his cynicism and bitterness, to the myths of the Navy, or to a prolonged exposure to the single hope that, as a midshipman and lieutenant, he had heard so fervently expressed by his peers. *A command* . . . ! A chance at last to exercise the skill and talents he'd developed . . . a chance to sail his own ship upon the seas, independent of the shore, to pick and choose the place of his own landfall, and survive by his own native cunning, free from the restraint imposed by subordination. How many of his fellows would envy him the chance, he wondered, and give all they possessed for the opportunity of commanding as much as a rotten old hooker of a scow in wartime? There were many, he knew.

Besides, *Experiment* was a lucky boat. Under David Porter she'd fought an epic day-long battle against Haitian pickaroons in January 1800, resulting in heavy casualties for the piratical forces of "General" Hyacinthe Rigaud; and later, under Charles Stewart, she'd captured the French privateer *Deux Amis*, and also the *Amphitheatre*, a British privateer captured by mistake and released afterward with apologies. She was almost as lucky as *Enterprise*, her sister.

There was also the matter of the Markham family. Almost the entire wealth of the various Markham branches had originally been won on the sea, as often as not in combat. It had been the legend of Malachi Markham, whose constant defiance of the odds during the Revolution had met with such spectacular success, that had inspired the sixteen-year-old Favian to join the Navy in the first place. Could Favian place his name alongside those of preceding generations? Would his own career be as successful as that of his father, Jehu, his uncles Josiah and Malachi, his grandfather Adaiah, who had commanded privateers against the French and died in combat with pirates off Formosa? Would Favian, in short, measure up?

If he turned down the command he would never know. Of the many thoughts flickering through his mind in the brief instant before he gave his answer, the most palpable was that of a long line of Markhams, some ghostly, some flesh and blood, watching him with cold, demanding eyes, their hands clasping the hilts of swords taken from other generations of defeated foes.

"I cannot," Hamilton was saying, "fault you for not accepting. It is no stain on your honor. There will be no stigma attached to you if you decline."

The devil there won't, Favian thought. He knew the service better than that.

"I am honored to accept, sir," he said. Hamilton smiled.

"I shall have the orders drawn this afternoon. I am pleased to have under my supervision men of spirit and patriotism such as yourself—*Captain* Markham."

It felt good, he had to admit it. Masters of Navy vessels were called captain whether they officially had the rank or not; and though Favian was a master commandant with a lieutenant's command, he was nevertheless captain of the United States brig of war *Experiment*, and would be until he was given another assignment or *Experiment* was blown out from under him. There was a giddy sensation that came as Hamilton pronounced the word. *Captain*: The word had such a sweet sound.

But, Favian wondered cynically, would there have been talk of "spirit" if he had declined? Would Hamilton or his successors have ever offered Favian another command, knowing he had once turned one down?

"Thank you, sir," he said. "I hope I shall prove worthy of your trust."

"Congratulations, Favian," Burrows said. The tone was grudging. Favian looked with surprise at his friend. Was there resentment in those solemn eyes? Had the jealousy begun already, and over such a poor command as *Experiment*? And then, in a frozen instant, Favian felt he understood: Possibly Burrows would have been offered *Experiment* if Favian had turned it down. Had he just, by taking a command below his own station, deprived Burrows of what might be his friend's first and only chance to distinguish himself?

"Mr. Burrows, I have good news for you as well," Hamilton said, a satisfied smile flickering over his features. Burrows looked at him cynically.

"I have received word that *Enterprise* has come into Portsmouth, after having sailed from New Orleans. Her captain, Lieutenant Johnson Blakely, has been promoted, and has relinquished command. As I am certain that your exchange will be concluded in a few weeks, I would be pleased, Mr. Burrows, to offer you the appointment."

Burrows said nothing. Neither did he move; he merely sat in the chair, his hands clasping its arms, his eyes fixed on Hamilton's face as if he expected the secretary of the navy to jump up and cackle "April fool!" before withdrawing the appointment altogether.

"Will?" Favian prompted.

William Burrows continued to gaze profoundly at Hamilton, his face set in its customary expressionlessness, and then he began to laugh. It was a strange, unpracticed laugh, akin to a high-pitched screech, Burrows's lips drawing back from his teeth and gums in a grotesque parody of a smile, his eyes still fixed on the astonished secretary. Burrows's face grew red, his body still frozen in a stiff attitude in the chair, his knuckles growing white as he fervently grasped the arms of the chair. His howls echoed in the small room. Tears began to fall down his cheeks. Hamilton stared at Burrows with nervous wonder.

"Will, for God's sake!" Favian said, astonished. He had never, in their entire acquaintance so far as he could remember, seen Burrows utter more than a polite laugh.

Burrows ran out of breath and began to cough. This seemed to break the spell; he huddled forward in his chair, coughing into his fist, and then looked up at the Secretary, his eyes still streaming.

"I—I am honored to accept, sir," he gasped.

"Er—congratulations, Captain Burrows," Hamilton said, a weak and nervous smile on his face. For some reason this set Burrows into another outburst of hilarity, quelled only when Favian, thoroughly scandalized, began to pound him vigorously on the back.

"I am sorry, sir," Burrows said as soon as he'd regained his wits. "I am—I am honored by the appointment, and apologize for my—my behavior. Perhaps you would be so kind as to give me and Markham each a glass of your North Carolina whiskey?"

"Are you—ah—entirely certain you are well, Mr. Burrows?" Hamilton asked cautiously. He poured whiskey and pushed it across the table. Burrows gulped it hurriedly.

"Never better, sir," he said. There was still a dazed smile on his features. He blotted the tears from his face with a handkerchief. "I can't—I can't explain what happened to me. I only hope I can persuade you to forgive me."

"Think nothing of it, Captain Burrows," Hamilton said, as politely as he could manage. "Both *Experiment* and *Enterprise* are at Portsmouth. Captain Markham may leave whenever he is ready. Captain Burrows, I am sure you will be prepared whenever your exchange is completed—"

"If I may, sir, I should like to leave with Captain Markham," Burrows said. "If you could send the orders after me, I could begin making arrangements as soon as I reached Portsmouth."

"Ah, very well, Captain Burrows. If you wish."

Portsmouth, Favian thought. The only town he could claim as home, the town from which the Markham clan had, over the last hundred years, sailed their wooden hulls upon the breast of the sea. Portsmouth. Favian, without quite believing in luck, hoped that Portsmouth would be lucky for him.

"Captain Burrows, your lieutenant will be Edward McCall," Hamilton said. "Captain Markham, your lieutenant has yet to be assigned. There are a number available; I have a list if you would care to indicate your preference."

"Thank you, sir." He took the list and scanned it. The privileges of a captaincy were coming quickly; he was given not only a brig, but patronage to go with it. It was a heady feeling, knowing he had at least the power to affect the life of one other officer. A bit of Decatur's cunning came to him. He looked up. "I can ask, sir," he said, "for no greater support than to request the services of Acting Lieutenant Archibald Hamilton."

The secretary flushed with pleasure. "I regret I must deny you your request, sir," he said. "My son is being reassigned to the *United States* in your place, as soon as his promotion is confirmed."

"I am sure he will bring honor to the appointment, sir,"

Favian said, his eyes already wandering once more down the list. He found he knew most of them, at least by reputation—the Navy was a small place—although he had not met some of the junior lieutenants.

"May I have Peter Hibbert?" he asked.

"A New Hampshireman, I see."

"I have known him for some time, sir."

"Very well. *Experiment* will have New Hampshire officers, and because she's fitting out at Portsmouth she'll have a New Hampshire crew as well."

"McCall and I are both South Carolina men," Burrows offered. " 'Twill be interesting, this little squadron. Which state will gain the most honor, d'you think?"

"I will lay you a wager, sir," said Favian.

"Alas, sir, I cannot afford to bet until I run aboard a few prizes," Burrows said.

"I hope you gentlemen will be at the President's house tonight, to celebrate the New Year," Hamilton said.

"I have not been invited, sir," said Favian.

"There is no need for an invitation to see the President," Hamilton said. "His house is open to all citizens."

"Strange, this custom," Burrows said. "I wish there were some certain commodores who held by it."

"Sir," Favian said, "I wonder if you have read my monograph on Massey's Recording Log. I think it would be of inestimable aid to the service—"

Hamilton waved his hand in dismissal. "I looked at it, Captain Markham, and I confess I could not make head nor tail of it. Interesting, of course, for those whose minds work that way. But it's wartime, and the office is a busy one. In peacetime I could afford to give the matter more attention."

Favian felt hopelessness rising in him. "Sir," he said, making one last attempt, "the recording log could be quite useful in wartime. Think of a long sea voyage, cruising 'gainst the enemy—"

"And then there's the patent problem," Hamilton went on. "How are we going to pay this fellow Massey his royalties when it would be considered trading with the enemy? No, it won't answer."

"We could make an improved version," Favian said. "We wouldn't necessarily owe Massey a thing."

"No, it won't answer," Hamilton repeated, genially pouring himself another cup of whiskey. "By the way, Mr. Markham, there's a question I've been meaning to ask you. Mr. Goldsborough, my regular clerk, reviewed the documents sent to us by Commodore Decatur, and brought to my attention a discrepancy. The sort of thing clerks love, of course, but still . . ."

"What is it, sir?"

"It's in the matter of a ship's boy named Jack Creamer. How did he manage to be enrolled as a member of the crew in mid-Atlantic, on the day of a major battle?"

Favian's mind spun furiously. "He—ah—his father was a member of the crew who died suddenly, last voyage," he said, hoping his improvisation would not be too absurd. "It was not until the day of the battle that Commodore Decatur remembered that we were carrying the boy's father on the rolls instead of the boy. We simply corrected the error."

"Ah, I see—yes," Hamilton said uncertainly, his brow furrowed.

"I see that you are busy, sir. We should take our leave. I'm sure we're both grateful for the chance to command." Favian fled with Burrows before Hamilton could take the opportunity to begin picking logical holes in the yarn Favian had spun him.

They sped from the Navy Department to celebrate their advancement at the nearest tavern. Burrows was not in uniform, but Favian was, and his opportunity to shift his epaulet from his left shoulder to his right, indicating command, had to be celebrated.

"What in blazes happened to you, Will?" Favian demanded as they splashed through muddy streets to the nearest saloon. "You looked like some mad ape laughing at the follies of mankind."

"That's what I felt like, Favian," Burrows said quietly. "I never thought I'd be promoted by a Republican administration. That's why I asked for a furlough and went to China. Even after I'd returned, I thought there'd be no real place for me. Third lieutenant of the *President* again, or perhaps a choice gunboat rotting in the Delaware. And

then when he offered me the *Enterprise*—my God!—
I swear, I thought it was some ridiculous prank. And then
when he called me captain I was off and laughing again.
After all these years, to finally have a chance."

"I would not break into such fits in front of naval secretaries again," Favian said, "unless you want to end up like
your Aunt Dotty."

They entered the tavern, scraped mud from their boots,
and ordered champagne. The tavern keeper accepted the
order without surprise; no doubt he was accustomed to the
early-morning drinking habits of young officers from the
Navy Yard.

"I hope you will be at the President's celebration tonight,
Will," Favian said.

"It's a little high-flown for me."

"We captains, Will, must learn to fly in these elevated
circles. Besides, you should thank Secretary Hamilton
again for your command, and reassure him as regards
your mental stability."

"There was going to be a celebration in a little tavern by
the Navy Yard."

"Don't be foolish. I think it would be to your advantage
to meet Washington society, and show Hamilton that you
can behave as something other than a baboon."

The champagne appeared; Favian smiled, paid, and
poured. They stood. Solemnly Burrows reached to Favian's
left shoulder, unfastened the epaulet, and shifted it to the
right; he saluted and raised the glass of champagne.

"To the captain of the *Experiment*, and to success on the
waters!"

"To success, and to the next captain of the *Enterprise*!"

They drank, and Favian tasted the first wine of command. It was light-headed stuff indeed; he supposed he
could grow to like it.

8.

"Can we make our excuses early, Favian? I have someone I'd like to meet at another place."

"We'll see how it goes, Will." The President's mansion, looking like a modest Georgian country house, was well alight, and echoing to the sound of music. Favian wondered if anyone present knew that the "Staten Island Reel" that was pouring out the windows was originally a song of American pirates, who, like Captain Kidd, had used Staten Island as a hideout one hundred and fifty years before.

Burrows, still in semirespectable civilian dress, carried a bundle on his saddle; this he gave to the servants at the door, along with his hat and cloak. Favian handed over his cloak and cocked hat, then walked with Burrows into Madison's presence.

The ceremonial East Room was decorated with the flags of the British captures that had flown over the Navy Ball a few days before. Most of the Cabinet were absent, but the secretaries of war and state were present, as well as the European consuls and a representative selection of both houses of Congress. A reception line had begun to form in front of Mr. and Mrs. Madison, and Favian and Burrows joined it. Any citizen could shake hands with his President. The line was delayed while a Philadelphia merchant subjected Madison to a graceless and seemingly endless peroration about some new kind of bomb-carrying balloon, meant to break the British blockade, which he proposed to inflict upon the military at only a modest profit to himself, the machine's inventor. Madison, dressed in a battered black coat, stood the narrative with far more grace than Favian expected, referred the merchant to Dr. Eustis, the

Secretary of War, and pointedly turned to shake the hand of the next man in line, leaving the inventor with no option but to touch the hand of the incomparable Dolley—dressed in a yellow satin gown with a pink cloak and, again, the white-plumed turban—and then withdraw, seeking Eustis among the revelers.

Madison remembered Favian and congratulated him on his promotion. "Thank you, sir," Favian said. "Allow me to present Lieutenant William Burrows, who has been made lieutenant commandant of the brig *Enterprise*."

"Mr. Burrows, it is always a pleasure to meet one of the brave men fighting to drive British tyranny from the seas."

"I hope I shall do the appointment honor, Mr. President," Burrows mumbled, his gaze directed toward the vicinity of the President's shoes.

"Captain Stewart is here tonight, gentlemen," Madison said. "His *Constellation* is almost ready for sea."

"A lucky ship, with a good captain," Favian said. "I trust the British will soon have cause to regret Captain Stewart's abilities."

Madison agreed and turned to the next man in line. Favian stepped on to the smiling Dolley.

"I regret I have nothing to lay at your feet, madam," he said, "but my loyalty to the nation."

Dolley Madison beamed at this declaration, which Favian had invented that afternoon and had been saving for the right moment.

"Congratulations on your appointment, Master Commandant," she smiled. "I hope I shall have the opportunity to decorate myself again with the symbols of your victories."

"I pray I may have that honor. British ensigns complement your coloring so well." Dolley Madison beamed again. Favian turned to Burrows. "May I introduce Lieutenant Commandant Burrows, just appointed to the *Enterprise*."

"It is a pleasure, Mr. Burrows."

"Thank you, ma'am." Burrows looked completely miserable. Favian, recalling that Burrows might suddenly break into another strange fit of laughter, took his friend in tow and, strewing compliments, left the presidential circle.

"Can we leave now?" Burrows asked.

"No, not at all. There is work to be done here."

"Favian, how can you do it?" demanded Burrows. "All those flowery phrases! I can't talk to these people at all. Never learned the language."

"Then it's high time you did. We can help the Navy at this party. The Secretary of the Treasury is not present, and we must find as many people of influence as we can and convert them to the Navy's cause while Gallatin is away." Albert Gallatin, the brilliant Swiss-born treasury secretary, was a vigorous opponent of the Navy, and had worked under Adams to prevent the Navy from being built at all, and under Jefferson and Madison to keep it weak and in harbor.

"I don't think I would be any help to the Navy's cause in my present state," Burrows said. "That champagne had me dancing all afternoon, but now I feel flat as a summer flounder. Perhaps I should fortify myself with a glass of punch. Complimenting the President's lady like that! You'd think you'd been to school at Versailles!"

"It requires but wit, education, and manners," Favian said. "If you are deficient in these categories, simply hang at my elbow, nod when I speak, and look agreeable."

They made their way to the punch bowl, where they met Thomas Tingey and his fiancée, and were soon joined by Charles Stewart.

"I've been informed of your new commands," Tingey said, smiling proudly. "It was I who suggested rerigging *Experiment* and *Enterprise* as brigs. Mr. Hamilton took my suggestions to heart, and I think you'll find them an improvement. No booms getting in the way of the guns, and you'll be able to back and fill to keep station. They've been given eighteen-pound carronades as well. You'll find them able to capture any enemy of their class."

"Indeed, sir," Favian said neutrally. "I hope I shall be able to receive the benefit of your innovations." He had caught Burrows's grimace: Tingey had taken two of the fastest cruisers on the seven seas and rerigged them with an unsuitable sail plan, overgunned them with heavy weaponry, and made them sitting ducks for any smart-sailing frigate, sloop of war, or sail of the line to come along and blow them out of the water. If he was captured, Favian would know whom to blame.

"I propose a boarding party, gentlemen," Favian said. "We may take Congress by storm while Gallatin's away, and spend some of his precious money for him."

"A splendid idea, Markham," Stewart said. "But you and I are strangers to this city—I suspect Captain Tingey will have to give us the benefit of his experience, yes?"

Tingey was happy to oblige. For the next few hours Tingey wandered through the room with his fellow officers, performing introductions, acquainting them with the powerful and influential. Most of the men Favian spoke to were surprisingly open to the ideas presented by the naval advocates—surprising, because these men had in large part been responsible for the shortsighted, incompetent naval policy of the last twelve years. Perhaps the Army's appalling defeats, and the Navy's successes, had caused them to reconsider their ideas.

Somewhere in the course of the busy evening Favian lost track of Burrows. Favian had been introduced by Tingey to a gaunt, somewhat wild-eyed legislator from South Carolina named John Calhoun, of whom Favian had never heard, but who, Tingey assured him, was a leading war hawk and a close comrade of the speaker, Henry Clay, who had led the fight to declare the war in the first place. Having been assured that the bill authorizing the four new ships of the line and the six new frigates would assuredly pass, Favian was urging upon Calhoun the need for smaller cruisers, sloops of twenty guns or so which could stay at sea for months, raiding enemy commerce, and yet be ready to defeat enemy ships of the same class.

"I think you will find my views in agreement with those of a countryman of yours, one Lieutenant Burrows," Favian said, and turned to discover Burrows had left his station at Favian's elbow and was standing among a group of men and ladies near the punch bowl. "I'll introduce you, sir, if you'll step this way," Favian said, and escorted Calhoun toward the busy bowl of punch.

A roar of laughter came from the group around Burrows. Favian was surprised to hear Burrows's droll voice coming from the midst of the laughter. " 'Mr. Burrows,' Captain McNeil says, 'I shall thank ye to keep yer fingers out of the rations we give to the rats!' " Another burst of hilarity came from Burrows's audience.

"Mr. Calhoun, may I present Lieutenant Commandant Burrows, of the—" Favian began.

"Oh, hi, J.C.," Burrows said laconically. "I heard you finally married Floride."

"Last year," said Calhoun.

"Congratulations, I suppose," Burrows said. "I hesitate to be overly fulsome to any of the marrying men of my acquaintance, lest it encourage the regrettable diminution of my bachelor friends."

"You should not despair. Marriages are made to create little bachelors—and little spinsters, as well."

"We were speaking," Favian said, trying to turn the subject back to naval expansion, "of the need for a new building program."

"Oh, aye," Burrows said. "More small ships, like the *Wasp* and the *Hornet*. And fewer captains like Daniel McNeil." This last sent the crowd roaring again. Favian realized with horror that Burrows had been entertaining his audience with stories of the Navy's most appalling captain, hardly the sort of tales suitable to set official Washington on a shipbuilding spree.

"Master Commandant Markham here can tell you more McNeil stories," Burrows said. "His first voyage to the Mediterranean was on McNeil's *Boston*. Never sailed within a hundred leagues of Tripoli, isn't that right?"

"He's out of the service now, of course," Favian said.

"I've told these ladies and gentlemen about McNeil's stranding his lieutenants in France, and kidnapping French officers to take their places," Burrows said.

"I think the story's exaggerated."

"Pish! You were there, you've told me about it often enough." He turned to his audience. "McNeil afterwards said that his officers' dinner-table conversation was dull, and he thought the conversation of Frenchmen might be an improvement. When his three lieutenants were ashore in Toulon, McNeil weighed anchor and sailed out of port,

taking French officers by force as he left, so that he could
have a good chat. They didn't serve either, because he
stranded them in Africa. He never communicated with
Commodore Morris, rarely wrote to the Navy Department,
and sailed about the Mediterranean at will."

"We did capture four grain barges heading for Tripoli,"
Favian added.

"But it was by accident. You never went to Tripoli, so
you never could have been looking for them. Eventually
the department orders caught up with him and brought
him home, and he was eased out of the service.

"Favian and I were both singularly unlucky in having
McNeil as our captain during our respective first voyages
as midshipmen. I was with him in his old command, the
Portsmouth corvette, and had to endure his company only to
Guiana and back, but poor Captain Markham had the
pleasure of his acquaintance all the way to the Mediterranean."

"Is this McNeil a typical product of the Navy?" asked
John Calhoun, a question Favian had been dreading.

"Indifferently so," Burrows said with a shrug. "The sea
breeds eccentricity. The loneliness of command, I suppose."

"There is no such man in the service now, Mr. Burrows," Favian said quickly.

"No, the Army's got most of the madmen now, I think,"
Burrows said. "But let me tell you fine people about Captain Dacres's hat. He was the British captain of the *Guerrière*—a talented captain, as those men go, young for the
command of a thirty-eight—and before the war he met
Captain Hull of the *Constitution*. He and Hull got to arguing the merits of their frigates, and each bet the other his
hat on the results of a contest between the two. 'Twas a
joke at the time, but when Old Ironsides beat the *Guerrière*, and Dacres came aboard to give Hull his sword in
defeat, Hull refused the sword, but he said, 'I'll trouble
you, Captain Dacres, for that hat!'"

Burrows's audience, which had enlarged somewhat,
burst into laughter. Burrows waited for an opening, then
deftly continued. "Captain Hull must have been a sight.

He's a portly fellow, y'know, and when he gave the order to fire they say he split his breeches clean up the backside!"

Favian watched in surprise as Burrows's audience dissolved into laughter and well-bred titters. It seemed as if Burrows had overcome his shyness in remarkably quick time, and also that his approach was perhaps more suitable to a New Year's celebration than Favian's higher-pitched appeals had been. Favian had been attempting to justify an increase in the Navy in terms of British prizes taken. Burrows, with a few drawling anecdotes, had somehow succeeded in making the Navy *popular*. Most of the administration and Congress were intelligent men, but they had no direct knowledge of the sea; the Navy had been an abstract to them, and, like all unknowns, somehow threatening—they had seen the Navy budget increasing for a number of years, and saw nothing concrete to show for it, not realizing that the Navy's primary function was to *prevent* unpleasant occurrences. Once they'd reduced the Navy budget, unpleasantness had begun to occur in plenty, which seemed to justify their original distrust of the service. These men had to know the service better to know that it was not full of imperialist adventurers eager to engage the United States in wars with every power in Europe; to know that it contained dozens of competent, tested officers, veterans of Preble's attacks on Tripoli or Truxtun's battles in the West Indies, who were eager to take command of whatever ships these congressmen voted them, and were both capable and prepared to win victories.

Favian listened as Burrows spun a few more anecdotes; then Burrows excused himself for a chat with his acquaintance Calhoun, and Favian found himself inheriting his friend's audience. He told them some Stephen Decatur stories, then began lamenting the Navy's lack of cruisers, illustrating his point with anecdotes of his father and uncles during the Revolution, and of naval exploits during the wars with France and Tripoli.

"But why cannot privateers perform the tasks of these sloops of war?" a rotund congressman asked.

"Sir, privateers function well as commerce raiders,"

Favian answered, his professional reflexes working automatically to create the illusion that his mind was dwelling entirely on the subject and that the congressman was an object of utter fascination. "But they cannot be expected to successfully engage enemy cruisers or convoy escorts, or provide prompt transportation for dispatches abroad or to our allies; they cannot deliver ambassadors to their destinations, or provide security for our merchant convoys. These tasks only a Navy ship can perform. Also, Navy ships can make extended voyages—into the Indian Ocean, or the Pacific, say—where there are no friendly ports, and where they could raid successfully for months at a time. Such a distance from home they'd have to destroy their prizes rather than bring them back over such a space of ocean. Privateers cannot be expected to destroy their prizes; prize money provides a privateer's livelihood. Privateers cannot sail very far from a friendly base, but Navy ships can. If we have enough sloops of war to spare, we can raid the East Indies and destroy the East India fleets. That will bring pressure on the British government to bring the war to a conclusion favorable to the United States."

The congressman nodded. "You sound as if you do not expect the British to give us a favorable peace otherwise. Don't you think we'll have Canada in a year's time?"

"I am not an Army man, sir," Favian said carefully. "Canada is not my department. I know only what the Navy can do if we are given the right ships."

There were a few more questions, and then Favian found himself talked out. He excused himself and poured himself a substantial cup of punch.

"Burrows seems to have made himself a success," said a voice. It was redhaired Charles Stewart, indicating Burrows surrounded by another roaring crowd.

"Aye. Becoming a commander seems to have done him good."

"And the Navy, I'll warrant."

Favian nodded. "Tingey was boasting earlier about the changes he'd wrought in our little boats," he said. "I'd rather have the schooner rig back again, whether we can back and fill or not."

Stewart agreed. "The *Experiment* is my old boat, you know," he said. "I knew how well she could handle. The brig rig will ruin her, I'm sure." He shook his head sadly. "You may be putting your head into the lion's mouth, my lad."

Favian felt a touch on his arm; it was Archibald Hamilton. "Pardon me for intruding, gentlemen," he said. "I wonder if I may speak to Captain Markham privately."

"With your permission, Charles?"

"Of course."

Hamilton drew Favian away from the others and spoke in a low voice. "I was wondering if you could help me get my father away," he said. "He's taken a drop too much. I've had the carriage brought around, and my mother's waiting, but he won't leave."

Favian turned and saw Secretary Hamilton, ruddy faced, in a circle of legislators; a glass was in his hand, and one arm was thrown around the shoulders of a sour-looking William Burrows. It looked as if the arm had been thrown around Burrows less in comradeship than for support.

"I'll do my best," Favian said. "Get his hat and coat."

He made his way to the secretary, hearing him declaim, in a loud voice, "That's right, Burrows! Give us the ships we'll be needing, and we'll finish the war without the blasted Army, and without the blasted interference of Dr. blasted Eustis!" The laughter that followed this denunciation of the secretary of war was decidedly strained, but Hamilton chose to continue. "I've always said," he declared, "that one American sailor can whip five—no, ten—Englishmen, and at least a hundred Mahometan Turks!"

"Pardon me, sir," Favian said, wondering if the secretary was going to obliterate, by a few minutes' impolitic inebriation, all that he, Burrows, and Stewart had achieved in the course of a night's earnest legislative influencing.

"I was wondering, sir, if Lieutenant Burrows and I might speak with you privately," Favian said. Burrows glared at Favian with resentment at being thus press-ganged.

"Of course, my'boys," Hamilton said jovially. "Always ready to talk to the brave men who serve, who serve—"

The Secretary, in the act of making an expansive gesture with one arm, had swung himself off-balance; Favian intervened to prevent Hamilton from toppling over.

"That's all right. Lean on me, sir. Shall we get some air, sir? I think it will do me good." With Favian on one arm and Burrows on the other, and without waiting for Hamilton's assent, the Secretary was propelled out of the East Room at a rapid pace.

"Air, d'you say?" Hamilton drawled. "Just what we need. You've been doing good work tonight, gentlemen. Let me just refill my glass. . . ."

"I was wondering, sir, if it might be possible to get my orders early on the second of January, sir, so that I could set out on the stage to Baltimore and thence to Portsmouth as soon as possible. It will take me at least a month to travel overland, and then of course I've got to have traveling expenses. I'm not sure the money advanced me by Commodore Decatur's agents will stand me the journey." Favian felt the words tumbling out as he ran his sentences together so that Hamilton wouldn't have an opening to speak; he sped the Secretary through the lobby and out onto the porch. Archibald Hamilton stood by the door of the coach. Still spilling words, his own incoherence increasing, Favian and Burrows propelled the Secretary, as politely as they could, into his carriage. Archibald Hamilton swiftly leaped inside, shutting the door.

"If you would take care of that, sir, we'd be greatly obliged," Favian finished, seeing his breath frost in front of his face.

"My hat and coat," said the secretary, completely befuddled.

"Sorry you're leaving so soon. I think we've done well by the Navy tonight. Young Mr. Hamilton has your coat. Thank you, sir, for all you've done." Archibald Hamilton called out to the coachman, and the carriage swayed off through the muddy ruts as words continued to spill from Favian like water from a chain pump.

"Can we leave now?" Burrows asked, as the carriage slipped down the muddy drive.

"Before the New Year? I thought you were finding your feet quite well."

"It was easy enough, once I discovered I didn't need your gift of courtly speech. I'm disappointed in our political superiors—I truly am. They're as interested as any shellback in service gossip. Let's step inside and get our cloaks. It's cold."

"I think we should say our farewells to Stewart and Tingey."

"Just so we don't have to shake hands with the President again. Don't know why we had to do it in the first place."

They walked into the East Room just as a cheer went up: Anno Domini 1813 had arrived. It proved impossible to leave just yet, for President Madison led a toast, hoping the New Year would prove a happy and triumphant one for the republic, and that her armed forces would triumph over tyranny. This sentiment was publicly appreciated by the French consul, who proclaimed another toast to the glory of the Emperor Napoleon, who at last report had captured Moscow, and would soon (doubtless) triumph over the Tsar and his treacherous anglophile advisors, uniting the Continent once more against perfidious Albion. Democratic-Republicans drank heartily to the toast; most Federalists scowled and looked down into their drinks—to them he was "Bonaparte the usurper," not "Napoleon the First."

Congressman Calhoun toasted, in advance, the certain capture of Canada in the coming year; Captain Tingey led a toast to the Navy; Dr. Eustis led one to the Army. Charles Stewart drank to Isaac Hull, and Favian, who knew a cue when he heard one, led another to Decatur. Burrows stumbled through a salute to David Porter, who had captured the *Alert*. Hopeful toasts were drunk to a few of the Army's generals, those who had distinguished themselves by somewhat less disgraceful conduct than the majority. But by that time most of the crowd had ceased to pay attention; so Mrs. Madison interrupted the chorus of toasts to announce the first song of the New Year: "Hail, Columbia." At this point Favian relented to the insistent tugging of Burrows on his sleeve and, after collecting cloaks, hats, swords, and Burrows's bundle, followed his friend from the President's House.

"This way," Burrows said, after they had called for their horses. He was leading Favian in the direction of the Navy Yard. "There is someone I would like you to meet."

"Who is this august personage, Mr. Burrows?"

"A most distinguished member of the college of musicians, Mr. Markham. So distinguished, in fact, that we shall have to disguise ourselves as members of his guild, utilizing the bundle which I have thought to bring with us."

"My God! What's that smell?" Favian groped for his handkerchief, held it to his nose.

"The slave market," Burrows said. "Within spitting distance of the President's mansion. A national disgrace."

"Don't they bathe the blacks, for God's sake?"

"Not until the day they sell them; then they bathe 'em and oil their skin. Waste of water otherwise." Burrows looked resentfully at the cold silhouette of the warehouse where the slaves awaited purchase by their new masters. "How many of our fathers, d'you think, expected slavery to flourish in the national capital of a free country, a quarter of a century after the Constitution was ratified?" Burrows asked.

"I shouldn't think the New England men did," Favian said. "You're from South Carolina; you should know the southern men better than I."

"It's an embarrassment, being from a slave state," Burrows said. "The institution should have died out by now, but as long as there's a frontier we'll be needing slave labor to clear it. Easier than soiling white men's hands."

"For the last four years it's been illegal to import slaves. Surely that will slow down the traffic."

"It might," Burrows said. "But it also makes the slaves already here more valuable. It's going to take a larger investment to buy slaves now, and the planters will be unwilling to forego such an investment once it's been made. The only thing that's slowed the growth of slavery has been that it was so easy to go bankrupt—after making such a huge capital investment just in labor, a few bad harvests could wipe a planter out. But now they have a new type of cotton called Mexican upland. It's resistant to the rot that wipes out cotton crops. Mexican upland and the cotton gin are beginning to make slavery pay. Mark my words: Cotton will be the main cash crop in the South in another score of years. Perhaps our great-grandchildren will see the end of slavery—we never shall."

"That's pessimistic, Will."

"I know South Carolina too well, Favian."

They had passed the slave market. Favian returned his handkerchief to his sleeve. Perhaps Burrows was right. The founders of the American republic had looked upon slavery with an attitude similar to that of Burrows: It was an embarrassment, but still a reality that had to be dealt with. The Constitution provided that the importing of slaves would cease twenty years following ratification; after importing ceased, it was assumed slavery could be gradually extinguished. It was thought that slaves would be needed to open up the wilderness, after which the need for their labor would be over. But the Louisiana Purchase had opened up enormous tracts of land, much of it suitable for slave-run plantations; and now, if, as Burrows said, slavery was beginning to pay, the institution might well last longer than the American founders had ever intended.

"That Calhoun you met tonight—he'll be part of the problem," Burrows continued gloomily. "John Calhoun came from upcountry, where there aren't many slaves—or many rich men, for that matter. But now he's married into the tidewater, and soon he'll be their voice, a slave owner himself. I've seen it happen to others; it'll be sad to see it happen to J.C. A man with his gifts could make slavery seem almost respectable."

"I'm surprised, Will, to hear you speak against your state's institutions."

"I'm a republican, Favian," Burrows said shortly. "Not a Democratic-Republican, but a republican with a small r. There are many of us left in the South; Calhoun was one, and may be still. But we're diminishing. It goes against my grain to see men abused under an institution like slavery. I've seen the slave markets in Tunis, where it's Americans and Christians they're selling. I don't see the difference. If we allow black slavery here, we can't very well object to it

in Tunis or Tripoli just because the slaves are white. . . .
Here's the place. Down this alley."

In an alley the horses were left munching into their feed
bags, while Favian was persuaded to doff his coat, cocked
hat, neckcloth, and cravat. The boots would have to stay.
He exchanged his uniform for a plain cloth cap, ragged
jacket, and scratchy wool scarf. Favian's uniform, along
with his sword, was rolled in Burrows's bundle, along with
Burrows's round hat and swallow-tailed coat. Favian tried
to remember a quotation about Harun ar-Rashid, the caliph
who legendarily used to amuse himself by dressing up as a
commoner and wandering about Baghdad; but the cold
night and the hearty series of toasts drunk earlier had
driven the verses from his mind, and he was perfectly
happy, after the transformation was complete, to follow
Burrows into a nearby tavern.

It was called The King's Head, the signpost outside
showing a gruesome but still recognizeable George III
hanging from a noose. Inside the tavern it was dark, lit
only by a roaring fire in the hearth and a few old battle
lanterns, probably acquired from some Revolutionary privateer. Favian cracked his head against a low beam seconds
after he entered. Seeing stars and feeling his throat
on the verge of clamping shut, assaulted by a pall of tobacco smoke as thick as gunsmoke on *United States*'s gun
deck, Favian was led to a back table by Burrows. He sat on
a rough bench.

Burrows produced a hand-carved pipe and some coarse
tobacco from a pocket, filled the pipe and lit it, adding
volumes to the cloud of tobacco already shrouding the
room. A frowsy woman in a dirty apron brought beer without being asked, and left without waiting to be paid.
Favian, recovering his vision slowly, glanced about him.

The inhabitants were obviously in the final stages of a
New Year's debauch. A gang of inebriated shellbacks was
playing at dice in a corner; others reclined with girls on
their laps; still others were comparing tattoos and swapping
yarns over mugs of beer or rum.

"There's the man I wanted you to meet," Burrows whispered, directing Favian's attention toward a man moving

slowly through the throng, in the direction of the dazzling fireplace. He looked forty, though if he were a seaman he could be younger, since the life tended to cut up a man's looks. He wore a leather cap, his light-colored hair in an old-fashioned queue, and carried a fiddle. He stepped up to the fire, set the fiddle in rest below his chin, and tuned briefly. A drunken growl of approval, and some applause, came from the crowd.

Favian sipped his beer. Burrows put his feet up on the table. The fiddler plucked the strings experimentally, then set to work. Favian recognized the opening bars of "Bonaparte Crossing the Rhine." It did not take much longer to realize that the playing was brilliant.

It seemed to be a Bonaparte medley, perhaps in honor of the United States's co-belligerent—maybe the fiddler was a Republican. "Bonaparte Crossing the Rhine" was followed in swift succession by "Bonaparte's Advance," "Bonaparte's Retreat," and "Madam Bonaparte." The tunes began to interweave with one another; it seemed on occasion that the fiddler was playing at least two separate tunes at once.

Most of the room was on its feet, mad with hornpipes and reels, the tavern shaking as the feet stamped in rhythm, punctuated by occasional crashes as one of the more comatose members of the crew plunged earthward, falling among the benches and tables like a Homeric warrior in his ringing bronze armor. Favian saw Burrows leap up and join the dancing throng, heard his high-pitched yells, a strange mingling of Indian war cries and fox hunter's yipping, echoing weirdly from the beams. One of the women dropped breathlessly from the dance and came staggering toward Favian's table.

"Buy me a cup of the bob smith, Jack?"

Oh, Christ, Favian thought, knowing this was not going to lead in any constructive direction. He nodded; the woman gave a signal across the room to one of the tavern workers and dropped herself on the bench next to Favian. She was a heavy, shapeless woman, wearing a heavy apron over a sack of a dress. A number of her teeth seemed to be missing.

"My name's Dulcey. Just been paid off, Jack?"

Favian shook his head. "Signing aboard the *Constellation*," he said. The waitress brought two cups of whiskey and this time waited to be paid. Dulcey observed Favian's purse with interest.

"That's a nice purse, Jack. I like them cuffs, too. You've got a nice shirt, eh?" Her hand slipped easily onto Favian's thigh. He sipped his beer, hoping somehow to conceal from Dulcey the fact that her caresses were producing the opposite of arousal. Inspiration struck.

"My wife sews small," he said. "She made the shirt."

"It's a shirt for a gentleman. Where's your wife, then?"

"Alexandria. She's a housemaid." That was just across the Potomac; he hoped Dulcey would realize he had not come to the tavern in search of carnal pleasures. At least it made her hesitate long enough for rescue to come. The medley of reels had ended, replaced by a lament Favian recognized as "The Hills Are Quite Silent," a song about a young man abducted by a press-gang on his wedding night and forced to serve in the Royal Navy. Except for a few dancers with female partners, against whom they leaned more for support than out of ardor, the dance floor cleared swiftly, and Burrows returned to land with a delighted exclamation into Dulcey's lap.

"Willy, m'dear!" Dulcey shouted, her face split in a gaptoothed grin. "You haven't found a berth yet? Your friend's goin' aboard *Constellation*."

"Th' Navy, that's the best berth next to a privateer," Burrows nodded, his arm going around Dulcey's shoulders. "Give me m'beer; I'm dry as a beached squid."

Favian passed him the mug, and Burrows drank. "Puritan Willy, if it's a privateer you want, you should go to Baltimore," Dulcey offered. "Cap'n Pasteur is shippin' men aboard *Snap Dragon*. Some o' the lads left last week, hopin' to find berths aboard her."

"She'll have her complement by now," Burrows said. "But I think I'll make m'way to Baltimore and see if I can find another."

"What's yer name, Jack?" Dulcey said, turning to Favian. "Are you as puritan as your friend?"

"My name's Favian."

"It isn't! What kind o' name is that?"

"Latin. It means 'man of understanding.' "

"It don't! D'you know the Latin, then?"

"Nay, o' course not," Burrows interrupted. "That's what the sky pilot on th' *Constitution* told him."

Favian, who was about to quote Horace, decided to keep his mouth shut. Seamen who quoted the classics might be more than a bit suspicious. He had not come prepared with explanations.

The fiddler concluded his lament, and with his fiddle still tucked under his chin he doffed his cap and made the rounds of the tables, the applauding sailors throwing silver. Burrows dipped into his pocket for a contribution.

"Lazarus!" he called as the hat passed. "Join us for a cup of bob smith."

"Aye, gladly," the fiddler said in a croaking voice. "Good to see thee again, Willy."

The fiddler made his rounds of the tables, then settled onto a stool across the table from Burrows. Favian pushed his whiskey to the man, who drank.

"You play a brave fiddle, Lazarus," Burrows said. "Your lament brought tears to many an eye."

"And so it should," Lazarus said. His keen blue eyes flickered over the crowd. "There are many here who have felt the hands of the press on their shoulders. Who is thy friend?"

"Favian, a Navy man."

"Those are dainty cuffs sticking from that old jacket," Lazarus said, his blue eyes flicking from Favian's wrists to his face. "Methinks thy jacket does not suit thy long limbs, Navy man."

"It keeps away the cold," Favian said, shrugging.

"I don't see that coat on thee, Navy man. I see a blue coat with gold buttons, and a cocked hat and sword."

"You dream, surely," Burrows said. Favian forced a grin.

"It's a dream I'll drink to," he said.

"I know what I know," Lazarus said confidentially. He touched his forehead with a burly finger. "I have *powers*," he said in a coarse whisper.

Favian felt a chill in spite of the warm air. The man's voice held conviction, even if his talk was nonsense. Lazarus's keen blue eyes held on him.

"Should we call you a *Navy* man, I wonder?" he grated. "I think you are not the Navy's, Favian. And I think you are not your own. You will become a schoolmaster in time, I suspect. But I see you in the earth at the end, buried in a uniform you never honored."

Favian's eyes locked with the fiddler's, and he felt the hair at his nape rise. Why, he wondered, did this local lunatic fill him with horror?

"Enough of your powers, for God's sake," Dulcey complained. She waved to a barmaid, her gesture nervous. "It gives me shivers," she said.

The fiddler's eyes turned to her. "Dost thou not know, silly wench, that I use my powers every time I tuck the fiddle beneath my chin? Dost not know that no fiddler can use his art without Old Nick's bidding, or how my powers were given by Old Nick himself, dancing on Virgin Hill beneath the sickle moon?"

Dulcey shivered again. "Tell us, Lazarus," said Burrows. The barmaid arrived with another round of whiskey, and Burrows paid.

"On Virgin Hill," Lazarus repeated, smacking his lips as he noisily sipped the potation. "I was one-and-twenty, and I was thought to have promise as a fiddler, so old Jimmy Davis took me to meet his Master."

"Virgin Hill," Burrows said. "That's the Quaker graveyard in Nantucket."

"Nantucket, aye," Lazarus said. "The Master was there, and twelve others. The Master was tall, aye, and black; and when he spoke the earth seemed to quake. *Dost thou know me, boy?* the Devil asked. *I do, sir*, I said. *Dost thou give me thy soul, if I give thee powers to make thy fiddle sing, and to see the hearts of men?* he asked. *I will*, I said, and the bargain was made.

"*Play then*, said the Master, and I put bow to string, and the power flowed through my arms and my fingers, and I played the wild dance that came into my heart. The Devil danced, kicking his shoes from his cloven feet, and Jimmy

Davis danced, and the others danced. Perhaps some of the graves opened, and the dead took shape and danced as well. A wild dance it was, beneath the horned moon." He glared at Favian, his gaze hard and defiant, as if daring Favian to doubt his words.

"That was in the twenty-second year of the reign of King Charles," he said, with utter conviction.

"Charles of Sweden?" Favian asked. "He hasn't reigned that long, surely."

"Charles of Sweden?" The fiddler laughed harshly, his croaking voice scornful. "Thou art a simpleton, boy! 'Twas in the reign of Charles Stuart, the Second, by Grace of God and General Monck King of England. A few years before they hanged the witches of Salem. And now I must earn my bread." He drained his cup of whiskey, and threw it on the table. It rattled in the silence, and then Lazarus stood and walked to his place before the flames of the hearth.

Dulcey's hands trembled as she raised her cup to her lips. "It's horrible, the way he speaks," she said. "Even if it ain't true."

Burrows glanced at Favian. His eyes were solemn. "It's the utter conviction of it," he said. "It's the fact that *he* believes it. It can shake your belief in what you know to be true."

Favian said nothing. Lazarus's performance—and Favian knew it was a performance, nothing more—had disturbed him. Lazarus had known him for a naval officer. But then, Favian reasoned, it was not a difficult deduction for a man to make. It was no great secret that Burrows enjoyed dressing as a seaman and partaking of common seamen's pleasures; Lazarus probably knew Burrows for who he was, even if Burrows didn't himself realize it. It had not required any powers given by satanic forces to penetrate Favian's hasty and unconvincing disguise.

Was it the prophecies that had made Favian so uneasy? Perhaps so. Despite a strange addition—Favian could never picture himself as a schoolmaster—Lazarus's comments had gone to the heart of Favian's dilemma. No, he was not entirely a Navy man; yet he was not free to be his own. *Free . . .* that seemed the heart of it. His fate, according to Lazarus, according to the Navy, was fixed; there was no possibility of any freedom of action, of taking any steps to avoid the ends of destiny. *No choice.* There was a plausible, horrible truth to that lack of choice. Since the age of sixteen, he'd had little option in what he'd done, in where he'd been sent, the wars and duels in which he'd fought. The battles had been determined by chance and by his superiors; one duel had been arranged by the lieutenant, the other determined by circumstance, when another chose to make remarks he knew would not be overlooked by any man who wore the uniform. As long as he wore the blue coat, Favian's destiny was fixed, and Lazarus had simply pointed it out.

All along there had been one choice: to resign, or to stay with the Navy. Resignation meant sacrificing all the last twelve years, everything that constituted his adult life. He could not throw them away—not in wartime, when a resignation could be interpreted as a lack of courage; not with a long line of Markham ancestors looking over his shoulder, hands clasping the swords captured from their enemy. . . .

Lazarus had begun playing "The Morning Dew." Favian and Burrows rose, bade farewell to Dulcey, and made their way into the cold of the night.

"That's the world in which our men live, Favian," Burrows said. "You don't have contact with it on the quarter-deck, not really. They don't often let us see it. But it exists, for them. Fiddlers acquire their talents from Old Nick. That's a superstition as old as sailing ships—older even than Lazarus claims to be. Like the one that says that bosun's mates can never be called to hell, so they can do what they like. We should know these things live in our men's hearts, Favian." Burrows looked at Favian solemnly. "Perhaps it lives in ours as well," he said. "Did you not feel a sympathetic little touch of fear when Lazarus spoke? Is that why you are so quiet tonight?"

"Why can't a bosun's mate be summoned to hell?" Favian asked.

Burrows shrugged. "I don't know. I suppose the story was invented by a bosun's mate to excuse his dissipation."

"It's late, Will." Favian took the nose bag from his horse and mounted the saddle. "I'll meet you at the Navy Department the day after tomorrow. Then we'll take the stage north."

PART TWO:
Experiment

The brig of war *Experiment* lay floating peacefully just off the Navy Yard, anchored near the sheer hulk that had just given her her masts; her rigging was not yet fully set up, her yards were still not crossed. She had been built in 1800 as a small schooner of one hundred thirty-five tons, at a total cost of $16,689. In 1809 Captain Thomas Tingey had refitted her at the Washington Navy Yard, converting her to a brig and replacing her guns; he'd exchanged her original armament of twelve six-pound long guns for fourteen eighteen-pound carronades, and crammed two long nine-pounder chasers into her bridle ports. Tingey's tinkering had increased her tonnage from one hundred thirty-five to one hundred sixty-five, and her authorized crew from seventy to ninety. Just what the overloading of her hull, designed for lighter armament and a schooner rig, had done to her performance remained to be seen, but it could not be good.

Just after her refit, in one of the odd, seemingly motiveless decisions that seemed to characterize Madison's naval policy, *Experiment* had been laid up in Portsmouth, her masts and rigging dismantled, her guns taken out of her. Since the declaration of war it had taken months to put her into shape again.

Favian compared her with the *Enterprise*, lying a little distance away. The decks of her sister brig were black with men, even in the chill of winter; a flag floated lazily from her peak; her paint and trim had been renewed after the long voyage from New Orleans. In contrast, *Experiment* seemed half-finished: There were only a few figures on her decks; her paint was in places worn clean away; her existing rigging seemed badly or carelessly set up; her trim in the water was bad, a streak of new copper under her bows showing she was down by the stern. There was work to do.

"Let's find the commandant of the yard," Burrows urged. They stood on the pier, their baggage around them, arrested en route to the commandant's office by the sight of their new commands. Favian gave *Experiment* another brief, longing look, and then set off to guide his friends to the commandant of the yard.

The commandant was not in his office, but his secretary, after reading Favian's orders, arranged for a boat to take him aboard his new brig. Burrows's status was more complex: As a released prisoner who had yet to be exchanged, he could not yet take command. He would have to stay on shore until his exchange was confirmed, or visit *Enterprise* on an unofficial basis, as a guest of Lieutenant McCall. It was, in any case, a matter for the commandant to decide, and the commandant was out of his office. Burrows would have to wait. Favian shook his hand and walked back to the pier to find his boat.

The journey from Washington had taken almost six weeks. They had gone by regular stage, a more comfortable means than the horseback journey Favian had made from New York to Washington; they'd stopped at inns each night, and stayed several days in Philadelphia, New York, and Boston as guests of the naval commanders of each city. In New York they'd seen Decatur, allowing him to host a celebration of their promotions. The party was held aboard *Macedonian*, the newest United States frigate. Decatur had presented Favian with a gift of the City of New York: a presentation sword worth several hundred dollars. Its blade was inscribed with the date of the *United States–Macedonian* battle; an elaborate hilt featured Liberty, an American eagle, thirteen stars, the pyramid from the reverse of the Great Seal, and the slogan "Free Trade and Sailors' Rights." In spite of its elaborate decoration, it was an excellent smallsword; it balanced well, and the blade, though narrow, was made of the finest steel. An elegant gentleman's weapon, less businesslike than the heavier Portsmouth presentation hanger Favian had carried since his return from Tripoli, but deadly in the hands of an expert fencer.

After picking up Favian's baggage from his old cabin on board *United States,* Favian and Burrows continued their journey, and arrived in a Boston wild with celebration. Just a few days before their arrival Captain William Bainbridge had brought *Constitution* into harbor, six weeks after he'd shot to pieces the British frigate *Java* off Brazil. It had been a dizzying victory for Bainbridge, whose tactics had been as brilliant, if not as original, as Decatur's, and who had finally overcome the streak of bad luck that had resulted in his capture in both the war against France and against Tripoli. Boston, that dour Federalist city whose population had greatly opposed the declaration of war, was nevertheless a Navy town, and with the rest of New England had always opposed the Republican cuts in the Navy. The Boston Republicans, few in number, were glad for a victory, any victory, in the war they'd forced on the country; and the Federalists could celebrate the fact that they'd been right about the Navy all along. And so New England was wafted along on a tide of, pro-Navy, bipartisan sentiment that laid to rest, at least temporarily, the quarrels that had driven New England almost to the brink of secession. The Boston that had been so hostile to the war had seemed to moderate its temper considerably.

From New London to Portsmouth Favian and Burrows had not had to pay for a meal or a drink; boys had appeared from nowhere at the sight of Favian's undress coat and sword, wistfully expressing their interest in becoming midshipmen; garrulous veterans had gone on at great length about their own wars; newspaper reporters from Federalist sheets asked pointed questions about the incompetence of Paul Hamilton and the others of the Virginia clique, while reporters from Republican papers seemed to insist Favian give paeans to Madison and Bonaparte. These Favian handled as well as he could, and tried to express support only for a larger, stronger Navy to counter the pressures of the increasing British blockade; he tried to avoid answering political questions.

His triumphal ride, which reached near-Roman proportions as it approached Portsmouth, was detailed in several letters to Emma Greenhow; now that he was ashore he had the time and leisure to make up for the long silence in his correspondence when he was aboard ship. A few of her letters had caught up with him during his dizzying ride up and down the East Coast of the United States; they were uniformly affectionate, observant, and witty, her humor a bit dry. It had been over two years since he'd seen her, since his two-month furlough before going aboard *United States*. He wondered if she had changed, if her father had changed; if she had gone riding with any rich young heirs.

But somehow none of the experiences with which Favian filled his letters were quite as memorable as the one incident he could not write about: his final night in Washington, when he had covered his uniform coat with his cloak and gone down a discreet alley, his pocket jingling with Zenobia's price. He'd been recognized as a privileged customer by the manager, who had evidently communicated with the owner while Favian was upstairs, for in the morning, when Favian descended to confront the madam's cashbox, he'd been told the night had once again been on the house.

Zenobia had been as ardent as before, and as inexhaustible; she'd been delighted with the gift Favian had brought her—a silver band for her wrist, which set off her dark skin admirably; she seemed truly sorrowful at his departure. He'd been lucky altogether that he'd headed north by coach and not on horseback. . . .

Favian's boat, bobbing on the choppy waters off the Navy Yard, drew closer to *Experiment*. Thoughts of Zenobia slipped from his mind as it became clear how worn the paint was on the brig's hull, how long it had been since the white trim had been renewed on the taffrail and false quarter-galleries. And what a strange addition those were! Little banks of glazed windows stuck onto the spar deck bulwark right aft, where the *United States*, for example, had windows that brought light into the interior of the roundhouse. But on *Experiment* there was no roundhouse, no poop deck, nothing but the open spar deck—the windows illuminated nothing, led nowhere, provided no additional visibility, and served only as ornamentation. They were more suitable for a French yacht, Favian thought, than for an American man-of-war. Perhaps, Favian conceded, they'd make her look larger, more menacing. Favian would have to hope they did; she was so slow and small that Favian would have to hope she could bluff well.

But slow, small, and tattered though she was, she was flying a commission pendant. And if she was commissioned, then he could take command of her.

"Boat ahoy!" *Experiment* was keeping a sharp watch, at any rate.

"Experiment!" The boatman answered.

There was a brief pause. "Say again?"

"Experiment!"

That set them bustling. Captains were known by the names of their ships, as dukes are known by their titles, or Shakespearean kings known as France or Poland. The boatman's answering *"Experiment!"* instead of "Aye aye" let the watch know their captain was coming aboard, and that they had better have a formal welcome ready by the time the boat drew alongside.

The twitter of the bosun's pipes as Favian ran up the battens on the brig's side, placed as an uncertain ladder leading to the entry port, sounded a trifle breathless, as if the bosun had run to his duty unexpectedly; and one of the midshipmen popped up the aft scuttle and joined the short line of officers a bit late. But all this was probably to be expected. There were no marines, not even a corporal's guard. Favian doffed his hat to the quarterdeck, then to the man in the battered uniform of a sailing master.

"Master Commandant Favian Markham, reporting aboard to take command as per orders from the Secretary of the Navy."

"Alferd Bean, sailing master." The master was a bit young for his position, still under thirty, brown and sturdy. His blue eyes were intelligent and inquisitive. Favian was almost certain their paths had never crossed before, which was unusual in such a small service. Favian pulled the Navy Department orders from the inside pocket of his boat cloak.

"I'll read myself in, Mr. Bean," he said. "Then you can introduce me to the officers."

"Aye aye, sir."

The pipes blew again, the crew shuffling to get a look at their new captain. The paper crackled in Favian's hand as he unfolded it; he stationed himself aft by the capstan and began to read his commission, letting all present know he had come aboard with the legal authority to command *Experiment* and require those aboard to do his bidding.

He had seen the ritual often enough; just two years before, he'd stood at Decatur's side when Decatur had read himself aboard *United States*. But now it was Favian's voice reciting the dry Navy Department phrases, and Favian who stood by the capstan, his epaulet shifted to his right shoulder, an object of curiosity for the jostling crew and the stiff officers. A real command at last: the object of every serving officer. What Favian had served for thirteen years in order to achieve. A breathless kind of exhilaration began to warm him. At last. A sluggish old hooker of a brig, but his. From the badly painted scrollwork under the bowsprit to the ridiculous false quarter-galleries—his.

He came to the end of the message. He folded it, hearing it crackle, feeling the eyes of the men on him. It was traditional for the captain to add words of his own, so the men could better gage his temper and know what to expect; and Favian realized that he had been so preoccupied with his other thoughts that he hadn't prepared a speech, as any sensible captain would. An idiotic situation.

The hands stared. There were only about forty of them, but they seemed to fill the fore half of *Experiment*'s eighty-foot deck.

"Some of you may know," Favian said, "that I was with Captain Decatur in the *United States,* in the battle that resulted in *Macedonian*'s capture. There was a special spirit aboard *United States*. I cannot promise that I can make that spirit blossom here, but I can promise that I will do my best. I can also promise you that you will be made to work harder, perhaps, than ever in your lives, as you prepare *Experiment* to meet the enemy. And I can promise you this: As soon as we fit out, and when you show yourselves ready, you will not have to wait for an enemy to find us, for *I will seek them out!* Mr. Bean, dismiss."

His last order was buried beneath a wave of cheers. Favian looked at the hands in some surprise; his words had been little but a pastiche of the many commissioning speeches he'd heard in his career, with a little blood-and-thunder, death-and-glory wartime rhetoric thrown in. The hands were waving their hats and cheering; the midshipmen looked half-mad with excitement.

Well, so much the better. A cheerful brig would find itself ready for sea all the sooner. The men would obey orders more willingly. Discipline problems would be fewer. And they'd die more readily, if it came to that, as instruments of their country's and Favian's united will.

Alferd Bean introduced Favian to the officers: John Miller, the bosun, who Favian remembered from the old *Constitution* as a stocky, reliable petty officer, literate, and one of the Navy's rare teetotallers; the midshipmen, Thomas Tolbert, Jim Dudley, and Homer Brook, all under nineteen and eagerly stumbling over themselves and each other in order to please the man who had promised them fighting; and the purser Ed Cook, portly and sullen, who looked resentful, Favian thought, at having to bond himself to the Navy Department to the tune of ten thousand dollars, only to be assigned to a miserable little brig, with an authorized crew of less than a hundred souls to cheat in matters of pay, rations, and perquisites.

"We have no lieutenant, sir," Bean said.

"We will shortly—Mr. Peter Hibbert, from the town. I hope to give him his orders later today." He glanced at the shrouds, hanging slack, the main yard, which lacked braces.

"How long is that main yard, Mr. Bean?"

"Thirty-four feet, sir."

"Miserable. Is there another spare available at the yard?"

"I have not inquired, sir."

"I shall do so, then. Why is the standing rigging so slack?"

Alferd Bean guiltily looked aloft. Favian watched him compose his answer. "We were given our masts only a few days ago. The weather was colder then. Last night it turned warm and the rigging slacked off."

Favian had no clear way of knowing if this was the truth. He let the answer pass.

"Call up the men and have it set up properly. Send for

Mr. Tolbert and have him show me over the brig. Send a party of men to sway up my dunnage and send it down to my cabin. I'll unpack it myself."

"Aye aye, sir."

"Immediately."

"Sir."

That was that. Favian could never make one of those hail-fellow-well-met "popular" captains—not that he would ever have wished to. His determination to make *Experiment* the smartest brig in the United States Navy, if not in the world, had might as well be apparent from the first day.

As Tolbert, the senior midshipman, took him over the brig, Favian kept an eye directed upward, watching carefully as Bean set up the rigging. Bean, the bosun, and the other midshipmen seemed to handle the job competently enough, but Favian wondered how many days it would have taken them to complete the job otherwise.

Favian went over *Experiment* from stem to stern, even stripping off his coat and going down into the bilges with a lantern, hearing the sounds of rats scuttling in the dark as he poked at the timbers with a knife tip to judge their soundness. He was not familiar with vessels of the *Experiment*'s class, and after having served on one of the big spardeck frigates, he found the brig minuscule by comparison.

Experiment's spar deck ran unbroken the length of the ship, lined on either side with the short-ranged carronades that constituted her primary armament. There was no wheel: the little brig was steered by a tiller right aft, unsheltered by the usual poop overhang from enemy fire. Below the spar deck was the berth deck, a tight and crowded place, where even the short Tolbert had to stoop. How close to ninety men were supposed to swing hammocks in such a space, Favian could not picture.

The officers lived aft in little lockers that were even smaller than the accommodations of the officers' cabins aboard *United States*. Following his tour Favian went into his own cabin and discovered that its only virtue was that it was the largest berth on the brig. He had naively pictured to himself something like the captain's cabin aboard *United States*, but he consoled himself somewhat forlornly with the thought that *Experiment*'s cabin was at least larger than his old lieutenant's berth.

Once in his cabin, he sent for the muster books and the master's log. There were forty-three men in *Experiment*'s complement, he discovered, less than half the allocated strength. The brig's papers showed copies of continued requests on the part of the commandant of the Portsmouth Navy Yard for a detail of marines, and numerous answers from the Navy Department claiming that the marines were on their way. It appeared that at one point the marines actually had been en route, but had been diverted to Isaac Chauncey's command on Lake Ontario.

After making a mental note to send another request for marines, Favian glanced through the punishment book. Bean had apparently considered few of the hands' offenses worth punishing; there were occasional cases of privileges or liquor rations being taken away for offenses such as drunkenness or fighting. One man had deserted, but not been caught, thus leaving moot the question whether to hang, flog, or imprison him. No lashes had been awarded: good. Favian detested brutal punishment, and regretted its occasional necessity; but if anyone was going to be flogged aboard Favian's brig, Favian wanted it to be his own decision and no one else's. He didn't want to step aboard his new command and be forced to pay the penalty for someone else's discipline problems.

He had been browsing among the record books long enough. He closed the punishment book, returned it to its niche, and went up the aft companion to the deck.

Bean might have been slack about starting the job of setting the standing rigging to rights, but Favian had to admit that once Bean had started, he'd made a good job of it. He tested the backstays and shrouds by leaning on them, and looked aloft, wondering whether to go up to the tops and crosstrees to test the topmast and topgallant shrouds. No, he decided; it would look too much like distrust.

"Detail a boat's crew," Favian said to Bean. "I'll be going ashore to see Mr. Hibbert. I will not be dining aboard tonight, though I hope to invite you to dine in my cabin when matters are not so pressing."

"Aye aye, sir. Thank you, sir."

"Tell the gunner and his mates that I'll be ordering a gun drill following breakfast tomorrow."

Bean seemed a bit startled. "With just a partial crew, sir?"

Favian gave him a deliberate frown. "I'd drill the brig's complement even if they constituted a cook and a ship's boy," he said.

"Aye aye, sir," Bean said, resigned to the change.

Once ashore, Favian went in search of the commandant of the Navy Yard, failed yet again to find him, found that Burrows had also disappeared, and then had himself rowed to Portsmouth, to the house where Lieutenant Peter Hibbert lived with his family. The house was a large one, though it looked as if it hadn't been kept up well: The Hibbert family had been wealthy merchants until Thomas Jefferson's embargo had ruined them, and they'd just begun to recoup their losses when the war began and forced them, as shipowners, to contend with the possibility that any merchant vessel they sent from their wharf might end up in a British Admiralty Court, prize to some lucky frigate captain. So far they, and the rest of the New England merchants, had been fairly lucky: for some reason the British had not made a regular blockade north of Sandy Hook, and the chief danger to the Hibberts, the Markhams, and their spiritual kin was from Royal Navy vessels en route between Halifax and the blockading squadrons farther south, and from British and Canadian privateers.

Favian knocked on a tarnished brass knocker. The maidservant who answered was barely in her teens, her knuckles red from her labor in the great house. Favian doffed his hat. "I would like to see Lieutenant Hibbert, if I may," he said. "I am Master Commandant Markham."

The maidservant nodded, bit a nail, and showed Favian into the parlor. Peter Hibbert came into the room a few minutes later, dressed in his shirt, a mallet and treenails in his hands. "Favian!" he said with a broad grin. "Did Annette get it right—have ye shifted your swab at last? Congratulations on your promotion!" He shifted the mallet into his left hand and clasped Favian's hand with his right.

"Thank you, Peter," Favian said. "Your father is well?"

"Yes. Better all the time. You'll have to join us for dinner one night."

"Thank you. I'll be happy to accept." Favian reached into the pocket of his cloak for Hibbert's orders, and brought them forth.

"I've brought your orders, Peter," he said. "You've been assigned."

"Have I, by God!" Hibbert said, beaming delight. He took the orders and broke the seal, and his grin faded. "It'll be gunboats again, mark my words," he said despondently.

Peter Hibbert was a broad-shouldered man just under six feet; his arms were long and heavily muscled, his neck short and powerful. He looked like a slightly less anthropoid version of William Bainbridge, whose service nickname had once been Gorilla. Hibbert was a few years younger than Favian, and his career had not been lucky: He had missed being one of Preble's boys by a few months, although he was a veteran of the later stages of the war with Tripoli, the unsuccessful attempt to put Hamet Karamanli on the throne to supplant the Pasha who had declared war on the United States, all of which happened after Favian had left the Mediterranean. Afterward Hibbert had survived the purges and ended up commanding gunboats on the Delaware. There Favian had met him, in those bleak years when Jefferson had imposed his embargo on American shipping; and it had become the job of the Navy to keep the embargoed ships in port, assisting in the wreck of American commerce. It had been a brutal time; Favian and Hibbert had been doing a nasty, political job, arresting men whose only crime had been an attempt to keep starvation from their doors. They had been commanding unseaworthy gunboats of a sort that were frequently running aground, foundering, or otherwise killing their crews. The fact that they were serving under Decatur had helped; Stephen Decatur had always been supportive of his men, no matter what vile job they had been ordered to do.

After Decatur had received the command of *United States,* he intended to take Favian aboard as his first officer, and Hibbert as another of his lieutenants; but Hibbert's father, whose health had been ruined at the same time as his fortune, had gone into a disastrous decline, and Hibbert had been forced regretfully to ask for a furlough in order to manage his family affairs. He'd asked to be returned to active duty at the declaration of war, but employment had not been found.

Although he knew Hibbert would not agree, Favian considered Hibbert's misfortune his own luck. He would have an experienced first officer, eager to prove himself, and a man who knew both Favian's methods and Decatur's.

The lieutenant's brown eyes scanned the orders, then rose in surprise to Favian's. "It says to report to you, Favian," he said.

"I read myself in this morning," Favian said. "You were my choice for lieutenant. Come aboard tomorrow, and we'll start learning our jobs."

"I'll come aboard tonight, if I may," Hibbert said, an astonished smile beginning to break out on his features. "I've been packed for weeks, waiting orders from Washington."

Favian felt a secret rush of satisfaction. He had chosen well. Hibbert had been a popular man with his crews, more popular than Favian had been; his style, though it demanded respect, was open, eager, and accessible. Most happy ships contained the combination of a stern captain and a more accessible first lieutenant, or a strict first lieutenant and a relaxed captain: Favian could expect *Experiment* to be the former. After years of frustration, Hibbert would be ready to prove himself. A fine, perhaps an ideal, subordinate.

"I'll be aboard after dinner," Favian said. "Report to me after you've stowed your dunnage."

"Aye aye, sir," Hibbert said, slipping easily into the formal speech demanded of a junior officer in the presence of his captain. Favian thrust out a hand, and Hibbert took it.

"Congratulations, Mr. Hibbert," he said. "We'll try to make something of the old hooker, eh?"

"Aye, sir. We will." The mallet slipped from his grasp and rattled on the floor. He grimaced.

"I've been making cabinets," he said. "A job I'd promised to do, but have been putting off. I'd better finish them before reporting aboard."

"Aye, you had," Favian agreed, picking up the hammer. He handed it to Hibbert. Aboard a small vessel like *Experiment,* relations between a captain and his men were necessarily more intimate than on a forty-four gun frigate like the *United States.* Favian and Hibbert were going to have to develop a working relationship, living cheek-by-jowl aboard an eighty-four-foot brig of war; they would have to tread a careful line between comradeship and discipline, neither too much of one nor of the other. He was glad Hibbert was enthusiastic; it would make things easier.

"*Experiment* is going to need looking after. By rights she ought to have a long shakedown cruise, but I don't know if we'll have the chance. Putting her right, after years of neglect, is going to demand a lot from both of us."

"Aye, Captain. I'll do my best." Favian nodded. The "Captain" had sounded right, and showed that Hibbert realized as well the difficulties of defining the formal boundaries between them.

"By the way, Mr. Hibbert, the sailing master is a man named Alfred Bean," Favian said. "I don't know him, and I wonder if you can enlighten me."

"The name is Alferd, sir, not Alfred," Hibbert said. "I knew him when he was a master's mate on the *Hornet,* off Derna. He's competent enough, and he knows his job once you point it out to him, but he hasn't a trace of inventiveness or originality. No initiative. If you give him orders, he'll carry 'em out well, but he won't volunteer a thought, or divert from his instructions."

"I see. Thank you, Mr. Hibbert," Favian said. That went a long way towards explaining the slack state of *Experiment*'s rigging. He and Hibbert said their farewells, and Favian left the house, hearing behind him the clatter and muffled curse that meant Hibbert had once again dropped his mallet.

2

A few days later Favian rode from town to visit his parents. He'd sent a letter announcing his arrival and his appointment to the *Experiment;* his father had sent a horse the next day, and put it at Favian's disposal for as long as the little brig called Portsmouth its home.

The horse was a plucky little roan mare with a traceable lineage going back several hundred years, all neatly recorded in Jehu Markham's ledgers: the passion of Favian's parents was now for horses, as once it had been for revolution. She was not a fast galloper, and would win no races, but she could carry him over miles of countryside at a steady, swift pace, and outdistance any stallion over the long run. Favian was happy to ride her, and knew that if he'd had such a horse on his ride to Washington, instead of the Navy hacks he'd been loaned, he would have finished the ride much earlier.

Snow lay on the ground in the shade of the rail fences, and a brisk nor'easter blew about Favian's ears as he rode. Since his return to New Hampshire he'd seen his eldest brother, Lafayette, and his cousins Obadiah and Jeremiah, the triumvirate who had turned the Markham family away from the sea, away from the business of carrying trade in a war-torn, unsettled world, taking the profits of earlier ventures inland, buying land, timber, businesses, small factories. Their talk at the dinner table had been of a new steel trap they were developing, to sell to the trappers of the North and West and bring beaver, mink, and ermine to the hungry eastern markets. They also spoke of a small arms factory they had set up, using Whitney's new system of interchangeable parts, and wondered whether the war would last long enough for them to turn a profit. There were also pitying remarks about Benjamin Markham, Jehu's second son, whose maritime insurance business had been brought to the point of bankruptcy by the war.

It had disturbed Favian to be reminded that while he and others were on the high seas risking their lives in a foolish and desperate war, others were at home plotting ways to turn the war to their own advantage. But he had concealed his growing annoyance, and responded as politely as he could when the subject came to privateering. The Markham families were also investing in privateers, and Lafayette seemed particularly interested in Favian's opinion as to what sort of privateers would have the greatest chance of success in the long run.

"Fast, large vessels, capable of making long voyages," Favian had responded. "Well-armed boats, like those our fathers commanded. Like that schooner Gideon has building in Joshua Stanhope's yard." They had listened politely and sipped their brandy, while Favian's inner eye brightened to the memory of that schooner he'd seen a-building. Apparently his cousin Gideon's initial privateering ventures had been successful enough to result in the laying down of a new schooner built especially for the trade. It was a radical design, built for speed almost to the exclusion of all else: very long, very narrow, masts raked outrageously sternward, oversparred. Dangerous to the enemy, and dangerous as well to anyone who sailed in her; oversparred as she was, she could be flung on her beam ends by an unexpected squall, or capsized by a hurricane. She was the kind of a schooner that would give most captains nightmares, but Favian would have given his left arm to have somehow been assigned to her instead of to a brig like *Experiment*.

The postprandial conversation had droned on: shares and holdings and leases and actions to recover debts. Favian excused himself early, saying he'd have to wake early in the morning to sight *Experiment*'s carronades. What had these men, these brothers and cousins—brilliant men in their own spheres, of that he had no doubt—to do with him? What could he tell them of his life, of the service, that they could understand? Nothing, he concluded. Nothing.

With his uncle Josiah, the next night, he'd been able to speak a little. Josiah still lived and breathed the sea; and in the way he leaned on his cane—he'd broken a hip some years back—could be seen the remnants of what had been a deep-sea rolling gait. Josiah's fierce eyes had gleamed as Favian told of the battle between *United States* and *Macedonian,* and a grim smile of triumph had lit his face as Favian had told him about the discrepancy of casualties.

"The Lord was with ye, youngster," Josiah said fervently. "I pray he shall always be with our nation in the struggles against these ungodly English."

"Amen," Favian had the presence of mind to reply. He knew Josiah hated the English with all the strength of a soul toughened by gunfire and the raging elements, and that this life of struggle against England and her minions was somehow confused in Josiah's mind with Old Testament battles, with the struggles of the Lord's chosen against the unbelievers, the godly against the profane.

Josiah was contributing a son to the struggle, the same Gideon Markham for whom Joshua Stanhope was building the radical schooner. Gideon was the fourth of Josiah's seven surviving children, and since early in the war had been commanding a privateer schooner in the West Indies, the same blue waters over which the three revolutionary Markham brothers had traveled in packs in search of British convoys. Gideon, Josiah's anointed, was carrying the old Markham standard, his guns roaring hot iron while his throat roared biblical texts. Favian knew Gideon well enough. He was a stolid, uncomplaining man, pious as his father, but without his father's fierce uncompromising nature, though his life would have seemed calculated to generate complaints and impious despair: Favian knew that Gideon had lost a wife and child to starvation during Jefferson's embargo, while Gideon had been pressed into the Venetian Navy. But from the evidence of the new schooner at Stanhope's yard, Gideon's luck had turned, and Favian wished him well, and urged Josiah to send his regards.

Even with Josiah Favian could not be entirely candid. It was not that Josiah would not listen to what he had to say, but rather that Josiah would not comprehend. Favian had stood on *Macedonian*'s scarred deck, ankle-deep in sloshing red water, bits of corpses rolling from beam to beam; and he had given orders, put the ship in order, later sailed it home. It seemed to Favian that any man with the tiniest ember of humanity would have heaved out his insides at the first glimpse of *Macedonian*'s well deck, and afterward been good for very little. But Favian had felt nothing but the desire to take David Hope's sword and run his country's flag up the splintered mast. The Navy had taken something from him, taken it for the Navy's own purposes, enabling him to stand on the enemy's deck and watch the rolling corpses unmoved. The corpses . . . Josiah would have rejoiced in them, and delighted in the thought of the impious English lying mutilated. Favian felt a vacant emptiness at what he'd lost, the humanity that would have allowed him to view such a scene in its proper horror.

And he felt angry at himself. Not only had he allowed the Navy to rifle his feelings, training him in the school of its sternness and extracting what the Navy did not need, but Favian, aside from private doubt, had not even had the character to resent it. He had obliged; he had spent a week in Washington working on the Navy's behalf, and had been duly rewarded with a small command and the promise of better to come. Trapped in the Navy's ways, he had accepted the *Experiment* and kept his misgivings to himself, and now he was training himself in another part, the part of a captain of a brig of war, once again for the Navy's behalf.

It was a confused mash of thoughts, of resentments and anger. Favian's father had served at sea, as merchantman and privateer; Jehu had raised Favian and had given his blessing when he went into the Navy. Perhaps Jehu Markham would be able to help him sort out this tangle of bitterness and spleen.

The brown deadness of the sprawling farm was streaked with windrows of snow, but the drifting smoke from the multiple chimneys spoke of warmth inside. His horse's pace increased as it recognized home. Favian passed through an open gate, the horse trying to trot as it smelled the warmth of the stables.

"Mister Favian." It was one of the stable hands, carrying a bucket of water.

"Hello—ah . . ."

"Henderson, sir."

"Henderson, of course." Favian brought the horse to a stop in front of the house and dismounted. The mare began to nuzzle Henderson's hand, greedy for the water.

"I'll take care of the horse, sir. Go right in."

"Thank you. Is everyone well?"

"Very well, sir. Congratulations on your victory and your promotion."

"Many thanks." Favian opened the great oak front door and walked into the hall, carrying his luggage. He looked into the study, where his father was usually found, and saw a roaring fire that gleamed off the captured swords that decorated the walls, and whose warmth made him hesitate, but no sign of Jehu Markham. Favian left his luggage by the door and wandered further into the house. There was a cry of delight from a doorway, a rustle of skirts, and Favian found himself embraced by his mother.

Anne Markham was still trim and agile and brown from daily exercise on horseback. There was little but her white hair to show that she was past sixty. Favian kissed her cheek. She grinned and twitched at the sleeve of his civilian coat.

"You haven't brought your new uniform, to show off your promotion?" she asked.

"I haven't got it yet," he said. He had "shifted his swab"—moved the epaulet from his left shoulder to his right—but his uniform coat, made for a modest lieutenant, lacked the quantity of lace necessary to support the dignity of a master commandant. Even the best of his old uniforms were beginning to grow worn, so he was having a new set made. "I've been to Mr. Tracey for the measurements," he said, "but he hasn't put 'em together yet." Tracey was his father's Portsmouth tailor, and had kept Jehu Markham in fashion for the last quarter-century; Favian had heard Jehu often wish out loud that he would be allowed to die before Tracey, so that he could present a respectable appearance at his funeral.

"Tracey's a good man," Anne said. "You look thin. Thinner than usual, anyway. Have you been well?" She looked up at him keenly.

"Some of the stomach trouble, a few months ago," he said. "I'm thin because I've either been on horseback or in a coach for almost every day of the last three months."

"I hope you will get some rest," she said. "I don't want—"

"Damme if it ain't Favian!" called Jehu Markham, stepping into the hallway in his riding boots. "I was in the stables lookin' after a colt with the colic, and Henderson came runnin' in sayin' you was returned. Damme if it ain't a pleasure!"

Jehu Markham's face was unlined by his sixty-seven years—very unusual in a sailor, come to think of it; the sun and exposure tended to cut up one's appearance. His hair had gone gray and had thinned, but his eyes still reflected an undiminished, acute intelligence, and his gestures showed a slim, agile body still subdued to an imperious will. He had given up boxing, but he still fenced and rode daily. He looked, Favian thought with a sudden flash of recognition, rather like an older edition of the face Favian had seen in engravings of the British general Arthur Wellesley, the Marquess of Wellington. Except that Jehu's nose, while aquiline, did not have quite the majesty of the arrogant beak of the Peninsular general. Jehu's face was a better-balanced version of Favian's: Favian had inherited his mother's height (Anne was an inch taller than her husband) and his father's cast of features, except that somehow the arching nose, the thin lips, and arched, skeptical brows seemed more awkward—unbalanced somehow—when stretched vertically to fit Favian's height.

"I've brought something for the study," Favian said. He returned to his baggage and pulled out David Hope's sword.

"From the first lieutenant of the *Macedonian*," Favian said.

Jehu looked at the blade, slipped it from the scabbard, weighed it in his hand. "Badly balanced old chopper," he said. "He's lucky he never had to board anyone with it. Still, it will look well enough in the study."

"Hope would be more at home with a cat-o'-nine-tails than a sword, I expect," Favian said. "He once gave a man three hundred lashes for stealing a handkerchief. And *then* he sent the fellow to prison. I heard him boast about it, a few months back, in Norfolk." Jehu carried the sword to the study, held it up against the wall, across Favian's other trophy, a Moorish scimitar. Favian warmed his backside against the fire, remembering the scimitar and the Tripolitan gunboat captain who had wielded it. A gross, fat man—turban, bright sash, greasy mustachio—who had come at the American boarders shouting Islamic imprecations, apparently used to intimidating an enemy by size and bluster. Favian, one foot still on the gunwale after a leap from his own boat, had found no difficulty, even off-balance, throwing the scimitar off and running the man through—the sort of easy beginner's stuff learned on the first day of fencing lessons. The hard fight had come later, leaping aboard the gunboat that had killed James Decatur. The Tripolitan captain who had killed James by feigning surrender and then firing a volley of musketry at the last instant before boarding had been armed with a blunderbuss that carried a curious spring-bayonet, and the man had known how to use it. The crafty little Tripolitan had jumped into the sea at the end, taking his strange weapon with him, and Favian's bloody survivors—two thirds of the Americans had been killed or wounded even before a maddened Favian, hearing of James Decatur's death, had charged heedlessly to the attack—had fired volleys at his bobbing head until it disappeared in a pool of red. Afterward there had been sharks. No trophies.

Jehu put David Hope's sword on a polished little table. "I'll have one of the servants mount it. The first of many, I hope."

"That's as the fates and the Navy Department decide," Favian said, the fire baking the backs of his legs. "I've been given the *Experiment,* and you know what she'll be like. Slow and overcrowded. We've already lost two of her sister boats, *Nautilus* and *Vixen,* run down by superior forces."

"There's no regular blockade off New England," Jehu said. "That will make it easier for you."

"I couldn't turn down the command once it was offered," Favian said.

His father looked at him unblinking. The fire snapped.

"Of course not," said Jehu. "Anne, ring for some refreshment. Would you like mulled wine, or does rum suit you?"

"Rum, thank you, sir."

"Straight? Or a toddy?"

"The latter, please."

"Sit down when you've warmed yourself. You must be hungry after your ride."

Favian received his toddy and his snack. There was a kind of shyness present in the room; he had not seen his parents for over two years, and there was simply too much to say. An involuntary sort of reserve developed; he didn't want to gush on about two years of sea duty, and they were hesitant about unburdening themselves of New Hampshire gossip to someone who had precious little contact with his home state and probably remembered few of the people of whom they'd had news. Jehu and Anne sat in adjacent armchairs, their hands sometimes clasped between them, swinging between the chairs. They were warm, polite, affectionate toward each other and Favian, indulgent—and it quite suddenly occurred to Favian that they had never been otherwise. He had never seen his parents quarrel; he had never seen them express intolerance, or even impatience. They had always made a point of adopting the correct public attitudes, in whatever situation; they had been balanced, articulate, responsible. Favian had never seen them lose their tempers. If they had ever fought with one another, they'd made a point of keeping it between themselves.

Favian had acquired from them his ability to keep his footing socially, his correctness; but somehow he had never entirely fit the pattern. There were parts of Favian that were not correct, not acceptable: anger, rage, resentment, fear, envy, lust. Somehow his parents' superb example had failed to teach him altogether how to deal with such elements of his own character; and living for so long under the shadow of Decatur—the chivalrous paragon of the Navy, from whom an unworthy thought had never been given expression—had not helped. Except for his occasional burst of temper, the terror of every midshipman in the Navy, Favian tried never to let the less desirable parts of himself show in public. Favian had neatly split himself, indulging his resentments and carnality in private, presenting a plausible, dutiful face to the world. In his more cynical moments he wondered if his parents felt as two-faced as he did, if even in Decatur there burned an inner, unworthy world.

But of course he could not ask. It wasn't the sort of thing one gentleman could ask another. It was one of the forbidden topics, like fear. If a naval officer were asked if he'd ever felt fear, he would stare at you with a strange, pursed, disapproving expression, as if you had just committed a social blunder the enormity of which was only being concealed by good manners. The officer might say Yes or No, but in a tone of voice that implied that the answer was meaningless. In the context of the question, the answer probably was.

The only context in which it made sense was in that of the Navy, the small, enclosed, competitive world, where officers were made by constant attention to a rigorous, often unspoken, unforgiving code that demanded the constant risk of their lives at every moment they wore the uniform. In that context fear existed, as did a good many other things, as facts of life, to be accepted much in the way one accepted storms at sea: The measure of an officer was not whether he was caught in storms, but whether he brought his vessel safely out of them. So with fear: one felt it, or not, but was judged by how one coped, whether one measured up or not. And it was never talked about: that was considered a bit redundant, a bit unmannerly.

Favian finished his toddy. "Uncle Josiah seems well. He mentioned that Gideon has taken his privateer to the West Indies."

"It's a good hunting ground," Jehu said. "A little far from friendly ports. In my war we had French and Spanish ports right at hand."

Supper was served. It was poultry, which Favian appreciated; pork and beef were his lot as a seagoing officer, but rarely a duck, chicken, or goose. There was good hock with the meal, brandy afterward, port later at night in the study. The procession of good wines was more welcome than the poultry, as a relief from the Navy's tedious ration of whiskey—called bob smith after Robert Smith, Jefferson's pinchpenny Secretary of the Navy, who had substituted it for the more expensive rum ration. Favian preferred rum, perhaps because he'd been raised on it, and always tried to stock some on board whatever ship he was serving on, as part of the personal liquor supply officers were allowed; but he'd never been able to afford the good wines that were always circulating about his father's table.

After supper they moved back to the study, and Jehu and Anne shifted to seats closer to the fire. The room was dark and quiet, lit only by the fire and the fire's reflection upon jeweled hilts, keen pike heads, polished blades.

"It's a strange life," Favian found himself saying. Too much wine, no doubt. "There's so much pressure—none of it very obvious, much of it unspoken—to be worthy. Not to be worthy of one's self, but of the Navy. It's not simply a way of life, it's a devotion to an ideal. Like olden chivalry—*chevalier sans peur et sans reproche.*"

Well, he'd said it at last. Jehu Markham, who could not have missed the bitterness, sat with the fire glittering in his eyes, saying nothing.

"My dear," said Anne. "My dear, do you think it was a good decision to send you to the Navy?" she asked. "Are you happy with it?"

Are you happy with it? Good God. Somehow the question of happiness had never before seemed to enter into it. The question was how one felt being torn between the ideal and one's own inclinations. Still, the question struck a facet Favian had never considered before.

"Happy?" he said in surprise. "I don't know. I suppose not." He floundered on, feeling himself mired more and more in the confusion of his own inchoate feelings. "It's a decision that was made a long time ago," he said. "I wanted it then, and we all agreed it was the best thing. It was such a major change that I've never thought to consider myself happy with it, or not happy—it's like being born in New Hampshire and deciding to regret it. It's a waste of your regret, because nothing can be done. I'm an officer in the United States Navy. It's a thing to take pride in, and I do. It's an important thing, and I've come a long way.

"But living up to such an uncompromising ideal can have its price. I've seen that with Uncle Josiah, you know. He's denied himself a good deal because of his religion, and he's undergone a discipline that's made him better at many things but narrowed him in other ways. It's what happens when you build your life around a single thing. I don't know how long I'll be able to do it.

"I began to have my doubts during the embargo. I spent five years commanding a little forty-foot gunboat on the Delaware. I was there, and so was Decatur, and Hibbert, and many other worthy officers—and our job was simply to stop people from earning a living at the trade they had followed all their lives. We were to stop and impound any American shipping clearing for foreign ports. I knew that every little schooner or brig that I stopped meant bankruptcies, families going hungry, good ships rotting or being broken up—enforcing a policy that everyone around me knew was wrong, that was on the verge of bankrupting the entire nation. Every day I'd have to turn away a score of men begging to sign aboard my gunboat, because the Navy was the only place a seafaring man could find work and hope to feed his family. They'd go down on their knees, some of them, begging, weeping. . . . Gideon's wife and son died of starvation, and here was I enforcing the laws that killed them."

It hadn't been the same as the chores the Navy otherwise carried out, Favian continued—the apprehension of smugglers, or those who tried to enter port without proper quarantine after leaving yellow-fever ports. Those people knew the risks they were running, knew the penalties for being caught. Catching the embargo breakers was different. They were desperate men, ready to dare anything, driven to break the law by their own despair. Some fired on the gunboat as it approached. One tried to run Favian's boat down. Others simply lined the rail and spat on the Navy men as they came aboard to do their work.

". . . Spat and cursed, and damned Thomas Jefferson and the Navy to hell fire," Favian said. "I almost threw up my berth then, but I realized that I would be condemning myself to the same kind of desperation in which these men lived every day—a seafaring man, without a job, without prospects. Starving like Gideon and his family. So I stayed in the Navy, and lived the ideal, and almost went mad because I knew I was serving a vicious, unjust cause, and I knew that if I had been one of those desperate men I would have done the same as they did."

The fire crackled in the flagstone hearth. Favian rose from his seat, threw more logs onto the blaze, stirred with a poker. He could feel the heat on his face and his bare hands. When he returned to his seat, he saw that Jehu Markham's gaze had lingered on the flames. Anne's serious eyes were still on him. He felt awkward, as if he had broken some unspoken law of etiquette.

"When I was a little younger than you are now, I made a decision," Anne said in her soft English accent. "I decided to marry your father, to cross the Atlantic, and to support him in his dreams of American independence. It meant giving up my family, my friends—not just giving them up, but striving to overthrow them. Treason. My father was a radical who supported the idea of a republic, but his wife and other children were not. There had to be a break. It was a severe one, especially when my father died and my brother Francis inherited the title. He sent me one frozen letter every year, to let me know he was still alive, and hadn't forgiven. A few years ago the letters stopped coming, and I knew he'd died."

The new logs had blazed up and made the room as bright as day. Part of her face was in shadow, part revealed with a blinding clarity; there was a memory of pain in her face, and a kind of pride.

"Here," she said, "I wasn't accepted either. I was the English bitch, the traitress, possibly a spy. After New London, I learned that I was blamed for the defeat, because I'd ridden down to see your father a few days before the disaster, and the people thought I'd somehow communicated with the British fleet. There were ugly scenes." New London, Favian thought, 1778. A British fireship raid on a major rebel port and stronghold. Jehu Markham captured, Josiah's privateer schooner taken, Malachi's *Royal George* blown up. Scores of other ships burned. A disaster of the first magnitude, for which Favian's mother had been blamed. He hadn't known.

Jehu Markham reached out to take his wife's hand. She smiled at him briefly, affectionately.

"I lived through those years. I helped your father fight my home and my kin," she said. "Sometimes I regretted the choice I had made, but I tried not to shrink from the consequences of the decision. Now, when I look back on it, I can say that I don't regret a thing. I hope that years from now you will be able to say the same to yourself."

Favian sipped at his port. "So do I, ma'am," he said.

Her eyes flickered with impatience. "What I meant to say," she said, "was that I know how it is to be torn in two, and all for a thing that most would not understand. Perhaps it's not much, to know that I understand. But it's what I can offer."

"Thank you," he said, and he found he said it with perfect sincerity. It was small comfort, but there was some consolation in her words, even if it didn't alter the situation. A different quality of consolation, perhaps, from what he had found in Zenobia's body, and the nimble hands that had massaged away the years of anger that lay buried in the muscles of his shoulders and neck. But there Anne's comfort was, and Favian found that it mattered. "Thank you," he said again.

3.

" 'Stood for his country's glory fast,' " quoth Miss Emma
Greenhow, " 'And nail'd her colors to the mast!' " She
stood by the two gray stone pillars that marked the main
entrance of Spanish Farm, her father's estate; she was
dressed in a bright green velvet jacket over a darker green
waistcoat and skirt, a new riding habit that set off her fair
coloring, and which somehow enhanced the appropriate-
ness of quoting Sir Walter Scott.

"What shall be the maiden's fate? Who shall be the
maiden's mate?" Favian thought to himself, as long as she
was going to throw Scott at him; but it was an unsuitable
reply, the more so because old Nicholas Greenhow had just
stepped out of the door to put his official seal of disap-
proval over the entire proceeding. Favian's memory—like
most Markhams, he was able to quote verse, secular or
biblical, on command—provided an appropriate answer.

" 'And ne'er did Grecian chisel trace,' " he said, " 'A
Nymph, a Naiad, or a Grace, Of finer form, or lovelier
face.' " Nicholas Greenhow scowled. Favian dropped from
his horse's saddle, handed the reins to a groom, kissed Emma's hand, and watched old Greenhow's scowl deepen.

"Hello, Emma. Sir."

"Markham," said the state assemblyman. "Fancy sword
you've got there."

"Gift of the City of New York. For the *Macedonian*."

"Silly custom."

Favian was dressed in the same civilian coat he'd worn
on the ride from Portsmouth the day before, but he'd chosen to wear the new presentation sword with the civilian
rig. He'd had an intuition the display might be useful, if he

were to carry a visible reminder of his victory and promotion, which might be expected to bring him a tidy sum of money, and a greater income than before.

That morning he'd sent a messenger to Spanish Farm with a note in which he proposed to pay his respects in the afternoon; a note in Emma's hand had come back, suggesting two o'clock and a ride on horseback. When he'd ridden to the door, he'd seen a groom holding a horse that had already been readied with one of Emma's sidesaddles. No other horses: That meant none of Emma's relatives were staying, and they would not have to endure the company of a chaperone, although possibly the silhouette of Nicholas Greenhow would occasionally be seen on a rise as the state assemblyman went about some obscure errand or other, pretexts for his scouting missions. That Greenhow seemed afraid that some afternoon he'd discover Favian and his daughter fornicating in a snowdrift seemed on one level laughable, and on another it proved that he didn't know his daughter—or anyone else, probably—very well. Nevertheless, the suspicious old character had to be dealt with, and courteously, for Favian knew that Greenhow would like nothing better than to find an excuse to eject Favian permanently from his company.

Greenhow chatted monosyllabically with Favian about the weather and about the last year's bad harvest and decline in income (at which Favian nodded seriously, though he did not believe it for a moment). Emma was helped by the groom onto her sidesaddle; then Favian leaped onto his mare and they trotted from the house.

Emma rode well and easily. A healthy flush came to her pale cheeks; loose strands of blond hair waved beneath the brim of her tall riding hat. Her gray eyes sparkled in the clear winter light; her rosebud mouth was parted in an exuberant, involuntary smile. She urged her horse to a gallop, leaped a gate, raced down a narrow road. Favian kept pace with her, enjoying the run that usually prefaced their meetings.

After a few minutes she took pity on her horse and slowed it to a trot; Favian drew up beside her and caught her smile, seeing her silhouette, as keen as the edge of a knife and as regal as a grand duchess's.

"Are you happy with your little ship?" she asked. She stroked her horse's neck, pleased with its run.

"It's a brig," he corrected automatically. "She's old and slow, but she's the first real oceangoing command I've had. And the only thing available."

"I thought you'd commanded gunboats."

"They don't count. Not to a deep-water sailor."

"Ah." She frowned. "You didn't mention that at the time."

They turned into a country lane sunken a few feet into a pasture, with dusty snow lying in the shadow of the steep banks. Flocks of brown sparrows flitted from rail fences as they rode. A group of rather mangy cows clumped in the road, sounding of bells and smelling of old hay, and Favian and Emma rode single file past their nonthreatening horns, Favian in the lead.

"You wrote that you'd met Mr. Madison," Emma said. "My father is wont to call him a traitorous ape. Does he at all resemble a monkey?"

Favian smiled. Traitorous, he thought, because he'd written most of *The Federalist Papers* and then become a Republican. For those who proclaimed the value of party over conscience, such was treason.

"He's short, very thin. Doesn't dress well. Gives the impression of having a good mind. If he's a monkey, then he's an old monkey. But I think he looks more like an old schoolmaster than an ape."

"And Mrs. Madison? The impression one receives is of someone monumentally indiscreet, not at all as Caesar's wife should be."

"She's demonstrative. Not very New England. I liked her, I think. The story goes," he said, lowering his tone confidentially, even though there was no one to overhear, "that Madison was having trouble keeping Gallatin in his cabinet, and that he needed Gallatin to keep the loyalty of the Republicans in the West. Dolley knew that Mrs. Gallatin loved playing hostess and so found excuses to avoid some official occasions. Mrs. Gallatin was always asked to step in as official hostess. Now Gallatin can't leave the cabinet without risking the wrath of his wife, who would be deprived of all her official grandeur if her husband becomes a private citizen again."

"It sounds very like Portsmouth politics," Emma sighed. "The sort of thing my father is always talking about." She eyed Favian appraisingly. "He disapproves of you even more, it seems. The Markham family is not as wholeheartedly Federalist as it used to be."

"Oh? That's news to me."

"It seems your brother Lafayette made what my father considers a quibbling address at the latest party convention," Emma said. "He actually expressed certain patriotic sentiments that are out of fashion among Federalists this year, and suggested that William Gray oughtn't to have been read out of the party simply because he loaned Isaac Hull money to outfit the *Constitution*. It was not received well."

"Lafayette hadn't mentioned the business to me," Favian said.

"There is talk of New England secession," Emma said. Favian glanced at her sharply. She rode along the lane, her profile turned to him, giving no indication of her feelings.

"That would be a disaster. If Lafayette spoke against secession, I'll support him." She rode on as if she hadn't heard. Favian wondered if her father was supporting secession, or something like it. Twelve years of Republican administration, he thought, and the country is on the verge of splitting apart.

"Do you think we shall take Canada?" she asked. The glance she gave him was nervous, half-apologetic. Favian wondered if Nicholas Greenhow had asked her to give him a loyalty test—loyalty not to the United States, but the Federalist party.

"No," he said. "We shall be lucky to hold the Niagara frontier."

She nodded. "That is the sentiment that prevails here, as well," she said. "That sentiment also holds that the Navy should stay in its ports."

Favian was baffled. "Why?" he blurted. The idea sounded absurd, particularly after the victories of Hull, Decator, and Bainbridge.

"The sentiment," she said carefully, "is that successful voyages by American cruisers will only bring a strengthened British flotilla to keep us blockaded, and that a larger British presence would be a disaster."

Favian shook his head. "The British will increase their strength no matter what we do," he said. "The Navy should take the opportunity to strike them when it can."

"And you will strike them, Favian?"

"Yes. If the opportunity arises." She absorbed this carefully, her gray eyes turned to his features as if studying them.

"Here's Hinckley's place," she said. "Shall we visit his orchards?"

The apple trees stood tangled and bare in the brown sod, crusted snow lurking among the roots and shadows. It was difficult to picture the apple grove as anything other than a dead thing, a ruin of some war or plague or biblical devastation; yet Favian remembered summers spent plundering here, standing in the trees with the scent of the apples, a summer breeze rustling the leaves, picking the fruit and pitching them down to Emma, who collected them in an apron. Years ago.

Emma gracefully slipped from her sidesaddle and walked over the cold brown grass. Her horse bent its head to nibble at the desiccated remnants of last year's fallen apples. Favian dismounted, walked to stand beside her. The dead limbs rattled in the wind.

"May I see your gift from the City of New York?" she asked. He slipped it from the scabbard, held it out by the blade in both hands. She took it, a bit daintily, wary of the edge, and looked along the incised decoration, the eagles and stars and mottos.

"A bit vulgar, isn't it?"

"I'm afraid so. I'll only wear it on formal occasions. The sword Portsmouth gave me years ago will be good for—for—" He stammered, realizing he's almost said "fighting." "For other things," he finished lamely. No good reminding Emma, who quoted Walter Scott so well, that swords could be used for purposes other than courtly ones.

She examined the smallsword a moment more, returned

the blade to him, and he slipped it into the scabbard. She wandered toward an old apple tree, touching it with a gloved hand. "Do you remember stealing apples from this tree?" she asked.

"Yes."

"I don't think Hinckley ever found out, he had so many. Or if he did, he didn't mind. There is something sweet about a stolen pleasure." She smiled bittersweetly, then turned abruptly away.

"But those are for children," she said. "No apples for us, Favian." She turned to him. "Was the battle very horrible?" she asked.

"You're very full of questions today."

"There is a lot I wish to know," she said seriously. She faced him. "Was it horrible, Favian?"

He remembered the mess on *Macedonian*'s well deck, the stench, the screaming. Funck lying on the litter with his leg off, blood dripping on the clean white planks.

"No. Not very," he said. "I was very busy. There was a lot of smoke making it hard to see." Not precisely a lie. The horrible part was after the battle, really, aboard the captured frigate. Emma Greenhow should be spared certain things. Everyone should, he thought. Part of being an officer was shielding civilians, ladies especially, from the more unpleasant realities.

She turned away, walking further into the grove. He followed. He had never seen her this way; usually she was fairly gay, chatting about poets and horses, about myriad relations who had married, been born or bankrupted, gone west, died, or entered politics.

"My father introduces me to men he hopes I'll marry," she said. "He feels I should marry someone stable, trustworthy, who has already proven himself a good businessman. Most of the people who fit his qualifications are his age, not mine."

"You are of age, and your father's sole heir," Favian said. "You can marry whoever you please."

She turned to face him. Her riding whip was twisted in her hands. "There is an attraction in my father's choices," she admitted. "The stability, the ease, the society. I am afraid of many things—hardship, toil, sacrifice—all the things I've never had to face. Perhaps it is life I am afraid of."

Favian's head swam. He reached out and took her gloved hands in his own, cold leather to cold leather.

"Marry me, Emma," he said. "I've got prize money now. My new rank will bring a good living even if I'm not employed. I may have more prize money before the war is over."

She looked at him unblinkingly. She was achingly lovely, her gray eyes wide, the flush in her cheeks. Wordlessly she shook her head. He let go of her hands.

"I can't—I can't now," she amended. "Not until the end of the war. I won't be a young widow. I can't face that prospect."

"Shall I ask you again after the war is over?"

"Yes. Ask me then. Perhaps I won't be so afraid." She turned, her heavy skirt rustling, and picked her way through the decayed apples to her horse. She turned, smiling broadly, her eyes sparkling. "Let's gallop, Favian!" she called, after he had helped her to the sidesaddle. "Let's gallop away from the war, and politics, and all responsibility!"

He sprang onto the back of his mare. The trees rattled like old bones as the horses pounded away.

4.

"Side party ready, sir," said Lieutenant Hibbert.

"Carry on, Mr. Hibbert."

"Aye aye, sir. Mr. Miller, pipe the side."

Accompanied by proper honors, William Burrows, lieutenant commandant of the brig *Enterprise,* climbed *Experiment*'s side with assistance from the sideboys, and uncovered to the quarterdeck and to Favian. Favian extended his hand, and Burrows clasped it. Burrows's exchange had finally come through, some three weeks following their arrival in Portsmouth, and he had officially commanded *Enterprise* for a week.

Burrows was followed by his lieutenant, Edward McCall. On the eve of *Enterprise*'s first cruise under its new captain, the officers of the *Experiment* were playing host to the officers of their sister brig.

"It's a good job you've made of her, Favian," Burrows said quietly, as he glanced over the little vessel. *Experiment*'s slack appearance of a month ago had altered radically: The deck was no longer lumbered with stores and coiled lines; the rigging was taut and well set up; the carronades had been sighted and repainted (bright blue, the only paint available), and the hull was now brightened by white trim on the false quarters, taffrail, and billet head. A fifteen-striped ensign flapped stiffly over *Experiment*'s quarterdeck. A file of twelve marines, in neat blue uniforms, bayonets fixed, lined the quarterdeck. The promised marine detachment had arrived the day before, having marched from Boston under command of their sergeant.

"Thank you, Will," Favian said. "Mr. Miller, pipe down." He showed his guests below. Favian's small cabin had been extended by removing the partitions between it and the cabins belonging to Lieutenant Hibbert and the master, Alfred Bean. The table had been extended with all the leaves available, and Calvin Davis, Favian's long-armed, melancholy steward, stood by with white gloves.

Favian directed Davis to open the first bottle of wine from his father's cellars, and the obligatory toast to James Madison was chorused and drunk. The second toast was to Captain Burrows of the *Enterprise*, the third to his officers. Burrows, more at ease in formal situations when only naval personnel were present, returned the toasts with a minimum of stuttering, and only a few involuntary nervous gestures.

"It's a smart-looking hooker you've made of her, gentlemen, in the last weeks," Burrows said, as the fish course was brought in. "I've been seeing your men chipping and painting, but it seems they've been a mite lax with the white trim. Didn't the yard send out enough paint?"

"We have trimmed the billet head, the rail, and the quarter-galleries," Favian said. "Masts and yards are white, hull black. I think we have been thorough."

"But the stripe over the gun ports, Captain Markham," Burrows reminded.

Favian sipped his wine. "Ah, but the white stripe's only customary, not required."

"But it gives a martial appearance, sir," said Edward McCall. "One cannot mistake a warship with a stripe over its gun ports, and the port lids themselves checkered black or red."

"Mr. Hibbert, if you would please enlighten our guests?" Favian asked.

"Of course, sir," said Hibbert. "We've left off the stripe because the appearance of a United States vessel is what we wish to avoid. Since the *Experiment* carries only sixteen guns, and can't hope to stand up against the most miserable ship sloop in the Royal Navy, let alone a frigate, we've decided to let a certain air of mystery be built around us. If the enemy can't tell we're a military vessel by the cut of our jib, then we're not obliged to tell 'em. If an enemy cruiser believes us to be a merchant, then he may receive a nasty surprise. And if we look like a merchant, we may attract enemy privateers. Capturing privateers is probably the only service we'll be capable of—we can't fight most of the enemy ships in these waters, and we're too slow to catch most of the ones we have a chance of thrashing. So our plan is to lure 'em in."

"Ah, I understand," McCall said. "But is it—beg pardon, sir—but is your plan entirely consistent with the behavior of a gentleman?"

Favian managed to control his temper, although his first inclination was to launch his fish course, plate included, at McCall's head. Another example of the hardheaded idiocy of so much of the officer class, he thought angrily. They would not lend a hand to any task that might get their palms dirty, because it was not consistent with the behavior of a gentleman. They would snub any officer who had risen from the ranks because he had not received a gentleman's training as a midshipman. Favian considered himself as much a gentleman as any of his fellow officers, and had fought duels to prove it, but that did not stop him from learning all there was to be learned about his duty.

"Gentlemen have practiced deception in war before," he pointed out. "It's customary to deceive the enemy by hoisting false flags, or by using enemy signals—which we also intend to do, by the way; we've got a flag locker choked with British, French, Spanish, Portuguese, and Cartagenian ensigns. What's the difference between passing one's self off as a merchant vessel and attempting to hide under colors not one's own?"

"Well said, Captain Markham," said Burrows. He was not a man to accept orthodoxy for orthodoxy's sake. "Let me know if your ideas work."

"There's another advantage to going without the stripe," Hibbert added. "The enemy can't count our gun ports."

"Not until your famous blue guns give 'em a broadside, anyway," Burrows added. "What possessed you to give the carronades that color?"

"The only paint available," Favian said, concealing more annoyance. He could tell he hadn't heard the last of the blue guns.

"Perhaps you should paint the shot an harmonizing color," Burrows said. "Pink, perhaps."

"I'll consider it," Favian said, and turned to Hibbert. "Can the yard send us any pink, I wonder?"

"Er—I'll find out, sir," Hibbert said, surprised. It was clear he wasn't used to the straight-faced raillery between Favian and Burrows.

"In fact," Burrows went on, "there is no earthly reason why you should keep your brig painted in the standard black and white, once you indulge in the innovation of blue guns. Why not gun ports painted in the same color as the guns? Or masts striped red, like a barber's pole, so that the British will know to come and have their blood let?"

"I shall leave these novelties to you, Captain Burrows," Favian said. "Ah—the next course, gentlemen."

The next course consisted of both wild turkey and leg of lamb; Favian carved one and Burrows the other. More wines were brought. Alferd Bean looked resentfully at the wine; he would probably rather have drunk rum or whiskey. But he grew merry enough, along with the rest of the company, even if he preferred day-old sour mash whiskey to fifteen-year-old Bordeaux.

After the final bottles of port the brigs' officers went on deck to puff their cigars in the cold, clean winter air. Favian and Burrows paced the quarterdeck, speaking to one another in low tones; the others congregated by the lee rail and chatted merrily.

"I'm envious of the state of your vessel, Will," Favian told Burrows. "*Enterprise* hasn't been neglected for years; *Experiment* has. If I had a full crew I'd sail with you, and give these men some sea experience. Curse these New Hampshire privateers! They're taking all the prime seamen, and leaving me with inland volunteers and dregs."

"Aye," Burrows said. "But *Fighting Yankee* has filled her complement, and *Rattlesnake* is shipping crew but can't find guns for love nor money, so things should be better for you soon. Merchant ships are still coming in and paying off their crews, and they won't go out again unless there's peace. You should have a fine crew shortly."

"I hope to be at sea by April first."

"That's All Fools' Day, Favian," Burrows smiled. "Take care you don't sail on a fool's errand."

Favian frowned. "There's a problem. Come here by the rail. I don't want the others to hear."

They huddled by the weather rail. Burrows, chilled, turned his collar up.

"You know our brigs can't hope to battle a frigate, or even an ordinary sloop of war," Favian said. Burrows nodded. "It may be necessary to run. We're slow, but we can get more speed by dumping boats, stores, and our water overboard."

"Or the guns," Burrows said.

"Aye, or the guns," said Favian. "That's the problem. I'd like to drill the crew at heaving the weaponry overside—but it's not the sort of drill likely to improve the hands' outlook. We can drill at firing the guns, boarding or repelling boarders, handling the sails, and so forth, but drilling to run away from a fight is not the sort of thing that will inspire the hands to confidence. Yet in a chase familiarity with the drill may save us—you know how mere minutes can count."

"Aye," Burrows said. "Running away is not a problem I'd considered. We're planning simply to trust to the luck of the *Enterprise* to see us through. But let me think a moment." He puffed his cigar meditatively. A fish broke surface below, fell back into the water with a plopping sound.

"You don't know how she sails," Burrows said. "You've warped her to the pier and back to receive stores; you've taken her across the bay to fire the guns and sight them, but you've never sheeted home anything more than a staysail. So you can't know for sure how to ballast her."

"I've been very careful with the ballasting, and the stores," Favian said. "When the stores were being lowered into the hold, I went out in a boat and rowed around the *Experiment* to check her trim. But still there's much I don't know. That's another reason why I wanted to sail with you. You know, you can never know if you're getting the best out of a vessel until you sail her against a sister ship."

"You've been diligent about it—so much the better," Burrows said. "Those long nines in the bridle ports weigh thirty-one hundredweight, and the carronades weigh less."

"Of course."

"Then after you've set off, keep shifting the guns to see if it improves her trim. Your complement will have practice enough in unbolting the cap squares and moving heavy weights, and you won't have to tell them it's an emergency drill."

"By God!" Favian said. The answer was simple, yet the question had been fretting him ever since he'd set foot aboard the brig. "I'm grateful, Will."

"We'll see how grateful you are if we ever sail our brigs together, and a question of prize money comes up," Burrows said with a smile. "It's cold tonight. I'd like to beg of you a warming draught in your cabin before we take our leave. Thank you for the feast."

"Aye, you're welcome," Favian said. "Give 'em hell."

William Burrows threw his cigar stub over the side. There was a hiss as it struck the water, and then it vanished on the ebbing tide. On the next ebb, Burrows would take *Enterprise* to the sea. Favian could only hope that *Experiment* would follow him before all New England was blockaded.

Favian was on deck when *Enterprise* hove its anchor short, made sail, and weighed. He called up the hands to man the shrouds and give three cheers as Burrows's little brig sailed past; the blue guns were cleared away, and the proper signal fired. *Enterprise*'s guns boomed in return, and as the brig made its way out of the channel, signal flags blossomed from its halyards, snapping out in the crisp air. "Signal one hundred two," Hibbert read. " 'Attack the enemy's rear.' "

Favian nodded, and understood. Their little brigs could never hope to fight successfully even the standard British brig of war, but there was a chance for successful employment as commerce raiders. "Attack the enemy's rear" was simply an acknowledgment of their situation; they dared not fight too openly, but would have to strike the British where they were most vulnerable. "Acknowledge the signal, Mr. Hibbert," Favian said. "Then reply, 'Good Hunting.' "

"Could we make it 'Good luck,' sir?" asked Dudley, the signal midshipman. "I'd have to spell out *hunting*."

"I said *hunting*, not luck!" Favian snapped, and then regretted his temper almost immediately. He was sorry Burrows was leaving, and it was making him irritable. He looked up at the receding brig, the bright United States ensign flying from her mainsail's peak.

Portsmouth would be a little colder without Burrows. Favian wished his friend success, and a safe return.

5.

"Mr. Stanhope." Favian nodded, doffing his hat.

"Ah, Captain Markham. I've been meaning to speak with you." Benjamin Stanhope was a shipbuilder, one of old Joshua Stanhope's two surviving sons, a bluff, broad-shouldered, self-confident man, with graying hair and a cheerful smile. He followed the trade of his father, who had built privateers for the Markhams during the Revolution, and whose father in turn had built fast cruisers for Adaiah Markham during the French and Indian War. One of Benjamin Stanhope's brothers, in fact, had been killed on a Markham ship in 1776.

"Sir, I am afraid I cannot speak for long. I'm expected at my uncle Josiah's."

"I won't delay ye for long, Captain Markham," Stanhope smiled. "Pray allow me to walk with ye a bit."

"You are welcome, sir."

"You found the cordage I sent aboard satisfactory? And the casks of salt beef?"

"Aye. I appreciate your being so prompt."

"If I or the Stanhope Yard can be of service in any other way, you have only to ask. Have ye seen the schooner we've built for yer cousin Gideon?"

"I have admired it, sir. It looks as if it would either sail rings around the fastest dolphin, or drive right under at the first opportunity. Either way I wish she was mine."

Stanhope beamed. "You'll be sailing soon, I take it?"

"We should enlist our complement in the next week. Sailors are volunteering now that most of the hard work's done, and there are no privateers in harbor. I've received my orders from the secretary, and I hope to be out by April."

Stanhope nodded. "Do ye have yer full complement of officers, Captain?" he asked. "Midshipmen, in particular?"

"Midshipmen?" Favian said, realizing what this peculiar conversation was about. He doffed his hat to a matron and her daughter, stepped aside to let them pass on the narrow sidewalk.

"We've three," he said.

"But ye could use another, as I take it?" Stanhope asked. "My son Phillip—he'll be sixteen in June, and has always wanted to go to sea."

"It won't be a very comfortable berth for a new boy, Mr. Stanhope," Favian said, meanwhile searching his memory for any reason, any gossip, why the family Stanhope should be so anxious to get rid of young Phillip. "It's a small brig with a new crew, and I have no great seniority in the service, nor any influence. In all fairness I should remark that an appointment to any of the large frigates would be more likely to keep Phillip under the eye of a senior captain who might be able to advance him more quickly in the service."

"Aye," Stanhope said, frowning. He looked up at Favian appraisingly. "Let's be frank, Captain Markham," he said. Do let's, Favian thought scathingly. "Young Phillip is determined to go to sea," Stanhope said. "In peacetime we could find him a berth without difficulty, but now that it's war we don't need him rotting away in some English prison. Just two weeks ago he ran away to the *Fighting Yankee* privateer, but her captain returned him after we applied to him. I don't think young men should ship out in privateers—they aren't gentlemen, those people, and it can give a young man bad habits."

"It is not always an edifying life," Favian said stiffly. Curious that a man so eager to have Favian do him a favor should so gratuitously insult Favian's father.

"No, it ain't. But if we sent him down to Boston to the *Constitution* or the *Chesapeake*, he'd be one of a couple dozen lads, all of 'em ready to get involved in duels or debt, with four hundred seamen to command, and no real reason to learn his job. But in a small vessel—*Experiment*, say—he'd learn what kind of a life the sea will give him, and in a small enough vessel so that he won't be getting up to much mischief."

"I see," Favian said noncommittally, although he reserved his own opinion about whether *Experiment*'s mids would furnish Phillip with the sort of companions the elder Stanhope wished.

"I will, of course, assist with any mess bills or any other such fees as may be required," Stanhope added quickly.

Stanhope was trying to bribe him. Well, it wasn't the first time he'd been made an offer, though it certainly was the first time he'd been offered money to take a midshipman on board. In the last few weeks he'd even had a bribe offered him by a clergyman who wanted to ship out as *Experiment*'s chaplain.

"You'd have to make those sort of arrangements with my lieutenant, Mr. Hibbert," Favian said. "It would be best if you'd arrange for an appointment so that Mr. Hibbert can meet the lad. I generally leave the business of the midshipmen to him." This was not exactly true, but at least it would serve to diffuse the responsibility if Favian and Hibbert concluded they would rather ship with Tecumseh himself than with Mr. Phillip Stanhope.

"There will be no trouble, I take it, acquiring the recommendation of a congressman?" Favian asked.

"Already done," Stanhope said briskly. "I'll write to Mr. Hibbert directly. I thank ye, Captain. Good day to ye. Give me respects to Captain Josiah."

"I will, sir. Good day," Favian said, doffing his hat.

He walked briskly to his uncle's house. His father's four-wheeler stood on the curb, the carriage horses having been stabled behind. The family was gathering, Favian thought to his surprise, probably to wish him off. He had been invited—*commanded* might have been a better word—to Josiah's house, at this hour, by a note carried by hand to the *Experiment*. As he'd written his acceptance, he'd wondered at the invitation's peremptory tone; he'd decided that it was simply Josiah's usual vehement manner of speech. But now that he saw the carriage at the door he began to wonder. His father had not sent him a letter informing him that he would be in town.

The door was opened to his knock by Josiah's elderly maidservant, a Hessian woman named Mrs. Ritter. She recognized Favian, took his hat and cloak, and led him to Josiah's receiving room. Favian was surprised to discover not only his parents and Josiah, but his brothers, Lafayette and Benjamin Franklin; his cousins Obadiah, Jeremiah, Abigail, David, and Jemimah; their assorted husbands, wives, and children; and, smiling wistfully from a settee that she shared with her chaperon—an elderly female relative whose name Favian had blissfully forgotten—Miss Emma Greenhow.

"Come in, youngster!" Josiah gestured. "We thought we'd give ye a boarding party before ye set forth!"

"Thank you, sir," Favian replied automatically. He made a circuit of the busy room, greeting each in turn, clasping the hands of the men, kissing the hands of the ladies. Emma Greenhow's hand was a fist, the fingers turned under; he kissed a taut knuckle and wondered if she had taken up biting her nails once again—an old habit—and was trying to hide it from him.

"I'm surprised to see you, miss," he said formally, altogether aware of the chaperone sitting by her.

"Your parents were kind enough to offer to take me to town," she said. "We are most happy to be able to attend. This is my cousin, Miss Arethusey Whitcomb."

"Miss Whitcomb," he said, and kissed a reluctant hand, while Miss Arethusey looked disapprovingly at him over her spectacles.

"Master Commandant Markham," she said, refusing absolutely to call him captain.

"How long will you be residing in Portsmouth?" Favian asked. "Will I be able to call on you?"

"I will be spending the night at Arethusey's," Emma said. "In the morning your parents will take me back to Spanish Farm."

"It's a shame you can't stay longer, miss," Favian said, ignoring Arethusey's tight-lipped, triumphant smile.

"My father would be lonely without me," Emma said.

"A rum toddy, Favian?" asked his brother Benjamin.

"Thank you, Ben. How is the maritime insurance business weathering the war?"

An expression of weary relief imposed itself upon Benjamin's plump face. "I've survived, Favian," he said. "God bless Commodore Rodgers for making the enemy concentrate to fight his squadron, instead of hunting all the vessels with cargoes that I'd insured. There are some hulls missing, but I've enough to cover the losses. And the missing might turn up after all, in some French port, or after some delay or other."

"And your rates, Ben?" Favian asked. Benjamin's face grew serious.

"Twenty-two percent, and climbing," he said. "There won't be many who can afford it."

Favian sipped his rum toddy. "I'll do my best to make the British underwriters charge the same," he said. Ben smiled.

"By thunder, I bet you will," he said.

"Apropos of nothing, Ben," Favian said, "d'you know anything about Phillip Stanhope, old Ben Stanhope's son? He's been offered me as a midshipman, and if the Stanhopes are intent on giving away one of their offspring, I can't help but wonder what's wrong with the lad."

"Phillip?" Benjamin's brows furrowed. "I've met him, but I can't say he's made any impression one way or t'other."

"He's mad about the sea," Emma offered, to Favian's surprise. "He's asked me about you often, when we were visiting his father."

"Indeed? An enthusiast," Favian said, wondering how Emma had come to meet Phillip Stanhope "often" at his father's. Perhaps Benjamin Stanhope, a widower, was one of the middle-aged businessmen Nicholas Greenhow considered a fair matrimonial prospect for his daughter. Favian felt a twinge of jealous annoyance. There was, unfortunately, no way he could ask.

"He bored the entire company on one occasion with a lecture on navigation," Emma continued. "He seems quite keen. I understand he attempted twice to run away to sea, but was prevented."

"Thank you, Miss Greenhow," Favian said. "Perhaps you also know the answer to a question I've been asking myself: Why would Mr. Stanhope send him aboard my little brig, when he could probably get Phillip a berth on a frigate?"

Emma laughed gracefully behind her hand. "I think I know the answer, Captain, but I don't know if it will please you." Ignoring the warning glare of Miss Arethusey, she gaily continued. "The Stanhopes feel that experience on your little ship—brig, I mean—will be so uncomfortable, and so discouraging, that his enthusiasm for the sea will be effectively put to an end. His father desires him to be an attorney."

"I see," Favian said, smiling at the revelation. He hadn't been at all convinced by Stanhope's glib explanation of how Phillip would learn his job better aboard a small, slow, cranky brig, as opposed to one of the big frigates.

The question that remained in his mind, and which would be impolitic to ask, was whether Phillip Stanhope was somehow lacking in intelligence: Anyone who had failed twice to run away to sea from a place like Portsmouth, where in normal circumstances at least a dozen vessels cleared the port each week, might well be mentally defective.

"Thank you, Miss Greenhow, for your timely intelligence," Favian said. "I hope I may be allowed to pay you a compliment on your appearance?"

"Thank you, Captain," Emma replied. "Could I trouble you to refresh Arethusey's cup of tea? I see her cup is being neglected."

"Of course," Favian said, mentally cursing the formalities. "Beg pardon, Miss Whitcomb."

Arethusey's tea was brought, and Benjamin launched into a long exegesis on the tribulations of insurance underwriters in wartime. At least they're not getting shot at, Favian was tempted to reply, but he kept his temper under control, and afterward was obliged to circulate.

The talk was chiefly political. The chief subject of debate concerned how it was possible to balance opposition to the war on the one hand with Federalist principles of a strong government on the other. It appeared the principles were losing: The declaration of war had produced such a rage on the New England coast that talk of separation was being heard—and listened to. The majority of the Markhams were caught in the middle. As merchants, they understood the war to be ruinous; but as patriots, with a family heritage of privateering and opposition to the British, they felt a pull of conscience asking them to stand by the republic.

The exception was Favian's eldest brother, Lafayette, the cold, brilliant businessman, whose leadership had helped the Markham & Sons Corporation weather the disaster of the embargo, and whose cutting, arrogant voice was put, with few reservations, against separation and in favor of the diligent prosecution of the war. Opposed to Lafayette was Favian's cousin David, the youngest of Josiah's sons and perhaps the most loved, whose considerable charm was deployed almost to the benefit of the British. "Let the republic go hang!" David said, smiling, and somehow mixed with David's smile the idea did not seem offensive. "We have no business consorting with those slave-owning Virginians in any case," David said. "Let's draw a new boundary at the Hudson, and make New England a republic of free men!"

"You would turn us into a colony again," Lafayette said, his voice frozen. "We would be dependent on the British for our protection, and cut off from the West. That is not what the American Revolution was intended to achieve."

Of Jehu's sons, Lafayette was the one who looked most like his father. The slim body perfectly controlled, the aristocratic demeanor, the intellectual brilliance, the superb dress—all were reminiscent of Jehu. But there was a heaviness, a solemnity, that did not model the original. Jehu could be cold when he wanted, and was usually reserved and polite—a quality often mistaken for arrogance—but Lafayette was both brilliant and icy. Jehu was friendly toward his relations, and openly affectionate toward his wife and children, but to hear Lafayette call his wife "my dear" was to be reminded of the tone used by a judge to address a confessed felon.

"It started as an American revolution, aye," David said, "but it's become a Virginian one. We were stampeded into this war by means both unethical and unconstitutional, and I say that if Virginia can break the Constitution with impunity, then the question of union ought to be reconsidered."

This was not strictly true: Every New England state except for Connecticut (which had voted solidly against) had been divided on the declaration of war, and New Hampshire had voted *for* the war by a margin of three to two, even though the two congressmen representing the coast, and the merchant interests, had voted against. If Congress had actually gone to the trouble of consulting the people it allegedly represented, the vote for the war would probably have been less substantial, and might have failed. Even as it was, though Congress had passed the war resolution, it had also showed itself completely unwilling to actually pay for the war it had started.

But somehow these objections, truthful as they were, did not alter the fact of war. The war with England was the ultimate political and national truth, and the sort of partisan political bickering with which the republic was accustomed to entertain itself during peacetime seemed both meaningless and absurd within the overall context. Perhaps the United States had made a bad bargain, but the bargain remained, and the realities had to be recognized. The war existed, and it was changing the lives of the entire body of citizens. The boundaries of the nation had been altered: West Florida had been seized from the Spaniards, and East Florida might be taken at any time; Detroit and much of the West had been overrun by the British and their native allies. The war was acting to alter the very thoughts of the nation as well. Never again would the public be able to shrug off a naval budget on the grounds that the Navy— that the very *idea* of a Navy—was a waste and extravagance and an invitation to mischief, not after the British built up their American squadron and began laying waste to the Chesapeake and Delaware. Never again would the Army and Congress blithely order an untrained, ill-equipped collection of militia, stiffened with a few regulars and generaled by superannuated, senile soldiers and politicians, in an ignorant attack on the greatest power in the world.

The war was making so much obvious that had before been the subject of puzzling debate: the need for a strong

Treasury, an adequate and vigorous military, and a coherent Indian policy, and the uselessness of commercial retaliations on the order of the embargo. All the Federalist ideas were proving their worth, but because it was the Republicans who were implementing them, the Federalists were crying "Tyranny!"

"What issue can there be," Favian found himself saying, "but whether we can end this war favorably or not? When the British land on our shores, they will not distinguish a Federalist house from a Republican house when they burn it, nor will they take care to plunder shipping owned only by Republican owners. The Indians will not inquire as to a man's politics before lifting his scalp, or the scalps of his wife and children. It is a national emergency, and the nation ought to respond as a nation, not as a collection of yapping children."

David listened to him with cheerful, though cynical, forbearance. "Spoken like a true servant of the Constitution!" he said, smiling. "It's a pity the Constitution has been cut up into ribbons."

"It's a pity some of us are so gleeful to see it cut," Lafayette observed in tones of arctic chilliness.

As bad as Washington, Favian thought. He went in search of another toddy and found his father's hand on his arm. "It was the same in my war," Jehu said with a tolerant smile. "The Continental Congress argued about matters of protocol while men froze to death at Valley Forge and the British plundered the Chesapeake and sat like kings in New York and Philadelphia. What one must remember is that the enemy are no better than we. Depend on it that the stupidity and waste in the American Congress and state houses is at least doubled by that of Whitehall and the Court of St. James's."

"We're supposed to be better," Favian said. "We have no lords, no king, no court intrigues."

"We *are* better," Jehu Markham said quietly. "In time the world will know it. Perhaps we will know it, too; I wonder if that knowledge will serve us good or ill."

"That's more than I can say." Favian poured himself a dash of rum, felt it burn his throat.

"I see Miss Whitcomb has gone discreetly in search of

the jakes," Jehu observed. "You may catch Emma without her chaperone if you seize the moment."

"I—thank you," Favian said. He heard David's mocking tones, Lafayette replying with words of ice, and he remembered the red water pouring from *Macedonian*'s scuppers. Why, he wondered, did he remember it now? Why had he looked upon it unmoved, as the red water climbed his white trousers, as bits of men sloshed back and forth, when he now found it so horrible, so unforgettable? He swallowed the rest of the rum and nodded to his father. His last chance to board Emma before he sailed.

She stood at his approach, put her arm through his. "It's getting a bit stuffy, Favian," she said. "Would you be so kind as to walk me around the block? I could use some air."

"Honored," he said.

She looked at him appraisingly as he held out her cloak and hat, and donned his own. "They've upset you, with their politics," she said. He opened the door for her. "They're not saying anything unusual," she said. "Nothing you can't hear in every coffeehouse, every day. On every front porch, on every street."

"It's nothing that isn't being shouted in Congress, either," Favian said. "I don't know why it upset me." She put her arm in his; they walked up the darkening street. Emma's breath frosted in the air; it had been an unusually chill day.

"It made me feel *Navy*," Favian said. "I've never thought of myself as being Navy, not really. And now I realize that I have so little in common with these people. I suppose I'm more Navy than I thought."

"What does it mean, being Navy?" she asked. Her eyes turned to his in the failing light. "I'd like to know, Favian."

"Be careful of that water—it's slippery," Favian said. *Navy*. How could he tell her about that orchard in Spain— how he had stood gazing down that pistol barrel, terrified out of his wits, but even more afraid to show fear? Or of how he had gone mad in the battle off Tripoli and jumped aboard a Tripolitan gunboat with only a few men at his back, leading a dozen against fifty?

"I don't know what it means," he evaded. She pursed her lips and looked at him sidelong, as if she sensed his deceit.

"I had always resented it," he said, "the obligation to 'be Navy,' never being able to drop it. I still resent it. But now it seems as if I couldn't drop it if I wished."

She stopped. Emma gazed calmly into his eyes. "Drop it, Favian," she said. "Resign the Navy. I can marry *you*, Favian, but I can't marry an officer. I need someone close." She groped for words. "Stay here. Take care of me."

He looked at her helplessly. "I can't resign. Not in wartime. Not after—" He took a deep breath. "Not after what I've said, tonight."

There were tears of frustration in Emma's eyes. "By God, I think I know what *Navy* means!" she spat. Emma turned and walked rapidly down the sidewalk, her heels rapping on the pavement. Favian followed, wrapped in hopeless gloom.

"The war won't last forever," he said. His words seemed to have no effect, but eventually she slowed and put her arm once more in his.

"I suppose I'm not used to people saying no to me," she said stiffly. "I shall try to be more gracious next time."

"I hope I shall never have occasion to say no to you again," Favian said. She gave a little smile.

"I was brave for a little while, wasn't I?" she asked. "I spoke out. It felt pleasant, while I was speaking thus. Years from now, I shall be able to look back on a moment of courage, before I turned back to a life of obedience."

Favian felt awkward and tongue-tied, and wished he had not fed himself quite so much rum. "You make it sound like a nunnery," he said.

"I wish we could run away," she said plaintively. They were at the door. She kissed him lightly, a little sadly, and then walked into the house. He followed.

Arethusey Whitcomb glared blackly at Favian as he returned to the company, and he nodded at her as politely as he could manage. The political argument was still droning on as the company went in to dinner. Favian took in his youngest cousin, Jemimah, while David escorted Emma Greenhow and Josiah was condemned to the company of Miss Whitcomb—which, fortunately, he seemed to enjoy; they found common ground in the active church lives they led.

Favian ate a cheerless dinner, despite Jemimah's attempts to make amusing conversation. What else could he have done? he demanded of himself. Even if he could bring himself to resign, Paul Hamilton would probably not accept the resignation. And if he succeeded in resigning, what then? For a young just-married man, with only a military career behind him, what prospects could there be? If there was anyone more penniless than an officer, it was an ex-officer.

The dinner over, brandy and coffee were brought in, and Jehu and Josiah were seen conferring at the head of the table. At last Jehu stood and called for attention.

"Ladies and gentlemen," he said, standing elegantly posed like an orator, with one fist on a hip and the other, knuckles down, on the table. "We are assembled this evening to welcome and honor Master Commandant Favian Markham, to congratulate him on his recent successes, and to wish him good fortune and attainment in his new command."

The others at the table broke into some small applause. "Hear, hear!" Lafayette intoned from somewhere at the table's waist, his deep, controlled voice rumbling unmistakably below the applause. Jehu held up a hand.

"But 'tis not the sole reason," he said. "The Markham family has not endured over the generations because we quietly accepted failure, or were short to praise achievement. Most of the gentlemen among us have been at sea at one time or another, even if the sea no longer furnishes us direct employment. Some of us present have had the distinction of fighting in the war for independence. Some of our family were killed in that war."

Jehu Markham paused, his eyes flickering somberly over the assembled family. Even the small children were silent, sensing the drama of his words.

"Favian Markham is a man of the sea," Jehu said. "He is following, to an extent, the family tradition. But he is doing more than that. As a gentleman, an officer of the republic, he is called upon to be many things: sailor, soldier, diplomat, at home both on a ship and in the corridors of Congress. His is a more difficult task than that of those who have gone before.

"We would like to make a presentation to him tonight. His uncles and I, in the war for independence, fought under a number of flags—under the Rattlesnake Ensign, the flag of New Hampshire, the Stars and Stripes, the privateer flag—but we sailed under one banner that we made uniquely our own. It flew over the *Royal George*, when Malachi and I took *Bristol*, and it flew over all Markham ships from that day. I know that Favian, a naval officer, may not be able to fly his banner from a vessel belonging to the United States, but I would like him to have it." Jehu raised his cup. "Ladies and gentlemen, I give you Favian Markham, and the viper banner."

Josiah, during this speech, had brought the banner from a drawer in a side table, and as the others stood, repeated the toast, and drank, Josiah walked down the length of the table to the stunned Favian. The banner was long, over twenty feet, and so was not unfolded except for the first few feet: It was a swallow-tailed pendant, a bright crimson, with a golden rattlesnake executed in formidable, unsightly detail, writhing down its length. Favian received the flag with shock. It had been designed by Malachi Markham, the Revolutionary prodigy of his father's generation, to proclaim *Markham* through the seven seas, and to cause the enemy to know the flag and fear it.

And again, as he felt the flag in his hands, he received the impression, as he had months ago in Paul Hamilton's office, of that long line of Markhams—the ghostly ancestors, Markhams in their generations, from Tom Markham in his bare feet and short jacket, a common seaman and a deserter from the Royal Navy, to the recent dead; and Markhams still living and watching him now, standing expectant with their cups in their hands—all pressing on him something that was both a gift and a burden: the naval heritage of the Markham family, the line of mariners, stretching to the present day, and now offering him a place. He could join that line, find a home within its coils, but only if he accepted the cost. There would be no way to avoid comparison with the others in the chain, no way to avoid knowing himself whether his shadow measured up to the others . . .

But then there had never been any choice, had there?

"I will fly it from the foretop," he said slowly. "I hope I will do it honor." He reached for his cup, raised it.

"To the family," he said. The toast's echo seemed to come from more throats than were present in the room, from Tom and Adaiah and Malachi, and from Gideon, who commanded a privateer in the Caribbean. . . . Favian's eyes turned to Emma Greenhow as he drank, and he saw her cup untouched. There was helplessness in her eyes. She knows, he thought with a chill, that she will never be of this family.

The company began to disperse. Markhams with children left to put them to bed. Emma and Arethusey Whitcomb left just after dinner ended. Favian kissed Emma's hand as she left, and saw—this time she forgot to conceal it—that she'd bitten her nails to the quick.

" 'Twas Josiah's idea, actually," Jehu said later, as Favian prepared to leave. "He'll be sending another pendant to Gideon at New Orleans, with Gideon's new schooner. Have you seen it building in Stanhope's yards?"

"Aye. I'd trade *Experiment* for that schooner without a second thought."

"Good as our Navy construction has been, the civilian shipyards have been better."

"I hope to have *Experiment* crewed before that privateer schooner touches water," Favian said. "Two weeks or so. Once the schooner starts to ship men, no sensible sailor will want to go aboard a Navy brig."

"I thought your crew was almost up to complement."

"Aye. In another week we can expect to have the ninety we're authorized, but if I can get more I'll take 'em. Ninety will give us an adequate crew, but there will be no reserve if I have to man prizes. And there are so many guns aboard that ninety men won't handle both broadsides efficiently—we're so slow we may have to use those guns if we can't run away."

"You have your orders?"

"Yes. The same as Burrows's—to cruise the coast up to the Gulf of Saint Lawrence, protect American shipping, capture or destroy enemy privateers. I don't think we'll be lucky enough to find a Royal Navy vessel we can beat."

"No." Jehu Markham's eyes were solemn. "Good luck." His arms went around Favian, embracing him. "I hope I will see you before you leave."

Favian kissed his mother and embraced her. He clasped his uncle Josiah's hand. Carrying the Markham flag beneath his arm, he went out into the chill night.

6.

Lieutenant Peter Hibbert stood by *Experiment*'s weather rail, feeling the brisk April winds tug at the skirts of his coat. Bile rose from his throat, and he fought it down, clenching his teeth. Seasick! It was outrageous, and humiliating. He gulped air, and moved forward toward the brig's center of gravity, where the pitch of the little vessel was not quite so disquieting. *Experiment* wallowed in the trough of a wave, and Hibbert gritted his teeth again.

Hibbert realized, as he watched the men at their work, scrubbing the decks and brightening the brass work, that he had not been to sea in a deep-sea vessel for almost eight years, since the *Hornet* had crossed the bar at Sandy Hook after the capture of Derna so long ago. Since then there had been the long, hated duty in gunboats, and the endless spell ashore, watching with never-ending anxiety as his father's body knit itself together after two catastrophic strokes. Hibbert had watched as his father took his first few steps, learning to walk all over again; he had spoon-fed his father in bed, like a child; he had watched as his father's clumsy hands picked up a pen and scrawled out a spindly, ink-spotted first alphabet, learning over again how to write. Hibbert had held his father when he wept, complaining that insidious surgeons had attached to his body the limbs of corpses, and taken his own living arms and legs to some dissecting table. But now the nightmare was over; his father was in excellent health for a man of his years, cared for by Hibbert's sisters, and perfectly competent to run his own affairs. Peter Hibbert, his son, could go to sea.

Hibbert battled his nausea and wondered how many

years it had been since he and his sisters had gone aboard
Ben Wohl's pilot boat for the picnic out to Saco Bay. Two
years, perhaps. The sea had been calm, and he had not
been seasick. He had worn his uniform, so that the crew
of the boat wouldn't treat him with the same condescension
they heaped on the other passengers—the well-dressed
gentlemen and giggling ladies who had chartered the schooner for their Fourth of July lark. Hibbert had felt his hands
itching to take the wheel or help haul on a line; he had
to restrain himself from calling out orders to trim the
braces or set the gaff topsails. He would have given anything then to be among the crew: yes, to be even the least
seasoned, most bullied, rawest-handed young lad among
them. But it was impossible. Had they seen him strip off
his coat and go forward with the hands, the upstanding
young gentlemen of the company and the delicate ladies
would have laughed.

He wished he *had* gone forward. He wished he *had*
helped work the pilot boat that day. It wouldn't have mattered if his friends had laughed to see him sweating like a
foredeck hand, and if his sisters had blushed for him. He
would have been a man among men for a short while, and
not a nurse.

Hibbert felt a gust of wind on his lee cheek, heard the
sails lift, then roar. He glanced up at the masthead pendant. The wind had backed eastward during the night and
had backed a point again. "Braces here!" he called. Miller
the bosun began to curse. His colt licked out, and the hands
scampered to the braces as the sails roared like distant
thunder. Hibbert stepped back out of the way as the sails
were trimmed.

Experiment had left Portsmouth six days before, on the
thirty-first of March. Her crew was up to a hundred and
twenty-three, thirty-three more than her official complement; men were packed below like salted cod in a barrel.
In the two weeks before the brig's sailing, two merchantmen had come into Portsmouth and paid off their crews;
after the usual debauch that followed a paying-off, most of
the tars found themselves without either money or employment. The privateers that had been recruiting were at full
complement; merchantmen in wartime were few and far

between, and the best berth available seemed to be the
United States brig of war *Experiment*. They had turned out
to be good men; some had been in the Navy before, and
these added a leavening of experience that proved good for
the little brig, crowded though it was.

The days at sea had, more so than usually, been full of
drills. There had been sail drills, accustoming the men of
each watch to their messmates. There had been boarding
drills, fire drills, boat drills, drills in shifting guns. And of
course there had been gunnery drills, performed for the
first time with live ammunition, with particular attention
being paid to the marksmanship of the two nine-pounder
chasers, to bring the accuracy of the ship's only two long-
ranged guns to the pitch necessary to strike out over a long
distance and bring a fleeing enemy to bay. The gunnery
drills were critical: The *Experiment*'s fourteen eighteen-
pound carronades had not yet been issued with the sheet-
lead cartridges that had so radically increased *United States*'s
fire in the fight with *Macedonian*. The brig would
have to fight with the old-fashioned flannel cartridges, and
that meant a slower rate of fire. Drill was necessary to
narrow the gap.

The hands were gaining confidence and skill, but they
were nowhere close to the high pitch of efficiency necessary to turn *Experiment* into the proficient cruising, fighting machine necessary to accomplish any wartime mission.
Not for the first time Hibbert found himself envying Edward McCall, his opposite number aboard *Enterprise*, who
had a seasoned, well-trained crew, many of whom had been
with the vessel for years.

Favian Markham's theories about gunnery, for example,
required a more disciplined crew than rival schemes: Firing the carronades by sections, rather than by broadsides or
at will, necessitated a high degree of matching competence
among the gun crews of one section; one laggard crew
could slow the rate of fire of the others. And Favian also
believed in each man being able to do another's job; gun
crew positions were rotated "with the sun" every day, so
every man had a different task. It would take weeks, probably months, before the crew of *Experiment* even began to
reach Favian's exacting standards.

Favian had other unusual ideas as well. The day before leaving port he'd ordered that a "naval square" be painted in black on the deck, on the white planking between the brig's two masts. He had borrowed the idea from Paul Hoste, a French naval theorist of the seventeenth century, whose works Favian had read in the original, having been introduced to them by William Burrows. The square (or *carré navale,* as Favian kept calling it) was two yards on a side, divided by a line (the "keel line") drawn fore and aft down the middle and by lines ("beam lines") drawn to opposite corners. The naval square was supposed to make easier the business of pursuing to windward: When the brig was close-hauled, one of the diagonal lines represented the brig's course after tacking, twelve points from the old course; the other represented the beam line to the new course. Standing by the square, a man giving orders to the helm could visualize the new tack much more easily. But Hibbert was a little suspicious. He admired the science of the device, but thought that a good seaman should be able to carry a naval square in his head, and perform the necessary maneuvers without reference to any patterns marring the clean pine deck.

But that was Favian's way: He aspired to being a scientific sailor, trying to avoid the seat-of-the-pants techniques of earlier generations of naval officers, to concentrate on finer and finer hair-splitting. He had been shifting the brig's long guns about, trying to adjust her trim; he had also redistributed the iron shot kept in the hold as ballast, hoping to better her trim in another way. Favian's orders to the midshipmen concentrated on the scientific as well. Their daily lesson plans included navigational theory as well as practical navigation, including spherical trigonometry and algebra; they were to exert themselves to learn French, which, in addition to being the international language and the language of diplomacy, was the language of such theorists as Hoste, Fournier, Bouguer, and Bourde de Villehuet—none of whom had been translated into English, but whose theories Favian considered important. Hibbert himself had never heard of most of them, and his French was rusty; but he'd borrowed the books and studied them in his spare moments. It didn't do well for the midshipmen to know more on any subject than the first lieutenant did.

Favian had even instituted the practice of inviting the officers and midshipmen to dine with him, the table conversation being held entirely in French. The emphasis on theory, however, made Hibbert uneasy. If the French had so many excellent theories, why were they always losing naval battles to the British? When, as tactfully as he could, he mentioned his doubts, Favian had an answer ready. "Midshipmen are fighters, and aggressive," he'd said. "They don't need to learn the principles of attack. Theory should not blunt their aggressiveness, but it might serve to temper their urge to combat with something that may be of use."

Favian's eyes had grown serious. "It was French tactics, performed properly, that defeated the *Macedonian*," he said. "Carden came charging in like Nelson at Trafalgar, but without Nelson's knowledge of when to attack and when not to. We slipped away to leeward and shot him to bits as he came up. We could have charged in as Bainbridge did with *Constitution*, and taken the kind of casualties that Bainbridge took when he captured the *Java*, but Decatur kept his head, laid the mizzen tops'l aback, and took his time. Both battles were victories, but Bainbridge lost three times as many men."

Perhaps. But Hibbert had been brought up in a school of aggressiveness, where attack was paramount, and where when the enemy was sighted and the guns run out, science was put back into the books where it belonged. It remained to be seen whether Favian would succeed in tempering the headlong impulses of the American sailor with his cool, intellectual additions.

"Flemish that line properly, you sojer!" Hibbert snapped. "Those coils look like some old rat's nest!"

There were too many landsmen aboard. They were learning fast, though. Thank the Lord for the veterans, who often knew what to do without being told. There were some who had served aboard *Constitution* and were now assigned as crews to the chaser guns.

The decks had been cleaned with seawater, holystones,

and prayer-books; the brightwork had been polished until it shone. Hibbert had the hands piped to breakfast, and sent below to the wardroom steward for a cup of coffee. The horizon was a misty blue, vague, the sun's outlines ill defined as it rose from the uncertain conditions ahead.

It was the Gulf Stream, the flow of warm water from the tropics to Europe that old Benjamin Franklin had been the first to chart. The warm water, contrasting with the cold water through which it ran, caused the fogs and mists and endless squalls associated with the Gulf Stream in these latitudes—or so the theory went. Hibbert had no opinions; he simply had to deal with the weather when it occurred. The Gulf Stream would help carry them to the Saint Lawrence, where their proper cruise could begin, searching for enemy merchant vessels and privateers setting out from Canadian ports, and hoping to avoid the British men-of-war based at Halifax.

"Deck thar! Sail ho! Off the larb'd beam!" The lookout's cry pealed down from aloft.

Hibbert glanced over the decks, saw a bosun's mate in the lee of the foremast quietly practicing his craft, making a long splice in an old line with his eyes shut. "You there!" Hibbert barked. "My compliments to the captain, and tell him there's a sail in sight to leeward."

"Aye aye, sir." The messenger vanished down the aft scuttle. Hibbert tilted his head back, his eyes narrowing as he looked up into the bright sky, finding the lookout at the masthead.

"Masthead there!" Hibbert bawled. "What d'you make of her?"

The lookout took his time before replying. "Deck thar! She's a brig, I think. On the opposite tack, so I can't be sure. Maybe two hundred tons!"

Hibbert nodded. He took a long glass from the rack and swept the horizon: nothing. The brig was visible only from the masthead; that meant she was perhaps twenty miles to leeward, give or take a few. No way, at this distance, to know if she was friendly, enemy, or neutral. Whether she might even be a warship, in which case she was almost certainly an enemy. Halifax and British Nova Scotia were there to leeward, perhaps fifty miles over the horizon. It seemed quite unlikely that any sail sighted so close to the British base would be friendly. Unless, of course, she turned out to be *Enterprise*.

Favian appeared on deck, in his shirt and wearing his undress round hat. Hibbert briefly gave him an outline of the situation.

"Give me the long glass, then, Mr. Hibbert," Favian said. "I'll go aloft."

"Yes, sir." Favian slipped the long glass over his shoulder by its strap and went up the weather main ratlines, a thin, ungainly figure in his shirt and hat, awkwardly swarming up the shrouds, unaccustomed to going aloft— like a longlegs spider, Hibbert thought suddenly. Favian's overlong limbs had the same kind of awkward look even when they knew what they were doing.

He watched as Favian hauled himself on the futtock shrouds, dangling inverted over the decks for a perilous instant, then levered his thin body to swarm up the maintopmast shrouds. Reaching the masthead, Favian swept the entire horizon, then concentrated on the invisible brig to leeward; he returned by sliding down a backstay, showing himself to be nimbler than he looked. He returned the glass to Hibbert.

"She's just forrard of the beam, Mr. Hibbert," he said. "I'd alter course six points to larboard to keep the wind of her, and clap on every stuns'l on the boat. I'm going down to finish breakfast. Call me if anything develops."

"Aye aye, Captain." Favian disappeared down the aft scuttle.

Well! Hibbert thought. The first sail they'd seen since clearing Portsmouth, and the captain didn't seem very excited. Perhaps it had been an exceptionally good breakfast.

Hibbert rapped with a belaying pin on the edge of the forward scuttle. "All hands on deck!" he roared, producing something like a groan from the men at their breakfast. "Smartly now!" Somewhere below the bosun was piping; he was joined in a few seconds by the brig's trumpeter. The companionway began to roar with the sound of bare feet. Hibbert straightened, looking resentfully at the aft scuttle where Favian had disappeared. The man could at least take an interest. He gasped for air, his stomach lurching. Seasick. Oh, God.

The helm was put over, and *Experiment* curved slowly to larboard, sails blossoming on her yards, the studding sails appearing on their out-thrust booms. *Experiment*'s motion increased with her speed, and Hibbert's discomfort multiplied until he felt he could barely stand. *Experiment* was pitching down into the trough of each wave with a shuddering lurch; Hibbert gripped his midsection and hung on for dear life. That motion was not healthy; it was not efficient. *Experiment* was not sailing as well as she should.

Hibbert concentrated on the problem, hoping to distract himself from his physical misery. Something was pitching the brig down each wave; perhaps all the sail was pressing her stem down too much. Should he have the royals furled and see if it improved the brig's motion? He considered.

Favian would have to give his permission; his last order had been to set every stitch of canvas, and that would stay in effect until he changed his mind. There were standing orders for the captain to be called as each sail was sighted; at first light, to take instant advantage of any sightings made at dawn; if the wind shifted more than a point; or if the brig's course had to be altered.

Experiment plunged down a wave and crashed into the water with a lurch. Hibbert fought down a flood of bile. Enough. "Mr. Dudley!" Hibbert called to a midshipman. "My compliments to the captain, and tell him I'd like to furl the royals. I think they're pressing her down too much."

"Aye aye, sir."

Dudley was back in moments and uncovered in salute. "Captain says do as you think best, sir."

Hibbert felt a glimmer of satisfaction through his misery as he barked out the orders. Sure enough, *Experiment*'s motion eased; she took each wave much more easily. Perhaps, he thought with relief, Favian's science was rubbing off on him: Most captains would probably never have thought that too much sail could be set in such conditions. Or perhaps, Hibbert amended, it would never have occurred to an officer with a less uneasy stomach.

* * *

Favian finished his breakfast and was on deck before the distant brig on the horizon was more than a fleck of snow above the cresting waves. He came up in his undress coat this time, and gazed aloft with interest. Topmast and topgallant studding sails had been set and were drawing well, with the wind coming over the starboard quarter. Staysails stretched between the masts like spread wings. *Experiment*, her motion eased by the furling of the royals, was shouldering through the waves like a boxer through a crowd of admirers. He glanced aft at the blackboard, where the latest workings had been scrawled, including the speed in knots after the last heave of the log (which had been moments before; he'd heard it through the cabin windows as he'd finished his breakfast), and found the brig's speed to be eleven knots—simply awful, in these ideal conditions.

Through earnest application to the superintendent of the Portsmouth Navy Yard, he'd managed to bring aboard a main yard of forty-two feet, replacing the thirty-four-foot yard Thomas Tingey had given her when she was rebuilt. But the new topsail and the new square mainsail that were necessary to fit the new yard had not yet been completed by the sail maker, and the old, smaller sail was aloft now, the buntlines, leechlines, sheets, and other controlling lines shifted awkwardly inward from their normal places to accommodate the smaller sail. The clumsy arrangement hadn't bothered Favian nearly as much as the fact that when the new sails were ready, they'd have to spend the better part of a day unrigging the old sails, topsail and square mainsail, sending them down to the deck, and rigging the new ones, shifting all the controlling lines and blocks to fit the wider sails. But still, when the new sails were sent aloft, they should be able to get another two knots from *Experiment* in these same conditions.

Favian's eyes lowered to the fleck of white on the horizon; already it seemed larger. Hibbert, presumably aided by Alferd Bean, had done well, considering the brig's inappropriate rig and poor sailing qualities. The sails were drawing well, their edges cutting the sky like a razor, the braces trimmed with care; and Favian was pleased with Hibbert's initiative in furling the royals and easing the

brig's motion. Hibbert had shown that the years ashore had
not dulled his seamanlike instincts.

Favian put the long glass to his eye, seeing the distant
royals and topgallants leaping into focus. He frowned,
walked to the helm. "Point to larboard," he told the helmsman.

"Aye aye, sir." He was straddling the tiller, the long fir
rod thrusting out from his groin like a grotesque wooden
phallus. He shifted, one eye on the compass riding in its
binnacle. "West nor'west half point north," he reported,
scrupulous. Favian glanced aloft again and ordered a minute adjustment to the sheet of the big fore-and-aft mainsail.
In the foretop he could see Homer Brook, the brig's fifteen-
year-old midshipman, with Phillip Stanhope. Brook was
pointing out lines and halyards; Stanhope appeared to be
repeating them. Stanhope's blue jacket was smart and new.
Favian, remembering his own first cruise on the old *Boston*, under crazy old Captain McNeil, was certain that
Stanhope could hardly wait until his neat blue jacket was
weathered and shabby, mended in half a dozen places,
stained with tar and salt: the jacket of a veteran seaman.
Brook, for his part, was probably happy he was no longer
the most junior mid on the brig.

Phillip Stanhope had come aboard the week before sailing. There had been no other applicants, and Hibbert, who
had interviewed the lad, had been impressed by his obvious
intelligence and apparent determination. It was clear to all
aboard that Phillip Stanhope was bent on learning his job,
and learning it well. It was equally clear that he took himself very seriously, far more seriously than did any of the
other midshipmen. It was a kind of pride, Favian supposed—the pride of a boy who is accustomed to being more
intelligent than most, and used to having his own way
much of the time, but thrown into a situation in which he
was abysmally ignorant of most of the facts of existence.
Favian hoped the pride would not flare into temper, and
that he, as captain, would not have to worry about settling
affairs of honor between Stanhope and the other midshipmen.

But that was anticipating. There was no sign of any
trouble. Stanhope seemed to be on friendly terms with his

fellows. In a larger ship there would have been more of a
capacity for mischief, with the usually headstrong, ambitious, competitive midshipmen all berthed together. The
United States Navy did not encourage bullying in the midshipmen's berth, like the Royal Navy did, but neither was
bullying or hazing unknown. But in the *Experiment*, eighty
feet long and with over a hundred twenty men aboard,
there could be no secrets. If there was anything wrong,
Favian devoutly hoped, he would soon know of it.

The midshipmen were probably going to be Favian's biggest problem—short of the British, anyway. Their education was at public expense, and was supposed to be conducted entirely aboard the brig. The problem was that,
short of practical seamanship, little of the midshipmen's
curriculum was best learned on a vessel sailing the high
seas. The life was coarse and active; a young officer would
have no difficulty learning to swear, drink, and trim a
brace, but when it came to such necessary elements as
mathematics, navigation, and French, life on shipboard
could prove an inordinate distraction.

Most midshipmen were made lieutenants following an
examination by a board of examiners, which tended to concentrate on the theoretical aspects of an officer's supposed
knowledge. Favian had known apprentice officers who
were perfectly competent in seamanship and gunnery—two
skills best learned on shipboard—but failed their exams because they had never fully mastered the arts of spherical
trigonometry. If only there were some place to pack the
mids off to, early in their careers, for a year or two of
intense study, Favian thought. In the meantime he and
Hibbert had to spend many valuable hours playing instructor, in order to give their boys a chance of passing their
examinations. It grated on Favian; the system was so
blasted *unscientific*.

Then, with a start, Favian remembered the mad fiddler
Lazarus in that Washington tavern: Was this what he'd
meant by saying Favian would turn schoolmaster?

A ridiculous thought. Favian brought his mind back to
the present situation and took another look through the
long glass. From the set of her sails, Favian concluded the
other brig was a merchantman.

The two vessels, on converging tacks, closed most of the distance between them before the other vessel was aware of *Experiment*'s existence. Then she wore about, and through the long glass Favian could see men running aloft to set studding sails. "Hoist the White Ensign," Favian ordered, and the British flag went up the halyards. More sails blossomed from the brig's yards, but Favian found himself delighted to discover that however slow *Experiment* might be, the other brig was slower. After an hour's chase had conclusively proved this, the merchant brig took in her studding sails and went onto the starboard tack, seemingly having lost interest in running away.

"Call the men to quarters, Mr. Hibbert," Favian said. Hibbert signaled the trumpeter, and the sound of the staccato call wafted over the brig. The deck drummed as men ran to their stations, as the lashings were cast off the guns and carronades, the clear sound of the trumpet being marred by the curses of officers and mates. Favian, out of the corner of his eye, saw Homer Brook sliding down a backstay from the foretop to the deck, while Phillip Stanhope, not yet having acquired the surefootedness necessary aloft, came carefully down the weather shrouds.

Experiment thrashed toward her prey with the wind on her starboard quarter. Favian kept close watch over the brig with his glass. She was a scarred vessel, the paint on her bows worn away to the wood, with old, yellowed, patched sails aloft, chafing gear hanging like old strips of seaweed, and broken ratlines dangling between the shrouds. There didn't seem to be quite enough men on deck to handle her very efficiently; perhaps she'd come out of Halifax and there had been a press in the town, although she didn't look as if she'd just come from port—she looked rather more like she'd just spent fifty-odd days rounding Cape Horn.

Half a mile. Favian lowered his glass. "Hoist our true colors, Mr. Hibbert," he said, and the White Ensign came down, the Stars and Stripes rising to the brisk wind. There was a stir on the battered vessel's quarterdeck, and she wore about in a last, futile hope of escape. This was a little silly. "Put a shot across her bows," Favian said with a frown. By now escape was hopeless, and the brig's captain should have known it. The larboard chaser's crew over-hauled its gear, aimed briefly, and fired, putting a water-spout half a cable's length in front of the brig's forefoot. Favian tasted the tang of gunpowder on his tongue. The brig came back into the wind, its square sails going aback, awaiting its fate. The Stars and Stripes came up its peak.

"What the hell—?" he heard Alferd Bean exclaim.

"Mr. Hibbert, have the launch swung out, and arm your party with cutlasses," Favian said. "I want to see that brig's papers and manifests."

"With pleasure, sir," Hibbert said, his face grim. "What's that man got to hide, I wonder?"

"It might be contraband," Favian said. "But perhaps she's a British vessel trying to fool us. That's what you'll have to find out."

"Aye, sir."

The brig drew near. *Experiment* came into the wind, took in her studding sails, threw her main topsail to the mast, and gentled to a stop. Favian took a speaking trum-pet from the rack. "This is the United States brig of war *Experiment*!" he shouted. His voice sounded hollow, ghost-like, through the trumpet. "What ship, from what port, and where bound?"

The brig's master was a giant, as tall as Favian, but with the broad shoulders and sledgelike fists of a prizefighter. His battered coat hung on him with a certain rude majesty, like the robes of a bankrupt king. "Brig *Pride of Rich-mond*, out of Hampton, bound for Bordeaux with a cargo of wheat!"

"I am Captain Markham. Why did you run from us?"

"I am Captain Buck Johanan Gardell, and it's none of yer fuckin' business! Maybe I just don't like uppity Navy bastards inquirin' into my affairs!"

"Stand by for a boarding party, Captain Gardell."

"I'll goddamn well protest at this harassment of a man goin' about his own business!"

Favian's temper snapped at Gardell's goading. "I'll be pleased to give you the address of the Secretary of the Navy, Captain Gardell—after my men have searched your vessel! And if you offer the least resistance I'll be altogether pleased to send your brig to the bottom—where, from the looks of it, it ought to have been long ago!"

Hibbert and his crew rowed across the fifty yards of ocean separating the two vessels. The boarding party were all wearing their boarding helmets, stout leather caps reinforced with two crossed bands of iron, and a slab of bearskin running fore and aft, hairy side up, with another strip of bearskin running under the chin as a helmet strap. The boarding party, bending to the oars of the launch, looked like a tribe of wild-haired, bearded savages, plumes waving, ready to wreak unimaginable violence upon their foes.

Hibbert and his men went aboard the brig. A petty officer required the brig's crew to start removing the main hatch, so the hold could be inspected for contraband. Hibbert himself vanished down the aft scuttle with a cutlass-bearing guard and Buck Johanan Gardell. Favian fidgeted on the quarterdeck and felt his stomach growl; although he knew about Hibbert's seasickness, and the misery it caused, he would have gladly exchanged his own touchy stomach with Hibbert's. At least the onset of seasickness was predictable, and it went away after a few days.

Favian, as he paced, saw Phillip Stanhope standing by the hammock nettings at the lee rail, staring intently at the other brig, his mouth set in a frown. The picture of a serious young officer studying a ship that might be an enemy. Favian smiled.

Hibbert returned to *Pride of Richmond*'s deck; spoke with the petty officer who had inspected the hold; then, leaving his party aboard the prize brig, returned in his boat to *Experiment*. "Their papers are in order, Captain," he said, after uncovering in salute. "She's carrying wheat, all right. Cleared customs in Hampton Roads. Owned by Buckley Brothers, in Chesapeake." He scratched his head as Favian laid the papers on the binnacle box and began to go through them. "There's something wrong, Captain, but damned if I can think what it is. And damned if I can think of a cause for detaining them in port."

Favian went through the documents, and knew Buck Johanan Gardell had won. There was no legal reason to send the brig back. The papers were in order; the cargo was as the manifests declared. The fact that Halifax was just over the horizon, and that the *Pride of Richmond* had behaved suspiciously, would be laughed aside in court. And in court it would certainly end, Favian could depend on that. The Buckley Brothers were a well-known merchant firm, based close to Washington, and nothing at all could be proved.

"Pardon me, sir. May I offer a suggestion?" Favian looked up in surprise to find Midshipman Phillip Stanhope standing quietly by Hibbert's side.

"Yes, Mr. Stanhope?"

"We—that is, my family—built some schooners for the Buckley Brothers," Stanhope said. "They needed the schooners as grain carriers to Portugal, where they had a contract to supply the British army in Lisbon. They're a rough crowd, and Gardell's one of the roughest. I don't think they'd stop a profitable trade just because we happened to be at war with their clients.

"Captain," Stanhope said, his eyes determined, "I respectfully suggest that we search that brig for a warrant from the British admiral on the Halifax station."

"By God," Hibbert said wonderingly. Favian's eyes flicked to the *Pride of Richmond*, seeing the brig's giant captain standing triumphantly on his quarterdeck, grinning insolently, hands in his coat pockets.

"Papers in order thar, Cap'n Markham?" Gardell boomed. "Or shall I spell 'em out for ye?"

"Take another ten men," Favian said. "Stand their crew up on deck, where we can see 'em. Search the brig from stem to stern for that warrant. Start in the captain's quarters, the chart room, the bread room—anywhere that seems likely. Ask for his keys. If he doesn't give them, smash your way into anything that's locked." He nodded to Stanhope. "Take Mr. Stanhope here with you."

"Yes, sir!" Hibbert snapped, smiling grimly. He and his men were across in moments. Gardell, protesting vigorously, was herded forward with the rest of the crew, the boarding party standing by with drawn cutlasses. In moments Hibbert was back on deck, waving a sheet of vellum.

"In his desk drawer, Captain!" Hibbert bawled. "Signed by Vice Admiral John Borlase Warren himself!"

"Put the lot of 'em in irons, Mr. Hibbert, and stow 'em

in the fo'c'sle!" Favian called, savage glee filling him. "I'll be sending the shackles across to you."

He gave the orders and returned his speaking trumpet to its place. Now there was another decision to make. Was the capture of *Pride of Richmond*, with written proof that her master and owners had been trading with the enemy, important enough to interrupt *Experiment's* cruise? He could escort that captured brig into harbor and tell his story in person to the authorities, or he could send a prize crew to do the job themselves. But that would require an officer, and with its inexperienced crew *Experiment* needed all the officers it had. He reached his decision.

"Call Mr. Miller," he ordered.

John Miller, *Experiment's* bosun, was an experienced sailor in his forties, with his hair in an old-fashioned queue and black tattoos on his muscled arms. He was fit, strong, and at least semiliterate; he was as broad and powerful as Buck Johanan Gardell, but at least a foot shorter. And Favian knew him for that rare seagoing creature, a sailor who refused to touch liquor.

Miller appeared and uncovered in salute.

"Detail ten men—take your pick, the more reliable the better—and take that brig into Boston," Favian said. "I want you to sail into the Navy Yard, and at my orders deliver the master and his crew to the garrison at Fort Independence. Keep them in irons. You can let them out of the fo'c'sle for exercise twice each day, but never take their irons off—particularly that monster Gardell. You'll deliver my letters to Commodore Bainbridge, or whoever commands at the Navy Yard, and to the commandant at Fort Independence. I'll also be giving you dispatches for the Secretary of the Navy."

"Aye aye, sir!" Miller boomed, his wide grin showing crooked, chipped teeth. "I'll be pleased to bring them bastards before a court, sir."

I'll be lucky if it's not me who's brought before a court, Favian thought. Interfering with a merchant ship owned by a rough and unscrupulous organization, men who probably had the ear of Washington . . . Favian had boarded and searched her, sent her under guard into Boston, imprisoned her master. . . . Of course there was the charge of treason, not easily overlooked; but then the Buckley Brothers might claim that Gardell was acting without their knowledge.

But fortunately, Favian thought suddenly, his own family was not unknown in political circles. The Federalists were out of power, but they were still a substantial minority, and could still speak, and there were three New Hampshire congressmen who had voted for the war. He'd write to his brother Lafayette.

Favian waited, however, for the sight of *Pride of Richmond*'s crew submitting tamely to being ironed hand and foot. Even Gardell mutely held out his hands and allowed himself to be shackled, although his tameness seemed not a result of his being cowed, but simply because he was so enraged as to be almost paralyzed.

Then, with a grim smile, Favian ducked down the aft scuttle to his cabin, took writing paper from his desk, and wet the tip of his pen. *Experiment* had taken her first prize, even if the prize had turned out to be another United States vessel.

7.

*

Experiment had been floating for three days in an ocean littered with garbage: coconut husks, orange and lemon rinds, banana peels, a streak of human refuse several miles wide, all floating toward Europe at a steady rate, carried by the Gulf Stream. The brig was carrying every sail it could set, the yards groaning with the strain, studding sails set even at night; for ahead, somewhere in the Gulf Stream, was a West Indies convoy.

A West Indies convoy! Perhaps one or two hundred merchant ships, their holds crammed with molasses, sugar, coffee, cotton, tobacco, sisal, spices, bullion . . . fortunes in prize money. There would be a formidable escort, but there was always the possibility of picking up stragglers, or running into the convoy at night and cutting out a few ships. The lookouts kept their eyes skinned, aware that in the case of success their share of the prize money would consist, for a seaman, of a small fortune. *A West Indies convoy!* A convoy would be even slower than *Experiment*. The ocean was big, but with luck they'd find the enemy.

They had encountered the streak of garbage a hundred miles south of the entrance to the Gulf of Saint Lawrence, while waiting for enemy prizes, and while Favian tried to make up his mind whether or not to venture onto the narrow Gulf. Coconut husks, banana peels—no products of Canada, these! They had set sail to the eastward, into the misty, squally Gulf Stream, encountering acres of refuse but, thus far at least, not so much as a distant sight of a sail.

Favian paced the deck, annoyed that his constant, involuntary glancing to leeward had given him a stiff neck. He had ordered himself to pay no more attention to the eastward horizon, but it had proved impossible; he mentally flogged himself every time he caught himself gazing toward where the convoy ought to appear, castigating himself for lack of self-control.

It had been eight days since they'd left Miller and the *Pride of Richmond* in their wake. *Experiment*'s crew had been drilled daily during its two-week voyage and had attained considerable proficiency in its craft. The gun drills were brisk and orderly, and although the men had not achieved the swiftness or efficiency that would come with longer practice, they had at least achieved a basic competence. Hibbert had been a good instructor, and Bean, though scarcely imaginative, seemed at least to have a solid grasp of the fundamentals.

The crew seemed eager, too, to put its newly acquired knowledge and practice to good use; the possibilities presented by the West Indies convoys had added an edge to the men's impatience. Their eagerness to do battle, while commendable, was having less desirable effects: There had been a fistfight the day before, and the participants had avoided a reluctant flogging only by virtue of the fact that Gable, Miller's beefy, giant-knuckled replacement as bosun, had while breaking up the fight beaten both participants so severely as to make any flogging redundant. One man had been sent to sick bay, nursing broken ribs.

Experiment was a small vessel, and overcrowded; the crewmen were aggressive, trained in combat, and beginning to get on one another's nerves. Favian ordered discipline tightened, knowing that he was taking the risk of setting off another outbreak; but he had little choice but to respond to the incident in some fashion.

Favian was rubbing his stiff neck when the hail of the lookout rang down from aloft. "Deck thar! Sail to leeward! Three p'ints off the starb'd bow!"

Favian controlled his impulse to look to leeward and forced himself to look aloft.

"Masthead there! What can you make of her?"

"Jest a sail, Cap'n! Can't make out no more!"

The men on deck were all craning their necks to leeward; others were standing in the ratlines, trying to see farther over the horizon. Favian saw off-watch men coming up from below; he could see the anticipation in their eyes. *A West Indies convoy!* Favian glanced over the deck, saw Midshipman Stanhope standing by the rail, crowding with the others, his dignity as an apprentice officer forgotten.

"Mr. Stanhope!" he barked. "Go aloft with a long glass and tell me what you see."

Stanhope grinned as he went aloft, moving nimbly on the shrouds, handling them with far more confidence than he had shown just a few days before. He wasn't swinging hand over hand down backstays just yet, but he soon would be.

"One sail, sir!" Stanhope called down. "Ship-rigged!"

Experiment caught the ship after a six-hour chase, ending when the quarry's main-topmast went by the board. She was *Alison Gross* of Plymouth, two hundred fifty tons, Captain Clark, twenty days out of English Harbor with a cargo of coffee and tobacco. She'd sprung her main-topmast in a squall two days before, while traveling with the West Indies convoy, and had fallen behind; *Experiment*'s pursuit had finished what the squall had started. Favian took the crew off, and *Alison Gross* was used for target practice for the next forty minutes, until the ship was obviously sinking. Favian set her afire to make certain and set off again in pursuit of the convoy.

The next day the new main topsail and square mainsail were finally finished by the sailmaker, and half the day was spent getting them aloft. Winds were fair from the west southwest: almost ideal for the pursuing *Experiment*, although Favian had to remind himself that they were ideal for the convoy as well. Another two days passed before they sighted a sail: Just before sunset they came up with the bark *Mandarin*, Captain Sims, three hundred twenty tons. *Mandarin* had lost the convoy two nights before, having apparently simply missed an order to alter course and sailed out of the convoy's sight by sunrise. Captain Sims's crew was added to the grossly overcrowded inhabitants of the berth deck; Favian took aboard some sacks of oranges and coconuts to vary the diet of his crew; and *Mandarin* was burned. *Experiment* sailed into the night, her sails reflecting the orange light of the destroyed prize.

The next day the horizon was clear. Caribbean garbage, though still present, was more scattered. Favian had a decision to make.

His orders had been to cruise the New England and Canadian coasts, in order to suppress enemy privateers and harass their merchantmen. The orders, though they allowed him to pursue targets of opportunity, in no way could be stretched to endorse a chase clean across the Atlantic. Yet if he continued the chase, that was exactly what he would do.

Just after the declaration of war, Commodore John Rodgers and an American squadron composed of *President, United States, Congress, Hornet,* and *Argus* had chased another West Indies convoy almost to the English Channel. Rodgers had never found his convoy and had turned back. Favian had been on that expedition as first lieutenant on *United States,* and he could remember Decatur fuming for days over the decision to return to the United States instead of tearing with the entire squadron through the Narrow Seas of England—the English Channel, North Sea, Irish Sea, and other bodies of water surrounding Great Britain, waters which the Royal Navy considered its own.

But Favian was not a commodore with a squadron of three fast frigates and two sloops of war; he was a very junior commanding officer with a slow brig and a complement still learning their jobs. The West Indies convoy might be just over the horizon. The lookouts might sight it in another few hours, or they might pick up another straggler that would give them a clue as to where the convoy itself might be. But *Experiment* might be no luckier than Commodore Rodgers; they might never see the convoy, and appear at the Narrow Seas' approaches only to make the same decision that Rodgers did. Favian did not have a squadron to back him, or orders that could be interpreted as authorization for a venture into European waters. But on the other hand, the convoy would break up as it neared the Channel approaches, each vessel heading for different ports, the escort scattered.

If Favian continued, the responsibility for what occurred, be it success or failure, would rest entirely on his own shoulders. He had considered calling a counsel of war with Hibbert and Bean, putting the matter before them, requesting their signatures on a written document agreeing with a decision to go ahead or to turn back. If disaster occurred, he could use the signed documents to spread the responsibility, to show that his officers deserved at least a share of the blame.

But no. The decision would be his, and he alone would bear the responsibility. It would not be fair to Hibbert or Bean if their careers were blackened by Favian's decision.

They would go on.

Day after day the horizon was clear. The winds blew fair for England, foul for America. The scattered Caribbean garbage was still present, but the distinct stripe of it that had littered the sea was no longer clearly to be discerned. Favian felt dyspepsia gnawing at his stomach, giving him sudden stabbing pains as he walked the deck and strained his eyes looking for ships that never appeared. The mood of the crew, formerly one of cheerful anticipation, grew sullen. Three prizes this voyage, Favian could almost hear them thinking, and one was American and the other two were burned on captain's orders, denying everyone prize money.

On the fourteenth night of the chase, when the lookouts had been cautioned to expect a European landfall at any moment and the sea had been bare of ships for almost a week, Favian heard a knock on his door as he was trying to decide whether he ought to eat dinner, for his stomach's sake, or try to fast the ache away. Calvin Davis, Favian's steward, opened the door, spoke in low tones with whoever had knocked, and then came aft alone, carrying a folded piece of paper. "Mr. Hibbert, sir," Davis said. "He said he didn't wish to interrupt your meal, but asked if I would give you this."

"Thank you," Favian said, surprised. He unfolded the paper and read:

19 April 1813.

To Whom It May Concern:
We, the officers of the United States brig of war Ex-

periment, wish it to be known that we approve and support the decision of Master Commandant Favian Markham, U.S.N., to Pursue the enemy West Indies convoy to the Narrow Seas of England, and are fully willing to bear our share of the responsibility for any outcome in which the decision may result.

> Peter Hibbert, *lieutenant*
> Alferd Bean, *master*
> Thomas Tolbert,
> James Dudley,
> Homer Brook, Jr.,
> Phillip Stanhope, *midshipmen*

Favian sat on his chair, feeling the brig creak around him, gratitude flooding him. Hibbert had understood the agony of his decision, the arguments he had mustered for both plunging ahead and turning back, and he'd understood that the decision had been made alone. He had wanted to show his loyalty and support. Favian felt an astonishing thankfulness. The letter had made him realize just how alone he had been.

Experiment had been made into a war vessel, a brig and its complement united in their purposes. Favian knew that it had not all come from him—that the support given by his officers, of which this letter was an example, had done its part. Favian swore he would never forget the part the others had played.

He thanked Hibbert the next morning, as *Experiment* swam through a dark mist, the rising sun a warming white glow ahead. "You're most welcome, sir," Hibbert said. "We're all grateful for the opportunities you've given us."

And then the lookouts were calling, at least two voices raised. "Deck thar! Land ho! Sails ho! Land off the larb'd beam! Sail dead ahead! Sail three points off the starboard bow!"

The land sighted was the treacherous, jagged rocks of the Scilly Isles, ten miles to the north. The sails sighted were English, and enemy.

Experiment had entered the Narrow Seas.

Eight days later, Favian stood on the quarterdeck fighting his exhaustion, as he strained his senses to the utmost trying to penetrate the clinging fog that surrounded *Experiment*. Over his head the big new main topsail flapped listlessly, then bellied out with a new gusting wind. He heard nothing but the sound of the sails, the low moan of wind through the rigging, the rush and splash of water beneath the brig's keel. Somewhere in the fog, probably hove to, were dozens of British ships. Probably some were warships, sent to hunt him down. And hidden by the mist, off the larboard bow or beam, were the Goodwin Sands, treacherous and shifting, which had been the death of many good ships and the Channel pilots they had carried. *Experiment* had no Channel pilots; a good lookout was all they could hope for.

In a way, the mist was a godsend. The Straits of Dover were narrow, and easily closed by British cruisers. If the mist lasted, and if *Experiment* didn't run aground somewhere in the unfamiliar waters, the fog could prove to be the slow, unhandy brig's salvation.

During its first day in the Narrow Seas *Experiment* had taken three British vessels: a brig, an hermaphrodite brig, and a full-rigged ship. Two luggers had made their escape. The three prizes were burned after their crews had been taken off.

Favian's viper flag, the Markham rattlesnake on its scarlet background, had flown over its first victims. The papers of the ship-rigged merchant showed that she'd been a part of the West Indies convoy, which had broken up the

day before. With her burned the hundred thousand pounds'
worth of sugar in her hold.

Favian thanked Providence for his privateering family;
he'd spent his youth in Portsmouth hearing tales of privateering, strategies used to lure merchant ships within reach,
tactics for avoiding enemy warships and escorts. The first
night in the Channel, *Experiment* had slipped into the shelter of a headland near Saint Austell Bay. The prisoners—
the eighty British sailor men and officers who had been
herded like sheep onto *Experiment*'s spar deck because
there was no longer room for them below—were put ashore
just before dawn, to make their own way to the nearest
town. As the sun rose in the east, *Experiment* had stormed
out from beneath the sheltering headland and caught five
sails within sight. Three were captured and set alight; the
others got away.

The hands, after a certain amount of gloom at seeing the
first prizes going up in flames, began to get into the spirit
of destruction. Obviously prizes could not be sailed all the
way back to the United States, to be condemned by a prize
court and sold; there was no money to be made here. But
still, the burning vessels made a fine sight—sheets of flame
roaring up the masts, flinging themselves aloft like shreds
of torn sailcloth in a storm; and the disbelieving, astonished
attitudes of the prisoners were gratifying: What, an American cruiser *in the Channel*? Besides, it was not unusual for
Congress to vote compensation for prize money lost in the
line of duty; and they had head money to look forward to,
twenty-five dollars per prisoner, shared out among the
crew.

But no sooner had *Experiment*'s complement resigned
themselves to no prize money than their forgotten hopes
were granted: The second night they'd hidden again near
Start Point and once more came storming out at dawn,
finding a startled post office packet a mere quarter-mile
from their hiding place. The packet had just left Torbay
with the mail and fifteen thousand pounds' worth of silver
coin, destined for paying Admiral Warren's squadron at
Halifax. The mail had been thrown overboard during the
capture, but the silver was transferred to a locker in Favian's cabin and a marine guard placed on the door. The

packet was burned by sailors made cheerful by the thought of money in their pockets.

For two days *Experiment* cruised between Start Point and the Bill of Portland, capturing five vessels in addition to the packet. The final night the blue-gray, crumbling cliffs of Lyme Bay glowed red with the light of merchant masts turned to torches. For the next two days *Experiment* swung farther out into the Channel, for Favian intended to avoid the great British naval base, shipyard, and fortress of Portsmouth, and Portsmouth's telegraph, which gave it instant communication with the Admiralty. Yet he came closer to the British shore at night, close enough to take a collier, which, when burned, sent flames skyrocketing hundreds of feet into the blackness, illuminating the sea for miles around. By its light Favian found another prize, a coastal lugger with a cargo of brandy smuggled from France, which Favian did not harm, but rather used to transport his mob of prisoners to liberty.

The next dawn *Experiment* appeared off Seaford Bay and took a coasting vessel at first light. Through his long glass Favian could see an alarm signal, a flag and two balls, hoisted above Seaford, and repeated at Beachy Head; but none of this stopped him from taking and burning a ship trying to slip out of the bay, and then sailing right into Cuckmere Haven to burn three prizes at anchor, with the battery thundering away for the better part of an hour. Here *Experiment* took its first casualty. The fire from the three-gun battery was almost completely ineffective, but one shot passed between the masts and, without damaging the brig or its rigging in any way, neatly beheaded Daniel Ferris, able seaman, on watch at the masthead. As the *Experiment* left the vicinity of Seaford, the Channel was seen to be full of sail scurrying away from the danger signal at Beachy Head, and no other prizes were caught.

The following day *Experiment* was completely becalmed, which was not to be expected in the Channel in May, and her complement discovered themselves ten miles southwest of Dungeness, with a big ship-rigged vessel four or five miles away, floating over her slack-sailed reflection. Favian put half his men into the boats, armed them to the teeth, and sent them for the enemy under Hibbert's com-

mand; a few hours later he was rewarded by the sight of a
plume of dense smoke rising from the becalmed merchantman. Hibbert, his face smudged with ash, returned with his
weary oarsmen a few hours later—he'd let the crew of the
captured ship row for England in their own boats—and
grimly handed Favian a captured newspaper dated just the
day before.

The prisoners Favian had put ashore had talked to the
authorities; this was no surprise. But they'd delivered a surprisingly coherent and perfectly accurate assessment of *Experiment*'s size, force, and crew, along with a description of
Favian, referred to as a "gangling descendant of John Paul
Jones and other American buccaneers." This amusing description was made alarming by an official announcement
of the Admiralty to the effect that no less than seven British men-of-war, including "frigates of twenty-eight guns or
greater," were being sent to scour the Channel from one
end to the other.

It was time, Favian decided, to run for it. *Experiment*
had burned eighteen British vessels, worth anywhere from
one-and-a-half to two million pounds, and had diverted
seven warships from their normal course of duty. It was
time to think about their own survival. *Experiment* lay becalmed on the rolling Channel, within easy sight of any
telescopes atop Dungeness, and with a burning ship just a
few miles away, calling the attention of any cruising warship to the spot.

Favian paced along the decks, wincing at the pain from
his stomach that had been nagging him, off and on, for the
last week and a half, and wondered which way to turn. He
doubted very much the safety of sailing back the way he'd
come, along the length of the English Channel: The enemy
would close off his path of retreat first thing. And yet the
Straits of Dover, to the eastward, were narrow, and easily
closed off by any one of those seven warships; and furthermore, if he ran that way, he'd have to return to the United
States by sailing clear around Great Britain, like the Armada, and possibly meeting the Armada's fate. Perhaps he
should head for the safety of a French port.

Favian looked over his crewmen, the men who were listlessly draped over the decks, leaning against the hammock

nettings, the bulwarks, the carronade slides. They had been granted only a few hours' sleep these last eight days; *Experiment* had been burning merchantmen day and night. The hands were nearing exhaustion, particularly those who had been forced to row with Hibbert's boarding party those long sea miles. They were in no condition to continue.

And what of *Experiment*'s captain? The days and nights he'd spent in the Channel were looked back on through a haze of fatigue; he'd barely eaten, snatching a bite on deck or a cup of coffee, and his treacherous digestion was growling its warnings and stabbing him with pain. He had turned into his bunk for only a few hours altogether, and turned in all standing, without removing his clothes, in case he was called. He knew he was not alert. Perhaps a few weeks rest in Calais or Boulogne was what they all needed.

With his mind still undecided he saw, in the late afternoon, the cat's-paws rippling the water to the south, an offshore wind from France. Mentally Favian sighed; with a southerly wind there was no way of making a French port. The sails began to roar, then the wind died and they fell silent. The yards were braced around to catch the next gust. When the wind blew, it blew cold, and brought the fog through which *Experiment* crept the next night, ears and eyes strained for sight or sound of the Goodwin Sands or cruising British warships.

Favian spent another night without sleep. His collar turned up to keep an irregular drizzle from the back of his neck, he slammed a hand down on the lee rail, hoping the sting of pain would force alertness. It did not. Even his dyspepsia seemed to have given in to weariness. The watch on deck murmured in low tones forward. There was a sudden clatter as something was dropped onto a carronade.

"Silence there!" he barked. A seaman bent forward to retrieve something—a knife?—from the deck. Favian rubbed his eyes and regretted his outburst of temper; there was no reason to have lashed out like that. In the fog, in the narrow and restricted waters, everyone was on a short fuse.

Then in the silence Favian detected something, a rushing sound or distant hiss, and suddenly he found himself wide awake, the weariness gone completely. He stared out into the blackness. What was it? A phantom of sound, he told himself, an illusion; yet he could sense something out in the fog, a presence. He cupped his ears, leaning over the rail into the blackness. The sound of water rushing beneath another ship's strakes?

And suddenly something came out of the fog, a giant jibboom appearing not three hundred yards away. Favian stared in fascinated horror at the figurehead beneath the bowsprit, some kind of mythological figure bearing a sword and heraldic shield, with great entrapping wings spread wide. The hull of the ship was black and enormous, with a wide yellow stripe running down its length of black-painted gun ports—the "Nelson checker." The air rang with the cries of a dozen lookouts from both vessels and the rattle of a drum from the enemy frigate.

She missed *Experiment* by fifty yards and vanished astern into the fog, on a diverging course. The brig's men were leaping to their stations, casting off the lashings on the guns, bosuns' pipes whistling down the hatches. Did I call them to quarters? Favian wondered, still staring into the fog where the enemy had vanished. Or is it something they're doing on their own? Perhaps Hibbert had given the order, or Bean. In any case *Experiment*'s trumpeter was soon blasting away to make it official, but Favian angrily hushed him. "Not a sound, men!" he called. "Clear, but quietly! Helmsman, alter course three points to larboard." That would bring them nearer the Goodwin Sands—if the Goodwins were in fact out there and not past an hour ago—but it would at least be farther away from the enemy frigate.

"Shake out the main-t'gallant." The order was given quietly and performed by men in silent bare feet, running up the dripping shrouds onto the footropes. It would probably be a mile—at least a mile, probably more—before the enemy frigate could wear around and begin a hunt through the fog, and the altered course would put more distance between them. Favian could only hope that the fog would not clear before *Experiment* was sailing free in the North Sea.

There was no more trace of the enemy. The wind quick-

ened at dawn, veering southwesterly, but the fog held; and
Favian breathed easier when he realized that there was
nothing but the North Sea under his lee, and that he was
well past the bottleneck of the Straits of Dover. He was
further cheered when he reflected that a southerly wind,
followed by a southwesterly breeze, was a perfect opportunity for French privateers to leave their havens and plunder the Channel, and that the seven British warships sent
to hunt *Experiment* might well have their hands full without troubling themselves about an escaping American brig.

"Foggy as it is, sir, it's the best weather I've seen on any
recent morning," Hibbert said, as he came up on deck with
his watch. Favian nodded.

"Take her northeasterly into open water," he said. "Just
give us plenty of sea room."

"Where shall we go from here, sir?" Hibbert asked. His
red-rimmed eyes were frankly curious. It was a little impertinent to ask such a question of one's captain, but
Favian knew he owed Hibbert an honest answer.

"Norway, I think. She's allied with France, and will be
pleased to see us, no doubt. But first we'll pay another few
visits to the English coast."

"Very good, sir." Hibbert smiled wearily.

"But for now we can rest. Just take her out of sight of
land. Once we've been free of pursuit for a few days, we
can pick our landfall and be certain of surprise."

For two days *Experiment* cruised out of sight of land,
without meeting another vessel or seeing sign of pursuit.
Then she returned to England with a vengeance. They
stood in with the land and cruised from Norfolk to the
mouth of the Humber, taking thirteen vessels in four days,
mostly two-hundred-ton colliers from out of the Tyne, craft
employed on the crowded, busy run from Newcastle to
supply the chimneys and gasworks of London. *Experiment*
would have caught more—sometimes there were fifty in
sight at one time—but that the colliers' masters, crafty men
who knew the waters better than the palms of their black-
nailed hands, would run close inshore among the sand-
banks and traps as soon as they knew the brig for an enemy, and *Experiment*, without a pilot, dared not follow.

The colliers' masters, once taken, were a pitiful sight; they'd beg for their ships, two actually going down on their knees and weeping. The run from the Tyne to London was considered so safe that most of the owners carried no insurance, bearing the risk themselves; their fortunes went up in flames with their ships.

Then *Experiment* ran out to sea again, beating into a northwesterly near-gale, salt spray rocketing over the weather bow. Favian, as he threw off his spray-drenched coat and hat before staggering to his cot, intended to go out of sight of land for another two or three days and then reappear, perhaps at Scarborough, off which Paul Jones had captured the *Serapis* back in 1781.

It seemed as if Favian had barely closed his eyes when Davis, his steward, was calling him: "Sail in sight, sir. To leeward. Mr. Hibbert sends his compliments and begs you come on deck."

Favian sat up, his head swimming, and groped for the coat that Davis had already opened for him. He inserted his arms, took his hat, and heard three bells strike. It had been half an hour since he'd gone below; he must have had some sleep after all.

Hibbert stood waiting, his face grave. He carried a long glass tucked under his arm. "A brig, sir," he said. "Came out of a squall about ten minues ago. Looks like a man-of-war, sir."

Favian felt the cold wind clear his head. He took the long glass and peered out to leeward, seeing topgallants and royals appearing over the crests of the waves. "Seven or eight miles, we think, sir," Hibbert said. "She's cracking on all sail to get to us."

"Keep her on this tack," Favian said. "I'll go aloft." He slung the long glass around his neck by its strap and stepped to the weather shrouds.

"Afternoon, Cap'n," the lookout said cheerfully as Favian hauled himself up to the main crosstrees. Favian grunted a reply, unslung the telescope, and put it to his eye. The masthead swung dizzily; Favian had difficulty keeping the glass on its target. A war vessel, with those smartly cut sails, almost certainly. A brig trying to claw upwind toward *Experiment*. Succeeding at the moment because she was carrying more canvas. The brig seemed very small at this distance, the black sliver of the hull occasionally buried, it seemed, by the surge of the sea.

"Seems about our size, Cap'n," the lookout said. Favian looked down at *Experiment*, at the eighty-five-foot hull surrounded by foam. Clear for action? Engage the enemy? It was what Stephen Decatur would do, what most of the captains in the young Navy would do without hesitation. Favian knew his men were good at the guns, could be counted on to fire steadily and accurately, if not swiftly. He had the weather gage, the advantage of maneuver. The battle would be swift: The introduction of the carronade, its heavy ball capable of rending a small vessel to bits, had radically altered warfare as far as brigs and schooners were concerned. Now such battles were short and bloody, like the fights between *Wasp* and *Frolic* the year before, or *Hornet* and *Peacock* early in 1813, and there was a high rate of casualties among the officers.

But for two weeks he and his men had been laboring almost without rest, capturing and burning thirty-one enemy vessels. Their drill had suffered, and all needed rest. No, Favian decided, there would be no engagement today. *Experiment* would run, then return to burn more enemy merchant ships, striking England in its pocketbook and making the underwriters at Lloyd's scream for protection. Even if *Experiment* won the battle, the American brig would still be in a hostile sea, possible damaged. They'd have to end the plundering expedition and run for the nearest friendly port.

Favian gave the long glass to the lookout and without a word came hand over hand down a backstay. As his feet touched the deck, he saw Hibbert's eyes on him and felt the expectant stares of the men. He saw the trumpeter standing nearby, his knuckles white as he gripped his instrument, ready to respond to the order to clear for action.

"Shake a reef out of the tops'ls, and set the t'gallants," Favian said quietly. "Run up the fore-topmast stays'l. I think setting any other stays'ls will give us too much heel, and we'll lose leeway in the long run. Set the catharpings so we can brace her up sharp—we'll hug the wind."

"Aye aye, sir." Hibbert's tone was flat, without expression, neither approval nor dismay. A brig's lieutenant, of course, stood no great chance of promotion unless his vessel won a fight. Favian could feel the wave of disappointment striking *Experiment*'s complement; there was a lack of enthusiasm in the petty officers' voices as they drove the men aloft. An American war vessel running from a fight with an equal. It had not yet happened in this war. "Pass the word for Mr. Tolbert," Favian said.

The short, stocky midshipman's face was sullen as he received the order to go aloft, take the long glass from the lookout, and keep the enemy brig under observation. "Yes, sir," he said, but his tone of voice might as well have proclaimed "Coward!"

Experiment came farther into the wind, the sails roaring as they filled and drew. The other brig continued to overhaul, but at a slower rate. Favian calculated that the enemy would fail to close the distance before sunset, and then *Experiment* could alter course and vanish into the night.

"Deck there! She's hoisted her colors, sir!" Tolbert called from the masthead. "Blue Ensign!" The midshipmen, of course, would be spoiling for a fight.

"Very well, Mr. Tolbert!" Favian returned. He put his chilled hands into his pockets. The men moved about the deck slowly, resentfully, deprived of the battle they'd been hungering for.

"Deck there! I can count her gun ports! Six this side!" Tolbert called.

Twelve guns altogether, Favian thought. Perhaps two more in the bridle ports, but even so she had two less than *Experiment*. *Experiment* would have a critical edge in any kind of fight. He could feel the hands' eyes on him again, hoping for the decision to throw up the helm and destroy the weaker vessel. For a moment Favian flirted with the idea. The battle would be quick, probably crushing. Perhaps *Experiment* could get away without any major damage.

But then he remembered the fight between *Wasp* and *Frolic* the year before. The American *Wasp* had shot the British *Frolic* to bits in a short, vicious action, killing or wounding ninety out of the enemy brig's hundred and seven men; but the American sloop had been cut to pieces aloft and was unable to run when, a few hours later, the British seventy-four-gun ship of the line *Poictiers* appeared and captured both the United States ship and its prize. Even a crushing victory could be Pyrrhic, this far from home.

Favian said nothing. Gradually he felt the hands turn away. Perhaps they felt embarrassment for him, a captain standing on his quarterdeck and quietly displaying his timidity before his entire crew.

The sun descended very slowly. "She's fired a gun to windward, sir!" Tolbert cried. "A challenge to battle!"

The Fates were not being merciful. "We shall make no reply, gentlemen," Favian said. He seemed very alone on the weather quarterdeck; the hands were supposed to show a proper deference by respecting the captain's privilege, but now it seemed less respect than avoidance. The sun finally descended behind the western horizon; night was falling rapidly.

Refusing to engage an enemy vessel of equal size, Favian thought: That was breaking the code with a vengeance. All his life he had lived under the shadow of the impetuous Decatur—as a midshipman off Tripoli, as a lieutenant in Decatur's gunboat squadron, and then aboard *United States*.

Decatur would have fought, of course. At least he could congratulate himself on breaking that particular leash. He found himself clenching and unclenching the arm that had been paralyzed just before the raid on Tripoli harbor, as if to prove to himself that it wasn't fear this time that had paralyzed him. He stuffed the hand into a pocket. No time to be remembering such things.

"We'll tack," Favian said. "Ready about!"

As he turned to give the orders, he saw Phillip Stanhope reluctantly leave the lee rail where he had been watching the British brig fade into the evening. Stanhope's face showed its usual blend of intelligent interest, without the sullen resentment of the other midshipmen. Perhaps, Favian thought, here was one who understood.

They went about while there was still enough light for the enemy to see the maneuver. The enemy tacked promptly, thinking, perhaps, what Favian wanted them to think: that the American brig had been impatient to run and had altered course while the enemy could still see it. Favian was perfectly willing that they should think it. An hour later, in pitch blackness with no moon and with scud whipping over the surface of the heaving sea, *Experiment* tacked again and sped into the North Sea. There were too many British warships about, Favian decided. *Experiment* could use a rest; she was short of water, and after a journey across the Atlantic much of her gear could stand an overhaul.

Four days later *Experiment* made her landfall off Norway, finding no British men-of-war. Off the craggy coast, she signaled for a pilot to take them into Bergen.

9.

Bergen was a tired city. Perhaps in normal times it would have been beautiful: built on a promontory, the buildings rising from the water's edge in tiers, dominated by the steeples of the cathedral and the Church of St. Mary, protected by the massive walls and threatening guns of the Bergenhus fortress. The weathered buildings had once been painted in gay colors, but they had faded; and as soon as *Experiment* cleared quarantine and warped into Vaagen, the inner harbor, Favian could see that Norway had been at war for a very long time.

Many of the inhabitants looked half-starved, and the pilot who had brought them into Vaagen informed Favian in his clear, London-accented English that the crops had failed the year before, and the British blockade had stopped the large shipments of grain upon which the health of the nation depended. There had been some attempt to decorate the town, Favian noticed, and the Danish royal ensign was flying from rooftops and hanging from windows; the pilot informed him that a royal personage—Favian didn't catch the name—was visiting the town, having smuggled himself from Denmark through the British blockade. But the gay bunting and colorful flags seemed only to accentuate the lifelessness of the town, Favian thought, and he wondered if this was what American port cities would look like a few years hence, when the British blockade had tightened and driven commerce from the seas. At least 80 percent of trade in the United States, he calculated, depended on deep-water or coastal shipping, and once that shipping was stopped, the entire American

economy would grind to a catastrophic halt, as bad as the
embargo or worse.

Experiment had been flying United States colors ever
since she'd been within sight of the Danish batteries guard-
ing the coast, and as the brig came into the inner harbor
Favian saw the stares of the inhabitants, both on the
wharves and aboard the ships riding at their bouys. Probably no United States vessel had visited Bergen since the
delaration of war the year before.

"By God, sir, look at that!" Favian heard Hibbert exclaim. "Those merchantmen there—they're flying the British flag! And they're lying next to that eight-gun privateer,
and those Danish gunboats!"

Favian took Hibbert's glass and confirmed it. With Denmark and Norway at war with Britain, there was clearly
something odd in British merchants sitting peacefully in
Vaagen, flying their own flag. There was very obviously
something complicated happening; Favian wondered if *Experiment*'s presence would make it more complicated.

Experiment had not been riding to its buoy for more
than fifteen minutes when a boat flying the Danish naval
ensign over its stern sheets came sculling toward them. A
Danish lieutenant came aboard, received the salute offered
him, and handed Favian a message. It was written in English, and in a clear, elegant hand.

> To His Excellency, Captain of the United States brig
> Experiment:
>
> His Royal Highness Prince Christian Frederick of
> Christiansborg, statholder in Norway, requests the
> honour of the attendance of Your Excellency and
> Your Excellency's officers this evening, at a dinner
> and ball at the Haakonshallen Palace, at seven.
>
> Peter Anker
> Secretary to the Prince Royal

"Good God," Favian thought. He asked the Danish lieutenant to his cabin for a cup of wine while he wrote out a
reply, in the meantime wondering just who the devil Prince

Christian Frederick was, and just exactly what a statholder might be. It would be impolitic, to say the least, to ask the Danish lieutenant, who was probably a member of His Royal Highness's household and capable of being offended by the question. Favian gave his reply to the lieutenant, saw him off, and passed the word for Hibbert.

Hibbert knocked, entered, and saluted; Favian offered him a seat and a cup of wine, and Hibbert thanked Favian civilly, his eyes hooded. Hibbert had been distant since the incident with the British brig, but not outwardly hostile. Possibly, Favian thought, Hibbert was simply thankful the decision had not been his. As the man who stood between the captain and the rest of the ship's company, some of the anger felt by the brig's complement was bound to rub off on him, and he would not have been human had he not resented it.

But of course there was no way to speak to Hibbert about the shadow that had fallen between them. They had worked well together until the British brig came from the squall, but they had not been close friends, they had not been on genuinely intimate terms. Favian, should he deign to speak of the crew's attitude toward him, would be divesting himself of too much of his captain's dignity—the hands' attitude toward the captain did not, as far as the Navy was concerned, matter in the least, so long as they did their duty—and Hibbert, if his captain chose to become intimate about such a matter, would be within his rights to resent it, for he might interpret the gesture as the captain trying to recruit him for a silent war against the crew.

No, Favian thought, there was no way to even approach, let alone solve, the problem between them, without solving it for the rest of the brig's complement as well. Hibbert was torn in many directions, and Favian sympathized: If he had taken it into his head to believe Favian a coward, or if resented the lost opportunity for glory and almost certain promotion, he nevertheless was obliged to Favian for being employed at all, and may thus have concluded that he owed Favian dutiful, if not enthusiastic, loyalty. No way of telling, of course; Hibbert might simply be doing his best to be civil to someone he despised.

"Mr. Hibbert," Favian said, after a pause, "we have re-

ceived a formal invitation to a dinner and ball this evening,
given by His Highness Prince Christian Frederick," Hibbert's face registered surprise. "I am informed," Favian
continued, "that His Royal Highness is the statholder of
Norway."

"I see, sir," Hibbert said carefully.

"Do you happen to know," Favian said, "who Prince
Christian Frederick may be, and what on earth a statholder
is?"

Hibbert's face showed a dismayed ignorance. "I have no
idea, sir."

"Prince Christian Frederick of—" Favian referred to the
invitation—"of Christiansborg?"

"Sorry, sir."

"I think, Mr. Hibbert, we should pool our ignorance
about Norway, and see if we can sort this matter out."

"Of course, sir."

Together they assembled an outline. Norway, as well as
Iceland, the Faröes, and Greenland, was a part of the kingdom of Denmark, as Pomerania and Finland had been a
part of the kingdom of Sweden until very recently. Both
Sweden and Denmark had been anxious to remain neutral
in the struggle between France and her enemies, but had
found themselves drawn into war on several separate occasions. In 1800 the two countries had been forced to join
forces with France and the mad Russian tsar, Paul, and the
result had been the Battle of Copenhagen, with a British
squadron under Hyde Parker and Horatio Nelson crushing
Danish naval power and driving Denmark out of the coali-
tion—which, due to the assassination of the tsar by his own
bodyguard, was short-lived in any case.

Denmark had thereafter attempted to maintain its neutrality, but had found the pressure to join one side or the
other intense. While Frederick, the Danish crown prince,
head of the government since the king had gone mad years
before, tried to make up his mind which way to jump, the
British government in 1807 made his decision for him by
attacking Copenhagen again with overwhelming ground
and naval forces, bombarding the town with rockets and
setting it afire, causing enormous civilian casualties and
seizing what amounted to the entire Danish navy in port.

Since then Denmark had been at war with England. The vital Baltic convoys upon which England depended for its pitch, turpentine, pine (for its navy's masts), and other vital northern products had been subjected to a constant attack by Danish gunboats and privateers as they threaded their way through the Great Belt and the Skagerrak. In return the British had subjected Denmark and Norway to blockade and brought much of their trade to a halt. Denmark was therefore fighting England at the same time as the United States was, though due to the cautious diplomacy of President Madison—who realized that an alliance with any of Bonaparte's allies meant war with Bonaparte's other enemies, such as Russia—the United States was in no formal alliance with any of the continental powers.

This complicated situation was made even more incomprehensible by the situation in Sweden. His former Swedish Majesty Gustavus IV had been subject to a kind of religious mania in which he considered Bonaparte the Antichrist, and had pitted his weak northern kingdom in an undying and unwinnable war against France. During this enmity Tsar Alexander, successor to the mad Paul, who had briefly been in alliance with France, had invaded Swedish Finland in 1808 and annexed it. Gustavus had been overthrown by his own subjects and replaced by a Danish prince; Hibbert remembered his name as being either Charles Augustus or Christian Augustus, but couldn't be certain. The newspapers, Favian recalled, had been full of the possibilities of Sweden uniting with Denmark-Norway in a kingdom of Scandinavia, just possibly strong enough to maintain neutrality in the face of Russian and British pressure. But Charles (or Christian) had died just after assuming power, effectively ending the dreams of those who had wanted to see Scandinavia united.

The Swedes chose as their new crown prince a French general named Bernadotte, one of Napoleon's marshals, who had ascended the throne as Charles John. After the French had occupied Swedish Pomerania prior to their invasion of Russian, Charles John had, surprisingly, taken Sweden out of the French alliance, and he was known to be negotiating with the Russians, presumably with the object of placing Sweden in alliance against France and

Denmark-Norway. Perhaps Charles John was eager to annex Norway as a replacement for Swedish Pomerania and Finland.

None of this gave Favian or Hibbert any notion of who Prince Christian Frederick might be, or just what a statholder was, but it served somewhat to clarify their hazy notion of Scandinavian politics. "No wonder all those kings went mad, sir, trying to sort out this kind of nonsense," Hibbert said. "Just think—the kings of England, Sweden, and Denmark, *plus* the tsar of all the Russians, all mad as loons at the same time!"

"They've all been replaced by now, at least," Favian said. "England's under a regency, and the rest are dead or out of power. I assume that whoever Prince Christian Frederick might be, he's at least sane. In any case, I'm sending you ashore to find out. We could use new cordage—you know how much—and fresh food for the crew, if there is any in this half-starved country. Do some discreet inquiring with the chandlers and anyone else you meet."

Hibbert stolidly tried to conceal his dismay. "Aye aye, sir."

"Call in the young gentlemen as you leave. I'll see if any of them can enlighten us."

As Hibbert left the cabin, Favian felt a breath of relief. They had just demonstrated that they could work closely together, if need be, regardless of the tension between them. It was nothing like open comradeship, but it would serve.

Experiment's four midshipmen, lined up in Favian's cabin, presented chiefly a picture of glowering hostility and contempt, with Stanhope, as usual, the exception, standing with intelligent dignity at the junior end of the line. Dudley and Brook, Favian saw, seemed to be taking their cue from Tolbert, the senior, a boy whom Favian had already marked as virtually certain never to pass the board of examiners unless somehow provided with the questions ahead of time—and even then he would have to be lucky. Yet Tolbert was the only one among them to have been in action, even if the action was a minor scrape with a Baratarian privateer a year ago; and the others looked to him to set the tone.

Favian did not ask them to sit.

"You young gentlemen will be pleased to know that we have been invited this evening to a dinner and ball given by Prince Christian Frederick, statholder of Norway," Favian informed them. "Can any of you gentlemen tell me who Prince Christian Frederick might be, or what a statholder is?"

There was a moment of silence, then a chorused "No, sir."

"Your ignorance is formidable, gentlemen, but nonetheless expected," Favian said, enjoying his conscious hypocrisy. "Mr. Hibbert shall enlighten you before we leave. What is more to the point is whether any of you can dance the waltz, which I gather is de rigueur in these parts."

"Er—I do, sir," Stanhope said. Silence from the others.

"Very well, Mr. Stanhope. That will save me the tedious duty of instructing you myself. Mr. Stanhope, you will teach these young gentlemen how to waltz. Let the ship's drummer give you the beat. Your instruction will take no less than a full hour; you will dance with each gentleman in turn. I shall be on deck later to observe your progress. It is perhaps needless for me to say that any gentleman whose dancing is a disgrace to this vessel will not be allowed to attend the ball. Gentlemen, you are dismissed."

This, Favian thought as they filed sullenly, and resentfully, from the cabin, will not increase my popularity with the midshipmen. "Disgrace to this vessel!" one of them exploded as soon as the door was closed. "I'll tell you who's a disgrace to this vessel!" The speaker was earnestly shushed by his fellows before he committed a court-martial offense, but from the thunder of their feet on the companion Favian knew that the name, if unspoken, was known to all. Favian sighed. It was not necessarily his job to cultivate the admiration of the midshipmen, but it was regrettable that they should have chosen to manifest their contempt so clearly. This was on the verge of mutiny; if one of them should choose to step over the boundary, Favian would have to act, with disrating or a whipping or, if the offense was grave enough, a full court-martial, with the offender in irons for the long journey back to the United States. And little good would come of a court-martial, either; the fact that *Experiment* had run from an enemy brig would be widely publicized within the service; and although the court-martial would no doubt support Favian, his reputation would be clouded.

Perhaps it deserved to be clouded, Favian found himself thinking blackly; perhaps he had simply been finding excuses for a decision made at the behest of fear. Again he found himself thinking of that long line of Markham ancestors stretching back into New England history: Had he failed them? Malachi Markham, that impetuous Revolutionary privateer, would have engaged without hesitation and won another of his spectacular victories. Malachi would have attacked even if there had been two enemy brigs. And if Malachi had been one of *Experiment*'s midshipmen, there would have been no concealing his contempt for anyone who failed to measure up to his standards.

He realized he was clenching the hand that had been paralyzed off Tripoli. He forced his fingers to open, worked them again, wondering if that secret paralysis on the eve of the raid would ever recur, staggering him at some critical moment, as he stood on the quarterdeck making decisions that would commit his vessel to battle, or fighting hand to hand in some melee.

Pipes whistled on deck, and Favian heard the echo of a challenge and reply: Hibbert returning from his mission on shore. Favian worked his fingers, feeling strongly the need for wine. There was a knock on his cabin door, and Favian stood. "Come in."

Hibbert's face was glowing; he was so bursting with information that he failed altogether to maintain the hooded distance he'd achieved the last few days. "I think I've managed to discover what we'll need to know," he said. He sat down, at Favian's invitation, and stowed his undress hat under the chair.

"I spoke to one of the customs agents," he said, "and two ship chandlers. They speak English remarkably well, which is understandable since this town survives on trade with the English, even though Norway is at war with them."

"I gathered that from the British shipping in the harbor."

"Aye. The inhabitants know how to make compromises. The British need Norwegian pine and pitch to keep their fleet in being, and Norway needs grain to survive, because even when there's a good harvest they can't feed themselves. The trade is done legally, under license. British ships leave the licensed merchantmen alone, allowing them through the blockade, and British privateers are instructed to do likewise. Bergen isn't even blockaded most of the time, because almost all their trade is with England."

"It will be useful, I think, for us to know that Bergen has an interest in keeping the British happy," Favian said.

"Aye. It will also be useful for us to know that Prince Christian Frederick of Christiansborg is the grandson of Frederick, the king of Denmark, and his current heir. They call him the prince royal, not the crown prince.

"The prince royal has been in Norway only a few months," Hibbert went on. "He was smuggled across the Skagerrak in the face of the British blockade, and made his appearance at Christiania, the capital, to take control of the government and hold Norway for the Danish crown. That's what a statholder is, I guess, though no one I spoke to could tell me what specifically it means. At least he commands the army and naval forces."

"That's fine, Mr. Hibbert," Favian said, relief flooding his mind. "We won't be expected to know the details." The Danish royal heir. The problems of dealing with court etiquette were minor compared with what could have happened had his entire party entered the royal presence without knowing whom they were addressing.

"There's more news, sir," Hibbert said. "A few weeks ago Sweden declared war on France and Denmark."

"So soon?" Favian was startled. "Bernadotte must have got all the assurances he needed from the tsar and the British."

Hibbert agreed. Favian called for Davis and ordered wine. Hibbert continued. "The prince royal seems to be a popular man. He is young, dashing, and a good orator. Opinion seems divided, however, as to whether the job he was sent here to accomplish is worth doing."

"There are people belonging to the Swedish party here?" Favian asked.

Hibbert hesitated. "I'm afraid it doesn't seem to be quite as clear-cut as all that, sir," he said. "Christian Frederick was sent to hold Norway for Denmark. It isn't going to be an easy task, as those British merchantmen in the harbor might tell you. There are those who seem prepared to give Norway to the Swedes, as you said—one of the ship chandlers was of this opinion, sir—he said it would be good for business. The customs agent I spoke to said there was considerable feeling—and I gather he was sympathetic to this view—that Norway should be independent from both Denmark and Sweden, with Christian Frederick as its king. That doesn't seem to make sense to me, sir."

"No," Favian said. "Not with Christian Frederick as Denmark's heir. Norway might separate now, but as soon as the prince royal inherits, Norway and Denmark will have the same king again. And it seems a little foolish to think that Norway can declare its independence while under attack from Sweden, England's ally, and dependent on British grain."

"Yes, sir."

The wine arrived, and Davis poured them each a cup. "The customs agent spoke of a minority," Hibbert continued. "Damned anarchists, he called them, who think that Norway should be independent and a republic without a king."

"I see. How does the prince royal fit into all this?"

"No one seems to know, sir," Hibbert said. "He seems to be sympathetic to Norwegian aspirations, but he also seems content to continue as the Danish representative. I'd guess he's waiting to see which way the wind blows, sir."

"I see. Thank you, Mr. Hibbert. You have performed splendidly. I think I should inspect the young gentlemen in their dance lessons."

Hibbert grinned. "I saw them, dancin' away to the beat of a drum," he said. "They looked quite unhappy about it, sir."

"The ball tonight will be full dress, of course," Favian said, standing. "That will mean white knee breeches and silk stockings. Pass the word to the young gentlemen."

Hibbert's face fell. "I—I have trousers only, sir," he said. "I didn't plan on attending any fancy dress balls this voyage."

Favian frowned. "And your legs are too short to borrow mine," he said. "Ah, well, we'll just have to wear plain republican trousers—blue trousers, I think. If they call us revolutionaries we'll just have to bear it. I hope you have a cocked hat?"

"Aye, sir, thank you. Sorry about the britches." Hibbert brightened. "At least I know how to waltz."

"Very good," Favian said. Above their heads they could hear the beat of a drum, thumping in waltz time, and the shuffle of the midshipmen's feet. As he preceded Hibbert from the cabin, Favian felt a growing satisfaction. *Experiment* might not be the grandest vessel in the United States Navy, but she was, by God, the only one in Norway, and Favian intended she should represent her country by making up in smartness what she lacked in grandeur.

10.

Experiment's watch officer, Gable, the acting bosun, barked an ill-tempered command, and the quartermaster hastened to invert the glass and strike three bells. Favian assembled his shore party on the quarterdeck to inspect them before leaving the brig. He was himself in full dress, substituting the trousers for the knee breeches, and was wearing his epaulet for the first time since leaving Portsmouth. It weighed heavily on his right shoulder, reminding him of the fact that he'd never encountered royalty before, that he was responsible for the conduct of his party of six while ashore, and that at least three of the six gave every indication of despising him for a coward.

At least he had no right to be ashamed of his own appearance. He had carefully combed forward the fashionable spit curls on his cheeks and temples; the four buttons on his cuffs that marked his rank gleamed with a soft golden aura; he was wearing the ornamented presentation sword given him by the City of New York. The gold tapes on his collar had been brushed, and his boots reflected the masts and the sky.

Favian was relieved to find that his inspection detected little that was wrong. Though the midshipmen probably loathed him, and resented fiercely being made to practice the waltz on deck in full view of the smirking hands and any telescopes from the town, they at least had made an effort to present a creditable appearance. Their buttons shone, their dirk scabbards had been polished, their shoes were bright with polish—although, Favian thought, a little more diligent attention to them during the course of the voyage might have resulted in a somewhat better reflection.

"White gloves," Favian said, and five pairs of kid gloves appeared from pockets.

"Very good. You will return the gloves to your pockets and put them on as we enter the hall. There will be no tobacco chewing tonight; I gather Europeans consider the custom barbaric. Mr. Hibbert, have the boat's crew stand by."

The pull to the water gate of the Haakonshallen was short; crammed into the stern sheets with his lieutenant and four midshipmen, wrapped in a boat cloak to keep spray from his uniform, Favian found himself enduring the stiff silence of the midshipmen and the sharp elbow of the coxswain, rammed into his ribs. He was pleased to find the journey at its end.

Their route led past giant fortifications, the Bergenhus, studded with embrasures and heavy guns. The fortress was large and well designed, its guns positioned to sweep the harbor; but Favian saw that the soldiers manning the walls were thin and dressed in tattered red coats, and that the guns were old and probably should have been replaced years ago. The Danish royal authority in Norway was clearly in decline, and he wondered whether the prince royal could possibly hope to alter the course of decay.

At the Haakonshallen's water gate they were met by the naval lieutenant who had brought Favian the invitation. The lieutenant saluted; Favian and the others uncovered in reply.

"Lieutenant Sverdrup, isn't it?"

"Yes, thank you, Captain Markham. This way, please."

Haakonshallen was an old, dirty palace, but managed to retain a certain weathered majesty; Danish flags flew above its roof, and well-dressed guards presented arms at the door. A string orchestra was tuning inside. Favian ostentatiously donned his white gloves, and was imitated by his party. Following Sverdrup, he came to the great hall, was announced in sepulchral tones by a uniformed major-domo, and was shortly thereafter introduced to Christian Frederick, Prince Royal of the Kingdom of Denmark-Norway.

The prince was standing, not seated; his reception line was more like Mr. Madison's than Favian would have expected at, say, the Court of St. James's. Christian Frederick was young, a few years younger than Favian, and well favored, with his dark hair combed forward in spit curls on his temples and dangling in romantic locks down his brow; his nose was long and aquiline, his eyes clear, his expression cheerful. He wore an elaborate uniform, with stars, ribbons, and giant epaulets upon which were embroidered three six-pointed stars. Evidently he was accustomed to keep some state, for in contrast to the ragged appearance of the Bergenhus garrison the company surrounding the prince was dressed to the hilt, as elaborately as he was, and the women glittered with jewels, some wearing stars. Favian was relieved to see that at least two of the prince's company were wearing trousers.

"I am happy to make your acquaintance, sir," the prince said, with an easy smile and schoolboy English.

"The honor is mine, Your Highness. May I present my lieutenant, Mr. Hibbert, and the midshipmen, Mr. Tolbert, Mr. Dudley, Mr. Brook, and Mr. Stanhope?"

"Pleased to make your acquaintance, gentlemen," the prince said. "Mr. Sverdrup, if you will be so good as to show the American gentlemen the admittedly limited attractions of Haakonshallen, I will speak with the captain." Hibbert and the midshipmen accepted this dismissal with grace and (Favian suspected) considerable relief; they bowed, and allowed Sverdrup to steer them in the direction of the punch bowl.

"Captain Markham, please allow me to present Count and Lady Lindenow, Count Gram, Miss Anita Courtois, Mr. Peter Anker, and Dr. Berg. Captain Markham, of the United States brig *Experiment*."

"Honored, gentlemen and ladies," Favian said, trying feverishly to remember their names and somehow keep them all straight in his head. Count Lindenow was the thin, stately man in his fifties with the iron-gray side-whiskers, dignified and a little supercilious, with a wife both thinner and taller than he was. Count Gram was younger, though by no means young, reddish haired and red faced, with his bull neck about to burst the collar of his uniform, and long, obviously powerful arms. Peter Anker was the prince's age, sharing his cheerfulness, dressed in a neat civilian coat, and apparently permitted to wear trousers in the royal presence. Dr. Berg was uniformed, bemedaled, and bore a sword, so Favian assumed he was a surgeon in the Danish armed forces; he was later to discover that this was how Scandinavia dressed its university professors, and wondered whether the swords were necessary to keep discipline in the classroom.

Miss Anita Courtois was, fortunately, unforgettable. She was tall, as tall as Anne Markham or taller, with short-clipped, curling blond hair, and a stunningly developed figure, hidden rather unsuccessfully by a white, high-waisted muslin gown, that made Favian suddenly aware that he had not had a woman since leaving Zenobia in Washington, four months before. Her voice, responding to the prince's introduction, was low, and showed that despite her French name her accent remained Norwegian—or perhaps Danish; Favian was not certain of the difference.

There were more introductions: military men and their ladies, of whom the men at least could be addressed as "sir," simplifying Favian's task of memorization. There was a Captain Beyer, who had the look of a successful privateer—the same weather-beaten, confident, vaguely insolent manner Favian knew from his own family and from other Revolutionary privateers. "I must excuse myself for the present, Captain Markham," the prince said. "I hope Dr. Berg will keep you amused. Dr. Berg, please find the captain a glass of punch."

"Thank you, Your Royal Highness," Favian said. Christian Frederick stepped into an adjoining room with Count Gram, and Dr. Berg—who wore trousers in addition to his military-looking uniform—escorted Favian to the punch bowl. Favian, glancing over the room, noted that there were spittoons placed in strategic locations: Apparently tobacco chewing was as fashionable here as it was in the United States. His shore party were separated, speaking to several different military (usually naval) figures in different areas of the room. No one seemed to be embarrassing himself or the United States of America. The string orchestra—twelve elderly men wearing long tailcoats and wigs;

mostly strings with a hammerklavier and a flute—began to play; it was a lively tune, not meant for dancing but for stimulating digestion.

"Count Gram is a man of influence," Dr. Berg said in a clipped brand of English, offering Favian a cup of punch as Favian sampled pickled herring. "His influence is felt throughout Bergen and the vicinity. His Highness will have much to discuss. Not very profitably, I fear."

Favian sipped his punch, finding his throat warmed by an unfamiliar tang. Berg must have seen his curious look, for he spoke: "Schnapps, I think. It's a sad state, but in our blockaded country we can offer you little else."

"It's very interesting," Favian said, taking another sip. He glanced behind him, seeing no one obviously listening to their conversation. "Why, sir," he asked, "did you say the discussions may not be profitable? With Count Gram, I mean."

Berg adjusted his spectacles. "I believe Count Gram's allegiance to the throne may be, shall we say, less well founded than his military reputation. He may believe that the Danish allegiance may be a greater handicap to Norway than that of . . . other powers. He also owns property in Sweden."

"I see," Favian said neutrally, listening while keeping the cup to his lips, his eyes darting about the room.

"His Highness will try to remind Count Gram of his obligations," Berg said. He looked at Favian significantly. "You may be able to help, Captain Markham."

Favian tried to conceal his surprise. "I, sir?" he asked. "I fail to see how."

"The very presence of your vessel is a reminder that Denmark has powerful friends," Berg said. "Bonaparte's star may be covered at the moment by clouds, but it is by no means eclipsed. It will shine forth again. The United States is engaged with England on the other side of the Atlantic; the British will soon be overtaxed. If your brig can cooperate with Danish naval forces, perhaps the blockade of the Baltic can be broken once and for all."

All this with a *brig*? Favian thought. "Your country," he said carefully, "has many vessels the size of mine, and larger. Your men are brave, your captains skilled, but the blockade is not broken."

"If our people could be assured that your vessel is but the first of many, they may take new heart," Berg said. "They may pay less attention to Count Gram and his ilk." His eyes looked unblinkingly at Favian from behind his steel spectacles.

"Sir, I have no authorization from my government to make such assurances," Favian said. The conversation was taking an alarming turn. Dr. Berg apparently looked at Favian as an emissary, and possibly a savior, from abroad, his presence to be used as another prop for Denmark's shaky rule in Norway. Berg was grasping at straws; the situation must be desperate here. Favian wondered what Berg would say if he knew *Experiment* was here entirely by accident, without authorization from the Navy Department—that the Navy Department, in fact, thought the brig was cruising North American waters, supposing, of course, it bothered to think about the brig at all.

Berg's eyes cut toward an approaching female form. "Careful now," he hissed, sounding like a stage conspirator. "Miss Courtois is a friend of Count Gram—please do not let her know of what we have been speaking."

Favian nodded, comprehending with effort the Dane's tortured syntax. "As you wish, sir."

Anita Courtois wore no ribbon or star, but diamonds glittered on her many rings, from silver pendants dangling from her ears. She walked on her low-heeled slippers as if she took pleasure in the act of others watching her walk.

"I hope, gentlemen, your talk is not political," she said as they bowed to her. "I have heard nothing but politics for weeks—the Swedish position, the Norwegian people, the view of the English government . . . all phantoms, warring with one another for the hearts of every man in the room."

"Would you care for some punch, miss?" Favian asked. She gave a sly, amused smile and assented.

"I can see that the viewpoint of the American Cabinet was being discussed," she said, "I can't seem to escape it. I feel as if I'm being neglected for politics."

"It is a political time, miss," Berg said stiffly.

"It has been a political time for twenty years," Anita Courtois replied, "and one would think any reasonable people would have tired of it by now. Come, Captain," she said, putting her arm through Favian's. "Let us walk, and speak of things other than the political aspirations of uninteresting people."

"If you like, miss," Favian said, allowing himself to be steered away. She leaned close to his ear and spoke with a lowered voice.

"Aren't you happy I took you away from that tedious man?" she asked, a low chuckle in her voice. "In another few moments he'd be asking you to make speeches assuring the Norwegian people that a convoy of grains and guns will be on their way from the United States."

Favian smiled. The hit was close enough. "You must enlighten me, Miss Courtois," he said. "I must confess I find myself a bit over my head here in Norway. My ignorance of local matters is matched only by my desire to learn."

"So that you can take part in those tiresome discussions?" she said. "I will not assist you, sir."

"Could you at least give me an indication of who Dr. Berg might be, and his relationship to the prince?"

"Ah, that is easy," she said, strolling toward a buffet table. "Dr. Berg is one of the Prince's creatures. He is a Norwegian, but has spent most of his life in Denmark, and owes the prince his entire loyalty. The same is true of that equally tedious Peter Anker."

"And Count Lindenow?"

"A Norwegian through and through," she said. "Have some of this fish on black bread."

"Thank you. You were speaking of Count Lindenow."

She looked at him with a certain exasperation. "His loyalty is to Norway, not to any king. He is a man of great honesty and influence." Favian nibbled at his black bread. Anita Courtois shrugged, then sighed. "I'll tell you the rest without your having to ask," she said finally. "Count Gram is a rich man who wants the war over with so he can make money in peace. He fought bravely in the war with Sweden twenty-five years ago, and has chopped up a number of men in duels for one silly reason or another. He hates Lindenow with a passion. Are you satisfied?"

"Not until you tell me about the prince royal," Favian said. That fish was vile. He put on a brave face and swallowed it.

"His Highness has brought a style to Norway which has been lacking for years, and for that I'm grateful. I'm not competent to judge the rest. Are you happy now? Would you like some more fish?"

"Thank you, no. You're a most fruitful source of information; I won't try your patience by asking for more. Except, of course, about the most interesting person in the room."

"I have told you all you are going to hear. For the rest of the evening, sir, I am a sphinx."

"I am referring to yourself."

She laughed. "Ah, no, no! Now you must answer my questions. Is it true that Red Indians cut out the hearts of their enemies and eat them?"

"I believe some did. That group is, I think, peaceful now. You must understand that there are at least as many tribes of Red Indians as there are principalities in Germany, and they all have different customs."

"That orchestra is playing very well this evening. These old stone walls provide interesting echoes, interesting effects. They used to be hung with carpets so that spies could hide behind them, and listen to the nobility plotting."

"As in *Hamlet*. I understand."

She halted, handed him an empty cup. "King Claudius would find himself very much at home here," she remarked. "My cup is empty, alas. Would you refill it? I confess that I've grown fond of schnapps."

"Certainly." He took the cup to the punch bowl and refilled it. Berg had gone, but Captain Beyer, the man Favian had marked as a privateer, stood by the bowl in consultation with one of his naval colleagues.

"With the Courtois, eh?" Beyer said, turning to Favian and giving him an insolent wink. "Careful does it, Captain. You're running onto shoal water there."

"Thank you, sir," Favian said formally. "I trust I have done nothing I shall regret."

"Not yet, you haven't," Beyer said, with another inti-

mate wink, and laughed into his cup of punch. Favian saw
he was missing a front tooth.

"Sir," Favian said, and bowed. He returned to Anita
Courtois and handed her the cup.

"Thank you, sir," she said, and smiled. "Here is the
prince and Count Gram—now I shall have to listen to politics all night."

Favian turned to see the two leaving the anteroom. The
prince did not appear displeased, but he seemed somehow
vaguely troubled, as if from indigestion, or as if he were
exploring a newly chipped tooth with his tongue. Count
Gram frowned as he came forth, scanning the company
until he saw Anita Courtois standing with Favian, whereupon his frown deepened and he strode across the room to
them.

"Anita," he said, taking her arm. "Captain Marley."

"Markham," she said with a smile. "His name is Markham."

"You will excuse us, please," Gram said, as if he hadn't
heard. "We are to go to dinner. Come with me."

Anita Courtois flashed Gram a look of exasperation, but
she obeyed, smiling as Favian bowed farewell. Straightening,
he glanced about the room to make certain none of his
charges were engaged in mischief, then reflected, as his
eyes lit upon Captain Beyer, that perhaps he had just run
onto one of the shoals surrounding the interesting Anita
Courtois. The dinner gong boomed.

Dinner was served in another chamber, on a long table
whose legs bore the graceful non-Euclidean curves of naval
architecture, and which Favian knew without a doubt had
been constructed by ship's carpenters. There were two gal-
leries. One was for the orchestra, which had to leave its
hammerklavier behind; even so, the space was so crowded
that several players were leaning over the gallery in order
to have room to bow. Another was for the common people,
who were traditionally allowed in most European courts to
watch the king eat, a custom that Favian was relieved to
discover was no longer followed. As he sat down to a royal
banquet, the last thing he wanted was to be stared at by the
half-starved inhabitants of Bergen.

The orchestra tuned, then began to play; Favian thought he recognized Carl Philipp Emanuel Bach. Favian, without great seniority, was seated halfway down the table, and had been asked to escort a Miss Margarette Tank, daughter of a local merchant. Miss Tank was young, graceful, and comely, but spoke no English; their conversation was limited to French, which she did not speak well, and soon languished. She soon began speaking animatedly in Norwegian to the man seated across the table from her. Seated on Favian's other hand was the formidable wife of one of the fort's artillery officers, who spoke only Danish and German, neither of which Favian understood. The meal was entirely of fish—fish grilled, fish stewed, fish pickled and broiled and sometimes raw, served with bread (black, white, and hard) and a choice of wine or cider. The party ran out of white bread halfway through the meal: Apparently the shortage of grain was extremely serious if the statholder's court was reduced to eating brown bread.

Counts Lindenow and Gram sat near the prince, at the head of the table; Favian could see that the prince seemed to monopolize the conversation, speaking cheerfully to both parties, who answered in monosyllables. Gram scowled; Lindenow kept his face carefully neutral; and Anita Courtois and Lady Lindenow tried their best to look interested.

It was the usual formal feast, complete with the usual toasts. The prince, in English, offered the health of Mr. Madison; Favian, in French, led a toast to His Danish Majesty Frederick. There were no toasts drunk to Bonaparte. Favian became aware, halfway through his meal, of the hungry stares of ragged soldiers standing guard outside the windows, and then remembered his boat's crew waiting in the cold night. He called a servant and sent his men a bottle of schnapps with his compliments.

After the dinner Favian found himself summoned by Peter Anker to the prince's side. After Favian's bow, and his untruthful compliments about the food, Christian Frederick led him from the chamber, the entire company standing as the prince rose, filing out whether finished with their meal or not.

The prince led Favian away from the Haakonshallen palace, into the Bergenhus fortress, and onto the ramparts overlooking the harbor, where *Experiment*, with the Stars and Stripes gleaming faintly at its peak, swung at its buoy in the fading light. They were alone, except for Anker and Berg, who loitered within hailing distance.

"Your ship, Captain Markham, has given rise to much speculation in town," Christian Frederick said. "My most difficult task here in Norway will be to prepare its defenses against the British. Your arrival has shown that we are not alone in the fight."

"Your Highness does me too much honor," Favian said, knowing better than to correct a prince who called a brig a ship. "The *Experiment* is small, and can do little to ease the British blockade."

"Captain Markham, I would like to visit your ship," the prince said with a smile. He propped his leg familiarly on a gun carriage, looking out through the casement.

"Of course, Your Highness. When would it please you to do so?"

"Tomorrow, if this is possible."

"Of course it is possible, Your Highness," Favian said calmly, while his mind secretly ran in panicked, shrieking circles. "Would you honor us with your presence for supper?" Favian mentally categorized what would be necessary for a royal visit: The brig must be full dressed, with flags from every halyard—he would have to find some Danish ensigns, and royal ensigns if possible; there was going to have to be a salute; fresh food would have to be found ashore, at any price; the brig's band would somehow have to acquire some practice. . . .

"I will be pleased to attend," the prince said. Favian suddenly realized that throughout the evening Christian Frederick had avoided using the royal "we." Or was that the privilege of kings?

"Shall we say noon?" the prince asked.

"Very well, Your Highness," Favian said calmly, trying to conceal his horror. He had said "supper" in hopes the prince would at least give him the afternoon to prepare. "How many," Favian asked, "may we expect in Your Highness's entourage?"

"Oh, three or four," the prince said airily.

"Very well, Your Highness."

Christian Frederick looked down at the gun he was resting his foot on, and his long face assumed an expression of curiosity. "What sort of gun is this, Captain Markham?" he asked.

"I believe it is a forty-two-pounder, Your Highness," he said.

"How far can it shoot?" the prince asked, staring abstractedly out into the harbor.

Favian hid his surprise at the odd turn of the conversation and answered. "At extreme elevation, perhaps three thousand yards."

"I suppose there is no great accuracy at that range?"

"No, there is not, Your Highness."

The prince looked seriously down at the gun, then took his foot off the carriage and stood erect, his hands in his pockets. On his face there was an expression of benign uncertainty.

"I do not have a military education, as my grandfather does," he said. "I am still learning. I must depend on the men I brought with me, to plan our campaign against the British. But I try to learn."

"I am sure Your Highness has competent instructors."

The prince seemed petulant. "My instructors have seen few battlefields," he said, "and fewer victories. You have yourself smelt the powder?"

"Yes, Your Highness. I fought in Tripoli, and I was lieutenant on the *United States* last year when we took a British frigate."

Christian Frederick looked sharply at Favian from beneath his sculptured brows, then nodded. "You have been victorious, then. Tell me, why have you and your ship come to Europe?"

"We were following a West Indian convoy, Your Highness," Favian said. "They avoided us, but since then we have taken over thirty enemy vessels in the Channel and the North Sea. We came into Bergen for rest and provision." There; he'd said it. He had not come to save Norway for the Danish crown, if ever that had been anyone's serious opinion.

The prince nodded. From the palace came the sound of

the string orchestra tuning. "I remember the first British attack on Copenhagen, under Nelson," he said. "I was about fifteen years old. There was a lot of smoke. I remember Danish ships burning, and the way the cannonballs skipped over the water, leaving a trail of white splashes in the sea. Afterwards I remember the boats coming back to the city, carrying dead men. We fought bravely, but we lost."

"The British have lost Nelson, sir," Favian said. "They can be beaten, even at sea."

"I don't want to see those boats again, with the dead men lying in their bottoms," Christian Frederick said, his eyes hooded and sorrowful. "To spare that I would do much." He sighed. "But it is my fate to be a leader, fighting the British."

"Yes, sir. It is our duty," Favian said. He had seen this before—men wrapped in their own tortured thoughts, trying to convince themselves of something. He wondered if Christian Frederick was trying to convince himself to fight or to surrender.

The string orchestra ceased its tuning. From Bergen came the sounds of bells ringing the hour. Favian saw a uniformed equerry walking from the palace toward them.

"That one will be reminding me that the ball cannot commence without me," the prince said, attempting a smile. "I have duties other than those of state, you understand."

"Yes, Your Highness."

The Prince called to Anker and Berg and walked with Favian toward the palace. They passed a squad of soldiers, dressed in their tattered red coats, coming out to relieve the guard. The squad grounded their muskets, then presented arms as the prince walked past; he acknowledged the salute with a wave, and looked after the half-starved soldiers with sorrow.

"They are brave, but we cannot find uniforms for them, and it's hard to find enough to feed them," he said. "What can I hope to accomplish with such men?"

"George Washington could not feed or clothe his troops," Favian said, "and he was able to defeat the British. It took a long time, but we achieved our independence in the end."

The prince did not seem to be cheered. "But there was a lot of killing," he said. "In a long war there is a lot of killing."

They entered the palace and walked to the ballroom. The prince took as his partner the daughter of one of the local gentry, whose father beamed proudly from the side of the hall as she and the prince royal led the cotillion. Favian found himself partnered with—good Lord—Miss Tank, who fortunately proved to be a far better dancer than linguist. Favian found himself thoroughly grateful for the instruction in dance given him by St. Croix, his father's friend and body servant, who had been a dancing master in France before some scandal connected with his employer's daughters had forced him into the service of an American patriot smuggler and subsequent privateer. Favian's limbs were too long to be truly graceful, but he knew the forms well, and had always enjoyed dancing; St. Croix's instruction had included dancing with a sword, so he avoided tripping himself or his partner, or lashing spectators with the scabbard, as several other guests—including Lieutenant Sverdrup and Captain Beyer—seemed to do regularly.

The moment came to exchange partners, and Favian found himself bowing to Anita Courtois. "You're doing very well for a seaman, Captain," she smiled. "I'll save you the second waltz." She made a face. "I must give the first to Count Gram, and he'll tread all over my toes. The fashion demands slippers for women and heavy boots for men—so unfair!"

"I'll look forward, miss," Favian said, occupied with being obliged to caper about her in a wide circle. There was a crash: Captain Beyer had tripped over his own sword and taken a dive for the floor. He seemed to have overindulged in punch and wine, and there was difficulty resurrecting him. The orchestra ignored the incident, and so, eventually, did the dancers.

The cotillion wore on. Favian exchanged partners again, finding himself with Miss Tank; the ladies performed a challenging little jig that gave the men a chance to admire their ankles—whoever it was the prince royal had picked as a partner, she was setting a daring and vigorous example for the other ladies to follow. Partners were exchanged once more.

"Your dancing is remarkably graceful, Miss Courtois," Favian said.

"Thank you," she said, without false modesty. "I was born to dance, I think. Your dancing is very nice," she said gaily, "but a little by the book. . . . I see you and His Highness were speaking alone by the battlements."

"We were speaking of customs in the United States Navy," Favian said. "I should think you would have been bored."

"So should I, my friend. Count Gram asked me to inquire, so I have. I have executed my spying mission faithfully."

"If a little indiscreetly, don't you think?" Favian asked. "Spies aren't supposed to mention their mission to the people they're spying on."

"Indiscretion," she said with a private smile, "has always been my chief weakness."

"You may rely on me not to report any little follies," Favian said. The dancers swirled, and Favian returned to Miss Tank, who curtseyed becomingly. Her color was high and her smile radiant; she was obviously having the time of her life. Favian glanced about: Miss Courtois was back with Count Gram, who was staring at his own feet with a pursed, fierce expression, as if he were willing them not to stumble.

The cotillion came to a flourishing ending and was followed by another line dance, something resembling a Virginia reel, in which Favian was partnered by a stranger whose name—something complicated and guttural—he was unable to absorb, but who was introduced to him by her former partner, Peter Hibbert, who probably mangled the name anyway. There followed the first waltz; the prince and most of the older folk sat out the rather scandalous dance, and Favian stopped by the punch bowl for refreshment. He watched Count Gram and his partner swirling across the floor; Miss Courtois had not exaggerated the count's lack of grace on the dance floor, but as far as Favian could see, she avoided having her feet trodden on through her own suppleness and agility. Favian began to see that it would be a pleasure to dance with her.

At the beginning of the next waltz Favian stepped across the floor, bowed to Gram and Anita Courtois, and announced that he believed she had engaged this dance with him. "If you will excuse us, sir?" he said, and took Anita in his arms, congratulating himself on a neat cutting-out operation performed beneath enemy guns.

She was a splendid dancer, as light and effortless in his arms as a breath of sea air, making him feel a better dancer than he was. He caught a glimpse of Count Gram's scowling, rufous face through the crowd, and found himself smiling down at her.

"Is Count Gram jealous of me?" he asked. "Or just of my dancing?"

"You will find him jealous of many things," she said, her tone indicating indifference. "Jealous of Lindenow's influence, the prince's popularity, Bonaparte's military reputation—oh, yes!" she said seriously, "jealous even of Bonaparte! That is how the prince royal should win him—offer him a chance to command, to become the Napoleon of the North."

"Should I tell this to the prince?" Favian asked.

"I do not care what you tell the prince." Midshipman Dudley whirled past with one of the local girls in his arms. He seemed to be enjoying himself, and Favian wondered if he was still resenting his afternoon's dancing lessons.

A week ago, he thought, he was trying to lose himself and his British pursuers in the North Sea, and contemplating his descent on the Hull colliers. Just that morning he had been concerned with little but warping his brig into the inner harbor, and hoping to give himself and his men a rest. And now he had met Denmark's prince royal, whom he was hosting in an intimate dinner aboard his brig the next day; he had found himself involved with Scandinavian politics, and was waltzing with the most beautiful woman at the ball. If he had been granted time to think about it, he would have been dazzled.

The dance whirled on. Favian whirled with it, his thoughts floating away on a vague haze of pulse and

rhythm, movement and swirling color. "What, no politics?"
Anita Courtois laughed. "Don't you want to ask me about
the other people here, whether they support Sweden or
Denmark or Norway?"

"I don't," he said, and found, to his surprise, that he was
telling the truth.

"Could it be, Captain, that you are enjoying yourself?"

"I am," he said simply. But her words reminded him
again that he commanded a small vessel in an alien, half-
starved, blockaded land, an ocean away from any safe harbor, and with officers and men who despised him for a
coward.

"But you are not enjoying yourself now," Anita said,
frowning. "What did I say?"

"You reminded me, Miss Courtois," he said, smiling to
reassure her, "that I must face tomorrow."

"You need not face it tonight. Come, let me help you
forget it again." But at that moment the waltz ended, and
Favian felt a rough hand on his shoulder.

"Pardon me, Captain. This dance is mine." Count Gram,
of course.

"My lord . . . Miss Courtois," Favian said, and bowed.
He went in search of Miss Tank for the third waltz, and
found her. At the dance's end, Gram and Miss Courtois
bowed farewell to the prince royal and called for their carriage.

Favian realized that despite the dancing and the roaring
flames in the fireplace, the ballroom was quite cold. A cup
of punch warmed him. The prince royal and Count Lindenow were gone; presumably they were conferring in an
anteroom. Favian saw Hibbert's uniform, plain and utili-
tarian in comparison to the other uniforms present, and
made his way toward it.

"Tolbert and Brook are half seas over, I'm afraid," Hibbert reported. "I've got Dudley walking them around the
courtyard outside until they're sober. Apparently they
didn't know better than to mix wine and schnapps."

"It's probably time to leave in any case," Favian said.
"We've got to be up early. Prince Christian Frederick and
his entourage will be dining aboard *Experiment* tomorrow
at noon."

"My God!" Hibbert's look was one of pure horror. "And we just in from a month at sea!"

"*Experiment* will be full dressed for the occasion," Favian said. "I'll have to send you ashore to find something suitable to feed the royal party—I doubt any of them will be used to hardtack and salt beef. You'll also have to see how many Danish flags you can find. It's too late to freshen most of the trim—we don't want His Highness getting paint on his royal breeches. But we can at least get most of the chafing gear down from aloft and harbor-furl the sails."

"Aye, sir," Hibbert said. "How many will be in the party?"

"Assume half a dozen. Ah, there's the prince. Send Stanhope to collect the other midshipmen, and we'll say our adieus."

"Aye aye, sir."

While Favian waited for the return of his party, the prince lingered arm in arm with Count Lindenow until the music came to an end; and then several equerries began to call for the crowd's attention. Christian Frederick stood on the orchestra leader's box and made a long oration, in which Favian could recognize few words but *Denmark, Norway, Great Britain,* and *Lindenow.* However much the contents of the speech escaped him, Favian did recognize a brilliant orator when he heard one; the cadences of the prince's speech were spellbinding, and the words repeated, echoed one another, and assembled themselves in battalions that marched, almost visibly, over the prince's audience. Christian Frederick's pauses were dramatic; at first they were filled with polite applause, but by the end of his address the audience was wild with enthusiasm, some cheering at the top of their lungs, everyone applauding madly.

The prince royal stepped down, handing his platform to Count Lindenow, who gave a low, polite-sounding address that everyone strained to hear. After Lindenow exited to applause, the prince spoke for a few more minutes and left the audience on their feet and shouting as before. At the conclusion of the second speech, the orchestra conductor returned to his box and led the orchestra in what Favian assumed was the Danish national anthem. He straightened himself to attention.

As the orchestra played, Favian became aware that *Experiment*'s midshipmen had filed in behind him. He waited for the end of the hymn, and as the orchestra struck up another waltz, Favian turned to speak to them. Tolbert and Brook were still more or less drunk, Brook leaning against Dudley for support.

"Mr. Hibbert and I shall be taking our leave of the prince," Favian said, realizing at once that he was not about to parade *Experiment*'s drunken mids in front of a royal personage. "You will get your hats and cloaks and wait at the water gate for us. Preserve the state of your uniforms; the prince royal will visit *Experiment* tomorrow, and I want you all presentable. Mr. Dudley, Mr. Stanhope, I depend on you to make certain that these gentlemen do not embarrass themselves on the way. Dismissed."

"Aye aye, sir," the midshipmen mumbled, and began their unsteady way to the door.

"Can't say as I blame them, sir," Hibbert said sympathetically. "None of 'em have ever been across an ocean before. It's not surprising they'd want to celebrate."

"Let them celebrate in the accustomed waterfront dives, and be robbed like gentlemen," Favian scowled. "Not at royal receptions. Let's say our farewells."

There was a long line in front of the prince, who was standing with Count and Lady Lindenow. The crowd was in an enthusiastic mood; Lindenow's hand was being pumped by every man in the house. Apparently he had done something spectacular. Favian found himself standing in front of Captain Beyer, and made a point of staying out of the range of the captain's scabbard. "What was the speech about, sir?" he asked.

"Patriotic horse shit," Beyer enunciated succinctly. "But Lindenow has agreed to raise a battalion at his own expense, for the defense of Norway. If he can find guns, uniforms, and food for them. It's a good thing for Norway, though. It's a pity there are so few like Lindenow."

"I see," Favian said. The significance of Lindenow's raising a battalion for Norway, and not for Denmark, was not lost on him.

"What Norway needs," Beyer said, "is more nobles like Lindenow, more privateers like me, and fewer kings like Christian Frederick and his granddaddy. No kings at all. A republic is what we need."

Favian remained politically silent. Beyer spat tobacco juice onto the floor, dribbling a bit onto his waistcoat. He leered. "I forgot," he said. "And more women like Anita Courtois, bless her."

"The United States could use a few of those, by Jove!" Hibbert enthused. Favian let Hibbert and Beyer compare notes on women they had each known. They crept closer to the royal presence, Favian being careful to step out of the way of the occasional pools of tobacco juice Beyer trailed behind him.

"Your Highness," Favian said, bowing to the prince royal when he finally got the chance. "We regret we must take our leave. We thank you for the invitation; it has been delightful."

"Must you leave?" the prince asked. He mopped sweat from his forehead with his handkerchief; the oration had warmed him as it warmed the crowd. "We will speak tomorrow, Captain. I think we have a great deal to talk about."

"I am at Your Highness's disposal," Favian said. He bowed again, then bowed to Count Lindenow. "My congratulations, sir," he said.

"Thank you," the count said, dignified, and Favian, with Hibbert following, left the hall.

In the courtyard outside there was a pool of vomit, which Favian devoutly hoped had not been left as a souvenir by one of his midshipmen. He found the boat's crew warm from their bottle of schnapps, and warm with their thanks; Stanhope and Dudley sat in the boat's bow, and Tolbert and Brook sat in the stern sheets. They looked sullen; perhaps they'd been waiting for a long time.

The boat set off from the water gate and rowed on the slack tide toward *Experiment*. The lights of Haakonshallen glowed softly behind them, and Favian saw that a bank of fog was slowly rolling in from the sea. It was very still. Favian found himself thinking of Anita Courtois—her scent, the way her agile body moved in his arms. . . .

Church bells tolled the hour. It was a pity he'd never see her again.

"Boat ahoy!"

"*Experiment!*" bellowed the coxswain close by Favian's ear. Even before the challenge was answered, Favian heard the sound of feet drumming the deck, the calls of the officers.

"Toss oars! Careful with that line there!" The coxswain's voice grated in Favian's ear. The boat thudded against *Experiment*'s side, and Favian stood, throwing his cloak out of the way, and went up the brig's side like a long-legged spider as Gable's pipes wailed an official welcome.

Gable stood by the entry port, his hat raised in salute. Favian uncovered to the quarterdeck and to Gable—and then saw the bruise under Gable's eye, and felt the pleasant dream that had been the evening evaporate beneath the onslaught of deadly reality.

"Regret to report, sir," Gable said, speaking mush-mouthed through swollen lips, "a breach of the brig's discipline."

"Report to me in my cabin in five minutes," Favian said, feeling the weight of that new golden epaulet pressing him down like some inevitable, unavoidable burden.

11.

It would be the first flogging Favian had ever ordered. There was no dispute about the facts, no excuse for the parties involved. Shortly after the boat party had left for Haakonshallen, Acting Bosun Gable had ordered Abraham Sedgwick, able seaman, to go aloft to overhaul the starboard inner main topsail buntline, which order Sedgwick had answered in a surly manner. Gable had lashed Sedgwick with his rope's end to get him moving, whereupon Sedgwick had growled an obscenity and blacked Gable's eye. Gable had had much the worse of the ensuing fight, but Sedgwick was eventually overcome by the entire corps of petty officers.

Disrespect, foul language, striking a superior officer, refusal to obey an order, perhaps mutiny. All admitted by Sedgwick. Favian, blinking in the early morning light that was streaming through his little cabin window, closed the book of regulations, John Adams's *Rules for the Regulation of the Navy of the United Colonies of North America, established for Preserving their Rights and Defending their Liberties, and for Encouraging all those who Feel for their Country, to enter into its Service in that way which they can be most Useful*, passed by Congress in 1799 and 1800, never amended. Old John Adams had based his concept of discipline on the British Articles of War, and the flogging penalty was clearly specified.

Well, time to get on with it. Sedgwick had been given the customary night in which to reflect on his crimes, and Favian would not prolong his wait. Favian groped in the halflight, found his dress coat, and shrugged into it; he took his hat and made his way out of the cabin. Hibbert was on

deck, as was Alferd Bean, both in dress uniform; they
knew there was going to be punishment and waited for the
inevitable, not relishing it, but knowing they would have to
be there.

Favian's breath frosted white in the blue morning. Overhead there were still many stars; eastward the sky had begun to lighten, Venus hanging above the dark bulk of the
mountainous land. Hibbert and Bean uncovered to him,
murmuring quiet "good morning"s. Favian took a breath.

"Let's get it over with," he said. "Then get *Experiment*
ready for the prince royal. Hands on deck to witness punishment."

Pipes whistled down hatchways. *Experiment*'s overlarge
crew, crowded forward of the mainmast, was an amor-
phous mass of shadows; the men's faces were obscured by
dark and by hat brims, their murmuring voices were indis-
tinct. The marines marched up in coats that matched the
deep blue of the sky, and grounded arms. The sound of
their fixing bayonets rattled unmistakably over the deck. In
theory Favian was supposed to use these marines to keep
order, firing into the crew if necessary, and unleashing the
bayonets if the hands tried to protest the punishment of one
of their own.

"Mr. Brook, you are not in your dress coat." Hibbert's
voice had detected a flaw in the dim line of midshipmen
on the quarterdeck. "Sedgwick has the right to be flogged
with appropriate ceremony. Go below and dress properly."

"Yes, sir," Brook said, his teeth chattering in the morning cold. There was a long pause while Brook rummaged
below for his coat, then a clump on the deck as Brook
skipped back to his place with a murmured apology.

"Abraham Sedgwick, step forward," Favian called out.
He could see Hibbert breathing onto his chilled hands, and
wished he could do the same.

Sedgwick was a brawny man, almost as tall as Favian,
with a neck like a bull and arms like twisted cables. He was
dressed neatly, in a clean shirt, white trousers, a necker-
chief tied neatly around his muscled throat. It was the custom, when reporting for punishment, to dress in one's best
clothes, so as to make as favorable an impression as possible on the captain. Sedgwick uncovered.

"You are charged with disrespect, foul language, refusing to obey an order, and striking a superior officer," Favian said. "Have you anything to say to the charges?" Favian thought his voice sounded hollow in the dawn. In awarding a flogging, he thought, the captain always acts alone. As first lieutenant he had reported breaches of discipline to Decatur, but it had always been Decatur who awarded the necessary lashes. In spite of the crowded deck, Favian felt very isolated as he awaited Sedgwick's answer.

"No, sir." Sedgwick's eyes fell to the deck. Good, Favian thought. He's not defiant. That will make it easier, flogging a man who accepts it instead of rebelling.

"Two dozen at the capstan, Abraham Sedgwick. Your liquor ration will be stopped for two weeks. Bosun, seize him up."

Favian sensed a stirring among the hands as Sedgwick, without a word, was led away. For the crimes enumerated, the penalty was light. Old Preble would have given two dozen for refusal to obey alone. But Favian was not Preble; he would exact his own style of punishment, and he knew that in part he had given a light sentence because of his own sense of abiding guilt.

A capstan bar was inserted in the capstan, and Sedgwick's arms spread-eagled on it, tied down with spun yarn. Lewell Sprague, *Experiment*'s surgeon's mate, fastened a leather shield about Sedgwick's lower back to protect his kidneys, and a thick leather strap was placed between his teeth to prevent him from biting his tongue.

"Mr. Parker," Favian said. "Commence punishment." Gable, as acting bosun, would normally have performed the punishment himself; but Favian had insisted on one of Gable's mates so that the flogging would not look like he was allowing Gable revenge.

Parker came forward with the cat-o'-nine-tails he'd spent most of the night weaving. Made of knotted cord, it would be thrown overboard after the flogging. Each man so punished was awarded the dubious dignity of having his own cat, which would touch no back but his; it was a ritual developed over generations by the Royal Navy and adopted in its entirety by the United States, even to the red baize bag that held the cat before it was used.

Parker took his position by the capstan and looked toward Favian for instruction. Favian nodded; get it over with. The bosun's mate returned the nod and brought his arm back.

The lash struck with enough force to knock Sedgwick's breath from him. *"One!"* The first blow would have opened cuts; the second would begin the job of tearing the cuts to ribbons. The bosun's mate, taking his time, separated the strands of knotted cord with his fingers, then brought his arm back again. Again Sedgwick's breath was knocked from him with an involuntary grunt. *"Two!"* That one must have hurt, and they wouldn't get better.

As the lashes came down one by one and Sedgwick's back began to be ripped open, Favian knew that he would never have had to order the flogging, that Sedgwick would never have blacked Gable's eye, if, six days ago, he had ordered the helm put up and engaged the British brig.

His men were all volunteers; unlike many of the men on British warships, they had joined of their own accord, wanting to serve their country at sea. They had wanted to strike back against the foreign navy that had pressed them unscrupulously into its service, that had involved them in its wars, that had taken American ships on the high seas and was even now strangling American trade. During the weeks spent crossing the Atlantic, Favian had trained them well; they'd been given a basic competence in the handling of the brig's armament, if not the smooth celerity resulting from months of practice. When Isaac Hull had taken the British *Guerrière*, most of his crew had been at sea just a little over a month; *Experiment*'s men probably knew that.

They knew they could have beaten the enemy brig, and Favian had not allowed it. They were in an ugly mood, resentful of authority, and it was in an ugly mood that Abraham Sedgwick had blacked the bosun's eye. Had Favian not promised them, within minutes after boarding *Experiment* for the first time, "You will not have to wait for an enemy to find us, for *I will seek them out!*"? Was a man, an officer and gentlemen, not to be held accountable for his promises?

"Twenty-four!" The cat-o'-nine-tails, dripping red, was returned to its baize bag. Lewell Sprague inspected Sedg-

wick's back, pronounced him fit to go below, and Sedg-wick's wrists were untied. He straightened. He had not cried out during the punishment, only the involuntary ex-halation when he was struck; his face now, facing the ris-ing dawn, was that of a drugged ox, a creature whose feel-ings are too insensate to react to pain. Why can't he at least feel? Favian thought savagely, wanting to punish him-self as well, feeling himself responsible for this spectacle. Why couldn't he cry out? Sedgwick spat the leather strap from between his teeth and was led below—like a dumb animal, Favian thought, a beast. A beast who knew only that a man had made him a promise, and the promise had been broken, and so he'd struck out. Favian remembered his own insensate behavior aboard *Macedonian*, the cool-ness with which he had viewed the slaughter, and knew that he was no better than Sedgwick, a creature only.

"Dismissed," Favian found himself saying. "Mr. Hib-bert, I'll want this deck clean. We have royalty visiting us at noon."

"Aye aye, sir."

The sound of church bells came tolling from the town. Favian saw the hands' faces, shadowed by the weak sun rising behind them, as he walked toward the companion-way. They were sober, a little resentful, as if they, too, sensed that their captain was as much to blame for the flogging as Sedgwick. The midshipmen fell out of their line, their usual chatter silenced for once. Stanhope looked a little green, and Favian remembered his own first flog-ging, with mad McNeil reading the punishment and the prisoner howling for dear life as the lash came down, and sympathized. Stanhope was learning one of many brutal lessons, and this one more brutal than most. This, too, could teach: Officers were to watch the torture unmoved, must order it when necessary. It was easier, really, than the next lesson, in which the officer had to watch with proper impassivity as fellow human beings were dismembered by roundshot, cut in half by chain shot, disemboweled by can-ister. Stanhope was beginning to learn what the uniform meant.

As Favian returned to his cabin, he heard the officers' voices barking out, the hands sullenly beginning their day.

The pumps would be manned, the decks scrubbed down, the brightwork polished, just as on any other day. By the time the prince royal came aboard, there would be no traces of Sedgwick's blood on the planking.

An hour later Hibbert knocked on Favian's door. Favian had just finished his breakfast, and written a laconic entry into his log: "5:30, punished Able Seaman Abraham Sedgwick with two dozen lashes and two weeks' loss of liquor ration, for striking the bosun. 6:00, washed decks."

Hibbert entered, uncovered, accepted Favian's offer of a chair. He seemed worried.

"I've received a deputation from the midshipmen's berth," he said. "Mr. Dudley has asked my permission to arrange for a duel between himself and Mr. Tolbert."

"Good God!" Hibbert's announcement had truly caught Favian by surprise. He leaned back in his chair to give himself time to recover. "What the devil has brought this about?" he demanded.

Hibbert sighed. "I gather that while we were saying our farewells to the prince last night, Tolbert was vomiting his guts out in the Haakonshallen courtyard." Favian remembered passing the pool of vomit, and nodded. "Dudley—who, you remember, was more or less sober—" Hibbert continued, "called Tolbert a simpleton and a suckling babe who needed a nurse to carry him about on shore. Tolbert resented this and called Dudley a bastard. Mr. Dudley would probably have laughed this off, but as you may know, Jim Dudley *is* a bastard, and sensitive about it—his mother was a laundress in New York, his father is unknown; some uncle or other arranged his midshipman's commission. So Dudley called Tolbert out, and Tolbert accepted."

Favian rubbed his freshly shaven chin. Dueling on his brig. Something else he could probably have prevented by fighting that British man-of-war; the mids would have had their fill of fighting then, and wouldn't have felt the need to prove themselves and their courage once they'd had a battle under their belts.

"And it was Mr. Dudley who made the challenge? The sober one? You're sure?" Favian asked.

Hibbert nodded. Favian steepled his fingertips and scowled. "I assume you've given them a lecture?" he asked.

"Yes, sir. I've informed them that I will not permit officers of the United States Navy to disgrace themselves in a foreign port, and so on—but they asked me to pass their request on to you. It's within their rights, sir," Hibbert conceded, ill at ease. No first lieutenant enjoyed having underlings appealing over his head to the captain.

"You did rightly," Favian said, trying to fix the problem in his mind. If Favian forbade the duel, they could always assert that it was a matter of honor, not under the jurisdiction of their officers anyway, and fight their duel on the sly. And then Favian would be left to account for one or two corpses or badly wounded midshipmen. Of course he could allow the duel, and excuse himself with the dubious-sounding pretext that affairs of honor were none of his business, but that was simply asking for trouble. Or, he thought slyly, he could allow the duel, and somehow arrange things so that no one would be hurt. That possibility was tempting, but if it should be discovered that he had tampered with a matter of honor, violating the code himself, he could be ruined. Better to let them blow each other's brains out, he thought savagely.

"Very well," he said. "You'll have to send them in to me, one at a time. All of them—Stanhope and Brook as well. Dudley first."

"Aye aye, sir." Hibbert seemed relieved to have that particular burden taken from his shoulders.

Dudley's knock was firm and defiant; after he entered, Favian kept him standing for a long ten seconds while he raked the boy savagely with his eyes. Dudley, he remembered, had just turned seventeen a few weeks before. He was slim, with clear, intelligent brown eyes, and an expression of furious stubbornness.

"You have asked permission to fight a brother officer," Favian said, keeping an edge in his voice. "Why?"

"I was insulted, sir."

"Mortally insulted?"

"Yes, sir."

"By a drunken man?"

Dudley hesitated. "I believe he knew what he was saying, sir," he said.

"He did not speak entirely without provocation, I believe?" Favian said.

Dudley frowned. Favian could see him searching for the right phrase. "I—my comments were not made with any intention to injure," he said. "They were not comparable to his deliberate insults."

Favian sighed. Dudley was obviously intelligent; he clearly knew that the challenge was not reflecting well on him. But he had made it; he would stick with it. It would be easier to fight than to work through to a resolution, picking over words, through the tangle of insult and counterinsult. And Dudley probably thought Favian a coward, or something close to one—that wasn't going to make this any easier.

"If I can persuade Mr. Tolbert to make an apology for his words, would you accept them?" Favian asked. When Dudley hesitated, Favian added, "It would not reflect well upon you to hold a man responsible for words spoken in a state of drunkenness. If he chooses to stand by the words after he has been given the opportunity for sober reflection, that is another matter entirely."

Dudley swallowed hard. "I will accept, sir," he said.

"Very well. I commend your attitude. It is mature and officerlike," Favian said. In something like this it was probably necessary to lay on praise with a trowel in the event of the least concession.

"It may be, however," Favian said, "that Mr. Tolbert will refuse to apologize until you yourself apologize for your words. As you inform me that your comments were not made with intent to insult, and were not comparable to his words, it should therefore be easy to make an adequate apology."

There. Trapped him. I've made it easy for him to apologize, and damned difficult to wriggle out of it if he won't.

Dudley grimaced, realizing he was caught. "If it will help, sir, I'll apologize for my words," he said, with far more grace than Favian expected.

"Very well. You may return to your duties. Tell Mr. Hibbert to send Mr. Tolbert to my cabin."

Tolbert's appearance wrecked whatever hope Favian had of arranging an accommodation. Short, square-jawed, just turned nineteen, pugnacious, and barely concealing his contempt for his cowardly captain, Thomas Tolbert refused outright to apologize for his words. Dudley *was* a bastard; Tolbert had only stated the truth, for which he had no obligation to apologize. If Dudley objected to the plain truth, it was time he was taught otherwise. If Dudley was willing to accept an apology, then it simply meant he was a coward as well as a bastard. "And that's that, sir," he concluded, with a defiant leer.

Favian began to sense there might be something more to this battle than an exchange of insults. Tolbert was the senior midshipman, ahead of the others both in years and in seniority, and the others had been following his lead. But perhaps Dudley, clearly more intelligent, had been challenging Tolbert's supremacy; perhaps, now that they'd all been under the fire of the Cuckmere Haven battery, Tolbert's skirmish with the Baratarian privateer did not seem quite so impressive. Tolbert might be feeling his authority slipping away, ebbing from himself to Dudley; the challenge might be the only way he had of striking back.

"Very well," Favian said, left no choice. "I hereby inform you that there will be no fighting among the men of this brig. We are thousands of miles from home, in a foreign port, and must therefore depend on one another to an even greater extent than we do normally. This morning you saw a man flogged for fighting. Due to your position aboard this vessel I cannot flog you—at least I can't flog you *yet*—but I can tell you my opinion, and it is this."

Tolbert stood at quivering attention, his mouth white and compressed, trembling with anger. Favian rose from his chair, his long body, bent beneath the deck head beams, looming above the little midshipman, speaking with scathing precision directly into Tolbert's face.

"Mr. Dudley called you a simpleton last night. This was perhaps lacking in tact, but I must say in all honesty that I agree with Mr. Dudley's perception. You *are* a simpleton, and a fool, and ignorant of both manners and tact."

"At least I'm not a coward!" Tolbert shouted, then bit his lip.

Favian stooped to bring his face within two inches of
Tolbert's, his own quick temper unleashed. "No one has
accused you of cowardice, Mr. Tolbert," he snapped. "How
could they? Your courage has not been tested. Only your
wit has, and it has been found imbecile.

"You've heard my orders," Favian said, standing,
breathing a little easier. "There will be no duel fought before our return to the United States. Any disobedience of
that order and I'll court-martial you on the spot—for murder. Murder of a brother officer. And the penalty for that
is hanging.

"There is nothing I can do to prevent your fighting once
we return home. I can just warn you that I will do my best
to lay court-martial charges, and in any case you will never
serve on a vessel of mine ever again, be it a line-of-battle
ship or a rowboat. You are dismissed."

Tolbert was sent off with flaming ears, and Favian, feeling his own burst of temper ebb, and regretting it, sent for
Dudley again. Dudley received much the same speech, delivered with considerably more moderation, and received it
quietly.

"It will be weeks, probably months, before we see Portsmouth again," Favian said. "I urge you to lose no opportunity to compose this quarrel. You will be living in close
proximity with Mr. Tolbert for the length of the voyage,
and bad blood between you can only injure the efficiency of
this vessel."

"I understand, sir."

"You are dismissed; return to your duties. Please pass
the word for Mr. Stanhope."

"Sir."

Stanhope came in warily, saluted, was asked to sit, and
complied. "I realize this interview will put you in a delicate
position with your fellows," Favian said. "I want it understood at the outset that I am not asking you to divulge
information that would harm anyone, or that could be considered a breach of confidence."

"Yes, sir." Stanhope's face showed his usual seriousness,
his usual intelligence. Perhaps here, Favian thought, is a
person who can help clean up this mess.

"I would like to know what happened last night to provoke this quarrel," Favian said.

"Aye aye, sir." Stanhope's outline was brief, objective, and thorough. Basically it confirmed what Hibbert had said; Favian speculated that perhaps Hibbert had acquired the main body of his own version from Stanhope.

"You couldn't have prevented it somehow?" Favian asked. Stanhope frowned.

"It was very fast, sir," he said. "One minute they were joking, the next Dudley was shouting out a challenge. I couldn't stop him. And Tolbert never backs down from anything."

"So I am given to understand," Favian said. He frowned, wishing he had managed to acquire some of last night's schnapps to drink now, privately in his cabin; he profoundly desired the taste of the fiery liquid to ease the tension he felt in his jaw. A duel. On his first command. Good Lord.

"There's nothing I can ask you to do," he said, "except lose no opportunity of making up his quarrel between them. I must urge you to act as a peacemaker."

"I'll do my best, sir," Stanhope said, after reflection. "But Tolbert is not in the mood for peace, and he hit Dudley in a sensitive place. Tolbert's a complete ass," he said surprisingly. His tone indicated that his judgment was based on long and sober consideration.

"I suggest you don't repeat that opinion in his hearing," Favian said. "I'd stay windward of him today; I gave him a long lecture. You may return to your duties."

"Yes, sir. Good morning, sir."

Well. That was unusual. Usually midshipmen made a point of sticking together, of keeping their thoughts about one another private. And even if they were a bit indiscreet, they *never* were so with superior officers. "Tolbert's a complete ass," Stanhope had said, in his serious, articulate tone. Very interesting. Stanhope was placing himself somewhat apart from the others, in the position of an observer, not a member of the midshipmen's mess. That was probably going to make problems for him in the future, Favian thought, unless he could successfully imitate being a mem-

ber of the band of brothers while secretly keeping his opinions to himself. At least this dueling incident had told him
something about Stanhope: He had an unusual midshipman aboard, one worth watching. He remembered Stanhope's quickness, weeks ago, to spot that Gardell was running goods to Portugal under British license. Yes. He'd be
watching Stanhope a little more carefully from now on.

Midshipman Brook could add little; he was fifteen, the
youngest of the mids, and had been made horribly drunk
by his fellows. His attitude expressed chiefly bewilder-
ment—that and the particular brand of morning misery
that follows a night's overindulgence—and Favian concluded that Brook had done well just to get to the boat,
without policing his fellow midshipmen's follies. Favian
sent him back to work.

Experiment was scrubbed down, the hands given breakfast, some of the white trim on the billet head and false
quarter-galleries renewed. Hibbert went ashore with a party
to secure extra Danish flags and fresh food for the party.
The blue paint on the carronades was freshened. Favian,
on deck to supervise the work, saw the midshipmen going
about their duties with varying degrees of grim determination. Brook was still having difficulty focusing his eyes, let
alone his mind; Tolbert and Dudley were white-lipped and
defiant, pursuing their duties with single-minded precision,
never glancing in one another's direction, avoiding each
other's company. The occasional necessary communication
between them was in monosyllables. Only Phillip Stanhope
seemed to be behaving normally, and that was becase his
normal manner was solemn; he was watching the others,
though, and with what Favian suspected was distant
amusement. He hoped, for Stanhope's sake, that Stanhope
would take pains to conceal his attitude.

The prince's barge was seen at its departure from Haakonshallen, and Favian had his men ready with time to
spare. The hands were dressed in their best clothes, white
duck trousers, blue jackets, and black neckerchiefs, and
were massed forward of the mainmast; the marines, their
crossbelts freshly whitened, stood at rigid attention on the
quarterdeck; the officers, back in their dress uniforms,
stood self-consciously by the entry port, Brook and Stan-

hope sandwiched tactfully between Dudley and Tolbert. Favian glanced over the brig: All seemed in readiness. He twitched his neckcloth and donned his white gloves. The barge came alongside; he could hear Norwegian commands, and then the thump. Sideboys dashed to the entry port to assist the prince, and Gable put his whistle to his puffy lips and blew an ear-splitting blast that caused at least two midshipmen, neither recovered from the previous evening, to wince.

The prince came up the side unassisted, dressed plainly in a black coat, tall hat, a small star, and, to Favian's surprise, black trousers. Favian raised his hat to the salute, caught Bean's eye, and nodded, seeing Bean give the signal.

The first saluting charge went off with a bang, and the prince royal was startled. His long, handsome face recovered quickly and glanced aloft in surprise, then in plain delight, as the second gun boomed. At the first charge flags had soared aloft from every halyard, springing as if by magic from the deck until they fluttered from every mast, from every stay. Count Lindenow came up the brig's side and stepped aboard, almost crashing into the back of the prince, who was standing delighted with the sudden appearance of the flags. It was an impressive sight, Favian thought warmly; full-dressing *Experiment* had taken just a few seconds, and it demonstrated a certain smartness and timing in which he could properly take pride.

But the prince royal was standing on the deck gazing upward at the whipping flags, and Dr. Berg appeared behind Lindenow in the entry port; it looked as if there would be a traffic problem unless the prince could be persuaded to stop blocking the path. Favian let his hat fall back to his head and stepped forward, taking the prince's hand.

"So pleased to see you, Your Highness," he said. "Shall I introduce my officers? You have not met them all, I believe."

"Oh—er—yes, of course," said Christian Frederick, looking down with surprise at Favian's republican fingers clasping his royal hand. Another gun boomed. United States regulations did not allow for more than eighteen guns to be fired during a salute, but Favian knew that roy-

alty expected twenty-one and had bent the regulations for
the sake of diplomacy. It was possible that no one in the
royal party was counting, but Favian preferred to be safe.

"Mr. Hibbert, my lieutenant . . . Mr. Bean, the master . . . Midshipmen Dudley, Stanhope, Brook, and Tolbert . . . Bosun Gable," Favian recited over the booming
guns, dropping the prince's hand as soon as he had steered
His Royal Highness from the entry port. Each officer saluted with bared head; the prince royal, still surprised at
the handclasp of a commoner, nodded regally in response to
each salute.

Dr. Berg stepped forward to introduce the members of
the prince's entourage: Colonel Count Lindenow, himself,
Lieutenant Sverdrup, and Captain Beyer, the gap-toothed
privateer, in a shabby brown coat stained with tobacco. Beyer had been given an office with a complicated title,
something like "special secretary on naval affairs," which
explained his presence. Evidently Christian Frederick liked
to pick his advisors from a diverse group of people.

Over Berg's introductions the saluting guns boomed, the
gunner's cadence coming loudly, ringing over the deck: "If
I wasn't a gunner I wouldn't be here—fire seventeen!
. . . If I wasn't a bastard I wouldn't be here—fire eighteen! . . . If I wasn't a damn fool I wouldn't be here—fire
nineteen!" Favian clenched his teeth.

"I see your guns are blue," the prince royal remarked
cheerfully. "Here we prefer them black. Is there some significance to the blue color?"

"No, Your Highness," Favian stammered, entirely surprised. "It's just the color paint we use."

"Most cheerful, truly," said Christian Frederick. He
glanced over the deck, as eager and curious as a small boy
on an outing. "What kind of guns are these little ones
here?" he asked, nodding—he was too princely to point—at
one of the starboard carronades.

Favian explained to the commander-in-chief of Norway's ground and naval forces that the guns were carronades, invented at the Carron works, in Scotland, though
these particular guns were made in America; that they
threw an eighteen-pound shot, which was large for a vessel
of this size, but were only accurate to two hundred fifty

yards. Favian could see Beyer listening with a cynical leer, scornful of the prince's good-natured incompetence in military matters.

"Would Your Highness enjoy a tour of the vessel?" Favian asked. The prince's eyes sparkled, and he nodded.

"Yes, if you please," he said in his formal, schoolboy English, and Favian escorted him aft—the Prince inspected the marines on the way, and pronounced them "prodigious fine"—and showed him the tiller, the capstan, the *carré navale,* the strange ornamental quarter-galleries, with which the prince was delighted. Then Favian conducted the prince royal forward, his own officers and the prince's entourage trailing obediently behind, bunching as they crowded through the gang of seamen that parted for them, smiling with true veterans' condescension for the royal landlubber. Christian Frederick was shown the nine-pounder chasers crowded into *Experiment*'s bridle ports, and Favian explained without being asked that their maximum effective range, mounted as they were right forward on a pitching deck, was nine hundred yards, but only three hundred yards with any great accuracy. Favian saw Hibbert listening to this elementary digression with a respectful face, and caught glimpses also of the prince's entourage listening with varying degrees of attention: Dr. Berg with a faint supercilious sneer (what did the nine-pounder guns have to do with the Rights of Man?), Lindenow with polite attention, Sverdrup with the same courteous mask worn by Hibbert, Beyer with his leer. And then, while Favian answered a question about the spritsail yard, he turned to find that Beyer simply wasn't there; he glanced back to see the back of the privateer's head disappearing down a hatch.

"This way, gentlemen. Your Highness," he said hastily. "We'll go below. 'Ware heads, and watch your step." He led them in Beyer's footsteps and discovered Beyer standing by the whiskey butt, hands belligerently on his hips, arguing with the marine who guarded it.

"Perhaps Captain Beyer would like a taste of what the men drink?" Favian said hastily, seeing the marine's knuckles grow white as they tightened on his musket.

"Yes, I would indeed!" the privateer barked, swinging

his burly frame about. "Tell this blue-coated bugger to take himself and his blasted musket out of my sight!"

"The marine was only doing his duty," Favian said. He stepped forward to the whiskey butt, drew off a cup, and handed it to Beyer. The marine stood with expressionless face.

"Thanks," said Beyer, and drained half of it at a drop.

Favian turned to the members of the prince's party. "Would Your Highness, or any of you gentlemen, care to taste the whiskey ration?" he asked. There was a general assent. Favian drew another cup and handed it with a bow to Christian Frederick. The prince royal sipped the nasty stuff, made a face, and passed it to Berg. Each man took a sip, Beyer intercepting the cup at the end of its journey and handing Favian the cup he had already drained. Favian, foreseeing trouble, called for Midshipman Brook and asked Hibbert to show the prince the delights of the berth deck.

"Take charge of the whiskey butt," Favian whispered to Brook. "If any of the prince's company wish a cup of whiskey, give it to them. But keep them from distributing the whiskey to any of the crew—just tell them it's a breach of discipline."

"Aye aye, sir," Brook said. Favian looked at him closely. It was plain that Brook was still suffering considerably from his overindulgence the previous evening, and if anyone was to prove a secure guard of the whiskey butt, it would be he.

Favian guided the prince past *Experiment*'s stove, where the cook and cook's mate were preparing the hands' noon meal of boiled salt beef and rice. Christian Frederick passed hastily by the unappetizing cauldrons and was conducted to the center of the berth deck, where he was shown how the mess tables were lowered from the deck-head beams during the hands' meals. During this speech, Favian saw Captain Beyer wandering forward for another cup of whiskey.

The entire party was then led aft for a formal dinner. Hibbert and his party had scoured the town in the early hours of the morning, searching for meat suitable for the royal party; hoping to find lamb or beef, he had been forced to accept a greasy lump of pork, some thin, gaunt poultry, and the inevitable fish. He had perhaps been too long ashore: Favian had received a private word from his steward to delay the meal as long as possible in hopes the pork would be done. But left with the unappetizing choice of a tour of the hold, the half-orlop with its cockpit and surgeon's table, or the bilges, Favian decided to announce dinner and run the risk of underdone pork.

Fortunately there were delays caused by the necessary formalities: the speeches, the toasts, the drinking to one another's health. Beyer appeared to be tossing off his wine with the same nonchalance with which he had drunk the whiskey; nothing but a growing flush testified to his advancing inebriation. The midshipmen had little to do but keep respectfully silent unless spoken to: Favian had avoided potential embarrassment by making Tolbert officer of the deck, where he could exercise his swagger in charge of the watch, while Dudley sat in the prince's company and ate carefully to avoid ramming his elbow into the nearby ribs of Midshipman Stanhope.

The pork, when it finally arrived, proved to be cooked to satisfaction, and after its consumption there was brandy and rice pudding. The meal had been a bit primitive by Europe's courtly standards, but for the brig it had been a major effort; and Favian was relieved to find that it had gone well, that the Prince had not been curious about the screened-off sick bay, where Sedgwick lay with his flogged back, looking like a side of raw meat, exposed, or that Tolbert and Dudley had not taken to shooting at one another with pistols while the prince toured the spar deck.

"If Your Highness is ready, there will be an entertainment on deck," Favian said as the prince contentedly sipped his brandy. "*Experiment*'s band will play, and there will be dancing."

The prince looked interested, but then Favian saw a veil slide over his eyes. "Perhaps our associates can attend the entertainment," he said, looking significantly at Berg and Lindenow. "I should like, Captain Markham, to converse privately, if we may."

"Of course, Your Highness," Favian said, taken by surprise. He turned to his officers, lined in a blue rank at the table's edge. "If you gentlemen will excuse us? Davis, leave the brandy bottle; you can clear the table later. Mr. Hibbert, please arrange the entertainment. We shall try to join you later."

"I shall be within earshot, Your Highness," Berg said, bowing, as he backed from the room. There was congestion at the door as the Danes and Norwegians tried to leave the small cabin without turning their backs on the prince royal and while the startled Americans tried to imitate them. Favian realized with horror that he had forgotten entirely about that particular branch of court etiquette; he had been casually turning his back on Christian Frederick throughout the tour of the brig. But apparently the royal dignity was prepared to make allowances for barbaric Yankee manners, Favian realized with relief.

As Favian resumed his seat, Christian Frederick, who had remained seated and perfectly at ease while the others filed out, turned to Favian with a serious look. "I've received, by special messenger this morning, the news that Sweden has assembled its army, and that Bernadotte has taken personal command. I must return to Christiania to take command of the government."

Favian felt a wave of empathy for the overburdened prince. If Bergen was typical of blockaded, half-starved Norway, then Norway could not possibly hold out against a determined Swedish attack.

"I am most sorry, Your Highness," Favian said. "Have you received word of an invasion?"

"No, there will be no invasion—not of Norway," Christian Frederick frowned. "Bernadotte will take the Swedish forces to Germany to fight the French. Denmark and Norway will be spared."

"I see," Favian said. The situation was clearly more Byzantine than it looked at the outset. "Your Highness will wish to take command of the Norwegian forces, to invade Sweden while their armies are elsewhere."

Christian Frederick gave him a look of astonishment. "Good heavens, no!" he said. "I don't want to provoke the Swedes! I intend to ready the forts, drill the army, and

hope to deal with the British before the Swedes can invade.
There is always the possibility that Bonaparte—I mean His
Majesty Napoleon—will defeat the Swedes on German soil,
and then there would be no invasion."

Favian carefully controlled his surprise. If the prince
could not understand why it would be to Norway's advantage to take the offensive while the Swedish army was occupied elsewhere—but perhaps Christian Frederick knew
political reasons why Sweden should not be attacked. Perhaps there was a reason of fundamental importance. But if
there was, it did not spring immediately to Favian's mind.

The prince was clearly not well informed about military
matters. Favian hoped, for Christian Frederick's sake, that
there were good advisors awaiting him in Christiania.

"Yes, we will deal with the British first," Christian
Frederick smiled. "After the blockade is lifted, we can receive food and military supplies from France and elsewhere abroad."

"Does—does Your Highness have reason to expect that
the blockade will soon be lifted?" Favian asked cautiously.
It seemed entirely inconceivable.

The prince royal smiled. He looked cunningly at Favian,
then leaned closer to speak in lowered tones. "A Danish
naval force will soon sail for Norway, to be placed under
my supervision. The ship *Najad* and some smaller craft.
They will break the blockade."

"I hope that is so," Favian said, without any hope. One
ship would not make any difference, he knew. "Is Your
Highness sure," he asked, as diplomatically as he could,
"that the presence of a Danish squadron will not attract
unwelcome British attention, instead of driving the British
off?"

Christian Frederick was still sublimely confident. "That
is what I wished to speak with you about," he said. "*Najad*
is a good ship, a frigate I believe, with forty guns, very like
the American frigates we have read about. Captain Holm is
a good man, but could benefit by exposure to the American
example. You are yourself the veteran of a victorious engagement with the British—there are not a hundred sea
officers in all Europe who could claim as much. Your appearance, Captain Markham, seems providential. I hope

that you will accept what I humbly offer—command of a united Danish-American squadron in the Baltic, to break the British blockade."

Favian was too stunned to reply, or even to fully absorb the import of Christian Frederick's words. Command of a squadron! The goal of every ambitious junior officer in United States service—a chance to become a Truxtun, Preble, a Rodgers. *Commodore*. The United States had no admirals as yet, and its highest title was an honorary one only, not a true military rank—but still, *commodore* had a magic ring. Commodore Markham.

"Sir—Your Highness—" Favian stammered, playing for time while his head spun. "You r-realize I have no instructions from my government to cover such a situation."

"Surely your government understands that situations can arise in which captains may act at their own discretion?" the prince said smoothly.

Favian poured the prince more brandy to gain time, poured himself some, sipped carefully. The dazzle was subsiding from the offer rapidly. Would Mr. Madison approve of one of his naval officers entering the service of a foreign country, even one fighting the same enemy as his own? No, the scrupulous Madison would not. James Madison had refused formal alliance with any European power, afraid of binding his own policy to that of an European despot, and spending lives for European goals. The United States had no quarrel with Sweden, Russia, Prussia, Spain, or Portugal, even though it was fighting their principal ally. It was a distinction most Europeans failed to appreciate, however; Spain and Portugal, warring officially against France but not against the United States, had nevertheless seized American ships and made prisoners of their crews.

But that would not alter James Madison's policy. The United States could aid the Danes indirectly, by fighting the British; but fighting alongside the Danes, let alone in command of them, was out of the question. Favian knew that the price of accepting the prince royal's offer would be his own resignation from the Navy of the United States.

And then what of Captain Holm and the other Danish officers who would suddenly find an American officer—

and a very junior American officer at that—suddenly promoted over their heads? And furthermore, an American officer who could not even speak a word of Danish, or Norwegian, or whatever language was spoken in the Royal Danish service? In the event of such an outrageous supercession, any self-respecting naval officer would have little choice but to resign; and though Christian Frederick would always refuse to accept the resignations and order the officers to continue their duty, it would not make for a good working relationship between the new commodore and his men.

And yet—and yet there was a half-witted attractiveness to the idea. It was a romantic concept, to be sure: taking command of a small, outnumbered squadron, stout Danes and Norwegians and his own experienced American crew; sailing from the crystalline Norwegian fjords to break the British hold on the Baltic. . . . Hopeless, of course. The British knew their Baltic trade was vital; they'd send another fleet, as they had twice before, and that would be the end of *Najad, Experiment*, and their commodore. And yet . . . and yet . . .) Perhaps all his life he would wonder if he could really have done it.

"Your Highness," Favian said, "I cannot." And before the prince royal could interrupt with a hearty, blind, enthusiastic rebuttal, Favian plunged ahead. He could not, because his government would not approve, because it would involve America with Sweden and Russia, with whom the United States had no quarrel. Because the Prince's own officers were stout and true and had no need of his advice, while they had every right to resent it. Because, in the end, Favian knew what he was, an officer of the United States Navy, and however much he might regret that fact, it could not be altered, and so he would stay.

"I will give you whatever advice I can, Your Highness, before I depart Bergen," he said, while Christian Frederick frowned, tapping one of his rings on the edge of the table in an irritated, rather petulant gesture.

"Captain Markham, I am disappointed," he said. The sound of a hornpipe came through the skylight, and soon there was the thunder of bare feet on the planking. Favian's mind strangely wandered to Sedgwick, lying in the screened-off sick bay, hearing the hornpipes dancing over his head, the thumping feet of his fellow crewmen. He wondered if Sedgwick felt isolated, or lost, or whether he accepted his separation from the festivities with the same oxlike stolidity with which he had accepted everything else, since his one outburst of temper had showed him the dangers of emotion.

"I expect much from this land," the prince said soberly. "In the Danish court we speak French; the women imitate French fashions and coquetry, the men sorrow that they were born in such a backward country as Denmark. In Norway there is much that is good, that is unaffected. I have been here a short time only, but already I love the land. There is work for a man here, to make the place strong, proud of itself. I imagine your America is much the same."

"Perhaps it is. I don't know Norway."

"The *Najad* will help Norway to feel pride in itself," Christian Frederick said. "It has been sent to break the British blockade that is keeping Norway hungry. The Norwegians will know the Danish court will keep faith. We will keep the ship here, in our fjords, and guard it until we can break the British." Christian Frederick's hand formed a fist, trembling, then crashed into the table. "It *must* work—it must. The Swedes are nothing without the British. It is the British we must destroy."

"Your Highness, one forty-gun frigate will make little difference to the British," Favian said. It hurt, somehow, to disillusion this charming, well-meaning man, to point out the realities that would bring his plan to nothing. "The British have a thousand warships. The Baltic trade is vital to them; their convoys go into the Skagerrak every week. They won't let you interfere with it. They will go into your fjords, and take the *Najad*, or if they cannot take her they will blockade her until winter freezes her in." The prince's gaze was abstract; he stared with empty eyes at his harmless fist on the cabin table. Favian did not know if the prince royal had even heard.

"Sir, there is a better way," Favian urged. "Send *Najad* into the North Sea, or the Irish Sea. Burn British shipping within sight of their home ports. That's the way to make them hurt. Once they know where to find your frigate, they will destroy it or render it useless."

"A national symbol means nothing if it is sailing on foreign waters," the prince said, his eyes filling with a melancholy that seemed just the tiniest bit affected, a little self-conscious, as if he were enjoying playing the part of a romantic hero, sacrificing for his subjects things they could never understand. . . . Whence came that intuition? Favian wondered, surprised at himself.

"*Najad* must stay in Norwegian waters. It will be a risk, but *Najad* will be protected."

"You will lose her," Favian said, and he knew with absolute certainty that he spoke the truth. The prince royal was an orator, a politician, a romantic. He would stake more on a dramatic gesture than that gesture could possibly be worth. *Najad* was meant to be a symbol around which the Norwegians could rally; but if it were lost, a lesson would be learned that the prince did not intend, and another bit of the earth on which he based his power would erode beneath his feet. Favian had been apprenticed, for almost his entire naval career, to Stephen Decatur, a man who possessed almost an addiction to gesture, but also the cunning and intelligence to know just how far to play each action, and how much to stake on each. Prince Christian Frederick did not. The prince was such an encouraging, friendly, well-meaning man that Favian almost ached for him, knowing him to be staking too much on *Najad*, unable to make him see the trap he was walking into.

"If the British feel they must—" Favian said, feeling he had to give another warning. Another hornpipe echoed eerily down the skylight. "If *Najad* provokes them, they will send another fleet to the Baltic, under another Nelson—or another Gambier," he said, naming the British admiral who had burned Copenhagen with mortars and bursting rockets.

"They won't have it," the prince royal said confidently. "They're diverting too much of their strength to America."

Favian felt hope ebb. The prince royal had set his course, clear-eyed, straight onto the rocks, and Favian could only be thankful that he had not been talked into becoming a passenger on the journey.

There was only one piece of information he had that could be of any possible use to Christian Frederick, and he might as well give it. "I am told—I do not know how reliable the rumor is, Your Highness—that Count Gram is lacking somewhat in enthusiasm for the Danish cause," he said. The prince looked up in surprise, then hooded his eyes carefully in a swift recovery of composure.

"Go on," he said.

"I am also told that Count Gram seeks a reputation on the battlefield," Favian said. "His loyalty might be assured were he to be given a command of some of Your Highness's forces, or even an important staff position. I am told this—Your Highness would know better than I if it is true."

The prince royal considered the matter, eyes narrowed, his face hard—a political creature; and Favian saw for a moment what the man might become in twenty years, his youthful, impractical idealism battered away, the romanticism gone sour, little to fall back on but autocratic instincts nurtured by the ruthless political environment into which he'd been born. At the moment Christian Frederick was a likable, ingenuous man, a republican and a prince simultaneously; but would the republican survive? Did he really like the handclasp I gave him? Favian wondered. What would Hamlet have been like had he not been poisoned, had he inherited the throne and had to spend twenty years fighting off young Fortinbras?

"You are surprising, Captain Markham," said the prince. "Probably you are right. I'll speak of it with Anker and Berg. And now," he said, standing suddenly, draining his cup of brandy, "I will enjoy your admirable entertainment."

"Of course, Your Highness," Favian said, standing. The prince was still a political man, distant, hard—no doubt he was not used to people saying no to his plans. As Favian escorted him from the cabin, he saw Davis, his steward, standing with a guilty face, suddenly busy, in his pantry. He wondered how much Davis had heard, remembering Anita Courtois's mention of the Haakonshallen palace walls, hung with tapestries so that spies could lurk behind them. No need for an arras on a brig the size of *Experiment*, he thought.

He escorted the prince up the companionway to the deck, where the entire brig's company had just commenced accompanying the band on "Hail, Columbia."

"Yankee Doodle" followed "Hail, Columbia," and Favian saw the prince's brow furrow as he tried to make out the nonsense lyrics, then saw laughter return to his eyes as comprehension dawned. The man was resilient, Favian saw; perhaps that would help him.

There were more hornpipes, more songs; and then the prince gave a courteous speech of thanks, addressed not just to *Experiment*'s officers, but to the men as well. The shellbacks visibly increased in stature with Christian Frederick's praise; he saw them look proud as eagles as the prince, with true republican instincts, gave them his royal thanks. Favian had arranged for the prince to get three cheers as he left the brig, but now he knew they would be heartfelt.

Captain Beyer was rounded up from the berth deck, where he'd been sitting on a coil of line near the whiskey butt and drinking round after round of the stuff. "He was telling Midshipman Brook about the whores of Copenhagen," Hibbert whispered in Favian's ear. "Comparing them with the whores of the West Indies, and of France. Brook's eyes were as big around as a twelve-inch hawse—I don't think the midshipmen's berth has heard the like."

"They will now, I suppose," Favian said, watching the remnants of the prince's party trailing over the side into the boat.

"Three cheers for His Royal Highness!" barked Alferd Bean, on schedule, and the crew roared. The royal barge slid from the brig's side, and Favian saw the prince standing in the stern sheets, waving in kingly, magnificent, solitary acknowledgment of the cheers that roared over the harbor. It was the last Favian saw of him.

The next day the prince royal left for Christiania, and the royal flags gradually disappeared from Bergen's tired, tattered buildings, and Count Lindenow began to raise from among his half-starved citizens his battalion of infantry, preparing to fight for Norway's hopeless cause.

12.

Favian looked down at the letter in his hand. It had come by hand from one of the local boatmen, addressed only to "Captain Markham, American warship," and Davis the steward had brought it straight to Favian's cabin. It read:

> Captain Markham:
> I would be honored if you would be my guest for a private supper this evening, eight o'clock.
>
> Yours truly,
> Anita Courtois

Repondez s'il vous plait.

Short and to the point. The address was on the back of the letter, which was sealed with a plain wafer. Private supper. That would probably be with Count Gram and half a dozen other acquaintances. Perhaps she simply wanted someone to talk to, someone ignorant of local politics. Count Gram. Favian grimaced. He wished he had thought of inviting Anita to the brig, perhaps with some other local ladies. A warship's company always enjoyed having ladies on board, at least in port.

But the boatman was waiting for a reply. Favian supposed he could endure the count's company for an evening. "Mademoiselle Courtois: I am honored to accept—Favian Markham," he wrote, and sealed the letter with a wafer. He copied the address from the back of the invitation, handed it to Davis, and saw it carried out. No doubt Davis would feast his eyes on the address as soon as he stood in the light of the companionway.

Well, there was no disguising the fact he was corresponding with a woman from the town, and there would be no doubt as to where he was going when he told Davis that he would not be requiring supper. It would be all over the brig in minutes. He might as well let them gossip. Whatever stories Davis and the others came up with, they would no doubt be more entertaining than the evening at Anita's, which would probably end around a whist table, with Count Gram and Anita partnered against Favian and some elderly relative who could not quite read the cards. There would be prodding questions from Gram, who would want to know what he and the prince royal conversed about during Christian Frederick's visit to *Experiment*.

But still, it would be good to sit near a woman, to bask in the sun of a female presence. To forget for a few moments the little brig so far from home, the midshipmen who were on the verge of pistoling one another, the crew that had grown restless with their own thwarted expectations of battle.

Experiment had been sitting in Vaagen for six days; it had been three days since the prince had ridden from Bergen in his carriage, surrounded by the dust raised by his cavalry escort. There had been visits back and forth from the brig to the town: A supper at the Bergenhus officers' mess had been reciprocated by a dinner held aboard *Experiment*; Bergen's mayor and town council had been invited aboard for wine and another exhibition of sailors' dances; and the officers had come ashore for a dry evening of tea with the town council and their wives, in which virtually the only common ground for conversation was the weather. The half-starved town had little to offer except the beauty of its natural surroundings. It was a shame. Favian would have liked to visit Bergen in peacetime.

Soon *Experiment* would have to leave Bergen and return to the North Sea. Two British merchant vessels had cleared Bergen since the brig had arrived; they would be carrying news of *Experiment*'s presence to the Admiralty. In another week, perhaps two weeks, there would be a cruising frigate in the offing, perhaps more than one. Favian intended to leave Bergen before he brought reprisal down on his hosts; that had been the principal reassurance he had offered the mayor and town council. The illegal but vitally necessary trade with England would not be interfered with.

Favian had received Anita's invitation while dressed in tar-stained white duck trousers and a canvas shirt, a marlin-spike hanging round his neck on a thong—he'd been aloft surveying the rigging, setting up and tarring down new cordage, and had just stepped down for a cup of coffee. To go ashore he wore civilian rig, a brown coat with a black velvet collar and buff nankeen trousers—these and his plain round beaver hat. He did not intend to be a uniformed naval gentleman for Anita Courtois to show off to her guests; but even so, he wore the New York presentation sword, a decorative, graceful object that went well with the dignified claw-hammer coat and would also serve, if necessary, to drive off any waterfront riffraff who thought to test what that tall dandy was made of. Davis had polished his boots without being asked; that dour New Hampshireman had turned into a good servant, even if he was becoming a bit presumptuous.

Favian was morally certain that Davis had overheard at least part of the conversation between himself and Prince Christian Frederick, and that to enhance his own superior position on the brig he had promptly spread the story over the ship. Favian wondered how the tale would affect his estimation in the eyes of the crew. Another example of his cowardice, that he refused to command a squadron against the enemy? Or an example of patriotism, that he refused a foreign command handed him by a monarch? Probably they hadn't yet made up their minds.

But there was no point in worrying over the hands' opinion of him; they'd make up their own minds, and probably change them half a dozen times per day. There was an evening with Anita Courtois to look forward to, even if there was going to be Count Gram, whist, and elderly relatives. Favian remembered the supple body held in his arms during their waltz together, the intuitive grace of her dancing. Yes. He was looking forward.

His boat's crew rowed him to the town, and he sent them back; he'd hire a local boat to return. He saw his coxswain give a knowing look to one of the other hands; so they'd already heard. He supposed that his status would be increased, if anything, by the rumor of a romantic conquest in Bergen. The boat's crew set out across Vaagen, and Favian turned to go into town.

Anita Courtois had rooms in a pleasant-looking, if faded, green building. A plump, red-haired, rather disapproving maidservant opened the door to Favian's ring, bobbed a curtsey while her scowling brows produced two V-shaped wrinkles over the bridge of her nose, and led him to the second floor. She opened a door and entered, showing Favian into the room, and in the first second of entry Favian knew that the conclusions drawn by his crew had been more correct than his own.

There were no other guests. The room was lit by perfumed candles that filled the room with the scent of roses, and a soft, subtle, flickering light emanating chiefly from a hanging bronze censer. There were tapestries on the walls, plump, tasseled pillows on the floor. The affect was meant to be Oriental, exotic; but it was spoiled somewhat by the sight of a thoroughly occidental table laid for dinner for two. Favian took off his hat and handed it to the maidservant.

And then Anita Courtois came through a curtained door, and the maidservant frowned again, bobbed a curtsey, and vanished. The white gown was of transparent muslin; Favian could plainly see the imprint of her nipples through the cloth, the staring eye of her navel, the dark shadow low on her abdomen. Diamonds and silver dangled from her earlobes, caressing her neck. "Good evening, Captain," she said, her eyes bright. He bowed, spoke his reply, and wondered why there was any need for dialogue. She walked toward him with a deliberate, provocative saunter and put her arms around his neck. No; no dialogue necessary.

There were a few maddening preliminaries to be gotten through before he could possess her: She had to be picked up and carried to the settee; her fingers had to nimbly remove his cravat and neckcloth; he had to stand on alternate legs for several awkward seconds while he got rid of his boots, after which his fashionably tight nankeen trousers, which were getting tighter by the second, had to be peeled off like a second skin, exposing his pale legs. It was easy, blessedly easy, after that; cares sluiced from his back like storm water from the nape of his sou'wester. But he never did get rid of the sword belt, and the New York presentation sword gave forth a syncopated rattle throughout their urgent, eager coupling, making its own vulgar commentary on the proceedings.

"*Oh!*" she said in wide-eyed surprise, some seconds after consciousness returned. "Oh, my dear . . ." She stretched out one arm, then rubbed her neck where it had been strained awkwardly against the settee. Her tones were lazy, languorous, entirely satisfied. "My dear, you've been on that boat for a long time. I had forgotten what it is to have someone new."

Favian felt stunned and a little self-conscious. His apparel was strewn over the floor like windblown leaves. He groped for the clips that held his sword belt, released them, and placed the sword well out of rattling range.

Anita took a handkerchief from his coat pocket and tenderly bent forward to touch a bit of sweat from his temples. "Shall we have supper now?" she asked brightly. "Yes, let's," answering her own question. "Beer or schnapps?" She kissed him searchingly.

"Beer," he said. "Beer would be wonderful."

"After our refreshment," she said, her white, chiseled teeth by his ear, "we can resume our indulgence, yes? I hope you have all night."

"All night and part of the day," he said. She dabbed herself with the handkerchief, uncoiled herself from around him, and straightened her dress.

"You'll have to put your trousers on again, I'm afraid," she said. "We mustn't scandalize my Irma."

The supper was fish, of which Favian was growing tired; but there was good, tangy cheese and a mug of yeasty beer. Irma served with disapproving stiffness and clattered the plates. Anita's eyes laughed in the candlelight, and he found himself responding to her mirth. Irma's obvious refusal to sanction their relationship made the whole business even more amusing. Eventually Irma was banished to her own rooms, leaving behind the cheese, a jug of beer, and a bottle of schnapps; and Favian was left to discover what he could of Anita.

Her eyes were a remarkably attractive blue, and were a little shortsighted. Her armpits were flossed with light strands. She had an agile, robust body, and entirely lacked modesty; she seemed at home on the settee, on the pillows, and once on a straight-backed chair. She surprised him with caresses he had experienced only at the hands of very expensive prostitutes, and coached his responsive ardor with knowing lechery; he found himself wondering hazily what he'd been missing all these years, confining himself entirely to professionals.

"It's been a long time since I've had anyone new," she repeated during a pause. It was approaching dawn, and Favian felt wonderfully refreshed, clearheaded, not in the least bit sleepy.

"You've been restricting yourself to someone?" Favian asked. "Count Gram, say?" He had found his curiosity rising; he wondered at whose hands she had learned her repertoire.

"Count Gram! The man is a selfish idiot. Let us forget him," she said with vehement finality. "He has been made a brigadier by the prince, and has thrown himself into the cause. Let him fight with the other dolts, and die." Favian seemed to have touched a sore point. He let it alone.

Anita poured herself schnapps, tossed it off with a contented smile, then nestled against him on the settee. He could feel the warmth and weight of her breast against his pectoral; she brought up a knee to stroke her smooth thigh over his stomach. An eyelash fluttered against his cheek. "No politics tonight but the politics of pleasure," she murmured contentedly.

Toward dawn there was a short breakfast of cheese, bread, and schnapps, and a final, lazy idyll on the settee that left them both breathless. Favian drew on his clothes, clipped on his sword, and kissed Anita good-bye, feeling her arms surround him. Lovely. Europe had its compensations. He promised he'd see her again before *Experiment* left port.

As he walked down the two flights of stairs, he tried lightheartedly to remember what they'd talked about during their hours together. No politics, as she'd insisted. No promises, no commitments except to another extended supper in a few days. She had not cared about his past; he had not asked about hers. Count Gram's name had been mentioned but once, and Emma Greenhow's not at all.

But most importantly, Favian thought with relief, he had entirely forgotten for the space of a few hours that his men thought him a coward, that two of his officers were planning to assassinate one another, that he was in a foreign port, without any authorization from the Navy Department, and hunted by the Royal Navy. Favian blinked in the pale dawn as he opened the door, and frowned, straightening his shoulders without realizing it. He was Captain Markham again, and he felt the burden descend on him like a leaden, crushing weight.

Across the street a coachman dozed over his reins; probably one of the local gentry was conducting a rendezvous of his own, Favian thought cheerfully, and the coachman had arrived to fetch him home. Favian, a fading contentment still lingering atop his sense of responsibilities, turned down the street, and saw from the corner of his eye two loiterers—perhaps revelers who had caroused the night away—ease themselves from a doorway. Favian walked obliquely to larboard to give them room, but they crowded him. Favian scowled, his contentment vanishing, and looked up at them.

What were they carrying? Pick handles? Axe handles? Something of the sort. Favian, leaping to larboard, managed to avoid the first blow that whistled within inches of his head. "Leave the lady alone," the man said. His face was bearded, his clothes mean. Not the sort of man usually chosen to bear a message. "You'll get what's coming to you if you don't," he warned. The bludgeon came up again. The other man, a little shorter, a little sharper, was maneuvering around the messenger's starboard quarter.

Favian's body flushed with energy, with brutal warmth. At last a problem he understood. He drew the New York presentation sword and let his assailants see the point directed at the nearest man's heart.

"Who sent you?" Favian backed slowly, letting them think he was afraid, and circling to his right to keep the larger man between himself and the other.

"Never mind that. Just leave the lady alone."

"Leaff her alone," the other said, a badly accented parrot.

"Go to hell."

"Then we beat the snot out of you," the first man said affably. Favian caught the blow on his sword hilt, thanking the gods of battle that the New York smallsword was made of good steel and hadn't snapped with the weight of the pick handle; he seized the other's weapon with his left hand and jerked it toward him. The pick handle's owner was jerked forward as well, and as the man watched in horror Favian ran him effortlessly through the left lung.

The bully wilted, dropping his weapon. Favian scaled it away, hearing it rattle on the cobblestones. The bully collided with his friend, then staggered in another direction. The sharp man swung hastily, unnerved by the fight's swiftness and by the collision; there was panic in his eyes. Favian stepped out of the pick handle's reach; the breeze of its passage tickled his knee. He stepped in before his attacker could recover and slashed his face open from forehead to chin. Another pick handle clattered on the cobbles.

The man staggered away, his hands over his face, weeping. His friend had fallen and lay in the street, his limbs convulsing involuntarily. Favian walked back up the street, threw open the door of the carriage that had been waiting, and thrust his sword inside.

"Come out so I can kill you."

"I don't have a sword. I didn't think I'd need one," Count Gram said, annoyance in his red face. He wore the scarlet Danish military coat. His coach smelled of fine leather work. "Your own men assured me you were a coward," he said. "I thought those two would scare you off."

"I'd advise you never again to listen to gossiping midshipmen. That was a very ill-bred trick. I'm not entirely certain you're not a coward yourself. I don't suppose you'd lower yourself to fight with your fists." Favian pictured the impact of his fist in Count Gram's face and grinned wolfishly.

"No. I will not."

"You *are* a coward, then," Favian said. "And a vicious cheat. And not a gentleman. How many times do I have to say it?"

Count Gram's eyes glittered coldly. "You have said it enough, I think. Who is your second?"

"Lieutenant Peter Hibbert."

"Mine is Baron Kurtz. He will meet your Lieutenant Hibbert in front of the cathedral at noon. Will that be satisfactory?"

"It will."

"Tell the coachman to drive on, will you?" Count Gram said, adjusting himself carefully in his leather seat.

"Tell him yourself," Favian said, and slammed the carriage door. He watched the coach rattle away, then turned to scan the street. The weeping man had gone; the other assailant still lay on the cobbles. His convulsions, and probably his life, had ceased.

Favian walked to Anita Courtois's building, his sword still in his hand, and climbed the two flights of steps.

13.

"My dear," Anita Courtois said in surprise. She passed a hand over her eyes, waking herself from the sleep that had probably just taken her. "Did you forget something? Why are you carrying your sword?"

"Your Irma has reported us to Count Gram," Favian said. "I killed one of his men out in the street. I am going to fight with Count Gram, probably tomorrow."

She looked up at him, her brows furrowed in annoyance. "Damn the slut!" she said. "She was supposed to tell him *today*. I didn't think she'd go sneaking out in the dead of night!"

Favian reached out and took a fold of her gown, drawing the sword's point through it, cleaning the bloody tip. Anita looked down at the smear of blood with distaste.

"I think," said Favian, sheathing the smallsword, "you had better tell me the whole story."

"Come in, my dear," she sighed. "Sit down. Have some schnapps. You could probably use it."

She sat opposite Favian and informed him that she was twenty-seven, from a poor family, and had been a courtesan for eight years. During that time she had been kept by four different men, had amassed a tidy sum of money, and had met many interesting people.

"Is your name really Anita?" Favian asked. She smiled.

"Don't be naive. I'm from Iceland, where everyone is poor. My name is Gudnỳ Ingimundardóttir—hardly the fashion. I took a French last name. French impresses these Danes, I don't know why."

"And Count Gram?"

Her expression was contemptuous. "The latest of my friends," she said. "He's lasted eight months. I've had enough of him puffing himself up, his endless talk about his enormous talents going to waste, and his going about ravishing chambermaids. One of them gave him the clap, and so I've banished him until he takes the cure, and I decided to take a lover myself to teach him a lesson or two. Show him that not everyone worships the image of Count Gram the way Gram himself does. I thought that I would see you once or twice, you would sail away, and Gram would either come back and ask forgiveness with a fistful of diamonds, or cut me off, and I'd move to Christiania and find a new friend—which shouldn't be hard, now I've been admitted to the prince's circle. Since Gram pays both for this place and for Irma I knew he'd find out sooner or later."

"Yes," Favian said with leaden weariness. "You'll go to Christiania. I'll kill Count Gram, since there's no point in letting former lovers clutter up your life. I'll sail away, and take an honest whore next time."

"No need to be insulting," she said, without any particular trace of offense. "Besides, I *am* honest." She poured herself schnapps and drained the cup. "I'm not making you fight him," she said. "You can sail away, and that will be the end." She yawned behind her hand, then apologized for it.

"It will not be the end," Favian said. "I'll have to fight him."

"My dear, that won't be easy," Anita said. "He's a crack pistol shot, and a good fencer. He's killed two people in duels and injured several more. Best to sail away. I'm not the kind that enjoys being fought over."

"I can't sail away."

"Who will know, or care? A few Norwegians you'll never see again? I'm not responsible for such idiocy," she said, with an airy wave of her hand. "If you fight him, you fight him for your own reasons. I wash my hands. I just wanted a good fuck, and by God I got one."

"How nice for you."

"I didn't hear you complain." She spoke sharply; a barb had finally lodged.

"I'm complaining now," Favian said. He stood up. "If you want someone to teach Gram a lesson, hire a schoolteacher. Or some stupid brute with a pick handle." She shrugged, plucking at the bloody patch on her gown. He walked out, went down the stairs, and took the rear exit to avoid facing the corpse on the cobbles, or any surrounding and curious crowd who might wonder why the velvet-collared gentleman was carrying such a nice sword.

"Pass the word for Hibbert," he said as he returned to his cabin. He'd ignored the knowing eyes of the men on deck, the satisfied glances and satisfied nods, men happily confirming the fact of their captain's having a woman on shore.

"It seems I'm fighting a duel," Favian said shortly, as soon as Hibbert had knocked and taken his seat. "I hope you will do me the honor of acting as my second."

Hibbert, too stunned to reply, could only nod.

"Thank you, Mr. Hibbert," Favian said. He knew his tone was cold, brisk, and probably unpleasant, but he couldn't stop it, couldn't moderate the harshness of his voice. "I will choose sabers," he said. "I will not apologize for my remarks to the other principal. The other second is a Baron Kurtz. You will meet him in front of the cathedral at noon. I suggest you wear uniform so that he will be able to recognize you."

"Yes, sir." Hibbert hesitated a moment. "Sir, if I may ask—what is the name of the other principal?"

"Count Gram."

"I see, sir."

Favian's next remark brought a startled expression to Hibbert's face. "I suggest you go armed to the cathedral," he said. "Nothing conspicuous. A sword, perhaps a small pistol or two in your coat pockets. I have been treacherously attacked once this morning. I think you will be safe, but there is no sense in being reckless."

"Er—aye, sir, I will."

"You may tell the other officers," Favian said, with what he hoped was a confident grin, "that there will be fencing drill this afternoon. If you have no more questions, Mr. Hibbert, you may go about your duties."

"Aye aye, sir." Favian could see dozens of questions al-

most bursting from him, but Hibbert reined them in and
left the cabin. Favian stripped off most of his clothes and
settled into his bunk; Davis appeared to ask if the captain
required breakfast and was answered in the negative. Overhead, Favian could hear the channel pump flooding the
deck with water for its daily scrubbing, and then the monotonous scrape of holystones.

Favian's fingers tingled as he remembered the shock of
the pick handle striking his sword hilt, the way the bully's
eyes had widened as the steel slipped between his ribs. He
remembered his own feeling of savage satisfaction at the
neat way he'd done it, left one man with a scarred face and
probably killed the other. It had been so pure, so easy—as
easy as the way he'd been led into Anita Courtois's arms.
He wondered if Count Gram would prove as easy, but he
doubted it.

He rubbed his eyelids, feeling the schnapps still warming
his body, and wondered, as he'd wondered after the *Macedonian* fight, what brand of monster the Navy had turned
him into. He had probably killed, and he had certainly mutilated—and with no thought other than a kind of aesthetic
pleasure in the simple, economic way he'd gone about it.
From their demands he had almost certainly known that
his attackers were hirelings, not thieves or murderers, and
yet he had planted six inches of steel into the breast of one
of them without a second thought. He hadn't even the excuse of passion; he had been cool throughout the fight,
quite cunning in fact. It was the trained officer who had
taken over, the Navy's creation, who had efficiently dis-
patched two opponents while the rest of Favian's mind was
still contentedly with Anita on her settee.

Tomorrow he would have to use the sword again, and
use it well. Gram had killed before, and would probably
have no compunction about killing again. Favian would
have to retain that efficient, deadly officer who lived
within him, and let him go about the business of massa-
cring Count Gram as skillfully as possibly. Favian would
have to let that part of him exist, and succeed, no matter
how much he hated him and resented his presence inside
him. He was a man who knew how to commit murder in
the gentlemanly way that meant he would never be

charged with the crime, following the strictures of the *code duello*: Kill a man for money and it was murder and theft, kill him in defense of an artificial sense of honor and the law would shrug. This was what the Navy, with its sublime indifference to paradox, had made of him: a killer and a man of honor.

14.

Hibbert returned by mid-afternoon. "It's been arranged for tomorrow morning at eight," he reported. "I've been given instructions to get to the place by boat. They will provide a surgeon, but I see no reason why we should not come with our own. It will be sabers, as you said. If they're treacherous, we might consider arming the boat party."

"Very good, Mr. Hibbert. I appreciate your efforts."

"I never liked that Gram, sir," Hibbert said. "He was too conceited, and acted like a bully. I wish you all success, sir."

"Thank you again, Mr. Hibbert," Favian said. "I think we may as well commence our sword drill."

The drill went well. Usually swords, cutlasses, and pikes were exercised two days each week; this drill made three, and probably caused comment, but Favian fenced each of his officers in turn and won a gratifying number of bouts. The rest of the daylight hours were spent on deck, supervising the minor but numerous tasks necessary to get *Experiment* out to sea again.

That night, despite weariness, he stayed up late in his cabin to complete all current paperwork; there would be less work for Hibbert to do if Favian was killed or incapacitated. A shrewd observer among the hands, who knew of the upcoming duel (and most did; the news was spread about by talented eavesdroppers who had kept their ears close to their captain's open skylight when he first informed Hibbert of the fight), might also have noted a nervous energy to Favian's activities, as if he were deliberately finding tasks with which to occupy himself, rather than face the appalling alternative of doing nothing and being forced to contemplate the livelong day the imminent possibility of his own nonexistence.

After Favian had finished his official duties, he paused a moment at his desk, hearing the slow pacing of the lookout over his head, feeling *Experiment* tug at her anchor as a cold gust of wind swooped down from the mountains. The brig was asleep; across the harbor only a few lights glimmered in the town. Favian contemplated the morrow and felt strangely at peace; he wondered why.

A few little tasks left to do. He wrote a letter to Hibbert, with "To Be Opened in the Event of My Death" written in frank letters across the back of the folded message. It was a simple instruction for Hibbert to take *Experiment* from Bergen back to the United States in whatever way he deemed best, en route doing whatever damage to the enemy he considered commensurate with the brig's mission, and justifiable with regard to her safety.

"With regard to engaging the enemy," he wrote, "the officer in command must make his own decisions, based on the information available to him, and on his own concept of the obligations of the service in time of war. It should not be judged dishonorable to run from the enemy, if by so doing the *Experiment* may survive to strike the enemy repeatedly and successfully elsewhere." Favian knew as he wrote the last sentence that it might well stand as his epitaph; it would go on record, and his actions in command of *Experiment* would be judged in its light. Future generations of officers might praise or condemn his action in declining combat with that British brig in the North Sea; and both sides would quote his letter to justify their attitude. Favian hoped they would understand, but he knew he had nothing to add. The words would justify his action or they would not, and there was nothing to do but put his opinions on record and hope that they would stand.

To his father he wrote another letter. The words came easily; perhaps deep within his consciousness, as he busied himself with readying *Experiment* for her return cruise, he had been composing it all day:

Sir:
      Yesterday, I was invited to the apartment of a

woman whose acquaintance I have made in Bergen,
and there spent the night. Early the following morning
I was attacked by servants of the man who, unknown
to me, had been keeping her, and I drove them off. I
engaged to fight a duel with their employer the next
day, and I was killed.

As I write this letter, I find myself at peace. I am
compelled to wonder, at this absence of agitation, with
what degree of compliance I have entered into this
affaire. I have been accused (it appears publicly) by my
own officers of cowardice, as I chose, for reasons that
seemed adequate, not to engage a British vessel of a
size similar to my own; and I am compelled to specu-
late that perhaps I have accepted this combat as a way
of proving to my subordinates that their accusations
are wrong. It may be that my death might be, in my
current situation, a preferable alternative to forcing
myself to return their silent contempt with a studied
indifference, or to continue admitting to myself the
possibility that they are right. In a way my acceptance
of the duel may prove that there is, indeed, a moral
cowardice in my nature, that I prefer risking my life
in some obscure, absurd personal combat in Norway
to enduring the oppressive disdain of my crew. In any
case I find myself content with the decision. If you
are reading this, you may in some way console yourself with the thought that I died at peace.

You may show any part of this letter to Mother, as
you best decide.

Your son,
Favian

Favian put down his pen, passed his hands over his eyes,
and then read the letter slowly, careful not to smudge the
drying ink. This will not do, he thought suddenly; he tore
the letter to bits and scattered the remains from his cabin
window. He sat down again and wrote:

Dear Sir and Madam:

As a result of an affaire d'honneur in Norway, I was killed. There was no possibility of avoiding the combat; the business was my choice; and I am content with the outcome.

Please retain in your thoughts of me my gratitude for the opportunities you made possible for me, and the affection with which you regarded

> Your loving son,
> Favian Markham

He turned in to his bunk and slept like a stone until Davis awakened him.

The morning was cold and clear. There was little reason to dress in black, since the fight would not be with pistols, but Favian put on a shirt of black silk that he had kept, since the age of eighteen, for encounters of this sort. He wore no stock or neckcloth, not wanting the heavy clothing to affect his agility; and he drew on blue trousers. In his pocket he stowed a loaded pistol, just in case, though he thought it would not be needed. He took the familiar Portsmouth hanger, the one he had worn since his return from the Mediterranean ten years before; he knew it better than the New York sword, and felt more comfortable with its less ornate hilt and its keen, straight, heavier double-edged blade.

He ate a very light breakfast, wanting to acquire energy without being slowed down by a heavy meal, and declined coffee; he'd probably be edgy enough when the time came. Putting on his boat cloak and donning his round undress hat, he walked up on deck and found Hibbert, his breath frosting in the cool morning, standing quietly with Sprague, the surgeon's mate, and the boat's crew of four. Hibbert looked at his watch.

"We have almost an hour to meet at the rendezvous, sir."

"Very well. Let's leave now; if we arrive early it won't matter."

"Yes, sir." Hibbert leaned forward to speak privately. "I'm carrying a brace of pistols, sir, in case they prove treacherous. Mr. Sprague also carries a pistol. I've stowed cutlasses in the boat for the boat's crew, and told them to come running if they hear shots."

"Thank you, Mr. Hibbert. I appreciate your efforts," Favian said. "Thank you, Mr. Sprague."

Sprague bowed stiffly, a frown creasing his face. It was clear that he disapproved of the whole business.

The boat's crew was sent down into the jolly boat, and then Sprague, Hibbert, and Favian descended, in proper reverse order of seniority. Hibbert took the tiller himself, acting the role of coxswain, and called the proper commands in a flat, emotionless voice.

"Fend off. . . . Out oars. . . . Give way smartly."

Their course took them out of the harbor and several miles to the south of Bergen, where another watery canyon opened inland, and the boat slid handily into the cold, still water. The sun had not yet risen above Norway's peaks, and Favian felt a chill working in past his boat cloak and uniform coat. He held out his hands; they were steady, absolutely steady, and he wondered again how much he was gladdened by the fight.

"Sir," Hibbert said in a low voice. "I wonder if I might venture to ask a question?"

"You may ask, Mr. Hibbert," Favian said. If the question concerned the causes of the duel, Favian had no intention of answering.

"There is a story going about the gun room, sir," Hibbert began, then hesitated for a moment, composing his thoughts. He licked his lips and began again. "The story, sir, is that Prince Christian Frederick offered you command of an allied squadron, and that you refused."

Favian was surprised by the question, and by the moment Hibbert had chosen to ask it. But since the story had gotten out—damn Davis anyway!—there was no real reason why it should be kept secret.

"I was wondering, sir, if—ah—the story was true," Hibbert said.

"It is, Mr. Hibbert."

"Sir, may I offer you my sincerest congratulations?" Hibbert said. Favian was surprised to find Hibbert's face showing unconcealed admiration.

"I am sure," Hibbert said, "that an officer of less dedication to the service, and less patriotism, would have accepted the prince's offer, and disgraced himself by serving in a foreign war."

"Thank you, Mr. Hibbert." So that was how everyone was reading it: a refusal motivated by patriotism rather than cowardice. Of course, in actuality it had been prompted by neither, simply by plain pragmatism; but Favian saw no reason to set this particular record straight. If he died today, that would be at least one thing remembered in his favor.

Hibbert consulted a hand-drawn map, and the boat came to shore three-quarters of a mile from the fjord's jagged mouth. Favian leaped nimbly to shore, glad of activity to warm his long, chilled limbs. Hibbert and Sprague followed, Hibbert windmilling his arms to bring blood into them. Hibbert led them inland to a twisting, ancient dirt road, so unused that sod had encroached upon the wheel ruts. He looked down at the road, then turned to Favian.

"A carriage has been along here just recently, sir," he said. "That would almost certainly be the other party. They will be perhaps half a mile farther along."

"Very good, Mr. Hibbert," Favian said. He took off his boat cloak, folded it, hung it carefully on a convenient bush. "I'd like to warm up here, I think. No sense in letting them watch while I do it."

"Good idea, sir."

Favian carefully went through the limbering exercises with which his father's fencing master, servant, and friend St. Croix had taught him to precede every bout. He felt the warm blood rush into his limbs, felt the skin tingle as it awakened. He stripped off his uniform coat and took his sword from his scabbard, balancing it, then briskly exercised with the sword for three minutes until he felt the sweat prickling his forehead and nape. He felt his limbs grow supple, the sword grow lighter and quicker. Warm enough. He stepped briefly into the bushes and emptied his

bladder; no sense in doing it while Gram watched. He
donned his coat and cloak to keep himself warm, and nodded to the others.

Hibbert reached into his pocket, withdrew a flask, and
offered it. "Would you care for a drink of brandy, sir?" he
asked.

Favian shook his head. "Thank you, Mr. Hibbert, but
no. It might take the edge off."

Hibbert nodded approvingly, stowed the flask, and led
the way down the road.

Count Gram's coach, with its familiar, sleepily nodding
driver, was found driven off the road in a dell. The choice
of place was perfect; there was a clearing obscured by high
ground, perfectly private. One man, short, top hatted, an
elegantly embroidered cloak dropping from his shoulders,
stood alone in the clearing. Hibbert stopped, narrowing his
eyes, and carefully scanned the trees to either side.

" 'Ware ambush, gentlemen," he said in a hushed voice,
and stepped toward the coach. Favian followed partway,
then, as the other man advanced toward them, lagged back.
The short man was presumably Baron Kurtz, Gram's second, and Favian stayed out of earshot as the seconds spoke
quietly between themselves. They paced over the ground,
which was good turf and fairly flat, beginning to turn
green after a hard winter, but soft with deadened grass and
leaves. The seconds spoke a final few words and then
parted, Hibbert walking toward Favian, Baron Kurtz toward the carriage.

"We're ready, sir," Hibbert said. Favian nodded and began to remove his boat cloak.

Baron Kurtz opened the door of the carriage, and a
portly man with a case exited, presumably the Norwegian
doctor. The doctor was followed by Count Gram, who cast
a single, contemptuous glance in Favian's direction and
then marched toward the trees, where he urinated quietly.
Then Gram turned to where his second waited and took
off his cloak. Beneath the cloak he wore a brilliant red
military coat, plated with orders and decorations, which he
unbuttoned and removed. Favian had stripped to his shirt.
Both principals handed their hats to their seconds, undid
their sword belts, and stripped the scabbards from their

blades. Swords in their hands, they were led by their seconds to the firm ground at the center of the dell, and for
the first time got a good look at one another.

Gram's face was a brighter red than usual, and bore a
ferocious, brutal scowl. He hadn't removed his collar stock
or neckcloth, and his neck looked as swollen as a bullfrog's.
His straight hanger, ornate, gold hilted, the blade dama-
scened, was held loosely but familiarly in his right hand.
Favian hoped the bulky neckcloth would restrict his movements, that the time spent in the carriage had cramped his
limbs.

The swords, both straight and double-edged, were approx-
imately the same length, but Favian's arms were probably
longer. Count Gram's round, powerful shoulders could be
expected to minimize that advantage.

"Gentlemen," Hibbert said, standing with Baron Kurtz
to one side, "as neither party has offered an apology, we
will commence at the word of command. At the word *advance* the principals will walk toward each other until their
swords touch. At the words *on guard* the principals will
assume the guard position. At the word *engage* the fight
will commence, and will continue until one party is defeated. The fight may be interrupted at any time for rest, if
both parties agree. Do either of you gentlemen require me
to repeat the instructions?"

Favian shook his head. Count Gram simply increased
the ferocity of his glare.

"Very well, gentlemen," Hibbert said. "Advance!"

The swords were extended and came together. Kurtz
came forward, took the swords in his carefully gloved
hands, and made certain they were in contact. Then he
stepped back.

"On guard!"

The swords drew back out of contact as Favian and
Gram planted their feet carefully and cocked their right
arms, bedding their left fists into the smalls of their backs.
Count Gram's eyes glittered blue. Favian saw the tip of his
own sword was steady, while his opponent's wavered
slightly: good. Favian's body felt limber and ready; his
heart rate was fast, but not too fast. He could detect an
edge of fear somewhere in his mind—enough to keep him

alert, but not enough to paralyze him. For a moment he felt a whirl of reckless optimism; he felt capable, certain, firmly in control.

"Engage!"

Both men stared at one another for a moment without moving, then cautiously moved forward to contact again. The blades clicked. Favian beat, thrust, was parried; the attack was not serious, the blades grating along one another as the participants tried to feel one another's strength. Favian's feeling of overwhelming optimism faded; Gram knew what he was doing. Favian could tell very little of Gram's style from the battle thus far, except that he was willing to bide his time. He would not, like the bull he resembled, attack heedlessly.

That was probably sensible, from Gram's point of view. Gram had not warmed up, at least not while Favian and his friends were watching; he'd spent his time in the coach and would warm up in the fight itself. That way time aided him. Time worked to his advantage another way as well. Both men's right arms were extended, holding their heavy swords. Before ten minutes had passed the arms would grow heavy, perhaps too weary for effective defense, and Gram's powerful arms would not tire as quickly as Favian's. It would probably be to Favian's advantage to force a decision early.

Yet caution warred with the impetus to attack and get it done. Count Gram clearly knew his business; he might well have the resources to fend off an early attack, or even end it fatally for Favian. Favian did not know enough. He decided to postpone an all-out attack for the present.

Beat, thrust: Gram attacking. Favian parried without giving ground and launched a counterattack; Gram, unperturbed, fell back a few feet, went on guard in the first position, with the hand at shoulder height, point down and across the body. Damn! Count Gram didn't mind giving ground when he had to, and that first position guard was a little unusual. Perhaps Gram could be tempted into a trick, though. Favian matched the first position guard, then feigned hesitation and shifted back to third, with the hand and elbow low and the point high. Gram fell for the trick, coming in with a cut at Favian's head, and almost lost his life to Favian's riposte—leaping back out of harm's way, off balance, and with his sword cutting air in a frantic attempt to parry, he lost instead a bit of fluff sliced from his shirt. If it hadn't been for his enormous strength, Favian would have finished him. For the first time, as they faced one another, Favian saw respect in his opponent's eyes.

Then Count Gram came forward into an attack, a little earlier than Favian had expected: The man recovered from surprises well. Favian felt his blade being drawn out of line by the succession of attacks—aha! St. Croix had taught him that trick!—and was ready with a counter when Gram's lunge came, the first lunge of the contest. Gram knew the counter, too, and beat the riposte aside. They parted, undamaged, and paused for some seconds to breathe and to ponder.

Favian looked at his own blade tip; it trembled slightly. His arm was growing weary. It wasn't dangerous yet, but it soon would be. The blood roared in his ears; his body felt amazingly alive, from toe to fingertip; his mind was working well, anticipating the movement of the blades. It was difficult to remember that the purpose was deadly, and perhaps that was just as well; thoughts of murder might slow him down fatally. Calculations flashed through Favian's mind, and he reached a conclusion: Attack, press him now.

Favian bore in. The blades clashed half a dozen times; Favian thrust, countered the riposte, thrust again. This was one St. Croix had taught him; did Gram know it, too? He did, but he kept giving ground; Favian pressed him harder, seeing the rough ground behind him. Gram beat Favian's blade aside with his full strength, giving too much power away, and Favian countered—that meant Gram was growing impatient, or perhaps frightened. The count's feet stepped onto a rough spot, and then he counterattacked with all his strength and power.

Favian gave ground, feeling panic for an instant as he felt his reactions just slightly inadequate, responding on instinct rather than from cunning, as if he were out of his depth; but the alarm faded as he stopped the counterattack and pushed Gram back again. How often had the blades

clashed in this exchange? Fifteen, sixteen times? Favian
pressed on, a cold, deadly impulse rising in him as he
sensed confusion in his enemy, and perceiving in his opponent what he had feared in himself: he was reacting more
and more on instinct. Favian fought for an opening, saw it,
and lunged. . . .

Count Gram saw the point coming and could not stop it.
His instinct was to push out with his hands in a child's
gesture of denial, and that gesture put his sword in Favian's shoulder. But by the time Favian felt the bite of the
metal his own blade had slipped between Gram's ribs and
torn open the beating heart. Favian drew back, his arm
dropping as he felt a pang of uncorrupted regret; he
watched Count Gram totter on the brink of eternity, and
fall. Curious that such a tartar of a man should die with
that little boy's gesture, he thought, and before the limbs
began to twitch, before he heard the rattle, Favian turned
his back on the scene and walked a score of paces. Only
when he felt the warm trickle running down his arm did he
remember the touch of Gram's barb, but by then Sprague
was there with his bandages, and Hibbert with his brandy
flask, and Favian felt only a weary desire to climb into his
coat and boat cloak and head for home.

The rising sun finally broke free of the mountains and
flooded the glade with light. Favian's minor puncture was
stopped, then bandaged. The red uniform coat was thrown,
medals clanking, over the scarlet splotch on Gram's chest,
and the heavy body was carted into the carriage. Hibbert
gently took Favian's hanger from his hand, cleaned it on
some dry leaves, and slid it back into the scabbard.

"Congratulations, sir," he said. "Well fought."

The journey to *Experiment* was made in silence. Favian
felt the sweat beginning to cool beneath his cloak, and he
huddled tighter inside it. When he saw *Experiment* riding
the waves in Vaagen, he realized that he was ravenously
hungry and could probably eat three breakfasts. He came
aboard to the usual formalities, but the whole crew was on
deck, and roared out three stunning cheers that drowned
out the wailing pipes, and made the harbor ring. Then
Alferd Bean was shaking his hand, saying, "Well done,

Captain," and the midshipmen were clustering around him, mouthing their congratulations.

"Thank you, gentlemen," he said, and made his way past them to the scuttle. It had cost a life, and made him a murderer once more; but in one of the Navy's ironies, Favian had regained the wholehearted regard of his crew. And again he wondered if he had used Gram as a pawn in the game of command—if he had fought the duel with this end in mind; to disprove the allegation of cowardice and regain the respect of *Experiment*'s complement.

Well, perhaps he had; and of course he'd done the prince a service, by removing the head of Bergen's Swedish faction. In his cabin he found the letters he'd addressed to Hibbert and to his father. He tore each of them across, once, and gave them to the sea.

15

Experiment took on fresh water and a pilot that afternoon, and in the early hours of the morning she weighed anchor and slid gently from Bergen's inner harbor, her blue guns saluting the Bergenhus. Favian stood by the tiller, feeling the cold breeze funneling down from the mountain passes, hearing the brig working, the planks and ribs and yards taking the strain, the water hissing and gurgling beneath the hull. They were leaving a native corpse behind. Bergen's Swedish faction was leaderless; the thankful Danes would probably not protest. Favian should be thankful he was so lucky. Lucky . . .

After dawn the pilot was put into his lugger, and in a few hours Norway sank below the horizon. Favian thought of Prince Christian Frederick, en route to Christiania, trying to keep his country together against the blockade and the Swedish threat; he thought of the frigate *Najad*, which would soon come to Norway's aid, and wished the ship well. He wondered if there were, somewhere in him, regrets that he had not commanded her, and decided there were not.

The land breeze gave out, and the wind veered southwest by west; the square mainsail was furled, and the big fore-and-aft mainsail spread. The hands looked at him strangely as he kept *Experiment* close-hauled westward against the wind instead of reaching southward toward the North Sea. *Experiment* would not do the obvious thing, and return to the Atlantic the same way she had come; there might still be British cruisers waiting in the Channel or coming with the wind for Bergen, and Favian meant to disappoint them.

It was a week before they finally sighted Fair Island on their starboard bow, signifying their passage between the Orkneys and Faröes; they saw fishermen, but left them strictly alone. The brig could be mistaken for a forlorn merchant brig at anything but close range, and Favian saw no reason to disillusion any observers. Another two weeks were spent circling the Outer Hebrides. And then at last *Experiment,* with a northwesterly wind behind her, plunged between Ireland and Scotland and again entered the Narrow Seas, the scarlet Markham rattlesnake snapping from the fore masthead.

Six British vessels were burned in the Firth of Clyde and the North Channel; a seventh, loaded with pipes of Madeira, had her cargo stove in and was turned into a cartel. *Experiment* sailed into the Irish Sea; three more sail fell swift victim. And then the American brig ran into a streak of luck: A convoy had broken up in the Channel approaches, and the squally St. George's Channel was full of its share of West Indian goods in British hulls; five were burned and a sixth converted to a cartel. And finally Favian concluded that it would be in *Experiment*'s best interests to get out of the Narrow Seas forever. There had been at least a dozen sails in that convoy that had made their escape, simply because *Experiment* could not chase them all at once; and they would soon be raising the alarm. *Experiment* had quite possibly bankrupted any number of British businessmen, and given Lloyd's underwriters collective apoplexy. It was time to move on. Favian put *Experiment* on a southwesterly course to enter the Atlantic.

The next day—a surprising day of mild, warm southwesterly winds—a laden collier fell prey to the brig, and as she burned she scarred the northern horizon with black smoke. Favian eyed that smoke uneasily, knowing it was almost a biblical signpost directing any inquiring eyes to the scene; and soon enough he found his unease justified. In *Experiment*'s wake, from out of the smear of black on the horizon, came a set of brilliant topsails and topgallants, a brutally efficient black hull with a narrow yellow strip over her gun deck ports. A frigate. She backed her sails briefly to pick up the collier's crew (since it was a mild day, with only a moderate sea, Favian had given them the choice of

imprisonment or sailing their ship's boats to shore; the collier's crew had chosen the latter), then set her sails in
chase, a bone of white water building in her teeth.

"Brace her up sharp, Mr. Bean," Favian said. "Set the
catharpings, and I'll have that t'gallant stays'l set as well."
He cast an anxious eye at the sun; it would be dark in two
hours, and then they'd have a chance of escape. Would the
frigate prove fast enough to catch them in time? Nothing to
do but wait.

The frigate was not fast as frigates went—not fast
enough to catch them before dark—but it was fast enough.
Any battle fought with that overwhelming force could have
but one conclusion, and even the most hotheaded of *Experiment*'s complement could not help but know it. Favian
had the weather battery run out to stiffen the brig, and
ordered the hands not actually engaged in the brig's business to stand at the weather rail, for quite the same reason.

The frigate still gained. Bucket brigades were sent aloft
to douse the sails (a wet sail held more air); the jolly boat
was hove overboard. The frigate's rate of progress was less-
ened, but it was still gaining. They could only hope for
night.

Favian stood by the tiller, gazing at the brig's foamy,
inefficient wake, the bright topgallants on the horizon that
were growing nearer. He would have the brig's chasers
shifted aft when the time came, hoping to disable the frigate's rigging. But that strategy would probably fail, and for
an ironic reason: The frigate would not be in range of the
chasers until after dark, and at night the guns' effective
range would decrease until the tactic was almost worthless.
Nevertheless, Favian kept the plan in reserve; if he
couldn't shake the frigate from his tail after the sun set,
he'd dump all his guns but the chasers, shift those aft, and
hope he wouldn't have to use them.

Favian turned forward; almost the entire brig's complement was on deck and idle, standing quietly by the weather
rail, staring with troubled faces at the pursuing ship. Midshipman Stanhope, his blue-jacketed back turned to
Favian, was supervising the whipping of water buckets
aloft to douse the sails. The other apprentice officers stood
with troubled faces, their eyes flicking from Favian to the

frigate and back again. Tolbert wore an aggressive scowl—looking, Favian thought suddenly, like a younger version of Count Gram at his most pugnacious. Dudley stood with a slight frown, as if he were calculating bowlines, or tonnage, or the weight of that frigate's overwhelming broadside. Brook was fidgeting with the buttons of his jacket and the hilt of his dirk; no doubt he wished he had something to do, like Stanhope, rather than stand on the deck and watch the enemy approach.

The midshipmen seemed to be wholehearted members of the brig's complement again, except during their daily working-out of *Experiment*'s position, when Tolbert, for example, was likely to be lectured for long minutes about producing a scrawled sheet in which the brig's latitude was wrong by at least a full five degrees, and at a longitude that would place *Experiment* somewhere on Lake Ladoga. But at least their resentments were the commonplace resentments associated with being required to learn spherical trigonometry and French, and not occasioned by doubts as to their captain's courage.

Unfortunately, Favian's duel had produced another effect: Tolbert and Dudley were less inclined to patch up their quarrel than ever. Favian's glorious example had inspired them to an orgy of sword and pistol practice, and no doubt as soon as *Experiment* touched Portsmouth they would be straining at the leash to go ashore and blow each other's brains out. Favian could not hope to keep them on the brig forever; sooner or later they'd have to be given leave to go ashore. He could only hope that the duel, when it came, would result in no more than minor injury.

Of course, Favian found himself thinking, they might all die of gaol fever in Dartmoor Prison, and the duel would not be fought. Calmly, knowing the hands' eyes on him, he went down the aft scuttle to his cabin. The barometer was falling slightly, but not with the precipitate drop that might mean a storm to hide in. He consulted the almanac and confirmed what he'd feared: The moon would be in its first quarter and would rise soon after sundown. He'd have to hope for a cloudy night.

He then calculated how much water *Experiment* could afford to dump—although he could lighten the brig that

way, he might also risk men dying of thirst on the long
journey across the Atlantic. He decided *Experiment* could
safely lose five hundred gallons, and returned on deck to
give the necessary orders. Then he, Hibbert, and Bean
went below to carefully choose the water butts to be broken
open. *Experiment*'s trim could be ruined if the wrong casks
were started; the frigate might catch her all the faster, just
as Captain Manley's *Hancock* was captured during the
Revolution. After consultation the casks were chosen and
marked; axemen burst them open, and the spilled five
hundred gallons were pumped from the bilges.

When Favian came on deck, he saw the hands were
more cheerful, arguing about the degree to which the frigate's progress had been checked; and he detected *Experiment* riding more easily on the waves, showing copper on
every roll.

Watched by every eye on the little brig, the sun approached the western horizon, and gray, low clouds began
to gather in streaks. Perhaps the moon would be masked
after all. Favian began to consider heaving overboard the
brig's launch, saving a few feet of leeway by getting rid of
that dead weight topside. He'd take *Experiment*'s hens and
goat out of the launch first, of course; it might be nice to
have fresh eggs and milk in Dartmoor Prison. He scowled.
There was an anchor they could get rid of as well, then the
guns. A pity some American privateer couldn't appear over
the horizon and draw off the frigate—or, better than that,
an entire American squadron, with Decatur flying his flag
in *United States*. Decatur, Favian knew, would relish the
role of rescuer.

And then lightning struck. One moment he was standing
on the weather quarterdeck, watching the frigate as she
drew nearer, and hoping idiotically for an American squadron; the next he stood gasping with the force of an idea
that might prove their salvation.

"Get the hens and goat out of the launch!" he heard
himself saying. "Rig the tackles! I want the launch in the
water. Mr. Tolbert, two lanterns on the double—*smartly*,
blast it!"

As his officers barked out their orders, Favian sped over

the plan in his mind, searching for errors. There was room for them, to be sure; but not for basic flaws. It could work, if the execution wasn't bungled.

His shadow stretched long over the deck and rail; the sun was very low, the eastern sky darkening. Most of the maneuver would have to be done after dusk, so the enemy couldn't see it and guess what was happening.

"Mr. Bean, I need you," Favian said. "And pass the word for Jarrod!"

Jarrod was the launch's coxswain, and knew the boat well. "Jarrod, does the launch have a weather helm?" Favian demanded.

Jarrod seemed surprised by the question, but the answer came readily enough. "Nay, sir, not really. A little touch o' the tiller will usually cure her."

"But you can trim the launch so that she'll sail on the starboard tack without a man on the tiller? Lash the tiller, say?"

"Aye, sir. If ye give me time."

"I can't give you much, Jarrod. Very little time at all," Favian said. It might work, by Neptune; even if it failed, it might give the brig a little more time.

Tolbert appeared with two lanterns and was told to light one and hang it from the taffrail, as if there were an unmasked light in the stern cabin. Tolbert looked thunderstruck, but did as he was told. Favian, burning with the heat of his inspiration, was explaining his plan to Jarrod, Hibbert, and Bean; his audience first goggled, then narrowed their eyes in thought, then nodded, then said it might work. Favian asked for volunteers who were good swimmers and got at least a dozen more than he needed.

Swift preparations were made. Lines were passed, and thirty men tailed onto them. The launch was given a lantern, a speaking trumpet, a slow match, and two coils of manila, each made of smaller lengths spliced to a combined length of five hundred yards, and run up through sheaves lashed to the main yard. The launch was raised from its cradle; men slacked off on the weather tackles while hauling in on the lee tackles, and slowly the heavy boat was moved out over the water, dangling between *Experiment*'s

yardarms. The transference of weight altered *Experiment*'s
motion, increasing her heel as she corkscrewed through the
waves.

They were going to have to lower the boat in such a way
that it would not immediately tip over or smash itself to
bits against the brig's side. And that would be tricky: *Experiment* was beating on the starboard tack, trimmed as near
to the wind as possible with her yards hauled around to
catch the wind, and her motion was considerable. Normally
the boats were lowered with the brig hove-to or anchored,
or at least traveling slowly; this was going to require careful control.

"Aft line there—lower away, handsomely, handsomely—
avast!" Favian chanted, his eyes narrowing as he watched
the launch slip toward the surface of the waves. "Forrard
line, lower handsomely . . . handsomely." The sheave
squealed as the line ran through it. "Avast!"

The boat was balanced over the waves, its bottom scraping wavetops on the brig's rolls to leeward. Each touch of a
wave set the boat trembling; if it were lowered any farther
there would be a depressing chance of its tipping. Favian
stared at the boat, trying madly to think of some way of
stabilizing it, but could think of nothing. He would have to
take the risk.

"Aft line, lower away handsomely—good. . . . Avast!
Forrard line, lower handsomely. . . ." He could feel his
nails biting into his palms. The boat was skiddering over
the waves, yawing wildly, spray leaping over it. "Lower
away, all!" For a heart-stopping second the boat rolled as it
was caught in *Experiment*'s bow wake, its lee rail under,
shipping water; and then it righted itself, salt water sloshing in its bottom, spray kicking up over its bow. It was
plunging into each wave and taking on water, and with the
yards braced up sharp the boat seemed dangerously near
Experiment's side—thank Providence for that extralong
mainyard! But as the seconds passed it was obvious that,
barring any freak waves or unusual motion on the part of
the brig, the launch would be safe for some minutes.

"Jarrod! Dudley! Aloft and into the boat with you!" Mr.
Midshipman Dudley followed Jarrod up the weather foreshrouds; they were both self-proclaimed good swimmers,

and good aloft in any case. They worked their way out along the square foreyard to where the line led from its block to the launch bobbing in the waves, forty feet below.

Favian could have had them in the boat all along, but he hadn't wanted to risk the boat's tipping with them in it, even with the use of safety lines, which could have proved dangerous if they'd gotten tangled with the lines that lowered the boat, or with the boat itself. Although climbing hand over hand down the boat falls was risky enough, in the opinion of Favian and both the volunteers it was considerably less dangerous than waiting in the boat to be overturned.

Jarrod crouched on the footrope, reaching with one hand for the line and seizing only empty air. *Experiment* pitched, and Jarrod grabbed wildly, unbalancing: another miss, and there were wrenching seconds when it seemed that he would fall. Then he tried another tactic, taking the footrope with both hands, then swinging his feet out into empty space, his feet flailing for the fall. Favian bit his lip. If Jarrod fell, that would be the end of him; *Experiment* could not afford to turn about and come to his rescue, and he would probably not survive in the water long enough for the British to reach him, even if they were in the mood to pick up Yankee strays and managed to find him in the dark.

But Jarrod's legs wrapped around the line, and within seconds he was lowering himself nimbly to the boat. Dudley, younger and nimbler, followed his example. Both men reached the boat safely, and Favian let out a long breath. "Slack off the aft fall!" he ordered, and saw the line slacked until Dudley cast it off. "Slack the forrard line! Smartly now!"

The line was paid out until the launch bobbed in *Experiment*'s wake, fifty yards astern, safely away from the turmoil of water created by the brig's inefficient hull driving itself through the water, safe from the danger of smashing itself against the Yankee vessel's sides. It was quite dark; the lantern fixed to *Experiment*'s stern seemed brighter than the moon. Favian, staring out over the taffrail, saw in his night glass only what seemed to be the inverted image of a dark shadow atop the water, where Jarrod and Dudley were struggling to step the launch's mast and ship its tiller.

Three lines ran from the brig to the boat: the towline from the launch's bow to the brig's yardarm, and the two five-hundred-yard manila lines that were coiled in the boat's bottom, leading to blocks on the new main yard—the lines that, if all went well, would bring Jarrod and Dudley back to *Experiment*. There had been debate about those safety lines. In one sense it would have been, simpler to leave them coiled on the brig's deck, and let them pay out as the boat was let go astern; but if one line jammed in a sheave the boat would upset, or Dudley or Jarrod might prematurely be yanked into the water. So the lines were coiled in the boat, and the best was earnestly hoped for.

Favian waited, hearing the pitch of the wind through the rigging go up half an octave as the wind freshened; seeing the moon's glimmer on enemy topsails as the frigate was revealed by a treacherous cloud. The frigate seemed less than two miles away. He mentally urged haste on the men in the boat.

A hollow, ghostly voice came over the sea. "We've stepped the mast, Captain," it said: Dudley's voice, distorted by the speaking trumpet. "The tiller's been shipped. We've raised the lantern to the masthead."

Favian looked at the sky, seeing a cloud approaching the crescent moon. He raised his own speaking trumpet to his lips. "Wait for the cloud to cover the moon," he said. "I'll give the word. D'you understand?"

"Aye, Captain. We hear you."

Favian walked to the taffrail, took the lamp from its bracket, and balanced it on the rail. The cloud approached the moon, wrapped it with tentative, misty tendrils, then blanketed it. "Now!" Favian bellowed into the trumpet. He waited until he saw a glimmer of light aboard the boat, then ducked the lantern behind the taffrail, where it was masked to the frigate, and extinguished its flame completely.

If luck existed in the world at all, the frigate did not notice the lighting of one lantern and the extinction of another over such a distance; the British would think the launch was *Experiment*. If they had been watching the glimmer of distant light and not the fainter gleam of moon-

light on the brig's sails, they would, at least for a few minutes, chase the boat instead of the brig. But in a very few
minutes, perhaps half an hour, unless the launch was set on
its own course, the British would overhaul it and realize
they'd been duped. They'd scan the horizon for the fleeing
Experiment, and quite probably find it, commencing another hopeless chase. Jarrod had to be able to raise the
launch's gaffsail and get the boat set on its own course
before the British were aware of the trick.

"Are you ready to cast off, Jarrod?" Favian called.

"Aye aye, sir," the ghostly voice answered.

"Are your safety lines rigged?" There was a moment's
hesitation.

"Nay, sir, they are not."

"Fix bowlines around your bodies, and snub the line
down. That's what it's for."

"Aye aye, sir." There was a minute's pause. "We're
ready, sir," came the voice.

"Cast off."

There was no reply, but in seconds the fall was hanging
slack, no longer connected to the boat. "Haul in that line!"
Favian ordered, not wanting it to get tangled with the lifelines when it came time to haul them in. The boat was on
its own. Favian pictured the frantic activity on board, Dudley working the jib sheets, Jarrod lashing the tiller, cursing
in the dark. . . . The little light at the boat's masthead
bobbed farther and farther astern. They'd have just a little
over three minutes before those five-hundred-yard lifelines
went taut; anxiously Favian looked at the two lines trailing
astern, counting the seconds, getting the count confused
with the rapid beating of his heart.

A muffled, tinny voice echoed from the boat, saying
something Favian could not distinguish.

"Did any of you gentlemen hear that?" Favian asked,
turning to the officers clustered on the quarterdeck. They
shook their heads. Favian raised his speaking trumpet and
shouted.

"We can't hear you! Please repeat!"

The voice came again, stronger this time, but not clearer.
Favian cast an anxious glance at the men near him. The

moon gleamed in their eyes as they shook their heads. Favian ground his teeth.

What the devil could they be saying? They were on their own out there; the only way the men of *Experiment* could affect their lives would be to haul in on the safety lines and bring them aboard. But had they finished their task? Favian strained his eyes looking into the darkness; aside from the gleaming lamp atop its dancing mast, he could see nothing of the boat, nothing at all.

"We're bringing you in!" Favian shouted into the trumpet. "Jump for it!" Favian finally ordered, taking a mental leap into the darkness. He turned to the men tailed onto the lines. "Haul in on both lines! Smartly now! Let's bring 'em home!"

The manila ran through the sheaves with a whirr, showering the men on deck with droplets of water. Favian stared aft into the brig's wake, trying to see into the blackness, hoping to see two heads bobbing in the cold waters. "Haul, boys, haul!" he heard Hibbert shout. A beam of moonlight revealed the pursuing frigate, its sails gleaming faintly, frightfully close. If this didn't work, there would be no choice but to dump the brig's guns, trading her fighting power for survival.

One of the splices caught momentarily in a sheave, and a petty officer cursed; but the stoppage was cleared without the necessity of anyone going aloft, and the ten men tailed onto each line hauled like fiends, drops pattering on the deck. Favian felt a surge of black despair wash over him. Even if they'd managed to get the launch running steadily on course, they would have balanced it for two men in the boat; once Dudley and Jarrod left, the boat may well have unbalanced and run up into the wind, spoiling the plan. But no—the light seemed to be moving off to larboard, on a slightly diverging tack, the boat pointing farther into the wind than could *Experiment*. It was under sail, independent of the brig's course!

Favian felt his heart lift, and he felt an involuntary grin tugging at the corners of his mouth. By God, it had worked after all! And now he could see two forms in the brig's wake, clinging to their safety lines, minute wakes trailing behind them.

Dudley and Jarrod were hauled dripping to the yardarm. Dudley was still, lifeless as a scarecrow; Jarrod's arms and legs moved feebly. Men ran aloft to help them in, and the two were lowered gently to the deck. Lewell Sprague, the surgeon's mate, came bustling on deck to see to them; he listened to their hearts and breathing and pronounced them alive. Favian ordered whiskey as a stimulant, and they were carried below to be dried and warmed.

Minutes after Dudley and Jarrod were carried below, Favian had his men standing by the braces. "Ready about!" he told the helmsman. "Put your helm down." The tiller swung to starboard, bringing the brig into the wind.

Experiment tacked and headed into the Atlantic. Astern, the light glimmered faintly, drawing the frigate away, until it fell below the horizon.

The next morning *Experiment* was alone on the waters.

16.

The most practical way to return to New England would be the same route used by *United States* and *Macedonian*, through the belt of northeasterly trades to the south, sailing past the coast of Africa on a wide southerly sweep rather than battling against the westerly winds and Gulf Stream of the North Atlantic. And so *Experiment* set her course to the south-southwest and vanished into the emptiness of the Atlantic, sailing free into southern waters while the Royal Navy frantically searched the Narrow Seas in the brig's wake.

The weather grew warm, and the hands grew browner as they spent the days in the sun. The mood on board lightened, and although drill continued daily, the hands had more time to themselves, doing their laundry, mending clothes, and yarning. Cheerfulness, in short supply after their pursuit across the Atlantic, and after the long days and nights of anxiety while they charged through the Narrow Seas, began to return. The brig's band gave concerts beneath the stars, with the entire crew singing along on such well-known favorites as "Yankee Doodle" and "The Yankee Privateer," filling the brig's tiny universe with its singing.

Favian felt the tension begin to ebb from him as he felt the tropical sun warming his shoulders. The hunters had been left behind, fallen astern with the Byzantine net of Danish affairs, and the cold and ruthless killer who inhabited Favian's soul was slumbering, unneeded. Favian felt a childish joy inhabiting his spirit in these balmy latitudes; the world was reduced to the tiny, isolated brig, alone on an empty sea, propelled by the steady, inexhaustible trades.

The European war was left behind; the American war was ahead, but still far away.

The daily drill at the guns was a reminder of the brig's deadly, inflexible reason for existence, but it was possible to subordinate that to mere routine. The continued enmity between Tolbert and Dudley, aggravated by Tolbert's jealousy over Dudley's success in the adventure of the launch, was disturbing to Favian's newfound contentment, but it was impossible for a quarrel between two juveniles to entirely spoil a day. Even Tolbert's mathematical incompetence moderated; his workings regularly placed *Experiment* within two thousand miles of where she actually was, and not exploring the banks of some Finnish freshwater lake.

But the long, summery gift eventually drew to a close. Early one morning Favian went on deck to search the horizon at sunrise, and found it chilly; he had to go below and return wearing his uniform coat, with the heavy gold epaulet that reminded him of his responsibilities, and of the sleeping murderer within. The wind veered day after day, until it blew from the southwest; *Experiment* passed inside the Bermudas and shaped a northward coast, heading for New England. Favian set the hands to work overhauling the brig's rigging and giving her a coat of paint, making her presentable for her return to harbor. She had been gone four months; by the time she made Portsmouth it would be early August. Favian knew that his family and friends would be anxious; he had set off on a short run up the New England coast, looking for enemy privateers; he'd sent in a prize and then vanished. In all probability English newspapers would have reached New Hampshire, informing them of *Experiment*'s unauthorized rampage through the Narrow Seas. By now New England and the Navy Department might have assumed *Experiment* had been lost, that the pursuit had finally caught up with her and she had been taken, like her fellow converted schooners *Vixen* and *Nautilus* the year before.

As they passed the latitude of New York, more lookouts were sent aloft; they had entered the area through which British warships would pass when sailing from Halifax to their blockading stations. They had been out of touch for some time, and there was no knowing whether the British had extended their blockade north to New England; the brig approached the land cautiously, ready to run if they encountered a British squadron.

At the latitude of Newport a sail appeared to northward; the strange sail, a schooner, approached until she was hull-up, then ran parallel for a few minutes, investigating the brig at long range. Favian did his best to counterfeit a vulnerable merchantman, but evidently the schooner saw through the disguise, for she ran. Probably a privateer belonging to one side or another, the schooner was the first sail sighted in four weeks, since the American brig had left the Narrow Seas. *Experiment's* trumpeter called the hands to quarters; Favian clapped on more sail, hoisted the American ensign, and shaped his course for the schooner, scarcely optimistic that the slow *Experiment* could possibly do more than give the swift privateer schooner a brief fright. But *Experiment*, with the wind behind her, was in one of her fastest possible relationships to the wind, while the schooner, with her different fore-and-aft rig, was in one of her slowest. Though the schooner drew slowly ahead, the pursuit lasted for some hours, and during that time another vessel appeared over the horizon, on *Experiment's* larboard bow. Since it was clearly impossible to catch the fleeting privateer, Favian altered course for the second vessel, taking down his battle flags in order to once again impersonate a merchantman.

The other vessel had probably been observing the chase for some time, and so the deception was probably as transparent as glass; but the stranger came steadily on, beating into the southwesterly wind on the starboard tack.

"That other sail is not behaving very sensibly, sir," Peter Hibbert said, frowning as he looked over the rail at the distant fleck of white. His brow was furrowed in thought, his eyes slitted against the sun.

"It's not behaving sensibly, Mr. Hibbert, for a *merchantman*," Favian corrected. "Hand me the glass—I'll go aloft to give her a look."

"I think she's a brig, sir," the lookout frowned as Favian came scrambling to the main masthead. "It's hard to tell, with her bows-on, but I think she's just a little thing."

"Is she, by God?" Favian murmured, and trained the

glass on the horizon, his arms and eye compensating for *Experiment*'s pitch and roll. The distant mote leapt into focus.

It was a brig, almost certainly, and almost certainly small. Her sails were cut extraordinarily well, and trimmed with a precision that most merchant vessels rarely attempted. The hull was black, with a yellow stripe. Favian felt his heartbeat increase at the mere sight of the strange sail, feeling his throat tighten and his mouth suddenly as dry as ancient bones. She was no United States vessel he had ever seen.

An enemy—a privateer or Royal Navy brig. And she was not running, but rather coming for a fight.

The brief summer of the *Experiment*, in which the tiny vessel had endured little other than brief, warm-water squalls, had come to an end. The brig would endure a storm: the storm of enemy shot.

17

Experiment had cleared for action when the privateer was sighted, so there was very little to do but watch the enemy approach, and make personal preparation. The schooner vanished over the horizon; if she was an enemy, she had probably assumed the other brig was another American; or perhaps she simply did not consider that part of her task was assisting the Royal Navy in a battle with a United States cruiser.

Favian went briefly to his cabin to don a plain black civilian coat over his blue trousers, with his brace of dueling pistols in his waistband; he strapped on the businesslike Portsmouth hanger and put on his boarding helmet, tying the strap beneath his chin.

The black coat was not an imitation of Decatur's informal dress during the *Macedonian* fight, but rather the result of a conscious realization that his six-foot-four-inch body made enough of a target without an officer's uniform to help enemy sharpshooters find their mark. As he slipped his arms into the coat, Favian wondered for the first time if Decatur had worn his battered old coat for similar reasons. Probably not, since he'd been wearing the coat before *Macedonian* was sighted, and in all probability simply forgot to change; but it was an intriguing idea. Favian knew Decatur's personality for an improbable mixture of the ambitious, the romantic, and the practical; and possibly Decatur, in retaining his black coat, had made a gesture in the direction of his own safety that dovetailed neatly with a wider republican statement. Perhaps his ambition had spoken as well; it would have made eloquent mention of the utter shame of cutting short a brilliant career due to a chance musket ball fired at a gold-laced coat.

This fight, Favian's fight, was going to be dangerous enough. *United States*'s battle with *Macedonian* had been at such long range that all of the damage had been fairly random, and it wouldn't have made any difference if the officers had been dressed in uniform or in rags. But *Experiment,* and almost certainly her opponent, were armed, exclusive of their chasers, with short-ranged carronades. Any effective fighting would have to be done well within musket range, and marksmen on both sides would be looking for the officers. And even leaving aside the marksmen, the danger from shot was inordinate at this range. Before the introduction of carronades, a battle between two brigs of *Experiment*'s class would probably have taken hours, neither side being able to mount guns of sufficient destructive power to do significant damage to their enemies.

Carronades had changed everything. Although their range was short, they carried a far larger shot and were capable of greatly enhanced destruction. *Experiment*'s broadside could tear her opponent to bits in twenty minutes of sustained fire, and presumably her opponent could do the same: There was a significant chance that one or both brigs would sink. The battle would be bloody, for human casualties would reflect the damage done to the hulls. Favian, calculating quietly as he loaded his pistols, came to the appalling professional conclusion that the chance of his own death was in the neighborhood of one third. One third. That would hold true for the other officers as well.

Favian finished his preparations and came on deck, ducking so as not to ram his boarding helmet into the deckhead beams. Peter Hibbert stood by the lee rail, examining the other brig with the long glass, speaking in low tones to Midshipman Dudley, who stood nearby.

"Mr. Hibbert, a word with you," Favian said.

"Certainly, sir. Take the glass, Dudley."

Hibbert wore his plain undress coat, with a little lacework around the buttonholes, but without the epaulet that marked his rank. Pragmatism seemed to have surfaced among the officer class. A one-third chance that Hibbert would be killed. A two-thirds chance that one of them would die in the next few hours. Ghoulish, but true.

Hibbert's pleasant brown eyes belied any anxiety about the forthcoming battle; his long-armed frame exuded confidence. Favian led him to the weather rail and spoke in low tones.

"We will engage the enemy, if they will let us," Favian said, and Hibbert nodded; there had, from the beginning, been little doubt. This was not the North Sea; *Experiment* was near home waters, and her crew well trained and rested; the enemy was a brig of equal force. This time there was no excuse. The aggressive tradition of the Navy demanded a battle, and failure to attack would serve as a reason for a court-martial.

"There is a significant chance I may fall, Mr. Hibbert," Favian said. "If I do, I wish you to know that you have my perfect confidence, and that there is no doubt in my mind that you can bring the engagement to a successful conclusion."

Hibbert's eyes widened at Favian's mention of his own death, but he nodded, knowing the odds well enough. It was simply a little unusual to speak of them.

"Thank you, sir," he said.

"Naturally, if you find yourself in command, you must follow your own inclinations," Favian said, "but it may help to know my intentions. We will shorten down prior to the action, but rather than furl the forecourse and foret'gallant we'll leave 'em hanging in their gear." This was *very* unusual; Hibbert blinked, but then nodded and said nothing.

"We have the weather gage," Favian went on, "so we can judge the moment of attack. The normal attack from upwind would be an attempt to cross the enemy's hawse and rake her; but any British captain who wasn't ready for that would be foolish indeed. We'll assume they're prepared. I think we're too slow to try a rake in any case."

Hibbert nodded again. "Yes, sir. I see your point."

"We'll haul our wind and engage the enemy yardarm to yardarm," Favian said. "Our sails will blanket the enemy's, and we will probably draw ahead. Once the action's under way, and there's a lot of smoke between us, we'll set the forecourse, and the t'gallant if necessary, and hope to pass 'em in the smoke. Once we draw ahead we can put up our helm and try to rake their bow."

Hibbert's eyes lit with understanding. "I see, sir. Very good, Captain, if you don't mind my saying so."

"There's a lot that can go wrong with it," Favian said. "And we'll have to be prepared." He paused. "Because of the danger to us both," he added, "I think you should stay forward of the quarterdeck. If we're not together, a single charge of canister won't be able to hit us both."

"Aye, sir. I'll do that."

There was another thought rising in Favian's brain, something he wanted to tell Hibbert—something like "If by chance they beat us, and I'm killed, give the *Experiment* up once you know it's hopeless. Don't prolong the killing."

But he couldn't say it. It would be disheartening for a subordinate to hear his superior anticipating defeat in such a way. The United States Navy never anticipated defeat. "Thank you, Mr. Hibbert," he said instead. "It has been a pleasure serving with you."

"Thank you, sir." Hibbert's eyes were frank and sincere. "It has been a distinct honor for me to have a place on this brig. I wouldn't have traded it for a first lieutenancy on the *Constitution*."

"Of course you would," Favian said. "But thank you anyway, Mr. Hibbert." Hibbert blushed, nodded, and mumbled something unintelligible.

Favian could feel a coolness beginning to envelop his mind, excluding all not relevant to the upcoming fight; he felt his brain slowly being absorbed in professional calculation. Those service reflexes were coming to the surface, the instincts and behavior drilled into him over the years, the things that made him a creature of the Navy, and its instrument. His mind raced with calculations. Not enough was known about the enemy, at least not enough to satisfy Favian's fastidious nature. They would find out more before the first shot was fired.

In the meantime the hands would have to be occupied. It would not be good for the crewmen to stand for some hours with little to think about but their own chances of survival, so Favian issued a ration of whiskey and asked the brig's fifes and drums to play a concert. As the fifes struck up "Yankee Doodle," Favian saw many of the hands throwing their whiskey into the scuppers.

"No Dutch courage on *Experiment*," he heard one of them say, and the words brought a flush of pride to Favian's mind. American sailors, volunteers to a man, taking pride in the fact they did not require artificial stimulus in order to fight for the republic. We're better, Favian thought. We're better than the slaves they have on board, and because of it we'll win.

For a moment pride roared like the ocean in his ears, and Favian experienced the pure, vaunting joys of command: a little brig matched against another little brig, alone on the wide ocean, a pure fight with matched opponents; and Favian knew that despite the daunting odds against his own survival, his brig would win. She would win because of the ceaseless training he had given his men, and the experience of victory he had given them in the Narrow Seas, burning the enemy with impunity and avoiding pursuit. If he had fought that other British brig in the North Sea, the battle might have come too soon; his men had not yet been forged into instruments of his will. Now it would be different; now would come victory, and the victory would be *his*.

The feeling faded rapidly. Brave words and thoughts would not win the battle. There was much he did not know for certain about his opponent: how many guns she carried, how she was handled, whether her crew was large or small, poor or elite. It was time to find out.

"Port your helm," he ordered the helmsman. "Put her on the starboard tack. Hands to the braces!"

Favian stood forward of the mainmast as *Experiment* began her turn, the *carré navale* beneath his feet.

Peter Hibbert watched as *Experiment* rounded clumsily onto her new tack, the yards progressively being braced around, the fore-and-aft mainsail blossoming out on schedule, the whole maneuver performed flawlessly. Favian, aided by the naval square, seemed intent on gaging the enemy brig's speed as compared to his own. Once Hibbert would have been impatient with Favian's finicking tactics, with the naval square and the careful measurement of the qualities of the two vessels. He was not impatient now.

He smiled to himself as he paced along the row of blue carronades, his eyes narrowing as he watched the enemy brig on the bright water. The large possibility of his own violent death did not bother him; such things were not his concern. He'd accepted the odds years ago, as matter-of-factly as he'd accepted most things. All naval officers lived on borrowed time. He was confident of the outcome, at any rate; whatever his personal fate, he was certain *Experiment* would triumph.

Hibbert glanced at Favian with affection. He had leaped at the chance to be first lieutenant of the *Experiment*, as would any officer who had been beached and forgotten for three years; but the acceptance had been qualified by a certain number of private doubts. He had wondered whether he would be able to work well with a captain of Favian's known fastidiousness, someone concerned so plainly with technical details, so overeducated, careful about dress and French pronunciation. Somehow the partnership had worked. Favian, the autocratic master of detail, and Hibbert, the plainspoken, plainthinking, patriotic subordinate, had made a team that, in Hibbert's opinion, left the result of the upcoming battle in little doubt.

Not that it had been entirely easy. During the interlude between Favian's declining the British challenge in the North Sea and the duel in Norway, *Experiment* had almost fallen apart. The men's spirits had plummeted; there had been a rebellion that led to a flogging; the midshipmen had gone berserk with blood lust. Hibbert had been forced to tread warily. He had not been entirely happy with Favian's decision—he knew that if he had been in command, he would have weighed the alternatives carefully, and then put up the helm and gone blazing into battle—but he'd accepted it, and understood the reasoning behind it as most of the midshipmen had not.

It was the lieutenant's job to serve as intermediary between the captain and his crew, and that task had grown difficult, often impossible, during those days. To support Favian unequivocally would have been to cut himself off entirely from the rest of the brig; to support the rebellious feelings of the hands would have been insubordinate and wrong. And he himself had felt, lingering at the back of his mind, the question that the others felt had been answered so decisively: Was Favian a coward? The unvoiced question had hampered him during that time. The news of Favian's duel had come almost as a relief.

Then, following swiftly upon the dazzling display of swordsmanship, had come the return voyage—another dozen merchant ships gone blazing to the bottom of the Irish Sea, and a swift frigate evaded with an unprecedented strategem. Lovely—oh, lovely. It had been a classic voyage, something to boast about in taverns for the rest of his days. Something to tell his children, to take pride in, no matter how the battle turned out.

He remembered that Fourth of July two years before, when he, his sisters, and their friends had hired Ben Wohl's pilot boat; he remembered the loneliness he'd suffered among his landsman friends, unable to show himself a seaman, unable to feel that he belonged with the passengers. Hibbert would never feel that brand of isolation again. After this battle, he would have earned his place on any ship in the world.

Favian still stood forward of the mainmast, gaging *Experiment*'s speed in relation to the other brig. Hibbert had been forced to conclude that perhaps those French theoreticians had been right about a few things, and he was glad he'd struggled with the alien language in order to extract from it the thoughts its texts contained. He had learned a great deal on this voyage. The rest of his career, if he survived, would be marked by Favian's presence, as Favian's, and so many others, had been marked by Preble's. Scarcely for the first time Hibbert wondered what he had missed by not serving under Preble, and commencing his naval career just as the old commodore left the Mediterranean forever. It had probably held him back, not being one of Preble's boys.

Peter Hibbert glanced over the brig, sharp-eyed, looking for something out of place, a rammer or a water bucket or a coil of rope, and he found nothing. He felt contentment seep through his broad-shouldered, long-armed frame. He may not have served under Preble, but he'd served under Favian Markham, and that was good enough.

Favian saw that the other brig was under fore-and-aft mainsail, topsails, topgallants, royals, and a main-topgallant staysail. *Experiment* had the same sails aloft, with the exception of the staysail, but that seemed to make little difference in relative speed: The British enemy was overhauling only slightly, if at all. It would be truly wondrous, Favian thought, if there was another brig in the world as slow as *Experiment*.

But there would be a difference, he reflected. *Experiment* had been designed as a fast schooner, and then given an inappropriate rig by a Navy Yard captain who cared more for theory than for practice. But the British brig had been slow and awkward from the start; it had been *designed* that way, by some incompetent in a British yard who held his position because his father had held it before him. Designers for the Royal Navy owed their positions to places in their hereditary craft guilds; they had no reason to improve the quality of their designs, and most of the successful ships in the Royal Navy were copies of captured French and Spanish ships. In contrast, the only mark by which American ship designers were known was whether their designs were a *success*. It was a big difference.

Favian took the long glass from its rack and peered at the other brig. It sprang readily into focus; he could see dark, anonymous figures climbing the shrouds, the white bone at the prow, a lighter patch on the darkened forecourse. She was bows-on, as she had been during her entire approach; and though she was close enough, Favian was unable to count the gun ports on her checkered side.

It would be useful to know their opponents' force. Favian lowered the glass and handed it to Phillip Stanhope.

"Mr. Stanhope, I'll thank you to keep your glass fixed on the enemy and report anything of interest. If you get the chance I want you to count their gun ports."

"Aye aye, sir."

"Mr. Bean, we'll be wearing shortly. I'll trouble you to send men to the braces."

"Aye, Captain."

The brig's band played "Liberty Tree" as the men took their stations. "Manned and ready, sir," Bean reported.

"Commence, Mr. Bean."

"Rise tacks and sheets! Wear-oh!"

The two helmsmen put up the tiller, and *Experiment* turned from the wind, wallowing clumsily in the trough of a wave before allowing her rudder, the doused fore-and-aft mainsail, and the squared-in yards to turn her bow downwind. Favian took out his pocket watch, as he had on *United States*'s quarterdeck during the *Macedonian* fight, experiencing a rush of familiarity.

"Shift the heads'l sheets. Set the mains'l. Set the forecourse."

Foam splattered over *Experiment*'s billet head as she came onto her new tack. She and the other brig were on opposite tacks; Favian would sooner or later get a glimpse of those gun ports, unless she tacked very soon. *Experiment*'s own sides were black on black, without the stripe that usually picked out a warship's port; Favian would very soon have the advantage of knowing his enemy's force, while keeping from the enemy the knowledge of his own.

"She's clewing up her fores'l, sir!" Stanhope reported, excited. "She's going to wear!"

"Very good, Mr. Stanhope. Count those gun ports when she shows us her broadside."

"Aye aye, sir. She's doused her mains'l! Her helm's up!"

The other captain was duplicating *Experiment*'s movements, trying to keep close, forcing an engagement. Favian made note of the time on his pocket watch. Out of the corner of his eye he could see Stanhope's lips moving as he counted the black squares on the enemy brig's yellow stripe.

"Seven this side, sir!"

"Thank you, Stanhope." Seven this side; she was a fourteen-gun brig, the same rating as *Experiment*. Of course, there might be a couple more guns crammed into the bridle ports, as *Experiment* had, making a total of sixteen; that would make it a perfectly balanced fight, at least as regards armament. Crew was another matter: Favian suspected that *Experiment* carried more men, and though the other brig's maneuvers were smartly done, Favian thought his own men were just that much smarter.

But still they were the same force, on the same sea. None of the sea duels thus far had been between vessels of equal force: *United States* had considerably outgunned *Macedonian*, and almost certainly would have won that battle in any case, even if Decatur hadn't been brilliant and Carden stupid; *Constitution* had borne the same preponderance of armament in its fights against *Guerrière* and *Java*. The British public, stunned by the defeats, had no doubt taken comfort in the fact that the odds had been heavily against them.

But the British could take no such comfort here. The fight would be a classic battle of equals—slow, overgunned, unhandy equals, to be sure, but equals nevertheless. No excuses for either side; the fight would be quoted for generations in texts on war at sea. Favian felt a thrill running through him, as the professional in him realized the consequences: his name and reputation made for certain, promotion guaranteed, assignment to a newer and better vessel, prize money, the thanks of the Secretary, the President, and Congress. Perhaps, another part of him added, the hand of Emma Greenhow as well.

All this if he survived. And if he did not, there would be another kind of immortality as compensation. There was always a special pathos, a special place in Clio's heart, for those captains who died at the moment of victory. Nelson had made himself a legend by dying at Trafalgar, and no doubt knew it as he received Hardy's kiss; Wolfe had achieved immortality by his death at Quebec.

"She's braced up on the larboard tack, sir," Stanhope reported. Favian looked at his watch; the other's crew seemed up to the mark. There was perhaps a hair's breadth of difference; the British crew's progressive bracing had seemed just a little tardy, and the topgallant yards had perhaps gotten ahead of the rest, but at this distance it was a little hard to be certain. There was equality in sail handling, or as near as made no matter.

"Good," Favian said. "We'll go about, just to see what

the British do. Hands to the braces!" He walked forward to
stand by the *carré navale*, plotting the course of *Experiment* after her new maneuver.

They tacked, flawlessly. There was a risk in tacking so
near to the enemy: They could have ended in irons, head
to wind and drifting backward in disorder. But Favian had
confidence in the hands' seamanship by now, and it was
justified. Shortly afterward the enemy tacked as well, proclaiming plainly that what American seamen could do, the
British seamen could do as well. Favian timed the move;
they'd done it smartly enough. There was nothing more to
be learned. It was time to begin the fight.

Favian assembled the hands first, and made the speech
they expected of him. There were references to free trade
and sailors' rights, the Liberty Tree, European tyranny, im-
pressment, giving John Bull his just deserts, John Paul
Jones, and the immortal trio of Hull, Decatur, and Bainbridge. And though it was a standard speech, given on any
United States vessel on such an occasion, it was not insin-
cere; Favian felt the words as he spoke them, knew their
essential truth and the larger truths behind them. Old Benjamin Franklin, at the close of the Revolution, had spoken
to the effect that the war had been won, but the War of
Independence remained to be fought. It was being fought
now: The entire continent of America, from Canada to
Chile, was embroiled in a contest to throw off the enshack-
ling weight of old Europe, and *Experiment* had her part
to play. Not that one little brig more or less would make a
major difference to either side; but *Experiment*'s defeat of,
or loss to, a naval vessel of equal force would stand as a
symbol to both continents of what the young republic was
capable of.

The brig rang with cheers at the conclusion of Favian's
speech, and Favian raised the biggest fifteen-striped battle
flag *Experiment* possessed to the peak, another gridiron
flag at the fore; and then allowed himself the indulgence of
raising the Markham viper banner at the main, the personal pennant of his clan. Again he sensed the long, dim
line of Markhams past and present: mad Adaiah; Malachi
with his hard, unforgiving eyes, glittering with a ferocious
hate of England; Jehu and his gentle strength; fierce Jo-

siah, uncompromising in his faith. He sensed approval in their faces, and the joy of battle in their ghostly hearts.

And then they were gone, and Favian stood alone on his quarterdeck, hearing the wind keen through the rigging, feeling spray on his face, the band rattling with fife and drum in the background. "Send the band to their stations," he said. "Starboard your helm. We're bearing down on them."

The hands went mad, cheering for what seemed hours, hats flung aloft to be caught by the wind and carried into the waiting wake. The helm went up, and the brig pitched as the waves came from its starboard quarter. The officers established control and sent the hands to the waiting guns, strapping on their boarding helmets, looking like a line of ferocious, plumed animals as they bent over their pieces.

The British, their own flags raised to the wind, waited for them, no doubt prepared in their own fashion.

18.

Favian came cautiously down the wind, on a converging course that would bring them together without any great haste, still studying his opponent. The long viper banner snapped overhead. The other brig shortened sail down to topsails and fore-topgallant, and Favian followed suit, taking in the royals, leaving both topgallants up and the forecourse set, giving him the speed he needed on the approach.

The brigs came slowly together. Eight hundred yards apart: easy range for one of *United States*'s twenty-four-pound long guns, but extreme, really hopeless range for anything the brigs carried, except for their bow chasers, which did not bear. Favian felt *Experiment* roll, heard the rigging keen with ghostly voices. His Portsmouth presentation sword rattled at his side. The enemy's flags were bright specks on the sea and sky.

"Steer nor'east by north," he told the helmsman. The angle of approach steepened: Both brigs were heading for an imaginary speck of ocean in front of them, but the British brig would reach it first. *Experiment* could try to pass astern of them, firing a full broadside through the British stern windows, a raking volley that would send eighteen-pound shot rocketing the length of the enemy brig, doing untold damage. Favian wasn't going to try that particular maneuver, since the enemy probably had a counterstrategy prepared, but he didn't mind them thinking that he might. Their preparing to counter an obvious tactic that he wasn't going to use might blind them to his real plans. . . .

The enemy brig fell off the wind slightly, as if ready to wear suddenly to prevent being raked, and Favian smiled. Very good. Favian could feel blood racing through his body; he was oddly conscious of the way his knees and hips compensated for *Experiment*'s roll and pitch, the unaccustomed weight of the boarding helmet on his head.

"Larboard side, triple-shot the first broadside," he ordered. "Even guns with doubleshot and grape, odd guns with shot, grape, and canister. Doubleshot after the first round—even guns with roundshot and grape, odd guns with roundshot and canister. Don't run 'em out yet." No sense in letting the enemy know which broadside he intended to fire first.

The enemy brig crossed the imaginary spot of water first. Favian could see its dark form beneath the forecourse. "Put your helm down," he ordered. "Furl the maint'gallant."

Experiment came into the wind, riding parallel and astern of the other brig, overhauling slowly. "Larboard broadside, run out! Number one gun, don't fire till you pass the enemy's mainmast!"

Favian took a glass and ran to the lee rail, leaning out past the main shrouds, his glass focused on the enemy for one last detailed look. The brig was trimmed well to the wind, clean and newly painted. Well cared for. There were silhouettes on her quarterdeck, men in cocked hats: officers, among them Favian's opposite. He focused his glass a little lower, picking out the golden letters that spoke his enemy's name: *Teaser*. Favian smiled and returned the glass to the rack. *Teaser* versus *Experiment*, 3 August 1813. A date for the history books.

Hands came down the shrouds after furling the maintopgallant. *Experiment* was still overhauling. Not too fast, or *Teaser*'s captain might guess Favian's plan.

"Clew up the forecourse!" Favian bawled. Men ran to the tacks and clewlines.

Bean's voice came clearly over the deck. "Ease the forecourse tacks and sheets. Haul away on the clew garnets. Belay. Haul away on the buntlines and sheets. Belay." The forecourse spilled wind and came smoothly up to the yard, without any dead men spoiling the neat doused sail. It could be set again, as swiftly as it had been clewed up, providing *Experiment* with added speed when it was needed.

Favian glanced aloft, seeing the marines in their blue coats manning the fighting tops, their rifles ready, six men in each top. One of them, the best shot, was assigned to fire accurately down into the enemy while the others loaded for him, thus keeping up a swift and accurate fire. Although Favian hadn't ordered it—it hadn't seemed quite the gentlemanly sort of order to give—the marines would no doubt make the British officers their special targets. No doubt *Teaser*'s marines would act similarly toward *Experiment*'s officers; Favian would have to remember to keep moving, spoiling their aim.

Experiment slowed, with her forecourse clewed, but it was still overhauling. *Teaser* bobbed just twenty yards ahead. Favian reached for his pocket watch and brought it out. "Ten fifty-seven, action commences," he said, and was surprised to find his voice trembling. With excitement, he thought, not with fear. Not with fear.

Experiment's jibboom crept up on *Teaser*'s quarter, thirty yards to leeward. "Starboard gun crews, lie down on the deck!" Favian ordered. The gun crews of the unengaged side looked at Favian questioningly, then lowered themselves to the deck. There was a resistance there, a bravado; it was clear they didn't like the idea of lying down in the presence of the enemy, even if it would be far safer for them.

Experiment's billet head drew level with *Teaser*'s aftermost gunport. Favian realized that in a moment the guns would be thundering, and his orders, thus far transmitted on the little brig without even raising his voice, might go unheard; he took up a speaking trumpet and tried to steel himself for that first broadside. It would be awesome when it came, the only broadside that could be aimed properly, and fired without the target being obscured by smoke. For a second Favian flirted with the possibility of lying down himself. There was no overriding reason why he should not; his orders had been given and would not change; for some time he would be superfluous. But the men on the engaged larboard side had to stand and take the enemy's fire squarely; they would not appreciate having their captain hide while they were obliged to endure the storm of

Teaser's fire. No, Favian would stand and make a target of himself.

A shot rang out, and Favian jumped. It was only a marine in *Experiment*'s foretop chancing his luck; for a moment he'd thought one or the other brig's main weaponry had fired prematurely. No, all was well. *Experiment*'s number one carronade had drawn even with *Teaser*'s aftermost gun port, and the two gun crews stared with mixed fear and hatred into one another's eyes, obedient to the command to wait. The marine marksman fired again, and Favian saw sudden movement on the enemy quarterdeck as enemy officers began to pace, making more challenging targets.

Favian saw the men of the number two carronade stiffen, and knew they were staring right into an eighteen-pound muzzle, and eternity. The marine fired again, and several men on the carronade jumped. Favian would have to credit that marine with a good grasp of tactics; his harassing fire would be making the British nervous, more likely to fire prematurely. The marksman in the maintop fired seconds after his fellow, and from then on there was a steady crackle from the tops. It was impossible to tell how effective the marines were—not, at least, until the battle was over and the winners could compare notes with the losers—but Favian hoped that at least they were serving to distract the enemy captain from his meditations.

The numbers three and four carronade crews were standing stiff now, staring into the British guns, their opposite numbers. Favian could hear a steady murmur of orders from Hibbert and Midshipman Dudley: "Steady, lads, steady. Not yet. Steady, lads. Wait for it. . . ."

Puffs of smoke from amidships on *Teaser*, and the humming of bullets through the air. The enemy redcoats were replying. It was not usually British practice to station marines in the tops. They considered there was too great a danger of the muskets setting fire to the sails, and a lack of accuracy from atop the swaying lower mast, so they lined their lobsterbacks on the deck and let them volley over the bulwarks. Favian suspected they were wrong. He saw Hibbert suddenly start moving, jerkily, as if he'd felt the twit-

ter of a musket ball near his ear, still murmuring his litany
of "Steady, lads, steady. . . ."

Any second now. The number two carronade was drawing even with *Teaser*'s mainmast. Favian was aware that
the litany had abruptly changed. "Wait for the next sea to
pass under us," Hibbert said. "Fire as we ride the crest."
Preble's old drill for accurate fire: Wait until the wave lifts
you, then wait a little longer, until just before you begin to
slide into the trough. Then, as your vessel hangs for a moment on the edge of the crest, there is a moment of perfect
steadiness, and a chance for planting your guns' shot where
they're aimed.

"Wait, wait," Hibbert said. The surge lifted *Experiment*,
the brig rolling, wind whistling through the rigging. "First
section, ready . . . *fire!*" Number one and two carronades
spat smoke. roaring back on their slides. Most of the British guns returned the fire instantly from sheer reflex, bad
fire discipline, and Favian saw smoke and flame belch
from *Teaser*'s side as the air filled with the eerie wail of
canister. Favian saw men going down, bits of the bulwark
dissolving into humming clouds of splinters. "Second section, ready . . . !" Hibbert was shouting over crackling
musketry. No need to be canny about firing the middle
three carronades; the enemy's firing on reflex had assured
the Americans that they would be firing at unloaded guns
and could take their time.

Favian had been outside of the arc of the enemy's fire,
his position on the quarterdeck not yet even with an enemy
gun port, a perfect observer. The British gunfire, triggered
automatically in response to the first carronade section's
opening fire, had not been well aimed, and it had almost
all gone high; there were pockmarks in the topsails, and a
few severed stays had coiled down to the deck, but the
casualties and real harm were small. Lovely. Let them keep
firing like that.

"Second section, fire!" Hibbert bawled. The three blue
guns bellowed, leaping back on their slides, their crews
jumping instantly to reload. The sheet-lead cartridges that
had enabled *United States* to so spectacularly increase its
rate of fire in the fight with *Macedonian* had not yet been
issued for the United States eighteen-pound carronade; *Ex-*

periment was using the old-fashioned felt cartridges, and the carronades needed to be sponged and wormed before being reloaded.

A British carronade fired, one of those forward that had not been able to bear on *Experiment* when the opening shots were fired. This was better aimed; Favian saw a section of hammock nettings tear open, spilling their contents, and men from the number one carronade crew, swarming about their gun as they reloaded, suddenly tumbled to the deck, staining the planks red. "Third section, ready . . ." Favian said, watching *Teaser's* stern sliding closer. "Train your carronades all the way forrard."

"First section, fire!" Hibbert bellowed, and the guns responded. Favian saw that the brigs were parting slightly, and looked at the dog vanes, then at the two helmsmen. They had allowed their helm to go down a bit, nervously steering *Experiment* slightly away from the enemy.

"Larboard half a point, blast you!" Favian said, seeing the helmsmen look in surprise at Favian, then at *Teaser*, then down to the tiller; they corrected, and Favian turned back to the quarterdeck carronades.

"Wait for it," he said. "Stand back from the recoil." He could see enemy gun crews working feverishly over their carronades, reloading, bringing them up to the ports by hauling on the side tackles. There was a bared, striped back beneath a nodding boarding helmet: Sedgwick, the man who had been flogged, returned to duty, his corded arms hauling on a side tackle as he tried to help train the carronade to bear on the enemy. Favian felt a wave rolling *Experiment*, saw the blue carronade muzzles point upward, then level. Not yet . . . *now!*

"Third section, fire!"

"Second section, fire!" Favian's order was echoed by one of Hibbert's. The carronades barked, one of the second-section guns flinging itself muzzle upward as it recoiled. Favian felt his breath catch at the tang of gunsmoke. Then the return broadside came, most of the British carronades firing together, almost all of them triple shotted. The air rang with whooshing, crying, wailing sounds, as if the sky itself had been wounded. Favian felt an invisible finger pluck his bearskin plume, saw men flung back from their guns, their hands scrabbling at wounds; the number five carronade was torn from its tackles and upended on the deck, lying forlorn, as what remained of its crew stared stupidly at its shattered slide.

"Load, lads, and let's give it to 'em again!" Favian shouted, knowing the encouragement might mean something even if his words were redundant. The number one section fired again. As Favian called out heartening words, his mind calculated rapidly. Even without the sheet-lead cartridges, they were firing faster than *Teaser*'s crews, and, with three sections firing each together, more effectively. *Teaser* was trying to fire whole broadsides and was being slowed down to the rate of the tardiest crewman.

The windward position was also helping *Experiment*, Favian realized. The smoke was being blown in the faces of *Teaser*'s gunners; soon they would be firing almost blind. *Teaser* and *Experiment* were both heeling over with the pressure of the wind on their sails. *Teaser* was firing high as her heel pointed her guns upward; but *Experiment*'s contrary tendency was to fire low, into *Teaser*'s water line.

"Third section, ready!" he called. "*Fire!*" Another two rounds of double-shotted fire were flung from the carronade muzzles into the enemy. The second section, slow in recovering from one of its guns being blasted out of action, fired shortly after. Favian felt a musket ball whistle by his ear; recalled he had forgotten to keep moving. He began to pace, walking back and forth on the short quarterdeck as the guns roared on.

The density of the smoke thickened until *Teaser* was seen only as a gray ghost on the sea to leeward, a gray ghost occasionally illuminated by the yellow burst of her own gunfire. Time to try his maneuver, Favian thought; *Teaser*'s visibility was bound to be worse than his own. He raised his speaking trumpet, then decided against it, not wanting the enemy to overhear. He ran forward instead, finding Alferd Bean standing planted on the naval square, encouraging the gun crews in his hoarse voice.

"Time to set the fores'l, Mr. Bean!" Favian shouted into his ear, and Bean nodded. A shot whizzed over their heads, and they both ducked, then straightened shamefacedly,

Favian walking back to the quarterdeck while Bean assembled his sail handlers.

When Favian returned he found Tolbert, one of the two midshipmen assigned to the quarterdeck, standing on the lee hammock nettings, one hand holding a backstay for support, the other brandishing a sword in the direction of the enemy. He was in plain sight of everyone aboard the enemy's deck, every marksman, every gunner.

"Get down from there, Mr. Tolbert," Favian barked through clenched teeth, despising this kind of pointless bravado.

"No, sir!"

"Get down, Tolbert, you ass!" Blue guns spat flame; British carronades replied. Tolbert's face was stubborn.

"I'm not getting down until *he* does!" Favian squinted through the smoke and saw another bold imbecile in a midshipman's jacket on *Teaser*'s weather hammock nettings, waving his own sword. A ridiculous test of courage.

"Everyone can see you're not running away, Mr. Tolbert. Kindly get down and do your duty!" Favian barked. A marksman's bullet ripped at the hammock nettings near Tolbert's feet. Tolbert's face was set in the stubborn lines with which Favian had become so drearily familiar during this voyage. He was not leaving the hammock nettings. Not voluntarily, anyway.

Fully aware that he was striding into space occupied by a man who was deliberately making a target of himself, Favian strode forward, seized Tolbert by the collar, and dragged him off the nettings to the deck. Bullets hummed through the air. Tolbert's sword fell from his startled hand and clattered on the planks. "Idiot!" Favian hissed through clenched teeth, and then as he straightened he saw the other midshipman, the British bravo on *Teaser*'s bulwarks, suddenly clutch his midsection, lose his balance, and slide slowly into the sea. Serves him right, Favian thought, and walked quickly away from an area that was beginning to fill uncomfortably with musket balls.

There was an attenuated ruffle of thunder, and Favian turned to see the forecourse being sheeted home, filling with wind and driving *Experiment* more swiftly over the waves. Already he could feel the brig taking the waves differently, with more urgency. If he was going to spring his surprise, he'd have to do it now.

"Starboard your helm." The helmsmen looked up in surprise, but obeyed. Flowers of flame blossomed from *Teaser*'s gun ports; musketry crackled. "Good," Favian said. "Amidships."

"Amidships, aye aye."

An eighteen-pound shot raged through *Experiment*'s hammock nettings; Favian saw hammocks and scraps of hammocks fling themselves into the air, settling over the decks. "Overboard with 'em!" he shouted, and the men obeyed; they were a fire hazard until they could be gotten off the brig. Through the smoke and rushing men Favian saw Midshipman Brook running aft, one hand holding his round hat on his head.

"Captain, Mr. Hibbert's down!"

Favian felt a pang of bleak dismay, and battened it firmly away before it could turn to sorrow.

"Killed?"

"I think so. Hit in the head by a grapeshot." That would bring death, aye, or horrible disfigurement. Favian saw the shadow of the enemy brig looming closer.

"Tell Dudley he's in charge forrard. Tell him to prepare for collision."

Brook's eyes widened. "Collision. Aye aye." He ran forward.

Favian peered through the smoke. *Experiment* was drawing ahead, and had turned to cross *Teaser*'s bows. Even with the increase in speed she might not make it: *Experiment*, though for the moment faster, had more water to cover, including the wider arc of her turn; *Teaser* might turn to larboard to keep her distance. It would be close. If the tactic failed they'd collide, broadside to broadside, and have to fight it out locked together.

Hibbert dead. The fact struck Favian with an almost physical sorrow. Hibbert was the only other who knew his plan. Favian would have to survive.

As *Experiment* drew ahead through the clinging smoke, its fore part was no longer in *Teaser*'s field of fire; for some minutes the enemy guns concentrated on the quarterdeck, where Favian paced briskly to avoid the bullets of red-coated marines. The volume of fire was terrifying for those minutes, the hammock nettings plucked and torn, bulwarks broken, men falling, streaked with red, as humming canister tore the air. The mainsail roared, wounded continually by high-sighted enemy fire. Favian paced quickly and waited stolidly for the splinter, or the roundshot, or the musket ball that would claim his life. It did not come. He saw Alferd Bean fall onto the *carré navale,* almost cut in two by an eighteen-pound shot, and still his own death did not come. He saw Sedgwick, his scarred back now streaked with powder, haul on a side tackle, and then die from a musket ball with the same oxlike placidity with which he had met his flogging; but still Favian's death did not come.

And then he saw *Teaser's* bow turning away, and he saw that the British had seen *Experiment* about to cross their bows and had responded, helm hard over, turning away. "Helm hard to starboard!" Favian shouted, turning to the helmsmen, but at that moment both helmsmen fell, snuffed by an invisible wind of canister, and Favian leaped for the tiller, his feet catching on something on the deck, something soft, like a body. He went to his knees, losing balance, the tiller catching him a blow on the cheek, but he put his shoulder beneath the tiller head and pushed, his booted feet scrabbling for traction. He half-rose, the tiller swinging, both his hands white-knuckled on the spar. *Experiment* responded, rolling on the seas.

For a moment it was a race, both vessels turning downwind, *Teaser* slower but on the inside track. If this continued they'd swing clean around until they came up against the wind, and then *Experiment* would have the leeward position. Favian didn't like that possibility, and his brain raced with plans to avoid it and somehow keep the weather gage: Clew up the forecourse and topgallant, slow *Experiment* down, then swing across *Teaser's* stern, raking her perhaps, maintaining the weather position. That could be tricky; it risked a collision, *Experiment's* bows into *Teaser's* side, that would give the enemy a raking shot, which at this stage would probably end the contest very quickly. . . .

But then the smoke parted for an instant, and Favian saw *Teaser*'s torn jib sheet flying free, the wind spilling. The jib sheet had been shot away. The careful balance of opposing forces that kept *Teaser* in trim was gone; the British brig's fore-and-aft mainsail would be pushing her stern to leeward, without the force of the jib to balance it. *Teaser* would find it impossible to continue her turn downwind until they brailed up the mainsail or got a new jib aloft.

Favian watched as *Experiment* won the race. The American brig slid across *Teaser*'s path, Favian's hands on the tiller, soon joined by the hands of two men he'd called from the unengaged starboard battery. *Teaser*'s jibboom came lunging out of the gunsmoke, striking just aft of *Experiment*'s mainmast, tearing a great gap in *Experiment*'s mainsail and tangling itself in the mainmast backstays. There was a grinding roar as *Teaser*'s bow crashed into *Experiment*'s side, putting out the eye of one of the false quarter-galleries. The number three battery cracked out just then, at Tolbert's command, both the aftermost carronades leaping back on their slides, their shot, canister, and grape tearing the length of the enemy deck.

It had worked, Favian thought dully as the brigs ground together, as the air filled with cheering and the brigs slowed, rocking on the seas, locked together like a pair of drunken dancers. *Teaser* slid back a few feet, as if contemplating *Experiment* at arm's length, and there she stayed, none of her broadside carronades bearing, ready to be torn apart by most of *Experiment*'s armament, hopelessly tangled and unable to get away without doing further fatal damage to herself.

It had worked. Favian could die now, having little more to contribute. Even the idiot Tolbert would know what to do now. Favian relinquished the tiller, shouting out commands for the unengaged starboard broadside to prepare to repel boarders. He doubted the command would be necessary; he couldn't see many Englishmen foolish enough to try to board over that narrow bowsprit, one by one, jumping down onto *Experiment*'s deck and onto the waiting pikes. But he reached into his waistband for a pistol just in case, and felt its balanced weight in his hands. There were figures on the enemy bowsprit, yes; but they seemed more interested in surveying the damage than in volunteering to be the first man slaughtered at close quarters by the waiting men in plumed boarding helmets. A marksman fired, and one of the figures staggered, falling into the green gulf between the two hulls. The second section carronades, trained as far over as their tackles would allow, fired at a command, the blue guns leaping back on their slides. Not a single British gun could bear on *Experiment*, not a single one. . . .

And then Favian saw it wasn't true. There were guns that bore, and he was looking straight into the muzzle of one of them. Six-pounders, long guns instead of carronades, crammed into *Teaser*'s bridle ports and bearing almost straight forward, used as chasers like the long nines in *Experiment*'s own bridle ports. They'd not been fired, since up until now they hadn't bore, and the red tampions with the carved lion's heads were still in place. But now Favian saw crews running to them, removing the tampions, ready to run them out. *Experiment*'s number six carronade stood within a few feet of the enemy's long muzzle, its own crew reloading madly, swabbing out the short blue-barreled weapon. It was a race. If the Americans won, they'd blow the British gun crew to bits, and prevent *Teaser* from striking so much as a single blow in response.

The crew of the number six carronade had taken casualties: A loader was down, and the gun captain sprawled on the deck, his chest a pool of blood, victim of an enemy musket. The enemy six-pounder was longer, and would take longer to load, but it hadn't fired earlier in the fight, and would not need to be wormed and sponged out. It would be very close.

Without conscious thought Favian stepped forward, took a priming quill from the gun captain's belt, and seized his powder horn, snapping the leather strap holding it around the dying man's neck. The gun captain looked up at him with hurt, uncomprehending eyes. One of the loaders was pushing the felt cartridge into the gun's muzzle. "A round of canister, lads!" he heard an English voice say.

"Canister on top of roundshot," Favian said, as the loader withdrew his rope-handled ladle; Favian jammed the priming quill into the touch hole, feeling it puncture the felt bag inside the gun. He glanced up, seeing the enemy gun crew working feverishly, shoving a tin bucket choked with musket balls down the barrel of the six-pounder. The eighteen-pound roundshot was rammed down the muzzle of the carronade. Favian poured powder from the powder flask around the touch hole, saw the assistant gun captain's hands cock the flintlock firing mechanism. "Run 'er out, lads!" he heard a triumphant English voice sing. Favian dropped the powder flask and snatched at the lanyard, hearing the rumble of the six-pounder being rolled up to the bridle port. The round of canister was shoved down atop the roundshot in the carronade.

He had lost the race. The enemy gun would be fired the instant it was run out. A round of canister was a tin bucket choked with musket balls; in another few seconds he and the others of number six carronade would be shredded by hundreds of lead bullets. His own carronade was ready to fire, but was not yet run out of the port. They would be lucky if there was anything left to wrap in canvas and commit to the sea. He saw the carronade crew reaching for the side tackles to run the gun out of the port.

"Belay that!" he barked. "Run for it!" They stood stock-still as they absorbed the command, then leaped for safety. Favian jumped to one side, the lanyard still in his fist, landed on his shoulder, hit hard, rolled. . . .

There was a tearing crash behind him; whether it was the enemy six-pounder or his own carronade was unclear. Favian staggered to his feet, seeing stars; his legs weakened and he went down again. His vision gradually cleared: The number six carronade was tilted muzzle-up on its side, having fired a split second before the enemy gun captain tugged at his own lanyard. Friendly hands bore Favian up; Stanhope's anxious voice asked, "Are you well, Captain? Have you been hurt?"

Favian shook his head. "I'm all right." He had taken an enormous chance. The recoil of a firing carronade was normally absorbed by the side tackles that had hauled it to the port, and by friction with the slide. Favian had fired it with the carronade fully back, with nothing but the strength of the carriage to absorb its rocketing weight. He had fully expected the heavy little gun to tear itself from its slide and go bounding across the deck, but the side tackles and the breeching had held.

He looked toward *Teaser*. The six-pounder was on its side in the bridle port, its barrel split across with the force of the eighteen-pound shot hitting it muzzle-on. Its crew was gone, as if it had never been.

The other British chaser fired, blasting away a piece of *Experiment*'s taffrail, but doing no other damage. It was pointed out at an awkward angle; unless the brigs' relative position changed, it would not be able to harm the Americans. The number seven carronade crashed and butchered the British chaser's crew at close range; after that the enemy gave up trying to use their forward guns and concentrated their efforts on trying to get the two craft apart.

They succeeded eventually—though not until they had been raked for five minutes by continuous American fire, not until Favian had seen with his own eyes an enemy officer in his cocked hat and blue coat go down to a marine marksman. The British bowsprit eventually tore free of *Experiment*'s backstays, snapping two of the big stays like thread, but fracturing *Teaser*'s jibboom. The two brigs scraped past one another, bilges grinding, broadsides blasting out into the faces of opposing crews. Then there was a reprieve from gunfire as both crews tried to regain control of their vessels: *Teaser* was running free, heading downwind; *Experiment* had been pushed almost head-to-wind and needed to fall off. Favian backed the jib and the foresails, throwing the helm all the way to larboard, and *Experiment*, after balking for a moment, turned downwind; the foresails filled with wind and she began gaining way.

The British tried to get a jib aloft to regain control, and they succeeded momentarily; but with the torn jibboom gone, much of the support for the foremast had gone with it, and the added pressure of the jib was too much—slowly the entire fore-topmast tottered, then crumpled, then fell in torn ruin across *Teaser*'s bulwark.

The British brig was entirely out of control now. The pressure from her mainsail pushed her stern downwind until she found a new balance, her bow pointing helplessly upwind; she hung there, at about a thirty-degree angle to the wind, drifting slowly backward, gaining sternway. *Teaser* looked very low in the water, listing perceptibly to starboard.

Favian sailed *Experiment* to within a hundred yards of her, backed the fore-topsail, and hove the brig to. *Experiment* could sit there forever, pounding *Teaser* into eternity. Presumably the enemy knew it; but the British brig's flags were still flying at her main and peak, and as *Experiment* neared, musket fire popped from behind her bulwarks. No surrender.

"Starboard carronades, ready!" Favian called, shouting into his speaking trumpet, hoping the British would hear his commands and, knowing what they meant, surrender.

"Starboard guns . . . *fire!*" The blue guns lashed out together, punishing the enemy. Favian gave them three perfectly aimed, perfectly coordinated broadsides, then called a halt. He raised the speaking trumpet to his lips.

"Do you strike, gentlemen?" he asked. There was no reply. "You have fought honorably and well," Favian shouted, trying to coat their embarrassment with as much sugar as possible. "There is no disgrace to surrender when the position is helpless." Give them time to think, Favian remembered Decatur saying, standing last year on *United States*'s roundhouse.

"I propose a three minutes' truce, while you consider your situation," Favian bellowed. "At the end of that time I shall call for your surrender."

Favian took out his pocket watch and opened it. *Experiment* rolled on the steady waves, wind keening through her rigging, men aloft to knot and splice cut rigging, others standing by their guns. The smoke of gunfire slowly dispersed; the Markham rattlesnake pennant flapped overhead. It was time.

"Gentlemen, your three minutes have passed!" Favian's voice echoed harshly through the speaking trumpet. "Do you strike to us?"

"Aye." The voice was very young. "We strike!"

For a few moments there was madness aboard *Experiment*, powder-blackened figures dancing impromptu hornpipes, their oddness increased by the nodding plumes of their boarding helmets; cheers roared out. Order was eventually restored, but not before *Teaser*'s beaten crew had been forced to endure the humiliation of Yankee celebration.

Favian was about to order away a boat, but then remembered that he had none: Both had been lost in the attempt to get away from the British frigate. He raised his speaking trumpet.

"You'll have to send us a boat, *Teaser*," he shouted. "Bring your captains and lieutenants aboard."

"Cap'n's wounded," called the young voice. "Boats're all holed, none of 'em can swim. We can't send a boat, sir."

Favian grinned. He had taken an enemy man-of-war, but had no way to take possession. "Stand by," he said. "We'll drift down to you."

"Yes, sir."

Teaser's wreckage over the side would slow her down, and with her fore-topmast gone she had a lower silhouette to the wind; *Experiment* would eventually drift very gently down to her.

Favian lowered the trumpet, then slid the heavy boarding helmet from his head, feeling a sense of wondering survival rising in him. He had remained alive throughout the battle, without so much as a scratch. He had been so prepared for death that the fact of his survival caught him by surprise. He'd done it, by Neptune! Captured an enemy warship, preserved his own, and lived to enjoy the prize money! He felt like joining the other survivors in their hornpipes. A bubble of laughter caught at his lips, but he restrained it.

There was work to be done. The carronades had to be secured, the hammocks spilled from their nettings had to be collected, the torn rigging had to be spliced, the dead had to be counted. There were twelve of the latter, Lewell Sprague informed him, when he found the time to come on deck and make his report. "Sixteen wounded. We think most of them will survive, including Mr. Hibbert."

"Hibbert—he's alive?" The words tumbled from Favian's lips. "I'd been told he'd—I'd been told otherwise."

"He was hit in the head by a spent grapeshot," Sprague said. "It must have bounced from one of the carronades and lost most of its force. It knocked him flat. I think his skull is not fractured; his helmet must have saved him. He's a lucky man."

"Lucky, aye," Favian said, relief flooding him. Peter Hibbert would be alive to receive his share of prize money and glory, and to accept his well-deserved, inevitable promotion. Idiotic happiness bubbled from Favian. "Thank you, Mr. Sprague." He walked forward to oversee the furling of the maincourse, and he felt the happiness die.

Midshipman James Dudley lay dead on the foredeck, shot through the breast. His glazed brown eyes, fixed at the sky, had lost their keen intelligence; he had not survived to fight his duel with Tolbert. Favian remembered Dudley sliding confidently down the boat fall when they'd given the British frigate the slip, and wondered why it was the good ones who died. Tolbert, the dunce, had tempted the fates and lived; Dudley had died unfairly in his place. Favian turned his eyes away from the body and saw the stricken face of Brook, Dudley's friend, struggling to hold back the tears. Death had not meant much to these boys until today; death had been a stranger, a phantom to be dared in bloodless duels or acts of bravery. Favian remembered his own first grim lesson in Spain, and sympathized.

He finished his task and walked aft to where the mainsail gaff was being lowered, where the torn mainsail would be replaced with one of the spares. "Congratulations, sir, on your victory!" Tolbert said, his powder-streaked face broken into a white-toothed grin. "It was brilliant, sir!"

"Thank you, Mr. Tolbert," Favian said, Tolbert's enthusiasm grating on his newly opened sorrow; but Tolbert did not hear the words. The stocky midshipman was staring wide-eyed to starboard.

"Captain!" he babbled. "The enemy brig—she's gone!"

Favian turned, sarcasm poised on his lips, to face the spot of ocean where *Teaser* had rested, awaiting boarding. She had gone, gone completely and in seconds, the sea empty save for wreckage, and drifting bodies, and a few bobbing heads frantically struggling to stay above the water.

The boats! Favian thought in anguish. *We've lost our boats! We can't do anything to save them!*

PART THREE:
Lazarus

1.

There were only five British survivors: three ordinary seamen, a corporal of marines, and a fifteen-year-old midshipman. They had been plucked out of the sea by men who swam out to the wreckage with lifelines, daring sharks and death by drowning to save men they had so recently tried to kill. The shivering survivors were given whiskey to warm them, and blankets and new clothes donated by their conquerors.

As *Experiment* spent the rest of the day hove-to, cleaning up her own damage and burying her dead, Favian heard the story of the British battle from the jigsaw fragments contributed by his captives. Their captain, Commander Bruce Keegan, had been wounded by a grapeshot during the opening moments of the fight; he was carried below, where he either died of his wounds or drowned when the Atlantic came pouring into the orlop; Lieutenant Reade commanded thereafter, until shot down by an American marksman. The water line had been torn open repeatedly; the chain pump smashed; but no one aboard *Teaser* had suspected she would go so quickly.

The captured midshipman was paroled, outfitted in Dudley's spare clothing, and given his hammock; the seamen and marine lived and messed with the American hands, fitting in well, submerging easily into the life of the anonymous and eternal sailor, hanging their hammocks in places once occupied by men they had killed.

Three days later they warped into Portsmouth harbor, the Stars and Stripes fluttering above a British ensign, the Markham rattlesnake pennant vaunting over all. There were old men of the sea in Portsmouth, men like John

Maddox or Andrew Keith, who had sailed with Malachi Markham thirty-five years before and who would know what flying the viper banner meant: that it was flown only over an enemy prize, during battle, or following a victory. The repaired battle damage and the patched shot holes in the sails were obvious in any case.

Burrows's *Enterprise* lay at anchor in the harbor, and *Experiment*'s anchor roared to the bottom nearby. Favian ran up a signal requesting boats, and oarsmen from the Navy Yard and the *Enterprise* raced to be the first aboard. Burrows's men won; the shabbily dressed, eager lieutenant was first aboard.

"So the truant is home at last!" he grinned, as he doffed his hat to the flag and to Favian. "We've all been very anxious; God only knows why. I hope you'll be able to explain your absence."

"I've written the report," Favian said. "You'll read it in the newspapers."

The smile faded from Burrows's face. Favian stood in his dress coat and cocked hat, the uniform he'd last worn to host the prince royal. His careful, fashionable spit curls were solicitously curled forward on his cheeks and temples; the gaudy New York presentation sword hung by his side. He was ready for his interview with the commandant of the Navy Yard, his packaged report in his hand; he was seconded by Hibbert, bandages wrapped around his head, carrying a package made up of the papers and manifests of all the ships *Experiment* had captured. His opening words to the commandant were ready; they were the same words he'd addressed to the Secretary of the Navy in Washington as the first sentence of his report: *We have swept the Narrow Seas of England of every enemy we encountered, and we have deprived King George of a brig of war.*

He knew what would happen when he spoke those words, and what would occur when his report reached Washington. The legend of the Navy, the legend whose circuitous marches Favian had been skirting, half-believing in its existence, half-terrified of its power—the legend would reach out to engulf him. He would become a part of it, whether he wished it or not. He was so *suitable* for the Navy's purposes: son of a celebrated privateering family, veteran of Tripoli, former apprentice to one of the Navy's untarnished heroes, a duelist who had successfully defended his own and his country's honor, and now the absolute victor over an enemy less remarkable for its size or efficiency than for the fact of its being a vessel of equal force to his own, beaten in "pure" combat, where the only difference was in the caliber of men on each side, and in the cunning of the captains.

Favian would accede to the legend; he could do little else. It would wrap him and make him its own, much as the well-trained, deadly serving officer had risen, just before the battle, to command Favian's heart and mind, and bring them under his cold sway.

From now on he would be judged according to the dictates of the legend. Minor divergences would be ignored; major ones would be explained away. The victory over *Teaser*—or rather the proclamation of it—would link the name of Favian Markham forever with the Navy. Strangers would drink to his name at distant tables; artists would beg to paint his portrait; entrepreneurs would trample one another in order to make him part of their schemes. He would be expected to make speeches at banquets; there would be more presentation swords. Of course he would be promoted, and the second epaulet would be attached to his dress coat. He would receive the thanks of Congress, and probably they would award him money for the ships he'd destroyed, making up for the loss in prize money; there would be no worries on that score. He would be very junior on the captains' list, so there would be no command at sea until after the war; perhaps he would be allowed to run some Navy Yard and count the number of prizes brought in by other captains. He would be able to afford to marry Emma Greenhow; perhaps, now that there was no prospect of his going to sea for a long time, she would even accept him.

The future was known. Soon he would be in its embrace, and there was little hope of escape short of some outrage. He could become a drunk, or a traitor, kill himself or murder children—that would be all that would halt the spread of the legend. Even if he should resign the service, he would still be Captain Markham, who sank the *Teaser* on August the third, 1813.

Part of him wanted it. The legend had its glamor and its glory; there was an attraction to living forever on the third of August, in the midst of triumph, and he wondered if his uncle Malachi, the subject of another legend altogether, had felt that same double-edged enticement. Malachi had gone from conquest to conquest, each spurring him to the next, each grander than the last. Perhaps he'd been unable to live for long in the glory of his latest adventure; perhaps he'd been trapped by the legend, forced forever to outdo himself with new feats of daring.

That was a danger, Favian knew; perhaps Favian would one day find himself unable to live forever on the third of August and would have to seek another battle, another ship to fight or another count to duel, in order to be able to live again in the present, if only for a little while. His father had survived the legend; but Jehu had always been his own man, and would never have surrendered his own carefully guarded sovereignty to an institution like the Navy. Yet Favian, who had thought he'd known his parents well enough, had always been puzzled by Jehu's turning away from the sea, moving inland to his estate and his horses. Perhaps the need to escape his own past had urged it.

"Favian," Burrows said, his voice lowered. "I have to talk to you privately."

"Not now, Will. The commandant's barge is—"

"Favian, for the love of God, I've got to talk to you before the commandant's barge arrives." Favian looked in surprise at his friend. Burrows seemed in dead earnest. "Privately, Favian," Burrows said urgently. "Now."

"Come to my cabin." Favian sped down the companion to his cabin, flung open the door, let Burrows in, closed the door behind them. Burrows looked thoroughly miserable.

"Favian," he said, "your cousin David is dead. Hanged in Fort Independence last month, for treason."

Favian looked at his friend in shock. "What the blazes—?"

"The evidence," Burrows said uncomfortably, "was very convincing. He'd had to leave Portsmouth; he was shown to be trading with the enemy, and he moved to Boston where such things are tolerated. They caught him stepping off a pilot boat carrying dispatches from the enemy. It was just after the British took the *Chesapeake* within sight of the city—you'd heard of that?"

"Yes. My prisoners told me. Lawrence is dead. But David . . . ?"

"Public opinion was hostile because of the *Chesapeake*'s loss; the trial was hasty, and perhaps a little irregular. I wanted you to know before you spoke to the commandant—the name of Markham may not be as popular as once it was."

"Yes, I see," Favian said, his mind aswim with dazed reactions. He'd have to contact Lafayette and Obadiah, find out how Josiah was taking it. . . . He heard the lookout hailing the commandant's barge, and reached out to clasp Burrows's shoulder.

"Thank you, Will," he said. "I appreciate your—your thoughtfulness."

"I just thought—I thought you'd best know now," Burrows said. Favian remembered his handsome, impudent cousin, eyes sparkling, cheerfully and unabashedly speaking in favor of New England separation at the family assembly in March. Caught trafficking with the British—a spy. Christ.

"Thanks, Will," he said, and ran up the companion to meet the commandant as he heard the barge scraping along *Experiment*'s side. The commandant proved not to be aboard; instead there was a junior lieutenant.

"The commandant wishes you to report to him ashore, Captain," the lieutenant called. His voice sounded harsh, disapproving. "He wishes you to bring your reports."

So. The commandant was not pleased with *Experiment*'s four-month absence. He was not pleased with having the complicated matter of the *Pride of Richmond*, the American hull filled with British wheat, dropped into his lap without having Favian present to answer the inevitable barrage of questions and demands. And probably David Markham's fate had not served to raise the commandant's estimation of other members of the family.

"Captain Burrows, if you'd care to join us, you're welcome," Favian said. "Mr. Hibbert, let's go. We're keeping the commandant waiting."

Hibbert, Burrows, and Favian jumped down into the barge's stern sheets in reverse order of seniority, and the coxswain called the stroke as they skimmed over the bright, summery waters toward the Navy Yard. Their boots echoed on the planking of the quay and the slats of the wooden sidewalk. A hunched fiddler in a leather cap played lively music outside the commandant's office, a few silver coins at his feet. He turned, gave a snaggle-toothed smile, and lowered his fiddle.

"Good afternoon, Cap'n," said Lazarus. "I thought I were right when I saw ye with a cocked hat and gold-laced coat. Like ye my tune? I call it '*Experiment*'s Victory.' I've been practicin' it these last few days. I fancy it'll be popular, don't ye think?"

Favian brushed past the demented fiddler without a word. Burrows waited outside the commandant's office while Favian and Hibbert entered.

"Blast you, Markham," the commandant said, scowling. "Where the devil have you been?"

Favian, standing at attention, opened his mouth and spoke the words he'd prepared. The legend reached out and made him its own.

2.

Favian and Burrows slipped quietly into the Navy Yard after nightfall. There had been an impromptu dinner at the house of the commandant in Kittery, with a flood of whiskey and an avalanche of baked ham, and Favian had complied with requests to describe in complete detail his voyage to Europe and back, and to diagram the *Experiment-Teaser* fight in dabs of whiskey on the commandant's polished table (much to the horror of his wife, who watched her fine lemon finish dissolve with each broadside). David Markham was not mentioned, for the commandant was being tactful, but Favian seemed to see David's smirk at every glass drunk to the honored dead, to poor James Lawrence and to the men of *Experiment* who had died while exacting an unknowing vengeance for *Chesapeake*'s loss. The dead seemed very much present.

Favian had desired little more than at least eighteen hours' sleep in his cabin; but when he and Burrows broke away, hastened to the ferry at the Navy Yard, and passed the sentry (and were stopped only twice en route by citizens offering congratulations), Favian knew the evening would go on: There had been a pattern set, at the commandant's house, of drink, and celebration, and mourning. This was not so much rejoicing in *Experiment*'s victory as waking the dead; it might well go on until dawn, this private, alcoholic ritual between Burrows and himself. The commandant, though well-meaning, was not of the same generation; he was not one of Preble's boys, and could not remember the long, tormented wake for James Decatur, followed within two days by another bloody assault on Tripoli that exacted revenge a hundredfold.

Burrows prevailed upon the corporal of the guard to rouse a boat's crew. "Will you join me in my cabin for wine?" he asked.

"Wine? God, no. Coffee."

"Coffee, then."

"Of course."

As they waited there was a hail from the marine sentry at the gate.

"Who goes there?"

The answer was equally plain. "Officer drunk on a wheelbarrow!"

"Pass, officer drunk on a wheelbarrow!"

The drunken officer proved to be Brook, escorted by some of the commandant's shorebound midshipmen and clerks. Brook was poured into the boat, with Favian and Burrows sharing the stern sheets; before they set off across the night waters the boat's crew paused for some extravagant praise of Favian's expedition. "I hope this will not be a frequent occurrence, Mr. Brook," Favian told the midshipman, but the fellow was already unconscious. The boat's crew promised to get Brook safely aboard *Experiment*, and Burrows and Favian went aboard *Enterprise*. Favian received yet more compliments and congratulations from Edward McCall, Burrows's lieutenant, before they could escape to the semiprivacy of Burrows's cabin.

"Did you hear what he was calling it by his fifth glass of bob smith?" Favian demanded, loosening his neckcloth, draping his cravat over the back of a chair. "Markham's Raid. My God!—Markham's Raid!"

"What's wrong with it?" Burrows asked. "Neal! Bring us coffee!" He kicked off his boots. "*Markham's Raid* has a nice flavor to it, I think."

"He makes it sound like some blasted cavalry skirmish, or a pillaging expedition, as if I was going to have to explain the possession of Lord Selkirk's silver plate like old Paul Jones," Favian said. "Make that coffee strong, Neal, or I'll end up like little Brook."

"Good news about the sloops of war, isn't it? I suppose you'll be given one."

"Nay, I'm too junior," Favian said. His and Burrows's efforts in Washington had paid off: Congress had voted

the money for six new sloops of war just after Burrows and
Favian had left the city. "Jacob Jones will get it, or Biddle
or Blakely or Warrington."

"There are to be *six*, Favian," Burrows reminded him,
"You've got a good chance."

"I almost said Lawrence," Favian said.

"Yes. It's hard to think of him as being gone, isn't it?
Such a lively man. 'What, not even Mr. Lawrence?' D'you
remember that story?"

"Yes. I first got to know him on the *Intrepid*, you know,
waiting outside Tripoli harbor to go in and burn the *Philadelphia*. A crew of seventy in a sixty-foot-long captured
ketch, crawling with bugs, enduring a week-long gale, living on water and hardtack because the beef had gone bad.
Decatur was sullen—impetuousness drowned by circumstance, you know—Morris wanted to go in in spite of the
gale, and risk drowning. Lawrence managed to keep us in
good humor; the flow of jokes and wit and good spirits
were irresistible. And later on in the fight he cut a Moor
through the teeth and just possibly saved my life, because I
was occupied with another enemy at the time. He was
damn foolish to fight *Shannon*, though, only a few days in
command, and with two of his lieutenants too sick to
fight."

"Aye. He was a fool, but you know how the gods love
fools," Burrows said. On the first of June, while Favian
had been in Europe, Captain James Lawrence of the frigate *Chesapeake* had left Boston to fight Philip Bowes Vere
Broke in the *Shannon*. The two frigates were equally
matched, but the British triumphed, and Lawrence had
been killed. It had been a "pure" battle, fought almost like
a medieval combat, with no other warships in sight and
with matched frigates, the only difference supplied by the
men who manned them. It was the first British sea
triumph of the war, and was being made much of by their
press.

"Yet Lawrence will be remembered, of course," Favian
said. "The commandant showed us the way, quoting Lawrence's last words over and over—'Don't give up the ship.'
The words will be remembered, and the fact that they gave
up the ship will not." The naval legend was protecting its

own, Favian thought. *Don't give up the ship*. The last despairing command of a mortally wounded, defeated man, already turned into a defiant battle cry. The British, of course, would remember only the victory.

The coffee arrived. Favian sipped it gratefully. "Poor Lawrence, poor James," he said. The taste of sour whiskey was washed from his tongue. "Whatever possessed him to do such a thing? The sneers of the Federalists on State Street? Is it an audience he wanted?"

"He got what he wanted, didn't he?" Burrows said. "A fight against a matched opponent. It's what you had, what we all want. He lost, but he had the opportunity."

"You take the damned matched fight," Favian said. "Give me heavy guns against light every time." He remembered Bean dead on the naval square, Dudley's glazed eyes gazing up at nothing; he remembered also his own keen eagerness for the fight beforehand, his glimmer of satisfaction when Stanhope had reported seven gun ports on *Teaser*'s side, knowing it would be a pure, matched fight and that he would win it. What a monstrous thought that was. Why hadn't he wished again for an overwhelming broadside that would have blown *Teaser* out of the water with the first blow, so that Dudley would have lived to hear the congratulations of Portsmouth, and come back to *Experiment* drunk on a wheelbarrow?

He and Burrows talked on long into the night, reviving old service stories, remembering the blue Mediterranean with the white walls of Tripoli set above it, remembering old griefs, old wounds: James Decatur, Richard Somers, Henry Wadsworth, John Funck, James Lawrence, the long roll of dead that they knew would grow longer before the war ended.

And for Favian there was another sorrow, unmentioned: David Markham. He had liked David—*everyone* had liked David, his charm, his careless good spirits—but he found, try as he might, that he could not mourn him. He was sorry that David was gone; he was pained for the effect David's death would have on his family, especially on Josiah, who had loved him more than his other children. But when he grieved it was for James Lawrence, Alferd Bean, Jim Dudley—even Abraham Sedgwick, the man he'd flogged. His mind swam with images of Lawrence, eyes blazing, fighting like a madman on *Philadelphia*'s deck; Richard Somers's last wave from the deck of the ketch *Intrepid* before sailing into Tripoli to blow himself to glory; Dudley swarming down the falls to the waiting launch. . . . Before these memories, David Markham's smile faded.

Implicit in naval mourning was the knowledge that it could have been any of them, that all their time was borrowed, all their lives potentially forfeit. Either Favian or Burrows, or any of Preble's boys, might have been treacherously shot in James Decatur's place; if the British six-pounder had been fired a split second earlier, Favian's memory would now be invoked in *Enterprise*'s cabin. David Markham was outside the circle; his life was not interchangeable with the others. He would have laughed, Favian knew, at the grim naval code, at the notion of comradeship and sacrifice in service to such an inflexible ideal. Let his memory fade, Favian thought; David would have wanted it. Filled as it was with false starts and heedless action, David had shown that he scarcely valued his own life; he would have despised anyone who placed a higher value on it than he himself had.

The Navy had won, Favian knew. It had his life, his spirit; the victory over *Teaser* had assured the Navy's own conquest. From now on Favian was, in everyone's mind, associated with the Navy; their tributes were to a personification of Navy spirit, Navy victory; they would be offered as much to the uniform as to Favian. The largely illusory spirit of rebellion Favian had cherished was deprived of whatever comfort it had given; how could he claim to be an internal rebel against the Navy's iron code when he found himself mourning James Lawrence and Jim Dudley, no kin of his, over David Markham, related by blood?

He found himself making a last protest before resigning himself to a life of obedience and glory. "Is it fair, d'you think, what we do to these youngsters?" he asked. "Take 'em at sixteen, fill 'em with honor, pride, and the Navy? Take Dudley—a bastard, put into the services by an uncle, his only schooling such as his captain cares to give him,

and you know what a bad captain can do—a whipping if
he objects. You remember what young mids are like—must
have a battle and blood before they're eighteen, and if not,
a duel will do, 'a matter of honor' on any pretext. What
does he know of the cause? What did we know, you and I,
when we fought off Tripoli?"

"We knew the Navy," Burrows said. "We knew each
other. I would have died for either."

"Is it natural—take a boy from his parents, from all natural life, and make him die for something so fierce and
abstract? 'I could not die anywhere so contented as in the
king's company—his cause being just and his quarrel honorable,' " Favian quoted, remembering the disguised Hal
going forth among his soldiers on the eve of Agincourt.
"But I always thought the quarrelsome soldier, Williams,
had the best of that argument—that the soldiers knew
nothing of whether the quarrel was just or honorable, just
that they were required to risk their lives for it. Henry
could only answer him by challenging him to personal combat, and that's no real answer."

Burrows looked at him curiously, as if thinking that
Favian was voicing some odd sentiments for a practiced
duelist. "We're not monarchs, you know," he said. "Henry
was the king; he alone decided issues of war or peace.
We're minor gentry, if anything; we come when we're
called, and fight when we're required to, and we can always resign. We and the men we command are alike in
that we obey; we're more like those soldiers than a disguised king."

Obedience. For a moment Favian wondered if his private rebellion had been occasioned by that military necessity. Perhaps he would have made a better privateer than a
naval officer; perhaps his schooner should now be cruising
with his cousin Gideon's in the Indies. Was it subordination
that made the code so difficult to accept? A privateer la-
bored on his own behalf; any profit was his alone, as was
the glory. How much of Favian's private bitterness had
been occasioned by the resentment of sharing his talents
and accomplishments with others?

Little, he concluded; such glory as he had won, in the

fight with *Teaser*, he grudged. Ultimately his resentment was personal; his temperament was unsuited to his occupation, and rankled in the Navy's mold.

"Perhaps it suits the New England pattern to be gloomy," he said, by way of apology. "I know I should be celebrating with young Brook, and driven home in a wheelbarrow."

"No, I don't think so—it's no longer our place," Burrows said. "It's funny you should mention Prince Hal, always disguising himself and going among the ordinary people. That's been my own practice, as you know, but I find the joys of it fading. There was a time when I could catch something genuine, unfeigned—but now I'm known for it, and people look for me, and whatever honesty and sincerity I found is gone once they know who I am. They love me for it, I suppose, but my own purpose is thwarted. If I were forced to endure society ashore, it should be the society of fo'c'sle men, but if I were given preference I'd stay on shipboard every minute, and never set foot on the land."

"D'you think the sea breeds purity, then, and the land corruption?" Favian asked.

"Nay, I have no illusions about the fo'c'sle crowd. They are as superstitious, ignorant, uneducated, and obtuse as they are open, generous, and comradely. They have their vices and pretensions, but because they are little men, insignificant in the scheme of things, their vices and pretensions do no harm. Besides, while trying to claw off a lee shore in a hurricane of wind, there is precious little room for ostentation or conceit. *There's* your purity for you—but a little of it goes a long way.

"No, I simply love the sea, and I prefer to associate with men who love it as I do. I hate the land, and I would avoid it if I could."

"And the Navy?" Favian asked. "Is the Navy an element of your scheme, or is it merely a means to get to sea?"

"Such as is best in the life of the sea, I find in the Navy," Burrows said. "I have sailed to China and back in a merchantman, and there is too much of the scent of land in the enterprise—crews half-starved and rebellious, niggling and haggling with merchants ashore to buy the goods—I tell you, the Navy is a better thing by far, even if there is too much of Washington in it. It lets a seaman be a seaman, and not a damned clerk."

Aye, true enough, Favian thought. The Navy, or privateering, was the purest form of sea service; but privateering flourished only in wartime, and the Navy would go on forever. He poured himself another cup of coffee. The commandant's whiskey still swirled in his mind.

"Will you get married, Favian?" Burrows asked. The question brought Favian up short, entirely surprised.

"I think—I suppose it would be good for me, don't you think?" he said.

"I think the right woman would. You need someone on the shore, something stable. Would make you less nervous, I think," Burrows said offhandedly.

"And yourself?"

"I follow the old Italian proverb: Praise marriage but stay single," Burrows said. "I am satisfied with various harbor Jills." Favian remembered the shapeless, gaptoothed Dulcey, and inwardly shuddered.

"I'm told that your affections are leaning in a particular direction," Burrows said. "I'm sorry if this is trampling on any private garden. You have only to say—"

"That's all right, Will," Favian said. "The whole town knows I have an understanding of sorts with Emma. And that her father disapproves."

"I've met the lady," Burrows said. "At a reception. Very lovely, quite intelligent. High-strung, I think, like you. Bites her nails, hates her father. She asked me about you, quite inquisitive. I think you may have captured her affections."

"The understanding," Favian said, "is that any formal offer on my part will have to wait until the end of the war."

"Quite sensible," Burrows said. "No doubt the father's idea. However, I think you may be quite justified in sweeping the lady off her feet, in your current situation. You'll have money, after all—that's the father's primary objection. She's of age, can marry whom she pleases."

"That's true," Favian said. The whiskey fog was beginning to clear. "I was going to try to see her anyway. I could renew the offer."

"I think you should. *De l'audace, encore de l'audace, et toujours l'audace*—the Navy's unofficial motto, I should suppose."

"Board 'em in the smoke," Favian agreed. Well, why not? he thought. He had stormed Washington easily enough. His star was in the ascendant; he was a popular man, if only for a moment. Why not take advantage of it? If the war went on any longer, naval heroes might become a surplus quantity. He should strike, he decided, while he could still be considered a rare catch.

3

Portsmouth, predictably, went mad. The unhappy outcome of the *Chesapeake-Shannon* contest had depressed naval partisans, and *Experiment* versus *Teaser*, another contest between equal combatants, helped redress the balance; and although presumably the enemy were happy with the exchange of a fourteen-gun brig for a thirty-six-gun frigate, Favian's action at least demonstrated that the United States could fight a battle on even terms and triumph at least half the time. And Favian was, of course, a Portsmouth native, a member of a prominent and respected family, commanding a brig crewed mainly by New Hampshiremen, and therefore due a triumph of Roman proportions.

Experiment's prisoners and the fifteen thousand pounds in silver Favian had taken from the captured post office packet were transferred to shore with a maximum of ostentation, accompanied by the brig's band and marines with gleaming bayonets. Later there was a parade, again led by *Experiment*'s little band, from the ferry to the town hall, where a benefit concert was given for the widows and orphans of the slain crewmen. *Experiment*'s band was followed by a group of local musicians and singers who performed Francis Hopkinson's *America Independent, or The Temple of Minerva*, a work written during the Revolution and celebrating its cause. There were banquets at which Favian's touchy digestion rumbled ominously, and speeches at which he soon learned to keep his face perfectly immobile lest he wince at the unending and flowery compliments, or at the fact that many of the speakers were blatantly attempting to turn the occasions to their own political advantage. He was being used by various local interests, he concluded; he also concluded he did not care, and used whatever platforms were given him to drum home his own message: an aggressive naval policy, the enforcement of statutes condemning trade with the enemy, the necessity to unite for the battle against the British. There was a thanksgiving service at a local church, and he was given a presentation sword in even worse taste than the one he'd been given in New York.

There were melancholy duties as well as celebratory ones. His six surviving cousins were each visited, and condolences made on David's loss; he paid a quiet, respectful visit to Josiah, who seemed quite baffled by the situation, well out of his depth. He learned the interpretation that the family was making of David's death: They seemed convinced that he'd been betrayed, led into treason by government *agents provocateurs*, who had decided New England needed an example and latched onto the guileless David as their victim. It was certainly possible; it might even have been true. Favian, from his first public appearance, wore a mourning band; he let Portsmouth draw its own conclusions as to whether the black band was worn for David or James Lawrence.

There had been changes in Washington: Favian was surprised to read a number of querulous letters signed by a new Secretary of the Navy, William Jones, wondering what Favian had done with the United States brig of war *Experiment*, entrusted to his command, which had seemingly disappeared. The secretary's curiosity would be satisfied as soon as he received Favian's official report, already in the mail; but Favian wondered what had caused Paul Hamilton's presumably forced resignation. His drinking? His hatred of Eustis, the Secretary of War? His unfamiliarity with ships? Any one of these reasons, in time of war, should have sufficed. But Favian was nevertheless saddened by Hamilton's dismissal; he had grown to like the man who had given him his first command, and he wished him well. He later sent Hamilton a long letter detailing his exploits, and wishing him happiness and prosperity; he didn't want the ex-secretary to think he'd been forgotten by those whom he'd promoted and favored.

It seemed there had been a complete shakeup in Washington: Dr. Eustis had gone as well, so perhaps the Army would at last grow serious about its task of defending the nation. But there was a practical side to Favian's concern: With Paul Hamilton had gone his chief source of patronage; as far as William Jones was concerned, Favian was simply a junior master commandant, a man who had more or less disobeyed orders to bring off a triumph, and whether Jones would consider the disobedience more important than the triumph only remained to be seen.

Peter Hibbert, recovered from his head wound, dove headlong into the swarm of activities, enjoying himself to the hilt. What ambitious naval officer had not dreamed of this? Second in command to a hero, promotion probably assured, he was attending an endless run of banquets, invited to the parlors of the most prominent men (and ladies!) in town, his opinion solicited on military matters, and on political matters beyond his ken, and then listened to respectfully—astonishing! He could understand how such things could go to a man's head.

Heady stuff this might have been, but Hibbert did not forget himself. There had been too many years of struggle, and there was struggle yet to come. His family had suffered badly in the war; their shipping business had been shriveled, and they'd invested in three privateers: One had been captured on her first cruise, another had been searching the seas for months without finding a single British prize. The only major return they'd had on an investment was on the *General Sullivan* privateer, commanded by Favian's cousin Gideon Markham, which had thus far returned a thousand percent. That, and Hibbert's pay, and his hope of money awarded by Congress in lieu of prize money, was the only income the Hibbert family could expect for some time.

And so Peter Hibbert kept his head and used his period of celebrity as a way of making and ensuring contacts that would keep the family afloat. Although he found attention being paid to him by ladies who would never have so much as looked in his direction when he was a half-pay, unemployed lieutenant, he remained cautious, courteous, and far from overpowered. He let it be known that he was available for social engagements only if others of his family were invited; and he was rewarded when one of his sisters dazzled, dangled, and was soon engaged to a young, propertied broker of maritime insurance.

In spite of all this activity, Hibbert had the leisure to observe that his captain was not content. He noticed that though Favian went to the same balls, celebrations, and parlors, and that he spoke the correct words and made the correct jests, yet there was something vacant behind his eyes, and something longing as well. His famous temper exploded more frequently aboard *Experiment* than it had in the past. Perhaps the absence of Miss Emma Greenhow accounted for it; Favian had invited her to travel to Portsmouth when Jehu and Anne Markham came into town for the celebrations, but she had declined, writing that she was staying with a cousin and could not get away. Favian had not returned to *Experiment* until late that night; he'd been brought back by William Burrows, with whom he'd apparently been carousing in seamen's taverns.

There was also some brand of antipathy between Favian and the lunatic fiddler, Lazarus. Lazarus had prominently displayed himself on the streets of Portsmouth, and had made *"Experiment's* Victory" a popular tune that other performers were now imitating; of course he'd been tipped extravagantly by *Experiment's* officers and crew, most of whom were engaged chiefly in spending four months' pay as quickly as they could, and had not yet absorbed a surfeit of flattery. Yet Favian, for some reason, avoided the man. Granted that Lazarus's insane conviction that he had sold his soul to the devil in 1682 was almost offensively fervid—and had been so loudly proclaimed that a local pastor had actually preached a sermon condemning Lazarus and all his works (which Hibbert considered excess of another sort)—still, Favian's attitude toward the man had been one of unusually chill avoidance. When Lazarus had been arrested for fiddling on a Sunday, thereby proclaiming his contempt for the Sabbath, Favian had gone so far as to remark that he hoped the man would be jailed until his satanic master came to collect him.

Eventually Favian's digestive complaint caught up with him, and put him in bed for a few days until the opiates prescribed by Lewell Sprague quieted his dyspepsia. When Favian emerged, he seemed pale, but his old self; his temper was not quite so likely to explode, and he seemed to regard social engagements with more cheer. Then William Burrows took *Enterprise* out of Portsmouth for a cruise down the Maine coast, in search of a Canadian privateer, *Loyalist,* and Favian vanished for a night, coming back after breakfast the next day with a private sort of smile and a series of ready jests. Hibbert kept his opinion of these activities to himself; an intolerant man rarely survived for long in an officer's mess.

A letter came for Favian at noon of that day, and Hibbert saw by the return address, as he took it to Favian, that it was from Emma Greenhow. Favian seemed inordinately cheerful when he came on deck to send a reply ashore, and Hibbert, because he had errands elsewhere in town, volunteered to bear it.

"Certainly," said Favian with a bright smile. "With my compliments, mind."

"Of course, sir." Hibbert tucked the letter into the sweatband of his round hat and was rowed to town. He saw by the address that Miss Greenhow was staying with her spinster relation, Arethusey Whitcomb, a ghastly old Congregational harridan whom Hibbert, and any sensible sailor, avoided on sight. Yet there was no choice but to approach the dragon, if one was to deliver a message to the maiden the dragon guarded. Hibbert made up his mind to deliver the letter into no one's hands but those of Emma Greenhow; he knew how easily disapproving relatives could lose one's correspondence.

The door was opened by Emma herself, much to Hibbert's surprise; she wore a green riding habit, her fair hair pulled back over her ears and held at the back with a comb *à la chinoise.* Her pale, fragile loveliness was more striking than he'd remembered. Hibbert doffed his hat and took out the letter.

"From Captain Markham, with his compliments."

Emma smiled, her eyes dancing. "Thank you, Mr. Hibbert," she said. "It is Peter Hibbert, is it not?"

"Yes, miss."

"I'm about to have tea; will you join me? Arethusey has gone to deliver tracts to the poor, informing them that their financial state is just punishment from God for some forgotten sin or other. I would have gone along, but I found myself with a convenient headache." She laughed mischievously.

"I hope the headache is gone," Hibbert stated, literal.

"I believe so. Please come in, Mr. Hibbert. May I call you Peter?"

"Of course, miss."

"I am Emma, of course," she said, showing him to a seat in Arethusey's spartan parlor. "I understand you were wounded in the fight. Have you quite recovered?"

"Oh yes, miss—Emma. Headaches and bed rest for a few days, and then I was well. I was very lucky."

Emma opened the note, read the message, and grinned. "An afternoon without Arethusey, riding with Captain Markham!" she proclaimed. "As cunning a maneuver as any of Captain Decatur's, wouldn't you say?"

"I'm sure it is, Emma."

She looked at him, still with the mischievous twitch to her lips, her head cocked to one side as if wondering whether to take his stolid performance seriously or not. She reached out to the teapot and poured for him.

"Phillip Stanhope—how is he?" she asked. "I see his father regularly."

"He's become a good sailor," Hibbert said, happy to discover a subject of conversation within his competence. "He's very promising; will make a good officer, I think. A very intelligent boy. A trifle serious, though—but I suppose he'll grow out of it."

"His father will *not* be pleased," Emma said. "They only sent him aboard *Experiment* because they expected the experience to sour him on the Navy forever."

Hibbert felt a smug grin tugging at the corners of his mouth. "Mr. Stanhope will make lieutenant if he wants it," he said. "Faster, perhaps, than some of the boys senior to him."

"No, Benjamin Stanhope will not be pleased," she repeated, a bit wistfully, her gray eyes far off.

Hibbert sipped his tea, blinking, wondering what Emma was reaching toward. "My father and Benjamin Stanhope have become political allies," she said. "They are trying to move the Federalists towards proposing amendments to the Constitution to forbid the government in Washington from prosecuting a war without the consent of all sections of the country."

"I see," Hibbert said, biting back what would, save for the presence of a lady, have been his usual reply. As a man who had been shot at, he had certain definite opinions regarding the conduct of politicians who, for their own political benefit, were trying to cut the ground out from beneath the country's fighting men. Yet, as the son of a commercial family, he understood the point of view of such men as Nicholas Greenhow and Benjamin Stanhope. If the war went on much longer the Hibbert family would be ruined, and all New England commerce with them. Honor versus bankruptcy: it was a savage dilemma, and Hibbert did not pretend to have the answer. Yet he was a Navy man; and with the Navy and a strong republic he would stand, even if it ruined all else he held dear.

"You do not agree?" Emma asked, her eyes intelligent, interested.

"I do not, miss," Hibbert said, his bitterness breaking free. "I do not enjoy seeing the men for whom I risk my life doing their best to make my risk larger than it is."

Emma accepted his harshness quietly. "Perhaps it would surprise you," she said, "to hear that I agree with you. That I have argued the point with my father, who informed me that, as a woman, my opinion is foolish and misinformed. That my sympathy for those poor pressed sailors, and my hatred of British arrogance and presumption, shows that I am feeble minded and too weak to live in the real world. I wish I could show him!" She raised a hand, clenched it into a fist. It trembled with the emotion of her words. "I wish I could show him that—that I do not—that I am braver than he thinks!" But the fist uncurled, showing a small hand with fingernails bitten to the quick—a girl's disturbing habit she had never entirely outgrown. She gave a wan, resigned smile.

"But I *am* a woman, am I not? The obligation to be brave is your lot, not mine. Mine is submission."

Peter Hibbert felt alarmed by this display; he felt a chivalrous instinct to leap up and offer to protect Emma Greenhow from whatever menaced her. But of course that would be foolish. There was no threat, nothing wrong—nothing, Hibbert thought, that a husband and children would not cure.

"I'm sorry, miss," he said. "Perhaps you would care to lie down?"

She laughed briefly. "No, I think not," she said. "But thank you, Peter. You are kind." She leaned back in her chair, relaxed, smiling; she had changed again. "I understand your sister will marry Gerald Catton."

"Aye," Hibbert said, relieved. They spoke about family, marriages, and births; Emma poured them each a fresh cup of tea. "Do you think," she asked, as he balanced cup and saucer, "that it is possible for the wife of a sailor to truly share his life? With the man absent for months at a time?" Hibbert stroked his long side-whiskers absently.

"I don't know, Emma," he said. "I'm not married."

She frowned. "There is such a risk, don't you think, of the husband and wife growing apart, separated as they are for such a long time? With the man immersed in a world she cannot know?"

Hibbert did not see any reason why a wife would *want* to share a sailor's life, but he answered the question as honestly as he could. "I think, Emma, that such marriages work. I can't say how; I can only say that they seem to."

"There are women who go to sea," she said hopefully. "The wives of captains."

"Aye. Merchantmen, mostly. It is not a common practice in the Navy."

"Is it not? Why is that?"

"It is not thought suitable for men-of-war to have ladies aboard," Hibbert said. "They must be looked after, and might detract from the ship's efficiency. And a warship must at any moment, even during peacetime, be prepared to fight, and during a fight the women, their servants, and possessions must be hidden below." He frowned, sipping his tea. "The Navy precedents haven't been very fortunate," he added. "The first captain of the *United States,* John Barry, built a roundhouse onto the frigate's quarterdeck for his wife, and ruined his ship's speed and handling. And Commodore Morris brought his wife to the Mediterranean during the Tripolitan War. She was not popular. It was said that Commodore Morris kept the squadron in European ports to oblige her, rather than inconveniencing her by fighting the enemy. The practice has been disapproved of in the Navy since."

"He was not much of an officer, if that is true," Emma said, her eyes narrowing. Hibbert, privately agreeing with her, said nothing; a naval officer does not criticize his superiors within the hearing of civilians. He had answered her question, but without volunteering anything, while he tried to discern what her true interest was. Obviously these questions were aimed at Favian, but Hibbert had no clear idea of the direction of her hopes. Hibbert had no intention of driving his captain's possible marriage onto any shoals.

"You Navy men, you're very closemouthed about one another," Emma observed. "You were very careful just now, speaking of Commodore Morris, not to give your own thoughts; you said 'it was said' and 'it was thought,' but you did not mention by whom such things were said or thought."

"It is courtesy," Hibbert said. "I was not there. My own service in the Mediterranean was under Commodore Barron."

"You don't speak of yourselves either, you Navy men," she accused. "You are as closemouthed as Freemasons about your craft."

"We are not accustomed—" Hibbert began, then interrupted himself. He sipped his tea for a moment, composing his thoughts. "Other people do not understand," he said. "It's not their fault, they just can't. They haven't been through it."

"Is that what *being Navy* means?" Emma wondered. "Favian—Captain Markham was once upset at a political discussion in his uncle's house; he said it made him 'feel Navy.' The discussion wasn't about anything out of the ordinary—it was the sort that can be heard anywhere. But it brought out something in him."

Hibbert held up his hands helplessly. "I can't explain, Emma. I wouldn't know where to begin."

"And Captain Markham? Is there some professional scruple about speaking of him? You've lived on the same boat for months. Can't you tell me what he's like, aboard *Experiment*?"

Hibbert sensed something in her pleading, and slowly nodded. "Aye. I can," he said. "Captain Markham is a brilliant captain, and a brave one. Braver than I am, in at least one sense." He told her of the day in the North Sea when *Experiment* sighted the enemy brig, and how Favian had turned from it and run for Norway. "It was a brave thing to do," Hibbert said, "and I did not realize it until later. His decision was not one that many officers would have made; I myself would have fought, I think. And many of the men just didn't understand it. They thought he was a coward—some said as much within his hearing. I'm certain Captain Markham knew, when he made the decision, that his courage would be questioned, yet he made the decision anyway. That's a special kind of bravery most of us don't have."

Emma's eyes glowed. "That's fascinating," she said. "And the battle itself? With *Teaser*? Was it very horrible?"

"I was out cold for most of it," Hibbert said self-consciously. "I really can't presume—"

"Peter, please," she said. There was a mute appeal in her gray eyes.

"I can tell you what others have said," Hibbert told her. "Captain Markham was brave as a lion. He walked into the line of fire to rescue a midshipman who was trying to get himself killed. He took the helm when the helmsmen were wounded, and later helped to man a gun himself.

"And I can tell you a thing that I learned myself," he said. "Favian won the battle in part because of his courage, and because his men were so well cared for and well trained—that's another measure of his skill, of course. But he also won it because he'd thought the battle out ahead of time, from start to finish. He told me how the battle would go before the first gun was fired, and I'll be capsized if it didn't turn out just like he said!"

Emma absorbed the information with a radiant smile,

triumph in her eyes. "I see," she said. "I've never known him as a sailor, never known what the Navy meant to him. We've been friends since we were little, but we see each other so seldom."

"He hasn't led an easy life in the Navy," Hibbert said. "Few of us have. But it should be easier for him now. He'll almost certainly be promoted to full captain. And when he gets a ship it will be a bigger one, a better one. They can't ignore his record."

"Ships," she said wistfully. "Phillip Stanhope always spoke of them as if they were the loveliest thing on earth. And of course one is denied them, as much else. . . . It has been lovely, Peter. Come again, and we'll talk." She seemed to grow even more cheerful as she stood, took his teacup, and led him arm in arm to the door.

"I think I'll know how to talk to Captain Markham now," she said. She seemed radiantly lovely, radiantly happy. Hibbert felt, as he said farewell, that at Emma Greenhow's request he would gladly have cut out his heart on the spot.

She shut the door behind him, leaving him on the streets of Portsmouth. He blinked, put his hat on his head, and remembered his other errands.

4.

Favian, later that afternoon, stopped by the stable to pick up his horse—the same mare his father had loaned him during his previous visit—and at the same time to rent another animal for Emma Greenhow. The beast he chose was a bright-maned gelding, obviously spirited, and slightly resentful of the weight of the sidesaddle—Favian knew that Emma was well capable of controlling the horse, and was never satisfied with docile mounts.

From the stable he walked both horses to Arethusey Whitcomb's, passing the fiddler Lazarus on a street corner. The minstrel was entertaining a small crowd, mostly children, with his selections. He leered as Favian walked past, but Favian stolidly ignored him. Lazarus the lunatic, with his prophecies, his fixed, immutable future. Favian had considered his future settled, in all but minor details, from the moment he'd walked into the commandant's office to announce his victory, but he did not appreciate Lazarus reminding him of it.

Emma Greenhow opened the door before he was able to knock. He was struck at once by an exquisite glow of happiness that seemed to surround her; he kissed her gloved hand and told her how lovely she looked.

She glanced down the street. "Let's ride away before Arethusey gets back," she said. Her eyes danced like gray fires. He helped her into the sidesaddle, then mounted himself. She set a brisk trot until they were out of town, then began her usual gallop down country lanes. He followed, feeling his own mount respond eagerly to the challenge, the mare moving easily under him. It was harvest time, and the countryside was dotted with reapers, swing-

ing their sickles in regular motion as they advanced their
swaths. Emma slowed the pace, then brought the gelding to
a walk, turning it off the road onto a grassy path that
wound among birch trees.

Favian followed, drawing abreast of her. The previous
night he had been repeatedly unfaithful to Emma with a
coarse-skinned York harlot, and although the woman had
been nothing exceptional, he still felt a mild erotic tingle in
his limbs, a sensation enhanced by the nearness of the
laughing, carefree Emma. She brought the gelding to a
halt, bent to stroke its neck with her gloved hands. It bent
to crop at the long grass. Favian circled her, then brought
his mount to a stop. Emma looked up at him and laughed,
her eyes merry beneath her tall hat.

"You will be promoted, and get a new ship," she said.

"I am certainly entitled to hope so. There will be quite a
wait for the ship, though."

"You deserve both, Favian," she said seriously.

"Thank you," he said, catching the shift in her mood.
Without his assistance she slipped from the saddle; she
picked up the gelding's reins and walked it over the turf.
Favian imitated her; they tied their horses to saplings
where there was plenty of grass for the animals and walked
onward into the trees.

"I'm feeling very brave, Favian," she said. "I feel as if I
could defy dragons. But I know that I will not be brave for
long, not without help. Can you help me be brave,
Favian?" He looked at her; there was an appeal in her
voice. "Your sailors were brave, in the battle; you must
have shown them how to use their courage. Can you show
me?"

"I'll be brave *for* you, Emma," he said. He felt her gray
eyes on him; then they flickered away. A jay scolded from
overhead. Her heavy skirt rustled over the grass.

"Favian, I must know," she said, turning to him. She
reached out and caught up his hands; he could feel the
strength of her grip, which managed difficult horses so
well. "You once said," she said, her eyes boring into his,
"that you 'felt Navy.' I want to know—I need to know—
how much of you is Navy, Favian? Is it a great part of

you? Is it—is it at war with the rest of you? And how
much of it can I share?"

Who the devil has she been talking to? Favian wondered,
astonished. He heard an outline of all his own conflicts and
doubts in her questions: his struggles with the Navy's iron
code and obligations, the narrow, confined pattern into
which he felt obliged to constrain himself. How much of it
could he truly share? he wondered. The duels, the gunfire,
the hideous, deforming wounds? The risk he bore whenever
he donned the uniform coat? The compulsion to deny fear,
to suppress parts of his own personality? The discontent he
felt when aboard ship, the alienation he felt on land, separated from so much of humanity by the gulf of his Navy
experience? For a second, possibilities swarmed through
him: Emma would understand; he could talk to Emma,
unburden himself. . . . But then the possibilities faded.
Why should he subject her to his doubts, his own torments?
It would be unfair to expect her to understand or to cope.
A gentleman did not so expose a lady to his troubles.

No, he would protect Emma from the war within himself, as much as he was able. He would present her as carefully formed a face as he presented elsewhere, and try to
draw comfort from the fact that he was sparing her exposure to his own anguish. He took a deep breath.

"My dear Emma," he said. "I should like to think that
you may have whatever I possess. I intend to make a success of my career, and I hope that from that success you
may have what you desire. I have enough now to give you
a home. It can be wherever you like, and as comfortable as
is possible, and it can be made more comfortable as I rise
in seniority. It is my earnest hope that you will lack for
nothing.

"But I should also hope that you will never need be exposed to the Navy side of my life. It's often unpleasant,
often dangerous. I hope I may spare you its anxieties, its
consequences. I think you may never have to worry about
such things."

He felt her hands fall from his, and she turned away,
her shoulders slumped in an attitude of defeat. Favian felt
his astonishment grow. She groped blindly for support, and
he took her arm.

"Favian," she said bleakly, "I do not want to be a widow for half our marriage. I am selfish; you know that."

"Emma, after I am promoted captain I won't have a command for some time," he said earnestly. "I'll be too junior. We can have a life together for quite some time, without interruption."

She looked up at him, torment in her eyes. "Favian," she said. "You have been in war. You have met men in duels. What is it like, to stand and watch a man point a pistol at your heart?" For an instant Favian remembered the feel of the turf beneath his feet, the scent of the orange groves, the struggle to control his trembling pistol; there was the memory, just weeks before, of hearing the enemy six-pounder rumbling out of its gun port, charged with enough canister to tear him to bloody scraps.

"I hope to spare you that," Favian said. Emma broke away, walking with quick, long-legged strides toward her horse. Favian followed. She reached the horse, clambered into the sidesaddle without his assistance, and looked down at him as he walked up to touch her rein. There was a flush in her cheeks, but her eyes were dull, pitiless.

"You encourage my cowardice; very well," she said. "I shall be a good little coward, as my father wishes. Benjamin Stanhope has offered me a proposal of marriage. When he tendered me this offer, he knew that you and I had an understanding; he was willing to wait until I'd spoken to you."

"Emma . . ." Favian said.

"Benjamin Stnahope is older than I," she went on, merciless. "He is not altogether my ideal. But he does not treat me as a halfwit doll, to be sheltered from the baser facts of his existence, and such life as he has he is willing to share. He is a brilliant ship designer, and will be able to keep me in comfort. Favian, I will accept his proposal."

"Don't, Emma," Favian said hopelessly.

"Too late. I'm sorry." She took the reins from his nerveless fingers, turned the gelding in the narrow path, and galloped away. Favian mounted and followed. They raced back toward Portsmouth, down the country lanes; and Favian saw Emma's gloved hand rising to her face as if she were wiping away tears. But by the time they entered the town her pace had slowed, and she had straightened in her saddle, apparently recovered.

"Thank you for the ride, Favian," she said as they drew up to Arethusey's little house. She dismounted again without his help, and handed him the reins as he dismounted. "I hope you will walk him before you give him back to the stables."

"Don't do it, Emma. Marry me. We'll work things out."

She shook her head wordlessly; and then her eyes suddenly brimmed, and she turned to flee inside the door. Favian watched the door close, two pairs of reins in his hand, the panting of the horse sounding in his ears. The door did not open again. Favian turned and led the horses down the street.

5.

The announcement of the engagement between Miss Emma Greenhow and Major Benjamin Stanhope (Stanhope held a commission in the militia) was made quietly, and produced little sensation; the consensus of opinion was that it was a good match. Not a great deal of public curiosity was wasted on whatever had become of her "understanding" with Favian; perhaps they had simply been friends all along, and her relationship with Favian one of convenience, to be used as an excuse for avoiding entanglements with other men until such time as she felt herself ready to marry. Such an arrangement, after all, was not uncommon, and it fit into the chivalrous standard of the Navy.

Favian was in the act of writing them each a brisk congratulation when there was a knock on his door. It was Phillip Stanhope, returned from some days' leave. For those days Favian had actually forgotten that he had Emma's stepson-to-be serving aboard his brig; the memory came as an unpleasant shock. As long as the younger Stanhope was aboard, Favian would have to be in regular contact with his father.

"Sir," Stanhope said, following his salute, "I've come back from furlough."

"I see, Mr. Stanhope," Favian said, wondering where this was leading. "I trust you enjoyed yourself?"

"Oh, yes," Stanhope said too quickly. There was a hesitation; the boy seemed to be groping for words.

"Sir," he said again. What followed was apparently a prepared speech. "Sir, I cannot be insensible to the possibility that, in light of my father's recent engagement, my presence aboard *Experiment* may be unpleasant to you. I therefore wish to remove any strain by leaving *Experiment* as soon as possible—with, of course, your permission."

"I see," Favian said, completely taken aback. "Have you spoken of this with your father?"

"No, sir," Stanhope said. Favian thought that Stanhope's tone indicated that he discussed important matters with his father as little as possible. "As far as my father is concerned, I would be going ashore at my own request in order to study French and navigation."

Favian's estimation of Stanhope's character rose. He had cut directly to the heart of a matter affecting his elders, and about which none of them would have spoken; he had, independently, evolved a plan for dealing with it.

"Mr. Stanhope," he said, "I will of course release you from *Experiment* if you wish. Nothing, however, would please me more than if you should decide to stay."

Stanhope's face showed instant, undisguised relief. "Of course, sir, I would prefer to stay," he said in a rush. "I hope this conversation will not be reported to my father?"

"You have my word, Mr. Stanhope." The boy saluted and almost skipped from the cabin. Favian picked up his pen and finished his congratulatory messages. When confronted with someone of Stanhope's honesty and integrity, he reflected, there was really nothing to do other than what he did. He just hoped that the words he'd spoken were true.

News trickled in as days passed, days that Favian deliberately filled with as much activity as possible. He busied himself readying *Experiment* for sea once more, in order that whoever succeeded him—presumably Hibbert would be promoted to fill his place—would have less work to do. In the meantime news came that the Canadian privateer *Loyalist*, which Burrows's *Enterprise* had been cruising for, was on the Maine coast again; perhaps Burrows would soon return with a prize. There was news from Boston that the crew of the *Pride of Richmond*, including her captain, Buck Johanan Gardell, had been released by the court on their own recognizance, prior to Favian's being summoned to testify at their trial, and now could not be found anywhere within the state. The prize court had already ruled, fortunately, that the *Pride of Richmond* constituted a fair prize; *Experiment*'s men had some money to scatter about the dives of Kittery and Portsmouth.

Social engagements occupied a great deal of time; there were receptions, balls, concerts, and earnest political meetings. Favian attended the latter in mufti. Surprisingly, the fiddler Lazarus vanished from the Portsmouth vicinity at the height of his popularity. Favian devoutly hoped that his satanic master had claimed him.

Favian's own period of celebrity was not yet on the wane, and he was much sought after to declare definite political allegiance to one faction or other; but he tried to confine his comments to the naval situation. Politically, New Hampshire was sliding toward neutrality, if not outright collaboration with the British. The Stanhope-Greenhow alliance was not only matrimonial, but political as well; they were trying to move the New Hampshire Federalists in the direction of New England secession. Whether they seriously intended to break New England from the rest of the United States, or simply intended to use the threat as a club to hold over Washington, was not entirely clear. Nevertheless, they were succeeding; Lafayette Markham was viewing his fellow Federalists with increasing disgust, and his speeches began to ring with warnings and denunciations.

There was an increasing illegal trade with Canada; there were stories of timber being shipped across Lake Champlain to help build the British squadron there, and other tales of entire herds of cattle heading northward to help feed the British armies. Greenhow's name was mentioned, though in whispers; Stanhope, who was making his money building privateers, had thus far stayed clear.

Of naval news there was little. Porter and the *Essex* were still in the Pacific, presumably doing good work. Charles Stewart and the *Constellation* had never left the Chesapeake; but, though blockaded, they had successfully beaten off British boat assaults. Decatur, flying his commodore's pendant in the *United States* and commanding a squadron that included the refitted *Macedonian* and the *Hornet,* had tried to slip out of Long Island Sound; but *United States* had been struck by lightning and driven into

New London, where the squadron was now being blockaded vigorously by a British flotilla. Favian's old messmate
on the *Constitution*, Thomas MacDonough, had effectively
seized control of Lake Champlain, which brought to an end
any possibility of a British invasion of New York, at least
until the enemy built more ships, which no doubt they
would.

In August Isaac Chauncey's squadron on Ontario had
fought a four-day running skirmish with the British squadron, and had lost four small schooners, two to capsizing
during a storm and two taken by the British. Favian, reading the accounts of the four-day action, wondered if his
intuition about Chauncey not being a fighter had been
right: His tactics, though innovative, had not been applied
with any vigor; and though the capture of the schooners
had perhaps been unavoidable—they had attacked the enemy without orders, were cut off and forced to surrender—Chauncey's not trying to rescue them did not look
good.

More could be expected from the Great Lakes. Chauncey's subordinate on Lake Erie, Oliver Hazard Perry, was
expected to battle the British any day now for possession of
the lake. Favian did not know Perry well; the man had not
served under Preble, although service rumor held that he
was talented. Favian hoped he'd be more aggressive than
his chief superior.

The situation, coupled as it was with the usual Army
blundering, made for unease. The war lacked any great
clarity; neither side had prosecuted it with any coherent
policy in mind, and the result had been a series of isolated
clashes resulting in isolated victories, none of which, because they had not been subordinated to any great, driving
strategy, could be decisive. Perhaps on the Great Lakes or
on Champlain a decisive victory could be won, a victory
setting a pattern that the war would follow. If Perry
triumphed on Erie, the United States would probably re-
capture all it had lost in the West; if Chauncey won on
Ontario and MacDonough managed to keep control of
Champlain, the most direct routes of invasion from Canada
to the United States would be controlled by American
fleets.

In the meantime skirmishing would have to continue, and brigs of war such as *Experiment* were as fit to serve as skirmishers as anything. Favian worked hard at making *Experiment* ready; although he had no intention of taking her out again, he would make her as prepared as possible for her next commander.

And then came news that shattered Favian's resolve. The first outline was sketchy, brought in by a coastal gundalow from Portland: There had been a battle off the Maine coast, and *Enterprise* had captured a British brig in single combat; Burrows and the enemy captain had both been killed, Lieutenant McCall had made prize of the enemy. Another variation came the same day by pilot boat: Burrows hadn't been killed after all, but he was seriously wounded. Favian did not wait for the third version. *Experiment* was hove to over her anchor; Favian sent a hasty dispatch ashore to a commandant he knew to be absent for a few days; and the brig raised its anchors, sheeted home its canvas, and, without bothering to pick up a pilot, raced madly from its anchorage.

Portland was made overnight, reaching on the brisk land breeze, Favian never leaving the quarterdeck all night as he kept watch. Cape Elizabeth was shaved by a margin that had all the men on watch standing wide-eyed on the foredeck, bracing themselves for the collision that never came. Two brigs were anchored under the fort on Great Diamond Island: Both were battered, with the scars of shot marring their paint work, and one with a jury mainmast. The more intact of the two was plainly *Enterprise*; the other was a twin of *Teaser*, clearly British built, the American ensign flying over the British on her peak halyards.

Favian brought *Experiment* in under a press of sail that must have had the men in the fort staring; *Experiment*'s anchor was kicked overboard and plunged to the bottom within two hundred yards of the anchored *Enterprise*, and the new launch was in the water before *Experiment* had even lost way.

McCall met Favian and Hibbert at the shot-scarred entry port. He had clearly not had much sleep; his clothes were stained and had obviously been slept in. He confirmed the first story.

There was much that was brilliant in the tale that emerged, and much that was reflective of William Burrows: the hours of maneuvering that opened the conflict, testing the sailing abilities of the opposing vessels; the opening broadside delayed until pistol-shot range; the fine maneuvering that had taken place while the guns were actually thundering—all plain Burrows, some shared with other graduates of Preble's school, but, taken all together, distinctly his. The Navy's legend would be supported by the addition of much romantic detail: the British colors nailed to the mast; the enemy captain killed and Burrows wounded at the first fire; Burrows, knowing the wound was mortal, refusing to seek medical attention until after the battle, giving orders and cheering his men until the end; his last words, after he'd finally clasped in his hands the defeated enemy's sword: "I am satisfied. I die contented." He had died in victory, and with a faint smile. The Navy as well as Burrows would be satisfied with the outcome.

Favian himself was not content with the tale of the battle; there was much he longed to ask his friend. How had Burrows known to shift one of the long nine-pounders aft to fire through a hole chopped in the taffrail? How could he have known that during the course of the fight *Enterprise* would forge ahead of the enemy *Boxer* and be in perfect position to rake her with three shots from that nine-pounder, shots that practically won the battle? How the devil had Burrows *known*? The tactic was without precedent. The fact that Burrows had sifted the long nine aft some hours before the first shot showed that he'd planned it somehow. Try as he might, there was no clear way Favian could understand Burrows being so certain a stern chaser would be necessary. Whatever Burrows's method of divination, he would take it with him to his grave.

William Burrows and Captain Blyth, his English enemy, were buried in a common grave in Portland. Favian, in full dress uniform, the mourning band around his arm and the epaulet heavy on his shoulder, delivered the eulogy—brother officers cut down in the prime of life, two gallant enemies who could in life have been friends, tribute paid by sorrowful survivors; standard naval fare, but no less true for all that—and then helped to carry the casket, its surface decked with a wreath, Burrows's seldom-worn cocked hat and epaulet, and (Favian had insisted) the sword of Captain Blyth, which Burrows had held in his hands when he died.

The minister gave his speech at the grave side; earth was thrown in the common grave; and seven marines, in rapid succession, fired twenty-one rifles into the air. One of the British midshipmen wept silently. As they filed from the graveyard it began to rain.

That night the officers of *Enterprise* and *Experiment* hosted the surviving, temporarily paroled officers of *Boxer* in a dinner ashore; plates were set for the dead captains, another for *Enterprise*'s dead midshipman, Kervin Waters. Captain Blyth had, by all accounts, been a man of considerable bravery and talent, and just a few months earlier had served as one of James Lawrence's pallbearers in Halifax, and was therefore deserving of compliment and courtesy. Favian's first toast was to "the crew of the *Boxer*— enemies by law, but by gallantry brothers." David McCreery, *Boxer*'s lieutenant, responded in similar high style.

A good many more toasts had to be drunk before the men present began to feel in any degree "brothers," but before the evening was out McCall and McCreery were refighting the battle, with salt cellars representing the brigs and toothpicks fallen masts, while Favian stepped outside into the rain, feeling it sluice down the planes of his face as he stared out into the bleakness of the water. Burrows gone, his closest friend, perhaps his only real friend. He had been smiling when he died; he'd not greatly valued his own life, and would have been happy to have given it in the service of the one thing he'd loved, his sole obsession, his mistress: the Navy. "I die content," he'd said; Favian believed he'd spoken the truth. He wondered whether contentment would be his own lot if his own time came. Probably not, he thought, though if necessary he could feign it well enough for the legend's sake.

The rain coursed down his cheeks, soaking down the back of his neck. He turned and went back to the dinner.

6.

Two days after the funeral Favian received, forwarded by pilot boat from Portsmouth, a letter from William Jones, the new Secretary of the Navy. It was brisk in tone; it offered congratulations for what Jones was pleased to call Markham's Raid—evidently that unfortunate name was going to become more or less official—and announced, subject to confirmation by Congress, Favian's promotion to full captain. The confirmation by Congress would come automatically, Favian knew; they would not hesitate to promote the man who had done much to erase the humiliation of the loss of the *Chesapeake*, even if he were kin to Federalists.

The second part of Jones's letter ordered Favian to relinquish command of *Experiment* and proceed "as quickly as circumstances permit" to New London, where he was required and directed to supervise the completion of the sloop of war *Shark*, now building, and take command of her as soon as she was built. This caught Favian by surprise; he had truly not expected to be offered the command of one of the six sloops of war he had helped persuade Congress to construct.

Shark. She'd be ship-rigged and fast, armed with thirty-two-pound carronades and two long twelves, enough of a broadside to destroy any equivalent British cruiser. There had been rumors about the design, an improved, smaller version of the *President*-class frigates: longer than the old *Wasp*-class sloops, with a great deal of drag to her keel, much deeper aft than forward, low bilges to stiffen her, a full fish-head entrance that would let her stand hard driv-

ing—a beautiful design. Favian suspected she might not
steer well, but that would be a minor fault: his professional
side itched to have her. With a ship like *Shark* promised to
be, Markham's Raid would have been even more successful
than it had proved with *Experiment*. There would have
been no need to run from the smaller enemy cruisers, and
the larger ones would have been outrun without difficulty.
All six of the new ships, acting together, could put England
under naval siege.

Favian penned a reply to the new secretary in the same
laconic style Jones seemed to favor, thanking him for the
appointment. *Shark* would not be launched for a year or
more, so Jones was not very serious about the speed with
which Favian would have to report to New London. Favian
would have time to conclude any business remaining with
Experiment.

In the letter to Jones, by way of being thorough, Favian
included an abstract of several articles in British newspapers captured with *Boxer*. There were several vitriolic edi-
torials about *Experiment*'s circuit of Britain, all of which
must have reddened ears at the Admiralty; there was some
bombastic crowing, to Favian's mind unseemly, about the
Shannon-Chesapeake fight. It appeared that Captain Philip
Bowes Vere Broke was about to be made a baronet. Favian,
in all fairness, concluded that the man probably deserved it.

Buried in one of the papers was a laudatory passage concerning an action by the sixty-four-gun ship *Dictator*, Captain James Pattison Stewart, assisted by two brig sloops and
a gun brig, in which the British squadron under Stewart's
command ran twelve miles up a narrow fjord in Norway to
destroy a Danish squadron composed of the forty-gun frigate *Najad*, three brig sloops, a number of gunboats, and
several batteries. The action, conducted with great gallantry at considerable risk, was to be awarded a naval
medal.

And there, Favian thought with great regret, went
Prince Christian Frederick's symbol of a united Norway,
battered to bits on a Norwegian rock by a superior force.
The British blockade of Norway would be tighter than
ever, and Christian Frederick's position further under-
mined. His gesture had gone only to provide a naval medal

for the British, honoring their own heroism. Favian felt relieved he had not accepted the prince royal's commission; but he also wondered—he would always wonder—whether he could have altered the outcome. The brief description of the fight indicated that all the British squadron were aground at one time or another; the battle might have been closer than the results indicated. Could he have done it? Favian wondered. Smashed the British while they were aground, capturing a sixty-four-gun ship? That would have topped, by a considerable measure, Malachi's capture of the fifty-gun *Bristol*, the most spectacular feat of the family.

Poor Christian Frederick. Favian had liked the man, and had sympathized with his dilemmas, his goals. Had it not been for the unshatterable code of the United States officer, demanding obedience to but a single flag, and for the gulf between a committed republican and a royal personage, Favian would have gladly served him.

As Favian finished his letter with a postscript mentioning his monograph on Massey's Recording Log, there was a knock on his door: Stanhope. "Boat coming, sir," he said. "Looks like the city fathers."

"Thank you, Mr. Stanhope," Favian said. "I'll be on deck directly." Stanhope saluted and ducked back into the corridor, and Favian folded, sealed, and addressed the letter. Since that extraordinary interview in which Stanhope had offered to leave *Experiment*, Favian had been relieved to discover there was no increased tension between himself and the midshipman. It would have been a knavish thing, and foolish, to have felt any resentment toward Stanhope on that score, and Favian was happy that he was not, even in secret, a knave or a fool.

The town council of Portland had come on business. The privateer *Loyalist*—the fast schooner *Enterprise* had been hunting when it found *Boxer*—had taken another prize, this one right inside Machias Bay, within sight of hundreds of onlookers. The merchants of Portland and other Maine towns were too frightened to send their vessels to sea; commerce was suffering; *Enterprise* was much too battered to sail out in search of her. In short, the city fathers requested that *Experiment* go in pursuit of *Loyalist* as soon as possible. Their request had something of the sound of command in it.

Favian reflected on their request. *Experiment* was still short of complement; the casualties lost during the fight with *Teaser* had not been made up, and the men sent off with *Pride of Richmond* had not yet returned. Still, *Experiment* was probably more than a match for a schooner privateer, assuming that *Experiment* could catch her.

The news of Favian's promotion created a certain difficulty: Favian was now a full captain, the highest rank the Navy offered. (*Commodore* was a strictly honorary title, applying to the senior captain on any given station.) He was far too exalted in rank to command a lowly converted schooner. But Hibbert was present, and Hibbert's promotion was probably pending as well. Favian could leave the brig as per Jones's orders, and give Hibbert the chance for glory and prize money with a cruise on the coast of Maine.

But what were *Experiment*'s orders? The commandant of the Portsmouth Yard had never superseded Paul Hamilton's original order to rid New England of enemy privateers; William Jones had not yet given the brig, as opposed to Favian, new orders. The commandant's cover letter sent with Jones's dispatch had been very brief, and had contained nothing that could even by implication constitute an order for *Experiment*.

In short, nothing stood in *Experiment*'s way if she wanted to head out for a short cruise of the Maine coast. The brig had her water, her victuals, and enough men to do the job contemplated. Favian assured the city fathers that *Experiment* would leave as soon as possible, and showed them off the brig.

Peter Hibbert, to Favian's surprise, proved less than delighted with the prospect of his first command. "Sir, I— I'm flattered," he said, sitting startled in a chair in Favian's cabin. "I'd like nothing more than a cruise of my own. But . . ." He hesitated.

"Go ahead, Peter," Favian said.

"Bean's dead, and hasn't been replaced," Hibbert itemized. "The bosun hasn't got back from Boston yet. I'd have to make one of the mids acting lieutenant, and there isn't one that's really qualified. Dudley would have been, but he's been killed. Brook isn't old enough, or experienced enough; Stanhope's learned the fundamentals but hasn't got the experience. That leaves Tolbert, and although we all know his bravery, his judgment has left a lot to be desired, and frankly I'd just as soon not trust my life to his navigation on a lee shore."

"I see," Favian said. Hibbert was perfectly right. *Experiment* would be critically short of officers, even with both captain and lieutenant; leaving the brig would put Hibbert in an uncomfortable situation. "I understand, Mr. Hibbert," Favian said. "I'll inform the city fathers of our situation, and our inability to comply with their request. Perhaps the commandant will be able to give you replacements when we return to Portsmouth."

"Sir," Hibbert said. "We don't have to . . ." He swallowed. "There's a solution, sir. I may be out of line to suggest it, since it may not suit your plans or orders. Sir, I think we can make the cruise if you stay aboard, in command of *Experiment*."

Favian leaned back in his chair. Yes, he could continue in command of *Experiment*; he was not officially a captain yet, not until word of his confirmation by Congress reached him. But did he want it? There was the chance of running into a superior enemy and getting captured, just when his promotion and appointment to the *Shark* would have guaranteed a brilliant future. But that chance was insignificant; there was no British blockade north of Boston. If Hibbert did not mind passing up a chance for a cruise of his own, there should be no problem. It would be a dreary little voyage of perhaps two weeks, with slim chance of even seeing *Loyalist*, let alone taking her; but Favian supposed he had no plans to be anywhere else.

"Mr. Hibbert, I can but commend your patriotism and willing spirit," Favian said. "We'll sail on the morning tide." Hibbert looked enormously relieved. Favian offered him his hand, and then a cup of wine.

7.

There followed an unfruitful week of cruising the Maine coast, seeking the *Loyalist* privateer. Between Portland and Machias Bay the Maine coast dissolved into a chaos of islands, peninsulas, capes, and bays; there were scores of reefs and mud banks, unpleasant currents and tides, dozens of little isolated villages, each sending plumes of smoke skyward in the dull light of morning, whose only contact with one another, and with the world outside Maine, was by sea.

It was fortunate that *Experiment* was carrying a Maine pilot, the Quaker Ezekiel Casterburgh, who knew the waters, but even so their task was a formidable one. The *Loyalist* was probably staying close to shore, anchoring among the islands at night and dashing out at dawn to snap up whatever the sunrise revealed, much as *Experiment* had done in the English Channel. They could have passed *Loyalist* a dozen times without seeing her; she could have been at sea as they threaded the islands, or hiding among the islands as *Experiment* rode off the coast.

On the morning of the ninth day of their search, Favian was prepared to conclude that it was hopeless to continue, and that *Loyalist* had probably very sensibly returned to Halifax to collect its prize money, or had gone to cruise another stretch of water. He stood on the quarterdeck with Hibbert and Ezekiel Casterburgh, squinting into the gray sea. The barometer was dropping, and the wind gusted strongly from the south-southeast. Favian was considering furling the topgallants. There was a strong swell pushing up from the south, the tops of the waves breaking and beginning to streak with foam. The sky was overcast, the sun hidden behind a pall of cloud. The signs were unmistakable, but Favian asked Casterburgh's opinion.

The pilot, a neatly dressed, thin, ascetic man of fifty, squinted to windward and tucked his hands into his armpits: a habitual stance when the man was thinking, Favian had learned. "Dirty weather, sir. This ain't a lee shore— not yet—but I'd get off it, or find a place to anchor."

"Is there a good storm anchorage near here, sir?"

"Mebbe so, but if there is I don't rightly know of it, not one thee can be sure of gettin' to in time. There's too much foul ground hereabouts, and there's a feelin' about this weather . . . 'tis strange. Don't like the signs."

"We'll clear this cape, look into this last bay, then run for the open sea," Favian decided. A gust rocked *Experiment*, the group of men on the quarterdeck moving suddenly as they sought balance, the rigging screaming.

"Aye, the open sea is best," Casterburgh agreed. "Captain, if I were thee I'd take in them t'gallants."

"I believe we shall keep them on a bit longer, Mr. Casterburgh," Favian smiled. "They're Navy canvas, not the local variety."

Casterburgh cast a gloomy eye aloft, then shrugged, as if to proclaim that he'd given his warning and was not responsible.

Then the deck rang with the cries of lookouts, and Favian looked astonished to leeward. *Experiment* had just cleared the cape, and the *Loyalist* privateer was in plain sight, British flags flying openly from her masts, caught in the act of pursuing a local ketch. The quarterdeck burst into a flurry of harsh-voiced orders.

"Clear for action! Trumpeter—where's the blasted trumpeter? Sound the call, damn it! Up helm—I said up helm! There . . . amidships. Mr. Casterburgh, how close can we shave that cape?"

"There are sandbars off that cape, extendin' sou'east at least a quarter mile."

"Thank you. Helmsman, half a point to larboard."

"Half a p'int to larboard, aye aye."

Spray whipped over *Experiment*'s quarterdeck as the sea rose behind her. The helmsmen wrestled the tiller; the waves right behind were smashing the rudder and making

it difficult to steer. Favian turned up his collar and tried to
ignore the storm building behind him. He scanned the bay.

The bay was wide, formed by two tree-crusted capes,
open to the east and southeast; there was white water rim-
ming the bay, indicating reefs or mud banks. Favian
scowled; it was a nasty lee shore to be embayed on, but if
the wind held south-southeast they could run out without
any trouble. There were islands in the bay, wooded and
rock edged; no shelter there. *Loyalist,* which had apparently not seen *Experiment* yet, was square in the middle of
the bay, heeling far over in the stiff breeze, her square
topsails set in addition to the fore-and-aft canvas.

"I don't know these waters well, sir," Casterburgh said.
"I can make some educated guesses, like, but it ain't the
same as knowin'. Thar's a fishin' settlement in thar, but I
only been to it a couple times."

"Thank you, sir. I'll try to be conservative," Favian said.
"Mr. Hibbert, we will furl the fore-t'gallant. Leadsmen to
the chains."

"Aye aye, sir."

The rising wind screamed through the shrouds. *Experiment* was cleared for action, the gun crews standing by the
blue-painted carronades, strapping on their boarding helmets and shivering in the cold wind; trimmers raced aloft
to get the fore-topgallant furled.

"And a half five!" the leadsman sang.

"Very well. Let her go."

"By the mark five!" Favian saw Casterburgh's eyes on
him.

"Very well," he said.

They crossed the mud bank in four and a half fathoms,
and then for the first time *Loyalist* saw them. The privateer schooner swung madly to starboard, yards flying,
booms swinging across as she jibed. An interesting tactical
problem, this: *Experiment* had the weather gage, and had
to keep *Loyalist* boxed in the bay, heading her off from
scraping past the northern cape, but also preventing her
from going about at the last minute and running under *Experiment*'s stern.

"Three points to starboard," Favian ordered. "Mr. Casterburgh, do shoals extend westward from that big island?"

"Don't know," Casterburgh said shortly. "Probably they do. I tell thee I do not like the looks of it."

"Neither do I, Mr. Casterburgh. We shall give it a wide berth. Mr. Tolbert, clear away the larboard chaser and give them a shot as soon as you think it practicable."

"Aye aye, sir."

"Another point to starboard. Tell the leadsman to keep sounding."

Favian felt himself grinning as the spray spattered on his upturned collar. There was a reckless feeling to this, as if he were deliberately tempting the fates: rising weather, an unknown lee shore, but yet they would give chase.

"And a half ten!"

It was a relief, sometimes, to let the cunning professional man in him take over, calculating bowlines and stresses, performing the automatic functions. Burrows's death had been a shock; his closest friend gone without his being able to prevent it, or give him succor. Let it down, this sorrow; feel only the wind on your neck, hear only the shrill of the rigging and the song of the leadsman.

"By the mark twelve!"

There was a crack and a roar, and the air filled with the sound of loose canvas; the main-topgallant had split and was flogging itself into tatters of flax. Casterburgh gave Favian a sour look, as if to say "I told you so."

"Mr. Hibbert, secure that canvas," Favian said, hiding his chagrin.

"Aye aye, sir. Hands aloft to furl the main-t'gallant! Clew down there. Ease the halyard! Haul round on the clewlines. Round in on the braces."

"And a quarter eleven!"

"Deck thar!" The new voice was the lookout. "That ketch has driven itself ashore. Topmasts fallen, sir."

Favian turned to see the ketch. It had deliberately run itself aground, presumably as much to escape the perils of a lee shore as to escape the privateer. Perhaps they'd thought *Experiment* was another enemy; he hadn't raised his colors yet.

"Raise our flag," he ordered.

"Ease the t'gallant sheets," Hibbert was still droning.

"Haul round on the clewlines, buntlines, and bunt leech-lines. Avast there!"

"By the mark ten!"

"Larboard chaser's cleared for action, sir."

"Fire as you bear, Mr. Tolbert." The range was long, and considering the way *Experiment* was being tossed on each wave, the chances of hitting were slim; but it would give *Loyalist* something to think about. The chaser crashed out. Favian didn't see the fall of shot.

The gridiron flag was snapping overhead. Favian thought he had the race with *Loyalist* won; he was keeping well to windward, forcing the Canadian to commit himself.

"By the mark six!" The water was shoaling rapidly as they approached the tail of the island. The rigging's shriek increased by half an octave; Favian glanced aloft and wondered whether he should reef the topsails. Not yet, he decided; but it was time to put a reef in the fore-and-aft mainsail.

The bow chaser cracked out again: clean miss. The mainsail was reefed and the water shoaled to four fathoms before they were past the island; Favian knew he'd won the race. Probably the Canadian captain knew it as well. If *Loyalist* kept on her present course, *Experiment* would rake her at close range, at least half a dozen broadsides before she cleared the northern cape, and that would put an end to it.

"Two reefs in the tops'ls," Favian said. It was probably not time to reef just yet—certainly not two reefs—but he wanted to slow *Experiment*'s progress, perhaps encouraging *Loyalist* to keep on her present course just a little longer before tacking and trying to slip under *Experiment*'s stern.

"Furl the forecourse, Mr. Hibbert."

"Aye aye, sir. Man the tacks and sheets."

The bow chaser roared. Favian saw a white feather in line with *Loyalist* as the ball clipped a wave top. "You've hit her, lads!" Favian shouted. *Experiment*'s cheers were almost drowned by a sudden howl in the rigging. *Experiment* rolled to leeward, spray sailing over her rail. If he hadn't already reefed the topsails, it was certainly time now.

"Deck thar! She's goin' about!"

Favian wiped spray from his eyes and watched *Loyalist*'s movements. She had chosen a bad moment to tack; she came into the wind just as the gust that had rocked *Experiment* reached her; her square topsails went flat aback and she hung in the wind's eye.

"She's missed stays!" He hadn't expected that. In another few minutes he could rake her with his full broadside. He watched as men ran to the Canadian's braces, as the jib was backed to help her fall off, as nothing worked and she began to gain sternway. The bow chaser fired, shot skipping within ten yards of the enemy. At last *Loyalist* fell off, back on the starboard tack, heading for the rocks. Nothing could save her now; there was not enough room to wear.

"Down helm!" Favian barked. "Brace her up sharp to the wind. Mr. Hibbert, rig the catharpings. Shake a reef out of the tops'ls. Let's get out of here before we end up on the rocks like *Loyalist*!"

The Canadian privateer gained way, hesitated for a moment, as if wondering whether to anchor or not and take its chances, then ran for the shore deliberately, trying for a gap between the mud banks and reefs rather than being driven on them. She succeeded, driving up onto the beach below the evergreens, her masts going at the first shock, her crew running down the broken masts into the white water, struggling up onto the beach. If the gale didn't finish her, she would certainly not be going anywhere for weeks.

Favian took another reef in the mainsail as the wind increased. *Experiment* was lying as close to the wind as she could; she would clear the northern cape by at least half a mile. Casterburgh looked at Favian with plain relief.

"Secure the larboard chaser," Favian was ordering. "Secure all guns. Double the tackles and breechings. Wedge the wheels. How's her head now?"

"East half-point north, sir," said the quartermaster.

"Very well. Let her go through the water."

Spray roared up over *Experiment*'s bow as the hands struggled to haul the carronades up to the ports and double the breechings so they ran no risk of breaking loose. The sky was all black to the southward.

There was a heart-stopping instant when all the square sails were a-thunder, and then the quartermaster corrected. "East by north, sir."

Favian squinted through the spray that dazzled his eyes. They would still clear the cape. "Mr. Hibbert," Favian ordered, "go below and tell Davis to fetch up my oilskins. Fetch up your own while you're at it. Here, take my boarding helmet."

"Yes, sir. Thank you." Hibbert had no sooner stepped below than the sails began to roar again. Favian glanced anxiously at the dog vanes, then at the quartermaster.

"East by north, half north," the quartermaster said. "The wind is heading us, sir."

"Keep her full. Let her go through the water." Favian felt anxiety wrapping him. This was going to be close. By the time Hibbert had come up in his sou'wester, and Davis had run up with Favian's, the wind had backed another full point, and *Experiment*'s bow was driving straight onto the rocks.

Favian scowled as he glanced to leeward, seeing white water streaming from jagged reef. He could be on that reef very soon, unless he somehow reversed the laws of nature and persuaded *Experiment* to sail straight into the wind. If a sleek schooner like *Loyalist* couldn't tack in this weather, a sluggish old brig like *Experiment* certainly couldn't. If he wore around, he'd end up on the rocks next to the privateer. The wind had foxed him; he'd have to go about very quickly or there was no hope at all. Box-haul her? Not in this weather; they'd probably end up on the point sternfirst. He reached his decision.

"Mr. Hibbert! Mr. Tolbert! Mr. Casterburgh!" He struggled into his oilskins as *Experiment*'s senior officers and pilot assembled on the quarterdeck. He clapped the sou'wester down over his forehead and blinked away the spray. "Gentlemen, I'm going to club-haul her. Double-bit the bower anchor and see her stoppered at twenty fathoms. Take the men you need for that and send the rest aft."

Hibbert ran; there was no time to lose. *Experiment*'s complement assembled just forward of the mainmast, a dark, soaked, probably frightened mass of men. Favian picked up a speaking trumpet.

"I'm going to club-haul her, men!" he roared. The howling wind almost drowned out his voice. "You'll have to watch me carefully, and you've got to obey orders instantly. And without panic, otherwise we're done for. Take your stations for tacking, and watch me."

The white-faced mass of men dissolved as they ran to their stations. It was turning black. Favian clung to the lee fife rail in the partial shelter of the mainmast. Hibbert ran aft, sliding over the slippery deck, to report the anchor ready.

"Very well. On my signal!" Favian shouted. "Quartermaster, keep her full!" They were within a quarter-mile of the beach; Favian could see Maine rocks jutting up dead ahead. This was going to be close. Favian turned to the helmsmen and ordered the helm put down. *Experiment* began to stagger into the wind.

"Stand by the anchor! Stand clear of the cable! Let go the anchor!"

The bower plummeted to the bottom; there was a flash of fire forward, from the friction, as the cable roared out. *Experiment* failed to make its turn, failed even to head directly into the wind; the brig lurched, then began to gain sternway, driving backward for the rocks. Then the cable went taut, water spraying from its tightening fibers, and the brig snapped head-to-wind with a lurch that threw half the men to the deck.

"Silence fore and aft! Haul all at once now!" Favian's men tailed onto the braces, their feet digging into the planks for traction as they fought to haul the yards over in the face of the opposing wind. Canvas crashed and thundered; *Experiment* tugged at its cable. Done!

"Cut the cable!" Axes thudded into the cable, and with a lurch *Experiment* was free; the sails were filling, and she was gaining way on her new tack.

"Keep her full," Favian ordered. "Mr. Hibbert, I think the sun's over the yardarm." The hands cheered as they coiled down, then ran for their liquor. Favian remained on deck, feeling *Experiment*'s motion as she corkscrewed through the water. Time to reef down again shortly, as soon as the main brace was spliced.

They weren't out of trouble yet. They'd have to clear the

tail of the big island again, then weather the south cape
with its shoaling mud banks. If the wind held, there should
be no problem. Favian smiled grimly. Hadn't he hoped
once before, just an hour ago, that the wind would hold?

But there was nothing to do about it. Favian remembered William Burrows saying, that night they'd held the
wake for James Lawrence, "While trying to claw off a lee
shore in a hurricane of wind, there is precious little room
for ostentation or conceit. *There's* your purity for you—but
a little of it goes a long way." Aye, this was pure seamanship all right; there was nothing purer than this elemental
struggle of a fragile vessel against an overpowering storm.
Favian felt his heart roaring, his face tingling as spray
etched his features. He tried to tell himself that he would
rather be at Portsmouth in a snug cottage, with mulled rum
and a roaring fire, but somehow he couldn't convince himself. So far as he knew, no American captain had ever successfully club-hauled a warship; this was a first, a professional triumph.

The hell with the profession, he thought savagely. The
triumph seemed entirely personal. He had bested the storm.
Perverse as the winds were, he had beaten off the shore
with the loss of only a topgallant sail, the bower anchor,
and twenty fathoms of cable; and he'd destroyed an enemy
privateer to boot.

"Mr. Hibbert!" They were in the island's lee; the wind
moderated, the waves' surging abated. Hibbert came bustling aft, bending his head to hear Favian's orders.

"Send two leadsmen into the chains," Favian said. "We've
got to keep as close to the island as possible or we may not
weather the south cape. I don't dare keep her off the
wind."

"Aye aye, sir."

"Another reef in the tops'ls." Spray curled from Hibbert's oilskin hat as he nodded.

"Aye aye, sir."

A chain of men was assembled to send the leadsmen's
information aft to Favian; with the wind howling, he
wouldn't be able to hear the chant directly. The first information was alarming.

"By the mark six!"

Favian nodded, worried. With this sea *Experiment* would strike in three. They were at least a quarter-mile from the island, and would have to pass close under its lee.

"A quarter less six!"

Damnation. Shoaling rapidly. Favian felt his heart race.

"And a half five!"

Favian kept *Experiment* driving on until Casterburgh's eyes were as big as saucers, until the leadsmen called three and a half fathoms. Favian turned to the quartermaster.

"A point and a half to starboard, if you please."

"P'int and a half to starboard, aye aye."

Experiment slipped gratefully from the wind. Favian could feel himself breathing easier; he could see Casterburgh clutching the fife rail, bracing himself for the crash.

"A quarter less four!"

"Down helm. Full and by."

"Full and by, sir."

They passed out from behind the lee of the island, and the wind heeled *Experiment* over until her lee rail began to ship foam. Rain splattered down on the deck. Favian peered ahead to see if they were going to clear the southern point. Quite clearly they would.

He felt like cackling aloud in riotous joy. They were going to escape the clutches of the coast! A piece of pure seamanship, unparalleled in the history of the United States Navy—wrecking a privateer and club-hauling off a lee shore on the same day! What an accomplishment! He had felt his distant halves unite, his whole will urging *Experiment*'s yards around; there was no rebellion in him, no distancing in the face of the elements. The seaman had triumphed over the officer and the cynic, uniting them. He'd never felt as alive.

"Barometer's rising, sir," Hibbert reported. "We'll have a nice day tomorrow." And we'll live to enjoy it, Favian thought. He saw the grin on Hibbert's face, and knew he was sharing the same relief and exhilaration.

"Congratulations, sir, by God!" Hibbert finally burst out, and then Favian and Hibbert were dancing like madmen on the deck, clapping one another on the back, the rain foaming off their oilskins.

Then suddenly the sails were roaring, and Favian and Hibbert were standing stock still on the deck, staring at one another in pure horror.

"She's heading us again!" the quartermaster gasped, utterly disbelieving.

Favian straightened, and gave the order in as expressionless a voice as possible. "Full and by. Let her go through the water."

"Full and by, sir."

They watched, doomed, as the wind veered and headed them for the mud banks off the southern cape. They were in narrower waters now; they didn't need the *carré navale* to tell them that even if they could go about once more, club-hauling twice in the same day, they would just run themselves onto the island.

Their luck had run out. The wind was behaving with unbelievable caprice, backing to put them on the northern cape, then veering to put them on the southern one. Favian had fought the good fight, but the elements had conspired to destroy him.

"Mr. Tolbert, I'll thank you to light a slow match, go forrard, and begin firing the distress rockets and the false fires."

"Aye aye, sir."

"Take Brook with you."

"By the mark eight!" Word was passed from forward.

"What does thee intend to do, sir?" It was the pilot, crouching down to minimize the lashing the wind was giving his back.

"Wait till she shoals to four and a half fathoms," Favian said. "Cut away the masts, then anchor."

Casterburgh nodded. It made sense; cutting away the masts would reduce the brig's drag, perhaps allowing the anchors to get a hold on the bottom.

The first rocket shot skyward, exploding red in the rain. Crimson shadows flickered across Casterburgh's craggy face. "It was brilliant, sir," the pilot said. "Wouldn't have missed it for the world." He stuck out his hand. Favian took it, curiously cool. In all probability they were going to die very shortly, and Favian could not find it within himself to work up much of a protest about it. He had done what he could, and through no fault of his own it had failed. He hoped someone would survive to carry the story of his efforts to the family.

Hibbert's hand came forward, and Favian clasped it. There was a wordless exchange in the red light, understanding in Hibbert's eyes. "Detail your men, Mr. Hibbert. Everyone else below decks."

"And a half six!"

They were coming up onto the mud bank. Favian gave the elements one last chance to change their mind as Hibbert prepared the best bower and one of the sheet anchors. Perhaps, on this foul ground, one of the anchors would hold. It was more likely that abrasion with some submerged rock would wear away the cable entirely.

"By the mark five!"

"Stand by!" Favian bellowed. Axemen stood by the weather shrouds, ready to begin their cutting. Favian raised his arm. He could see word being passed aft.

"And a half four!"

"*Cut!*" Favian roared, and dropped his arm. Axes thudded against the taut backstays. One by one they sprang free. Another rocket shot up, and a false fire burned brightly from the stem. In the white-hot light of the false fire the mainmast went over, toppling into the water with a wooden moan, a torn ruin of hemp, pine, and canvas. Then the fore-topmast toppled, men leaping free. *Experiment* wallowed in the waves, rocking wildly without the pressure of the sails to keep her heeled over.

"Stand clear of the cable! Let go the best bower!" He had gotten rid of the masts first, before anchoring; otherwise they would have crashed down on deck instead of over the side, probably killing half the crew.

Even as it was, the deck was a litter of broken spars and scattered lines. No one seemed to be hurt. The sheet anchor followed the best bower; the cables were veered out. *Experiment* pitched madly, the broken masts grinding alongside. As the strain came on the cables, a titanic sea came aboard, washing her fore and aft. Favian clung, blinded, to the fife rail, feeling the water threatening to tear him free;

at last the wave poured aft, and he glanced about him. The two helmsmen were miraculously staying at their stations; Casterburgh had been knocked to his knees, but was struggling blindly to his feet.

"Head for the hatch, boys!" Favian shouted. "No point in staying on deck!"

They ran for it, managing to duck down the aft scuttle before the next sea came aboard. Hibbert was waiting for them; he gave his report in a subdued voice.

"I think we may have lost a few men overboard in that sea," he said. "Mr. Sprague reports a broken arm."

"Take a head count. That'll keep everyone busy for a few minutes."

"Aye aye, sir."

"Can you tell if we're dragging?"

"Not yet, sir."

"Nor can I. I'll be in my cabin."

The cabin seemed as good a place as any to await the end. *Experiment* was pitching like a mad thing, and Favian knew she couldn't stand it for long. The anchors would drag, or the cables part. This storm was unbelievable; it must be a West Indian hurricane that had climbed high into the Atlantic before thrashing itself to bits on the New England coast. That was always a danger this time of year. At least Favian could console himself with the thought that British Bermuda had probably been hit a lot worse.

Favian broke out some of his father's wine he'd been saving for a special occasion, and poured a cup for himself and for the pilot.

"Here's to the hereafter," he found himself saying, knowing there was a diabolical grin on his face, a reckless acceptance.

"Amen," Casterburgh said solemnly, and drank. Favian seated himself in his chair, hearing the little trickles as his wet clothes drained themselves onto the deck. He could feel the little shocks as the anchors dragged, and calculated what would happen when they struck. Stern-first onto the mud banks, then they'd broach-to and probably break in half. The safest places would be clinging to the masts in the lee of the wreck; they would be sheltered from much of the waves' force there, and from much of the wind. Hibbert knocked, then entered.

"Two missing, sir. Sprague has splinted that broken arm."

"Have some wine, Mr. Hibbert."

"The anchors are dragging, sir," Hibbert said.

"Just so. Have some wine."

This would make a tidy little story, Favian thought as the wine warmed him: the officers drinking wine in the cabin while *Experiment* went on the ground. But what else was there to do? he wondered. Nothing at all, nothing but take the little pleasures that remained.

They sipped the wine gratefully, speaking little, until one of the cables parted. It would not be long before the other went as well, and then the end. Favian rose, shook hands with his companions, and said, "Mr. Hibbert, please go forrard and pass the word that the safest place will be clinging to the masts."

"Aye aye, sir. It has been a privilege."

"The privilege was mine."

The other cable parted before Hibbert returned. Favian decided to head for the companionway. He drained his glass. "Will you join me, Mr. Casterburgh?"

"I shall join thee in a moment." The pilot took off his oilskin hat and began to pray. Favian left him in peace and went forward to the companion.

The first shock tore the rudder from its gudgeons and flung the brig sideways. Favian braced himself in the corridor and went up the companion, ripping open the hatch. A sea poured down into his face; he lurched blindly upward, then ducked as he heard the new launch break free of its lashings and fling itself to leeward. Wreckage scraped against the coamings. There was another roll as the sea lifted the wreck, and Favian was bracing himself in the hatchway with all his strength as *Experiment* went over on her side, her hull scraping along the mud with a tortured, grating sound; then she swung upright violently, suddenly free of the ground. She'd been hurled clean over the first mud bank, but would soon be on a second.

Favian flung himself out of the scuttle, heading for a pinrail; he seized a length of line and tried to secure himself before the next sea came. Dark figures were scurrying over the deck, pouring up from the fore scuttle, some flinging themselves into the water as they struck out for the masts. The next wave lifted *Experiment*, boiling over the weather rail, then brought her crashing down onto the next bar. Favian heard timbers breaking. She wouldn't last long.

More men were on deck, trying madly to lash themselves down or peering off to leeward, trying to guess their chances of swimming to the masts. A small figure bolted from the aft scuttle and ran to the shelter of the stump of the mainmast, arms wrapping around the fife rail as the next sea came aboard. *Experiment* lurched; Favian saw one of the weather carronades break free and hurtle across the deck, a tumbling juggernaut, until it smashed its way through the lee bulwark.

A head popped out of the after hatch; apparently Casterburgh's meditations had been disturbed. The head popped down as another sea burst over the wreck, then Casterburgh scrambled up with surprising agility and flung himself into the sea. Favian heard a clattering by his foot; a brass speaking trumpet was lolling in the scuppers, torn from its locker. He reached down to pick it up.

"Make for the masts, those who can swim!" he shouted. He saw heads turning on the foredeck. "This is the captain! Make for the masts if you can swim!" he roared. He saw nods.

Another sea tore at the wreck, lifted it, brought it crashing down. The figure at the mainmast fife rail lost his grip, spinning to leeward; Favian dropped the speaking trumpet, reached out, and seized oilskin. He felt his fingernails being torn out one by one—there was no pain yet, but it would come soon enough in the salt water—but he kept his hold, and the water receded. It was Mr. Midshipman Stanhope. Favian seized a length of line and began lashing him down.

"Can you swim?" he roared into the boy's ear. Stanhope, his eyes wide, overwhelmed by the suddenness and completeness of the disaster, stared wildly, then nodded.

"Wait till the next surge, then follow me!" There was slow comprehension, then another nod.

The next sea brought grinding, breaking sounds from below; planks were starting everywhere, and the stores in the hold were shifting. *Experiment* had no life left in her; soon she'd be kindling washed up on the rocks. Favian cast off his safety line, seeing Stanhope doing the same; he timed the seconds between the waves, saw a moment of stillness below the rail, and leaped.

Foam, roaring madness, blackness, wet. His crippled hands struck out, bringing him up; somehow he got rid of his boots. Stanhope was nowhere to be seen. The next wave carried him toward the wreckage of the masts, drifting fifty feet from the wreck, still connected by the lee shrouds. It felt as if he were breathing in pure seawater; he could hear the thundering of his heart above the shriek of the wind and crash of waves.

He saw the fractured mainmast looming overhead like a great broken spear, and lunged for it; he felt a trailing shroud under his hands and seized it. He hauled himself in, then grasped the mast itself. A head swept by and he recognized Stanhope, hands flung up, despair on his face; and Favian reached out again, finding Stanhope's hair, and gripped. A little of such purity goes a long way, he thought, and probably would have grinned if it hadn't meant opening his mouth to the foam. The next sea almost parted them; but here in the lee of the wreck it was calmer than on whatever remained of *Experiment*'s deck, and Favian held on. Stanhope's hands clutched Favian's arm, and then the mast; Favian passed a line around them both and lashed them firmly.

Favian gasped for breath until he felt the weariness begin to ebb from his limbs, until his trip-hammer heart began to slow. He looked up. Others were clinging to the mast; he saw one of the helmsmen lashed safely, the pilot Casterburgh with his hair streaming, other heads bobbing in *Experiment*'s lee.

"Is that you, Captain?" It was Gable, the acting bosun; he was straddling the lower mast just below the fighting top, which lay like a great upright shield in the water.

"Aye," Favian said.

"There are a score of men here!" Gable roared. "We're all snug! It's easier t'other side of the top, sheltered like!"

"Good!"

"I can see men on the foremast! I think I can see Mr. Hibbert!"

Hibbert had survived; wonderful. Favian hauled himself up until he straddled the mainmast, then he lashed himself down again.

"Gable!"

"Aye, sir!"

"Is there room behind the top for more men?" There was a hesitation.

"If some really need it, sir!"

"Very well. I'll remember that."

The brutal storm raged on. The sea grew darker as night fell. Favian's crippled hands began to throb. *Experiment* broke in half about midnight, having lasted far longer than Favian had expected; he never saw what happened to the men on the foremast. The stern half rolled over the mud bank, then stuck fast to another, still providing shelter for the men clinging to the mast. Favian tried to sleep, and may have succeeded in snatching a few minutes' rest.

Toward dawn Favian saw Casterburgh was suffering, only half-conscious; the Quaker pilot was passed behind the shield of the fighting top and lashed down, but it was too late. Just before dawn Gable reported that the pilot had died.

The storm had been moderating for some hours. Dawn produced a sickly yellow sun, and cheers. Favian looked around him: *Experiment*'s stern half was near-buried in a mudbank, surrounded by foam. There was no sign of the fore part; presumably it had broken up entirely. The foremast was gone as well, along with Hibbert and whoever else had been clinging to it.

"Get a head count," Favian said.

There were twenty-three survivors clinging to the mainmast, including the indestructible Tolbert; the total was more than Favian could reasonably have expected. The trick now was to keep them alive. Favian began making drowsy plans to wait for the sea to moderate and the tide to come rolling in, then to cut the mast free from the wreck and drift in as close to shore as possible before beginning the last swim.

The clouds had torn themselves to fragments and streaked the sky. The tide began coming in; the waves were smaller. No vessel would have had a hard time beating out against this weather, but it was still formidable enough for anyone trying to navigate a piece of jetsam.

Stanhope's eyes opened wearily; he climbed up to straddle the mainmast next to Favian. "Good morning, sir," he said politely, and yawned. It appeared that he had upheld the proud tradition of midshipmen that claimed they were able to sleep anywhere.

"Good morning," Favian said. His hands ached like hell, and the night's activity had finally caught up with him; he felt wretched. Sixty men dead, he thought—not bad for a day's work. Not a great cost, considering they'd made a new chapter to the naval legend. And then, of course, there would be the automatic court-martial that came to any captain who lost his ship. He supposed he would be cleared; he was a hero, after all . . . a hero who would have to write a letter to Hibbert's father and to Casterburgh's wife, to Brook's parents, to the purser's wife, and to so many others. Favian wondered if he would feel himself obligated to explain the perversity of the wind, that it really wasn't his fault that sixty men died. Compared to the horror of composing those letters, the court-martial held no terrors for him.

"A sail! A sail!" Gable's hearty voice roared over the waves. Favian craned his head; a little cat-rigged vessel was coming out of the bay, bucking each wave. Someone must have seen the rockets, he thought dully, or the crewmen of that ketch had watched the wreck.

The men set up a weary cheer. The catboat came closer, hesitated at the edge of the mud bank, then began sliding in. She drew only a few inches without her leeboard; she was safe enough.

Favian looked up, seeing the heads clustering at the gunwale, hands reaching out to drag the half-drowned men aboard. The wreck's survivors were babbling their thanks, their joy. Favian felt the salt crusting on his forehead and thought of the letters.

He untied his lashings, then slipped off the mast. There were men with broken ribs, arms, and legs; he helped them free, handing them to the men on the catboat. He saw Stanhope go over the gunwale, then Gable, Tolbert, and the body of Casterburgh. He was alone in the sea, treading water near the mast. The last to leave the ship, he thought . . . what was left of it.

A man in a leather cap leaned over the gunwale to help him into the catboat.

"Here ye go, Captain. I was hoping we'd meet again. Take thee my hand."

"Thank you," Favian said. Hadn't the storm had the calling of destiny in it, a certain implacable inevitability? Why shouldn't the symbol of his fate appear in the morning of the storm's conclusion? For whatever reason, he was not surprised.

The man who helped him over the gunwale was, of course, Lazarus.